The LOVE HEIST

THE LOVE HEIST

UNLUCKY IN LOVE

ANGELA CASELLA

ALSO BY ANGELA CASELLA

Apple Ridge

Falling for Mr. October (September 2026)

Hideaway Harbor shared universe

The Holiday Hate-Off

Babes of Brewing

Best Served Cold

Worst Nanny Ever

Best Kind of Trouble

Worst Faking Idea (May 2026)

Unlucky in Love

The Love Fixers

The Love Bandits

The Love Losers

The Love Destroyers

Spin-off Standalone

The Thief Who Saved Christmas

Finding You

You're so Extra

You're so Bad

You're so Basic

You're so Vain

You're so Phony (coming soon!)

Fairy Godmother Agency

A Borrowed Boyfriend

A Stolen Suit

A Brooding Bodyguard

A Reluctant Roommate

Bringing Down the House (Nicole and Damien's story)

Highland Hills

(co-written with Denise Grover Swank)

Matchmaking a Billionaire

Matchmaking a Single Dad

Matchmaking a Grump

Matchmaking a Roommate

Matchmaking a Player (novella) by Angela Casella (May)

Bad Luck Club

(co-written with Denise Grover Swank)

Love at First Hate

Jingle Bell Hell

Fraudulently Ever After

Matchmaking Mischief

Asheville Brewing

(co-written with Denise Grover Swank)

Any Luck at All

Better Luck Next Time

Getting Lucky

Bad Luck Club

Luck of the Draw (novella)

All the Luck You Need (prequel novella) by Angela Casella

CHAPTER ONE

LAINEY

Both of my parents are con artists. *Bad* con artists.

But if wishing for status they weren't born into and money they didn't earn were an art, they'd be Matisse and Rodin. Sometimes they get little wins, though, like the time my mother acquired a rich lady's wallet when I was ten. I helped her cut her hair to better match the photo on the license, and we snuck into the woman's private club for an afternoon of bliss. We ordered food and charged it to her account, swam, got massages, and then booked it before anyone could notice.

I might have only been ten, but I wasn't stupid. I knew it was wrong, and my mother *definitely* did. It also felt really, really good—like we were playing a game and winning, and no one else knew about it. I don't think we've ever enjoyed each other's company more than we did that afternoon.

When we left, my mother had a glimmer in her eyes and a bounce in her step. She was *happy*, which I wasn't used to seeing, and I felt some of her shine rubbing off on me. I remember thinking, *So this is what it feels like to be rich.*

My mom brought me home, to our cramped fourth-floor walkup in Inwood, although my mother liked to say we lived on the

Upper East Side. And once we were sitting on the couch, directly in front of the fan, because it was hot as the seventh circle of hell outside and in, she leaned in close and said, "This is going to be our little secret, Elaine. Don't even tell your father."

"Can we do it again?" I asked, because acting rich had felt pretty damn good, and I wanted more.

She laughed so hard her head tipped back.

"Not as Marjorie Eccles," she finally answered with a wink, wrapping her arm around my narrow shoulders. "But she's not the only one who doesn't know how to hold onto her handbag."

That was news to me, because I'd thought she'd found it lying on the sidewalk. A feeling of misgiving pricked at me—*finders keepers* was one thing, but snatching a handbag was a definite crime.

"You really nabbed her purse?" I asked.

She shrugged and leaned toward the fan like she wanted it to swallow her. "You know stealing is wrong, Elaine, but she needed someone to teach her the golden rule. I saw her kick a homeless man's hat, and the money he was collecting scattered everywhere. Who would do a thing like that?"

"Did you give the cash in the bag to him?" I asked, getting caught up in the picture she was drawing.

Robin Hood was my favorite story—taking from the rich and giving to the poor. I wanted to be like him when I grew up, but when I'd communicated as much to my best friend, Claire, she'd bitten her lip and said, "*But you can do that in a legal way. Like, maybe you could become a civil rights lawyer.*"

"*That sounds like a lot of work,*" I'd replied. It went without saying that it sounded like *boring* work.

"*Probably,*" she'd said thoughtfully, "*but learning how to steal from people without getting caught would be hard too.*"

But apparently I already had a thief in the house, so maybe it wouldn't be impossible to become Robin Hood.

I watched my mother expectantly as she sighed and leaned in even closer to the fan. "Well?" I prodded.

"Of course I did, Lainey," she said without flinching.

She said it so seriously, without any hitch in her voice. Then again, she'd always been a good liar. So I—

"IS THERE any point to this story?" asks my business partner, Nicole, kicking back in her chair. Her pink hair is a pop of bright color beneath the low lighting.

We're sitting at a round table in the kitchen of a cabin in Marshall, NC, drinking beers. My best friend—Claire, of the well-intentioned advice—inherited this place with Nicole from their biological father. Since Claire is the closest thing to a sibling I've ever had, I followed her here.

It didn't hurt that my life in New York City had crashed and burned.

But that was a few months ago. Claire recently moved in with her boyfriend, who lives next door with his sister, and Nicole doesn't stay at the cabin much anymore because she and her husband own a much nicer house in Asheville. So I'm the last woman standing, living in this cabin that I've lucked my way into, owned by two people who don't charge me rent.

My parents taught me well.

Nicole came over to discuss the new business venture we've been working on together, The Love Fixers, services for people who have been screwed over by love. It's a work in progress, because I have to balance it with a part-time job as a personal assistant for an older rich woman who dislikes me, and Nicole is a private investigator who keeps unpredictable hours.

Claire is basically here as our cheerleader, giving us what little energy she has left after waking up at four a.m. to get ready for the morning rush at her bakery. Her brownie-slash-donut creation,

Bronuts, are already on several "best of Marshall" lists—although admittedly those lists aren't long and there aren't many of them. In the tourism race in Western North Carolina, this town is usually an afterthought, a pit stop. It's a refreshing difference from living in New York City.

"Well?" Nicole says, lifting her eyebrows and rocking some more.

Claire, who's sitting at the table with us, shoots her a dirty look. "Of course there's a point. She's getting to it. It's called dramatic timing."

"Thank you for the encouragement," I say with a smile.

Nicole rolls her eyes. "You're not a kindergarten teacher, Claire. You don't have to give out star stickers."

"I know where she's going with it," Claire says with a nod.

"So you've been bored by it before," Nicole replies, but there's a hint of amusement to her mouth.

"You know you want to know what happens next," I say.

She waves her hand, which is as much of a go-ahead as I'm likely to get.

"I went looking for Marjorie Eccles. It wasn't hard. My mom had hidden the purse and the wallet. She was probably planning to destroy them—"

"Or keep them as a souvenir like a serial killer," Nicole says.

"Maybe," I concede with a shrug. "Anyway, I went to the address on her license and returned the rest of her things. Pretended I'd found her purse thrown out on the sidewalk."

"Like if a mugger had tossed it after taking the good stuff," Nicole says with a nod of approval.

"Well, yeah," I say, "which is basically what happened. Anyway, I took it to her building, and she came down to get it. She told me I was a good citizen and the sweetest little girl she'd ever seen. And then she gave me fifty bucks."

"Did you give it to your mother?" Nicole asks.

I give her a flat look, remembering the shame and sense of wanting I'd felt as I took that bill. Because I'd *wanted* to deserve it but had been very aware that the only reason she'd lost her bag in the first place was because my mother had stolen it.

"So you're not entirely stupid."

"Hopefully not. Anyway, it turns out Marjorie was on the board of a charity geared toward ending homelessness."

"One kicked hat at a time," Nicole says with a glimmer in her eyes.

"My mother was lying."

Claire shrugs and nods at the same time, her expression sympathetic. She knows my mother's a liar. She's been to a dozen MLM parties for everything from shitty makeup to shitty tinctures, and my God, my mother acts like every bad product she decides to peddle is going to end world hunger. Her hustle is so dedicated it's almost admirable.

Almost.

I suppose I'd have spoken to her more recently than a few months ago if either of us found much to admire about the other.

"Maybe," Nicole says. "Probably. But you're naïve if you think being on the board of that charity means she's never kicked over any hats. Besides...you took advantage of her too."I nod. "Good people get taken advantage of. They get fucked over by people who don't mean well, like my mother, and even people who do, like me."

"Your point?" she presses, rocking in her chair again.

"Women like Marjorie need our help. I also have a lot of karma points to build, and sending out glitter bombs and 'fuck you very much cookies' to people's exes isn't going to do it. We've been thinking too small with the Love Fixers." Our jobs have been small and sporadic, nothing Robin Hood would write home about. I want to make a real difference—to soak up people's pain and then rain it down on the people who deserve it.

"I'm proud of those cookies," Claire interjects, tapping the table with her finger. "My sugar cookie recipe is to die for."

I give her a sympathetic look. "Claire, do you really think someone who gets a cookie that says 'fuck you very much' from their ex is going to eat it?"

She visibly deflates. "Well, crap. It feels like I've wasted a lot of effort. I should just be frosting graham crackers."

"But it's the effort that goes into it that really sends the message home," Nicole says, which is her version of a sisterly pat on the back. She picks up her beer and swigs it, then shifts her attention to me. "So, let's have it. There's something you want to do, and it's dangerous, and for some reason, you think you need my blessing."

"You're my business partner." Meaning she's the one who's bankrolled this thing, in as much as it's needed to be bankrolled. Right now all we have is a vague website, an LLC, and a brick and mortar office in this house. But I'm not my parents' child for nothing—I can think big, even if I can't achieve big. In my head, I can see it growing into a real business, one with employees and salaries and maybe even a bonafide snack room.

"Which means I trust you," Nicole continues.

This penetrates more deeply than she probably meant for it to. It pinches like a pair of pretty shoes that refuse to fit, no matter how many times you try to jam your foot in. I *want* to be a person who's trustworthy, but I was raised by parents who taught me to lie and manipulate. To climb social ladders and then destroy them so no one else could follow me up. And, I'll be honest, sometimes I fall into that behavior without even realizing it's happening.

Maybe I told the story, in part, as a warning.

Don't trust me.

And here she is, saying she does.

First, Nicole told me she believed in my idea and wanted to help me make a go of it, and now, in her own way, she's saying she believes in *me*.

I want that so badly it hurts. Which gives me pause, because I have to wonder: did I manipulate my way here? Was I dishonest without realizing it?

It's fucking exhausting to constantly second guess yourself.

Sighing, I take a swig of beer and pull my phone out, then scroll to the email, pulling it up. I've already told Claire about it, but I didn't want to play show and tell with Nicole until I'd done a little ground work. I'm not embarrassed to admit that I want to impress her.

I slide the phone over to her.

"Assume I'm illiterate," she says, squinting at it before sliding it back. Based on the way she was studying it, Claire's far-sightedness is probably hereditary.

Nicole would die before admitting she needs reading glasses.

"The client went to a party with her boyfriend," I say, "and later that night, they fought and broke up. But she left her heirloom heart pendant necklace in his apartment. And, get this, he won't give it back. He claims it's not there, but she knows exactly where she left it. He's lying."

"Why are you so sure of that?" Nicole asks shrewdly, watching me.

"It's worth a lot of money," I say, "and it has sentimental value for the client." I think of the signed Yankees bat I stole from my ex-fiancé, Todd, which has a place of dishonor in my room here. He used to talk about that bat at parties for so long people's eyes would glaze over, but he'd keep going for at least another two minutes because he wanted to make sure to establish his dominance—it was his privilege to bore them while talking about his privilege.

"He wanted to take something that would hurt her," I continue, "because she hurt him."

It's probably hypocritical for me to care about her emotional pain and not Todd's, but I didn't find a stash of vanilla sex emails exchanged between her and her childhood sweetheart. *She* didn't try to break me like I was a recalcitrant horse.

"Why'd she split up with him?" Claire asks.

"Was it porn?" Nicole puts in with fresh interest. "Let me guess, she found out he was into some really bleak shit."

I roll my eyes. "She broke up with him because she suspected he was a cheater, one of those guys who wanted to have his cake and eat it too."

"That's such a dumb saying," Nicole says. "Who the fuck would buy a cake but not want to eat it?"

"The 'fuck you very much' cookie people," Claire says sadly, and I can't help but laugh.

"My point is..." I say, waving my hand. "She didn't trust him, and he couldn't come up with a good explanation for his behavior. So she decided to cut her losses, and now he's holding her necklace hostage, thus proving his unworthiness. Someone needs to step up and deal with this jerk, this absolute waste of humanity. I'm going to get that necklace back for her, and I'm going to make him regret the day he was born."

"And it will be therapeutic," Claire says sadly, giving Nicole a significant look that probably flies right over her head. "Because Todd was a cheater."

"That has nothing to do with this," I insist.

Another lie, although this time everyone knows I'm lying. Still, there's a lot Claire doesn't know about the Todd situation...things I would prefer not to tell her.

"I don't care," Nicole says flippantly. "Sounds fun. I like a good heist. I'm in."

"We could get into trouble," I admit. "The business could get into trouble."

We set it up as an LLC, but I'm pretty sure 'limited liability' doesn't cover stealing stuff for people.

"I wouldn't want to do it if that weren't a possibility," she says. "Did you run a background check on this woman?"

Nicole showed me how to do it, so I took that step on my own, wanting to prove that I could follow instructions.

"I did. And I met with her too."

"Here?" Nicole asks, raising her eyebrows.

"Starbucks."

Cleo's a little woman, with long black hair and big brown eyes, more Bambi than Disney princess, and I instantly felt an urge to protect her. I mean, what monster would want to inflict emotional damage on *Bambi*?

One who deserves to have his fortress stormed—and I'm more than ready to do the storming.

"Good," Nicole says after I tell her about the meeting. "Let her know it's a go. We're in."

"Good," I repeat, feeling a smile slide across my face. I instantly feel ten times better. I feel a rush, not entirely unlike what I felt the day my mother and I left that private club.

"You know," Nicole ruminates, "the best way to get close to him is probably to pretend you're interested in his dick."

I shrug, grinning at them. "Revenge as therapy. I don't hate it. And get this...the guy's actually a therapist."

"I feel the need to point out that actual therapy, with someone other than the man you're trying to trick, would be less dangerous and more dignified," Claire says.

"Probably," Nicole says with a smirk. "But I'm guessing she'll never know. And the therapist will be spared thirty-minute long stories about her mother."

I shake my head at her, then lift my bottle toward the ceiling and say, "Jake Jeffries, I'm coming for you. You hear me? I'm coming for you."

CHAPTER TWO

JAKE

I'm so bored, I've been reduced to counting the flecks of peanut shells on the bar top, wondering what would happen if my brother or someone else with a peanut allergy walked into this dump without knowing it was the place that might murder them. We're just outside of Asheville, so you think they'd have some sort of ordinance about peanuts, but this place is probably intentionally giving the middle finger to tourists and anyone who might give a fuck about trying not to poison people. Maybe I should send the bartender an anonymous EpiPen. *Use in case of balloon face.*

Then again, my brother Ryan is an idiot, and it's his fault that I'm here, listening to Anthony Rosings Smith drone on—his ability to complain seemingly as deep as the Mariana Trench—so maybe I'll invite Ryan out for a drink as soon as Roark lets him go.

"You okay, Jake?" Anthony asks, pausing with his beer halfway to his mouth. His brow is furrowed. The look he's giving me would probably be called patrician. Everything about him, from his expensive hair cut to his houndstooth jacket—which has *patches* on the elbows—makes him look out of place here. He's a sore thumb, a hundred dollar bill in a dirty tip jar, and I wonder if he always feels fingers reaching for him.

I fist my hand under the bar, letting my nails bite into my palm as a reset. I can't let my mask slip again. That was one of the first rules Roark taught us: *Never let your mask slip,* usually followed by "dumbass."

I grin at Anthony, then slap him on the back like he's my best buddy old pal. "Never better, my friend, never better. You were telling me about your mother?"

Anthony runs a hand over his face. "Jesus, when you say it like that... It's just...you're easy to talk to, but I didn't mean to spend the last half hour venting."

Yes, he did.

"Not at all!" I say, lifting my hands, palms out. "My mother's a pain in the ass too. Always complaining about..."

Shit, what would a mother always complain about...?

"She tries to control your love life too?" he asks with understanding.

I snap my fingers. "Yes, always. Like, find yourself a girlfriend if you feel so strongly about it. She really hated my last girlfriend. Told me I was a fool for choosing her."

He smiles, and I feel a smooth certainty slip in—like a fine wine. This is it. It's time. I've built the framework, and now it's time to slap up the house.

"You know what, my friend," I say, nudging his arm. "I'm good at getting to the bottom of problems."

"Because you're a therapist," he says knowingly.

I nod, accepting the lie as truth. "Exactly. You said your mom's having an engagement party for you and your fiancée next Saturday."

"She only agreed to it to make a point," he says darkly. "She's always trying to make a point about something. And Nina only wants to go because *she's* trying to make a point. God only knows what any of it is really about."

Man, this guy's really got the whole poor little rich kid thing going on. I wonder if he'd be making this same argument if he knew my mother took off when Ryan and I were just four, and the only thing I remember about her other than that is the fact that she named us Jake and Ryan after the dumbass main character of *Sixteen Candles*. Or that the only parental figure who stuck around for more than a year or two is the man who's currently holding my brother hostage for trying to steal from him.

I sneak a sidelong glance at Anthony, who probably got a pony for his fourth birthday. Yeah, I'm guessing he'd still complain if he knew. Makes me feel better about playing him at least. That's rule four or maybe five. *Demonize your mark. It helps you strengthen your defenses against them.*

I grin at Anthony like I could honestly think of nothing I'd like more than to sweet-talk another grown man's mother.

"Sure, sure," I say. "Why don't I come along, see if I can get her to communicate what's really going on? Wouldn't that be something?"

My pulse kicks up. I've been working up to this moment for two weeks. If he says no, I'll be wasting all the groundwork I put in, from running his wallet over to him—after I pickpocketed it—outside the gym to saying I'd only accept a drink as a reward. Not this drink, mind you. No one likes someone who acts too eager, even if they mean it. And if they don't...well, a person can tell. Maybe not the person sitting next to me, but when I commit to doing a job, I commit to doing it well.

So this is the third time I've had a drink with Anthony Smith. He's primed...he's ready...I think.

A slow grin spreads across Anthony's face, and I feel a thump of excitement in my chest. I'm in. Success is always a good feeling —like when your number comes up in a game of roulette or four cherries in a row. The bad feelings come later, creeping in at night or on the edges of an otherwise good experience, but this time I'm being an asshole for my brother's sake. Maybe there won't be any bad feelings.

"You'd really do that?" Anthony asks, as if I just offered him a platter of those fish eggs rich people pretend they enjoy.

"It would be my pleasure to help you and your lovely bride. Besides, I'd like to meet your mother."

That part's not entirely untrue. I've heard so much about Mrs. Rosings over the last couple of weeks that it'll be like coming face to face with a celebrity.

"Well, okay," Anthony says with a grin. "It starts at seven o'clock at Smith House. Are you free?"

Five days from now, because it's Tuesday evening—the only night Nina could "spare" Anthony this week.

Saturday's party will be the beginning of the end, thank fuck, because I am beyond done with this situation.

I make a show of checking my calendar on my phone, then nod. "Yeah, I should be able to swing it."

"Thanks so much, man."

His phone buzzes from its place on the bar, set out because he probably knew he was going to get summoned. He picks it up, frowning when he sees the screen. "Duty calls."

I'm tempted to ask him which of the women who controls him sent the text—his fiancée or his mother—but instead I say,

"And a true man always answers that call." I'm laying it on a little thick, but from the look of him, he doesn't mind.

He gives me one final clap on the back, then slaps some money down and leaves. He's the one who chose this dump of a bar, and I have to wonder if he picked it because he didn't want to be seen by anyone he knows. Maybe he wanted free rein to complain about his mother and his fiancée without being overheard. I can't deny the man has his own gilded problems. Sounds to me like he's having serious second thoughts about going through with his wedding to his controlling, gold-digging fiancée but would rather die than admit his mother is right. Although I've never come close to getting married—no woman in her right mind would *want* to marry me—I understand the sentiment. I don't like giving any ground to Roark either. In fact, I've done my damn best to break free of him and go legit—working on designing websites freelance—but my brother has unintentionally reeled me back in.

Sighing, I lean back in my chair and press out a text to Roark:

I've got an in on Saturday.

A second passes before a follow-up text comes through. It's a photo of Ryan sitting on his couch, watching TV. He's acting like he's on vacation, not being held hostage, but that's Ryan for you. If he were careful, he wouldn't be in this mess. I know Roark enough to understand the threat is still very real—sure, he's the closest thing we have to a father, but I believe he'll still hurt Ryan if I don't come through. "*You can do whatever you like, sure,*" he used to say, "*but there are always consequences.*"

He's made it clear what the consequences will be this time: *steal from me, lose a hand.*

It hasn't happened yet. But I have no doubt it will if I don't come through. Sure, Ryan's bulkier than I am, and he could physically best Roark in hand-to-hand combat, no problem. But Roark has a few very discreet, very unemotional people who work for him, people who aren't afraid of a little violence. People who have guns.

I'm pissed at my brother, and before all of this went down, I hadn't talked to him for almost a year, but I'd prefer for him to keep all of his body parts. Besides, I can't overlook that he was trying to mend our relationship, even if he unintentionally made everything worse.

I leave the bar and drive to the Airbnb apartment I've been renting under my assumed name, ready for a celebratory beer and some down time. I feel myself sighing as I head inside. It looks like a home...someone else's home. I'd sure as fuck never frame "home sweet home" needlework and hang it up next to the door.

Still, it's not a bad place. Too quiet, though. At home, I can hear so much of my neighbors' bickering that a few weeks ago I knocked on the wall and confirmed that Mick really *had* said that yesterday—and agreed with his girlfriend that it was uncool of him to have lied about it. Obviously, Mick didn't find that nearly as amusing as I did, but you can't please everyone.

Here, there's crickets.

Obviously, it's better to keep a low profile if you've gone somewhere to steal something, but I'm someone who craves noise, bustle, and conversation—even if it's light and meaningless. Maybe *especially* if it's light and meaningless. Because people can't be trusted, but they can be fun.

Asheville's busy enough, but I've kept in character. I don't want to be seen in the wrong places, talking to the wrong people.

Still...there's only so much quiet a guy can take. I've made some mistakes since arriving in town, including one really bad one, but I won't be making more of them. As much of a dumbass as my brother is, he's the only person I've allowed to mean anything to me.

I've collected a beer from the fridge and am sitting down with my sketch book and pencils when I hear a knock on the door. My back goes rigid, but I have no reason to worry about anyone coming after me, so I make my way to the door without pocketing my knife.

When I look out of the peephole, I see a perfect stranger. I know she's a stranger, because she's the type of woman a man doesn't forget—short, wavy black hair, eyes the color of a glass of fine whiskey, and a curvy figure showcased in a red sweater and a pair of shorts so short it looks like they're about to quit and move to Florida.

Don't be stupid, I remind myself. I don't know if this woman's here to preach to me about the second coming in an outfit that looks like sin, or if she's selling chocolate bars or magazine subscriptions no one wants, but I have to send her on her sexy way—even if my natural inclination is to invite her in for a drink.

I open the door slightly, nod to her.

"Hi," she says, giving me a look that lingers in a few places, sending a warm awareness through me. Then her hands worry at each other, and a little crease forms between her perfect black brows. "I'm sorry to bother you, *sir*, but I lost my cat, Professor X. I've been going up and down the hall looking for him."

I'm not even tempted to ask her if the cat is one of those hairless ones who bears a resemblance to Patrick Stewart. Hearing this woman call me *sir* from those red-painted lips is nearly a religious experience. "No, sorry," I say, then cock my head. "I thought no pets were allowed in these units."

Not that I give a shit, but it's always good to know who else is breaking the rules. Leverage isn't just a big word; it's a lifeline.

Her cheeks flush, but she doesn't look away, holding eye contact like it's a challenge. It just so happens that I like challenges. They fill my cup. "Are you a man who believes in following the rules?"

I lean against the door frame, enjoying myself now. "When it suits me."

She gives me another assessing look, that blush in her cheeks long gone, and I feel a prickle of something. Interest, sure. Attraction, hell yeah. But this is something else...something I can't put my finger on. Cocking her curvy hip, she plants a small hand on it—all sass and attitude—and I feel an unwanted appreciation, along with the thought that I'd like to wrap my hand around that hip and squeeze. "And does it suit you to help me look for him before I get into trouble?"

Don't do anything stupid. Don't do anything stupid.

"If it suits you to have a drink with me afterward," I say,

because I've never been very good at listening to sound advice, even if it comes from my own damn brain. "What's your name, lawbreaker?"

"Elaine," she says, holding my gaze. "And yours?"

"Jake."

Jake's a common enough name that I usually only change my last name when I'm posing as someone else. It helps when you can respond without the kind of hesitation that could give a person away.

She nods, then lifts her brows. "No time like the present, Jake."

It hits me that she doesn't seem particularly torn up over this lost Professor X. I'm grateful for that, but at the same time, it feels a little off. A woman who'd bother getting a cat would probably care about it going missing.

I've learned to trust my gut, so I ask, "You don't seem too worried about Professor X."

"He has a wanderer's heart," she responds. "It wouldn't be the first time. I've been careful because this place—" She waves her hands, silently referencing the stringent no-pet policy. "But there's no keeping him contained. He always comes back, though. Always."

"What's he look like? I need to know so I don't collar an unsuspecting cat."

"He's all black."

My suspicion eases, and the need to not be alone with my thoughts right now is powerful enough that I decide I'm going to do it, consequences be damned.

"Just a second." I dip inside to grab my keys, then lock the door behind me while Elaine watches.

"Are you from a big city?" she asks, her voice a little low and throaty, like she should be singing in a lounge somewhere.

I pocket the keys. "It's not that," I say, sidestepping the question. "I just don't believe in asking for trouble. My buddy here told me the cops don't respond much to B&Es."

"Or lost cats who aren't supposed to exist," she says with another half-smile that would make Mona Lisa jealous.

I glance down the hall, taking stock. My apartment's the last on the left. "So have you already checked in with everyone, or do you have one apartment left?" I motion to the place across the hall. It's occupied by an elderly, half deaf man who tells me the same joke every time I see him. *Where do pencils go on vacation? Pennsylvania.* I figure he doesn't get many sympathy laughs in his day-to-day, so I always give him a good one and offer him a beer. He accepted one time, and we had a twenty minute bitch-fest about traffic that was more engaging than anything Anthony Rosings Smith has ever said to me.

If I said that to Ryan, he'd shake his head and tell me that I have a chip on my shoulder about rich people. He'd also tell me it's ridiculous to have it out for the kind of people I'd love to become. Fair point.

"I haven't stopped by that one yet," Elaine confirms, "and then I was going to check the stairwell, maybe, and look around outside the building."

I have a feeling she's not going to see this cat until he wants to be seen, but I'm not too fussed about finding him. I want the company. The enjoyment and distraction of being out with a beautiful woman instead of stowed away in my box for the night.

She's your neighbor, you idiot. Abort. Abort.

At the same time...I'm only going to have to be here for another week or so, right? What's the harm in having a little fun?

And, sure, maybe that attitude is exactly what got Ryan into trouble in the first place, but we're not brothers for nothing.

CHAPTER THREE

LAINEY

If you pretend you have a pet, people are more likely to trust you. Pretend you're *looking* for that pet, and they'll probably offer to help you.

Yes, I know that sounds horrible. It *is* horrible.

It's a ruse my parents have used to introduce themselves to important people, and they formed a friendship with a couple who brought us to the Hamptons one summer.

I decided to pretend I'm Jake's neighbor for a couple of reasons.

Reason One: Cleo told me Jake has only lived in this place for a few weeks, so logic suggests he hasn't had a chance to meet all of his neighbors.

Reason Two: People are more likely to invite a neighbor into their apartment, and I need to get in there if I'm going to retrieve her necklace. It's not exactly safe to go inside a strange man's apartment, but I have mace and a Bowie knife and years of self-defense training. Besides, Nicole is my getaway driver and knows where I am. If he tries to cross me, he'll regret it.

Jake's certainly an attractive, charming devil, not that I'd expected anything different. Cleo had texted me a photo of him— slightly curly brown hair, light hazel eyes with long black lashes, and a tattoo of a fox made of fire on his forearm. He's drunk in the photo, judging by his bleary expression. I've looked at it a lot over the last few days, preparing for this moment.

He looks exactly like he did in the photo, and yet he doesn't...

He's got more...vitality, I guess. Everything about him seems alive, from the dancing flames on his intricately designed tattoo to his fit, muscular body and the mischief dancing in his eyes. It lights him up from within, making it hard to look away.

Or maybe it's the fires of hell that light him up.

Men like him have a seductive power, and after being in Jake's presence for twenty minutes, I'm positive he knows it and twists it to his advantage.

The only surprise so far was his rapport with his elderly neighbor, a grizzled man with wispy white hair and pitch-dark eyes who introduced himself as Mr. Tim. Jake clapped the old guy on the back, and they told each other terrible dad jokes. It was, I regret to admit, adorable. But for all I know, he's been stealing the guy's social security checks on the sly.

Jake sneaks another glance at me as we leave Mr. Tim's closed door and enter the stairwell. "Interesting name for a cat. Are you an X-Men fan?" he asks as I pretend to glance around for the fictional cat.

"I liked the comics when I was a kid," I tell him as we descend the stairs. When we reach the bottom, I peer around the small, decidedly empty space before reaching for the door handle. "I enjoyed imagining I was a mutant," I say as I open the door and step into the alley beside the building, Jake following me.

I'm not lying. I *did* like it. I normally felt like a cog in my parents' plans, but Lainey with X powers was in control.

"Me too," he says with a grin as the door clicks into place behind us. "My favorite character was Gambit."

I contain a snort. Of course he prefers the character who was a notorious thief. Not that I can talk...Gambit is my favorite too. I liked the thought that someone who was a villain could also be a bit of a hero—that we're not destined to only be the worst parts of ourselves.

"Let me guess," I say, clearing my throat. "Do you like playing cards?"

"Sure," he says, his grin spreading wider. "I like it a lot when I'm winning. The secret is knowing when to stop playing. My brother's never figured that out."

"You have a brother?"

He nods, glancing around, and I remember I'm supposed to be looking for my fictional cat. "Let's check out the area near the trash bin," I say, gesturing to the huge black dumpster in the alley. "Professor X has a thing for rotting garbage. It's the feline in him."

If he's disgusted by the thought of hanging out by a pile of trash on a hotter-than-usual October day, he doesn't let on. He strolls by my side, his pace easy and his stride confident, then says, "You got any siblings?"

"No, it was just me," I say, realizing belatedly that I could have made up a passel of brothers and sisters for "Elaine." Then again, it's always easier to stick to the truth so long as you don't dole out identifying details. There's also something surprisingly freeing about talking to a stranger, someone you're never going to see again. "But I have a close childhood friend. I used to pretend she was my sister." And also that her sweet-as-pie father was *my* father, but I don't add that. I haven't even told Claire. Jealousy isn't the kind of feeling you should ever admit to, according to my mother. It's something to act on, not get lost in.

He gives me another sidelong look, pausing, which prompts me to stop moving and turn toward him. His gaze moves slowly over my face, sending awareness in its path. Then he surprises me by slowly reaching up. I'm not sure what he intends at first, but he tucks my hair behind my ear, curling his fingers briefly around my ear. My breath catches, and an almost painful zing of awareness shoots through me. It's...disarming, but it's been a long time since a man's touched me; that's all.

"I get it," he says softly. "My brother's a bit of an idiot, but I don't know who I'd be without him. He keeps me grounded."

My mouth drops open, because I'm taken aback. I didn't expect him to have a sensitive side, but maybe he's just throwing out a lure to pull me in for that drink he requested.

Then something furry brushes against my legs. The only furry things to have ever unexpectedly brushed against my legs in New York City were rodents the size of domesticated pets, so I scream. And practically leap at Jake, who reflexively wraps his arm around me, pinning me to his hard, hot chest.

"What is it?" he asks, his tone urgent, his breath at my ear, and even though my nerves are still as raw as if someone took a cheese grater to them, I feel a hot shiver run through my body. I lean in closer—for protection, obviously, and also so we present a larger target.

"A rat," I say, my voice breathy. "It brushed against my leg."

Even as I report this gruesome fact, there's another brush of fur against my bare leg. I yelp again, but this time I look down—and see a black cat rubbing against my leg.

Huh.

My brain takes two seconds to absorb a few facts. Fact One: the cat's wearing a filthy red collar with no tag. Fact Two: the cat looks like he hasn't had a good meal in at least two weeks. He's either a stray or on one hell of a walkabout. Fact Three: the cat meets the description I gave earlier, and he's acting like I'm made of catnip. If I claim he's not mine, Jake will be suspicious. But if I claim he is, he might assume I'm a jerk who doesn't feed her cat...or suggest that I bring him home before coming over for that drink he promised me. I'd have nowhere to bring him but back out here, and if he's really a stray, he might need some help, and—

Jake has released me and is looking down at the cat expectantly, and I know I need to do something...

"Professor X," I croon, getting down on my haunches to pet the cat. "Mommy didn't realize it was you." In my peripheral vision, I can see Jake making a face, and I almost laugh. I've been overdoing it, but I feel the perverse urge to dial it up rather than down—to toy with Jake to see how he reacts. "Oh thank goodness, my widdle mister, Mommy was so worried this time, but you always come back to me, my baby boy, don't you, my darling?"

The look on Jake's face...

He's not even bothering to hide his reaction now. He's watching me and the cat with horrified fascination.

I try to hold it together, but I can't help it, I burst out laughing, and the cat leaps up onto my bent legs. He's small, but the maneuver catches me off-guard, so I land on my ass on the smelly pavement near the trash dumpster, laughing, the cat clutched in my arms. The absurdity only makes me laugh harder.

I used to be good at this kind of stuff, but I'm not anymore. I'm *glad* I'm not. But it's inconvenient at this particular moment.

Jake looks surprised, understandably, then he reaches for the cat and says, "Let me help you up, Catwoman," followed by a smirky smile that's hard to look away from, damn him.

I hand him the black cat presently known as Professor X, and he cradles him to his hard chest, holding out his other hand to me. I let him pull me up, trying not to feel too grateful for the assist—or to notice that he has nice, strong hands. Capable hands.

He's an asshole. A liar and a thief. He's only helping you because he wants something.

The something he wants is me—and I can't deny that thought is a little...exciting, even if I have no intention of giving myself to him.

I bolster myself against his smile, against the moment of shared humor. You can get along with anyone for twenty seconds. It doesn't mean they're a person worth knowing.

"You had me going for a minute, you know," he says, handing Professor X back to me gently, his hand brushing my arm. Another hot shiver has the nerve to work its way through me, especially when Jake meets my gaze, his eyes still full of mirth. I pointedly look away.

The cat surprises me by nuzzling his furry little head under my chin. I'm surprised by the heat building behind my eyes, the warm emotion drowning my chest. It's just...

I never had any pets growing up, but I'd always wanted one. Someone to take care of. Someone who'd love me no matter what and demand nothing in return. That was the precise reason my parents had said pets were a waste—you give and give and give and they couldn't ever return on the investment.

Because love didn't have any value on its own.

Coughing the emotion out of my throat, I say, "I'm very fond of my cat."

"Clearly."

"I color coordinate my outfits to his collars."

For a second, he looks uncertain again, like he can't tell whether he's in the presence of a psychopath or a person with a twisted sense of humor, and then a sparkle lights up his pretty eyes. "No, you don't. You're fucking with me."

"So why's he wearing a red collar?" I ask.

"Coincidence."

"I don't believe in coincidences."

That's true, mostly. Except...

The cat in my arms *seems* like a coincidence.

At the same time, there are any number of stray cats in Asheville. There's even a Facebook group called Asheville Cat Weirdos. I know this because I infiltrated it to get the goods on a woman who'd stolen her girlfriend's cat.

"But do you believe in keeping your promises?" Jake asks.

I can tell where this is going. He's going to ask me upstairs for a drink. While that's exactly what needs to happen, I can't deny there's a stubborn part of me that wants to laugh in his face again. He may seem funny and charming, and there's no denying he's very attractive, but he's wearing a mask as surely as I am. I know what he did to Cleo. I know who he is at his core—rotten. Wrong.

A little bit like you, a voice in my head whispers.

But I straighten my spine and tell that voice to keep its unsolicited opinions to itself.

"It just so happens that I do," I tell him brightly. But the little cat rubs his head against my chin again, and I register that the hand holding him to my chest can feel his ribs.

Nicole would tell me not to be an idiot, but I can't let this cat starve. He may not be my "Widdle Mister," but he deserves more.

"I need to feed my cat first."

I don't have a plan for that, but I'm a reasonably intelligent woman. Surely, I can figure something out.

He rubs his chin, then says, "There are a few cans of cat food under my sink. You're welcome to them."

"You have a cat too?"

He shakes his head. "It's a short-term rental. My best guess is that some rulebreaker left them in there, and the cleaning service didn't find them. There's also enough single-serving condiments to either make a person really sad or stock a Wendy's." He inclines his head. "I guess they could do both at the same time."

This is good. This lets me stick to the plan. But I have a strange feeling of misgiving. My gut tells me something is off, but I can't decide what unless it's the unexpected presence of this cat.

As we get close to the door leading into the building, I fuss over Professor X so Jake will know it's on him to take out his key card. But I make sure to reach the door first, because I don't want him to think I'm hesitating for any reason other than that I don't want to let go of the cat.

Jake doesn't seem to notice, easily slipping ahead and using his key card. We walk upstairs companionably, but I notice the way he's eying the cat. Professor X has one ragged ear, and he's skinny and gangly. My mark is probably wondering why someone who makes such a show of caring for her cat is neglectful, which makes me feel like a jerk even though Professor X isn't my cat—or wasn't until today. After I leave, I'm going to make sure to look for his people, and if I can't find them, I'll be his person.

The thought fills me with a warm glow, even if I'm not sure how I'll make my getaway with an unexpected sidekick.

"He been gone for a while?" Jake finally says as we reach his door.

I look down at his matted little head. "No." I adopt a grave tone. "He's just sick."

I feel like I'm cursing poor Professor X by implying he has a serious illness, but surely Jake will stop asking questions if he thinks my friend is on death's doorstep.

"What kind of sickness?" he asks, proving that an asshole will do whatever it is he wants. He unlocks the door and waits for me to step inside. I do and glance back as he follows me in and shuts the door behind him.

Frowning at him from over the cat's head, I say in an undertone, "I don't like discussing it in front of him."

Two minutes too late, it occurs to me that I should have told him that I'd only adopted Professor X a couple of weeks ago, which would have been a much more convincing story.

Jake lifts his eyebrows, probably teetering back toward his "she's crazy" estimation, then says, "You can take a look at the containers of food under the sink. See if there's something you think he'll eat."

Probably every last can Jake has, and the sink too, but I just set the little cat down, and he follows me into the kitchen.

"Would you like a beer?" Jake asks as he enters the kitchen behind us—it's open concept, so I guess we were technically in the kitchen as soon as we entered the apartment. That makes things easier, because I won't have to struggle to pretend I'm familiar with the layout of the apartments in this building.

Cleo told me she thinks he'd keep the necklace in his bedroom, and I have to agree. It's the only really private place in here, other than the bathroom, and most people wouldn't keep valuable belongings next to the toilet.

Which means I have to think of some excuse to go into the bedroom. By myself.

I glance down at my red sweater, covered in cat hair, and think, *You were a good sweater, and you didn't deserve this. But we all have a part to play.*

"I'd *love* a beer," I say brightly. "Thank you so much."

In truth, I don't love beer, other than some of the fruity flavors a few of the breweries around here have gotten creative with, but I won't be drinking much of it anyway.

I pull out the cans of food, and Professor X gives an excited yowl and scratches at them. So I open three and set them out in a row, and he's finished the third one before Jake can even pop the tops on the bottles of beer.

He takes in the scene without comment, but I see the questions forming behind his eyes. Not good. I have to speed this mess up. Still, the cat's mewing, so I open a fourth container, then grab a bowl from the drying rack next to the sink and fill it with water, setting that out too.

Jake hands me one of the beers, his gaze a little shuttered. I can't imagine what he suspects, but I have a feeling he hasn't caught on that his ex-girlfriend hired me to steal back the necklace he took from her, so at least I have that going for me.

"Shall we sit on the couch?" I suggest.

"Sure," he says, leading the way—and my traitorous eyes dip from his broad shoulders down to his ass. He's several inches taller than me but not huge, like Declan and Damien, and he fills his clothes out well. So what? The same could be said for bodybuilders with protein powder for brains. He certainly doesn't deserve any props for being good-looking and making the most of what genetics gave him.

We settle onto the couch, Jake a few inches away from me, and it's only then I realize I forgot to take the beer. I'm off-kilter. Unbalanced. Maybe that's because of the way he's sitting—so damn close, his thighs angled toward me, his knee almost touching mine. One arm is stretched over the back of the sofa, his fingers close enough to burrow into my hair.

I take a deep breath to settle myself, ignoring the prickling sensation across my exposed skin and the warmth that seems to radiate from him.

My gaze lands on the coffee table. There's a sketchbook on it, a pencil layered across the top.

"Oh, do you draw?"

"It's nothing," he says. Setting down his beer, he moves his other arm—the one that was nearly wrapped around me—and reaches for the book. He goes to stuff it into the drawer of the plain but serviceable end table next to the couch. But Professor X appears from nowhere like an avenging angel and takes a swat at it.

Jake swears and fumbles the sketchpad, and it falls open on the floor, revealing a hand drawn comic that makes me gasp. I see two little boys with curly hair in one panel, and a pair of foxes covered with fire in the next.

"That's really good," I say, surprised.

I've never seen such detailed pencil drawings in person before. I want a better look at it, but judging by the way he's already slapping it shut, he's not up for sharing. I study him with interest as he tucks the pad away. He's upset and showing it. For only the second time since I knocked on his door, I feel like I'm seeing something real from him. The first was just before I ended up on my ass next to the dumpster.

"They're only doodles," he lies.

And there the moment ends. Rest in peace, moment of truth, you were good while you lasted.

"Cool," I say, raising my eyebrows. "I like putting dumb little doodles together too when I'm on the phone."

Get it together, Lainey. Stop antagonizing the man.

But I can't seem to help myself. I take a minute to consider why, and come to an unwelcome conclusion. I'm doing it because I find Jake attractive, and just now, I found him a little interesting too.

I tell myself it's no big deal, because I'd probably find a mop attractive right now—if it had a vibrator attached. It's been a long time since I had sex, and much, much longer since it made me come. A good session with my vibrator is all it takes to send me over the edge. But Todd never did. He was a rich, attractive, white man, he was used to pleasing people simply by existing. So even though he had a big dick, he absolutely did not know how to use it.

I was also hyper-aware of everything I did when I was with him. Which angles were best for my face, my breasts. Which sounds he found the most appealing. I could never lose myself in the moment. The stakes felt too high. I'd decided to marry him, and I'd gotten lost in that goal, to the point where everything I did was about placating or impressing him.

So here I am, sexually starved, sitting next to a very attractive man whose opinion I couldn't care less about. It's natural I feel a little drawn in by him.

But I can't forget why I'm here. So I offer him a big smile. "What do you do for a living, handsome?"

He's watching me a little warily, which isn't great, but I still can turn this around.

"I'm a therapist."

I nearly snort on the sip of beer I just took, but I clap myself on the chest and say, "Sorry, went down the wrong way."

He angles his head. "I haven't seen you around the building before."

"I like to keep to myself, usually. I'm reserved."

The doubtful look on his face says it all.

"Around most people," I add flirtatiously, batting my lashes at him. "I feel *very* comfortable around you."

Something flickers in his gaze. He's not buying it.

Professor X strolls back into view with a tuft of feathers he got from who knows where—possibly a pillow he decimated within the last five minutes—and then rolls onto his back right in front of us, giving us a good view of his—erm—her privates.

Jake frowns. "Is that cat...female?"

I don't think, I just lean over and kiss him.

CHAPTER FOUR

JAKE

This woman is a tornado of chaos. One minute she's giving me shit, the next she's coming on too strong, and then there's her cat, who seems intent on ruining this apartment...

There's a story with the cat, and it's not the one she's telling me.

It was stupid to invite Elaine in here—the kind of stupid that gets a man in trouble. It would be stupider to ask her to stay. But she just kissed me, and my dick is at war with my brain. So I shift on the couch and lift a hand up into the black satin waves of her hair and kiss her red-painted lips, needing them to open for me and let me in.

I have the stupid urge to impress her. She might not think much of my drawings, or my fake career in talk therapy, but I'm good at some things. Maybe, if I play my cards right, she'll let me show her all of them. I suck on that bottom lip I've been eying for the past hour, full and lined with red, and she releases a gusty sigh and leans in closer—then surprises the hell out of me by climbing onto my lap.

Oh, hell yeah. My hand finds her curvy hip and slides around it, drawing her closer, letting her feel how much I appreciate her.

My dick was already half-mast, and now it's painfully hard. But I haven't gotten the green light to involve my dick, so I focus on her sweet lips opening to me, her legs straddling me, knees on either side of me on the couch cushions. I pull her closer, deepening the kiss and rocking her against my body, and she rocks back harder, her teeth clashing against mine almost as if she wants to bite me.

We're all over each other, feral, and it hits me that this has escalated quickly. Too quickly. I don't know shit about this woman, other than that she's lying about something, possibly multiple things. So am I, but I haven't really lied to her. Not about anything except for Jake Jeffries being a head shrinker.

Lying isn't something I do because I like it. It's a survival tactic, a job, a trick of the trade.

She meets my gaze, and something glints in her eyes before she really *does* bite my lip—sending a bolt of pure need straight to my dick. I'd meant to back off, to guide her back to her own square of the couch, but damn it, I don't have it in me. At this particular moment, she's my own personal kryptonite. The sweet distraction I didn't realize I needed after my evening with Anthony Rosings Smith. She wants me, and I want her. Can't I just shut off my brain for half the night? Won't that help me mentally prepare for what's ahead?

I slide my hand around her hip and squeeze her ass, bringing her closer. Sighing into her sweet mouth when she grinds against my dick, the friction the kind of sweet torment that has driven men to acts of insanity.

I guess bringing a strange woman home to the apartment you're staying in for a few weeks before you steal a priceless piece of jewelry qualifies one of them.

And this isn't even the first time I've made that particular mistake. Last time, at least I had the excuse of being so drunk I could barely stand.

Then there's a crash and a yowl from behind the couch, and Elaine practically leaps off of my lap.

I get up, my dick jutting against the zipper of my pants, and see that the cat has emerged from behind the refrigerator with a glue trap attached to the side of his—or I guess her—body.

"Oh no," Elaine says, running to her. The cat steps back and hisses, and again I have an itch in my brain—a feeling of something not being quite right with the two of them.

I scratch my head, trying to get my brain working again, but too much of my blood is still down south. "The guy who owns this place must have put them behind the fridge. They're glue traps, for—"

"I know what they are," she says, biting her own lip this time, glancing up at me with those whiskey eyes. "I don't think he—she's going to let us get it off. We have to find the closest animal clinic."

"Isn't there a vet you go to?"

"Yes," she says, reaching for the cat, who swats at her with a paw and hisses, clearly not into the idea of letting anyone near her or the glue trap. "They told us never to come back."

What, now?

"Why do I get the feeling you're not telling me something?" I ask, that once mild brain itch turning into a poison ivy patch. My dick has deflated, because this situation feels strange, to say the least.

She made it sound like the cat's dying of incurable cancer, but if that animal's sick, she's spry as hell. And cancer doesn't explain why she looks like she's been living hard for months.

Besides, who the fuck doesn't know whether their own cat is male or female?

Is the cat even hers?

The more I think about it, the more the whole thing stinks worse than those trash bins outside do, even though I can't wrap my head around what she could possibly be up to. She can't know who I really am or why I'm here.

So maybe she *is* crazy.

Elaine just stares at me and grabs the beer she left on the kitchen counter, taking a long pull of it. "Can you look up the closest place on your phone, Jake? *Please.*"

The cat's pawing at the glue trap now, and it hits me that it's a hell of a way for a mouse to go out. Stuck where it stands, no ability to escape. Trapped. Doomed. Celestially fucked. I decide I'm going to look behind the fridge later and remove any traps that might still be back there. No one deserves to die like that.

But first I have to get Elaine and her cat out of my apartment. There's something off with her, badly off, and I would have noticed if my dick weren't such a fan of her.

So I grab my phone off the coffee table and start Googling. But I've barely entered in a search when I hear the sound of something spilling, followed by an *oh shit* and another yowl.

When I turn around, Elaine has somehow managed to spill what looks like her entire beer down the front of her shirt.

How? The opening in the bottle shouldn't be large enough.

"I'm sorry," she says, lifting a hand to her wet chest. For a second, my gaze is drawn down to the slope of her tits, pressing against the front of the wet fabric...but I force myself to look away.

"I don't even know you," she says, looking at me with gorgeous whiskey eyes full of worry. "You must think I'm..."

"No," I say quickly, even though the real answer is *yes*. "But you're right. You should get Professor X some medical treatment."

"Except..." she pauses. "Could I please borrow one of your shirts? I don't really want to go to the clinic smelling like a brewery." She smiles at me. "I know it'll be *much* too big, but I can tie it up with a knot—and return it later of course."

It's a reasonable request, and to tell her no would make me a jerk. So I nod. "Yeah, no problem," I say, even though I have no intention of collecting it later.

I bring her inside the bedroom, feeling her presence like it's branding me, because even though I've decided this is a no-go, dead-end situation, she's still a gorgeous woman, and she's about to strip down in my room. Put on one of my shirts.

My attention shifts to the feathers all over the floor and the murdered pillow lying amidst them.

There goes Jake Jeffries's security deposit.

"Sorry," she says self-consciously. "She really likes feathers. I have to sleep on foam."

"No problem," I lie.

I tug a navy blue T-shirt out of the drawer, gritting my teeth, and then back out of the room. Trying not to think of her perfect tits exposed to the functional dresser and the ugly Home Sweet Home prints on the wall.

The door slams shut in my face.

Yes, this woman is a fucking tornado, and I already have whiplash.

"This was a bad idea," I tell the cat in an undertone, then run a hand through my hair. She yowls and bats at the glue trap, eyes full of fire.

I have to keep a low profile until Saturday, then I need to blow town as soon as possible.

CHAPTER FIVE

LAINEY

I tell myself she'll come around. I have to believe it, because there's no way I can bring myself to leave the cat behind.

I start rummaging through Jake's drawers like a contestant on a shopping spree show, knowing the clock is ticking down. *It's okay, Lainey, you've got this.* Then I get a glimpse of myself in the mirror attached to the dresser top, seeing my smeared lipstick and beer-soaked shirt. My fingers lift to my kiss-swollen lips.

I climbed onto his lap like a woman possessed.

Nope. Don't got this.

This situation has gotten way out of control, from the way I climbed that jerk like a tree—my hormones lighting up like a string of Christmas lights, delighted to be plugged into the wall—to the glue trap attached to the poor, apparently female cat. I swipe at my lips as I open another drawer, swiping a hand along the sides and then the bottom. Nothing.

This is not good. It only takes a reasonable person a matter of seconds to put on a shirt, and sure, I haven't been coming off as particularly reasonable, but he won't want to leave an unreasonable woman alone with his things for long.

"Elaine, is everything okay?" Jake calls.

My pulse kicks up a notch, my breath coming in pants. I need more time. There's a chance the necklace isn't even in here—that he hid it somewhere in the living room—but my gut tells me he'd want to stow something valuable in the bedroom, where most visitors would never see it. Maybe I need to remove the drawers?

"Elaine?"

"Sorry," I shout, my mind working fast. Then, cringing, I use the one excuse guaranteed to buy any woman a few minutes. "I just got my period, and it's a real bloody mess. I'm so sorry, but I'll be a few minutes."

There's an en suite bathroom, which makes it a reasonable excuse.

Quiet hangs on the other side of the door, and there's a pause as I carefully remove the bottom right drawer, trying not to make any noise. It's a new dresser, thankfully, not like the old, creaky piece of furniture I have back at the cabin, and it slides out without much fuss. Then Jake calls out, "Do you want me to go ask one of the neighbors if they have any..." There's a pause. "Tampons?"

I halt what I'm doing, taken aback by his offer. It's not the kind of thing you'd expect a cheat and a thief to say, but then again, it wouldn't be the first time he's surprised me tonight. He's not what I thought he'd be. Still, I'm here for a reason, and if accepting his offer buys me some time, I'm all for it. The only neighbor I know is the one who's across the hall from him, and there's no obvious reason why the joke guy would have tampons, but presumably Jake knows a few more people. If I get lucky, this could give me enough to search his whole room.

"That would be so sweet of you. Thank you so much."

There's another pause, and I can imagine him shifting on his feet just outside the door, maybe running a hand through his messy hair. My mind darts to his tattoo—did he come up with the design himself? It looks a lot like the drawing in his book.

Then I remember that I'm holding a drawer full of his pants because I'm looking for the necklace he stole from his ex-girlfriend. My resolve firms.

"Ask them if they have super tampons for a heavy flow," I say sweetly as I gently lower the drawer to the thick carpet and feel the vacant area it left behind. Nothing.

I hear his footsteps walking away, followed by the sound of the door opening and closing.

My blood pounding harder in my veins, I return the pants drawer to its usual position and go for the one next to it, on the other side of the dresser. I pause when I notice the contents— sketchpads, like the one he hid in the other room. Colored pencils.

I'm tempted to look inside the books, but it would feel like a violation of his privacy—a thought that makes me laugh at myself as I slick the drawer out and set it on the floor. *All* of this is a violation of privacy, and he deserves it. I have to remember that. Sure, he may have some artistic talent, and he may be man enough to discuss periods with his neighbors, but he's also a player and a thief. He's the kind of guy who inspired me to start the Love Fixers.

I slide my hand around at the bottom of the dresser again, on the left side this time, and find a strip of condoms. Frowning at it, I toss it back in, telling myself this is further proof that he's been up to no good. I return the drawer to its position, stumped, then head into the connected bathroom, feeling around the floor for any loose tiles—none.

Where the hell would he have hidden it?

My mind circles back to those sketchbooks, and I return to that drawer, working quickly.

I open the first book and see more pencil sketches. My finger traces a picture of the same little boys from the book in the living room. Both of them look a bit like Jake.

What a strange combination of things he is—a therapist who draws and steals. What made him this way?

It doesn't matter. You don't need his fucking origin story. He's an asshole. A liar.

My heart thumping, I open the second book, and this time my heart lodges in my throat because there's a cut out in this one, with a little box nestled inside. I pull it out and click it open, and there it is—a gorgeous blue heart pendant set in swirls of white gold.

For some reason, I'm disappointed for half a second. Disappointed that Jake is exactly what I thought he was a couple of hours ago. But this helps me push him squarely into his bad guy box. In fact, his decision to hide the necklace in a hollowed-out book speaks of a level of deception that's frankly unhinged. He may know how to charm, and I have to admit he *definitely* knows how to kiss, but he's not good news for anyone.

He took this necklace from Cleo, and now I'm going to steal it back for her. Fair is fair. And sure, he's going to know it was the crazy lady with the cat, but he could hardly report me to the police when he stole the necklace himself. Even if he did, he doesn't know anything about me other than my legal first name.

I remove the necklace from the box, stuffing it into my shorts pocket, and then return the box to the book and the book to the drawer.

I'm about to clean up the mess I made in the other drawers, but it occurs to me that I shouldn't. It'll take him longer to notice the missing necklace if the rest of the room is a horror show. So I start scooping clothes out of the drawer and throwing them everywhere. A T-shirt over the lamp. A pair of pants strewn over the bed. A real clothes murder scene. I reach for the bottom left drawer, for the sketchbooks, and then...don't.

I tell myself it's because it'll tip him off to check the necklace box sooner rather than later, and not because I like his drawings.

The damage done, I exit through the bedroom door, shutting it behind me.

And slam right into Jake. A jolt shakes me before I regain my senses enough to take a step back, but his shirt is left with an imprint of my boobs...because I didn't change out of the beer-soaked shirt.

He looks at me in obvious bafflement—

I was in there for at least twenty minutes, and I'm still wearing the same shirt.

"I got distracted by all the blood," I explain. "It was like a murder scene in my pants."

He lifts his brows. I can't tell whether he's disgusted or just unaccustomed to women speaking like this to him. "Uh. Ohh-kay. Sorry, no tampons. Joy in 2G said her monthly visitor stopped coming twenty years ago. But she offered to pack up some menses tea for you. Apparently she makes it for a small business, so that's good news, I guess."

I study him for a second too long. Does he actually have a neighbor named Joy, or is this some kind of test, to see if I say something like, "*Yes, that sounds like Joy, all right,*" so he can catch me in a lie?

"Well, thanks for asking," I say breezily. "I think I'd better go take care of that situation. A wad of toilet paper will only last for so long."

I'd wanted to see him flinch, so I'm gratified when he does. I feel a little...testy after finding the necklace like that, hidden away in a book, as if he can conceal his shame. He *should* be made to feel uncomfortable, and I'm happy to take on that duty for all of womankind.

Crouching down, I call to Professor X, feeling Jake's gaze on me. "Come here, kitty, kitty. Come here, Professor X."

"Cats don't typically come when called," he says, doubt layered into his voice.

"She's an exception," I insist as she hisses at us, pawing at the glue trap. There's no reason for me to be nice to him anymore—all the better if we get out of his apartment sooner rather than later—so I add, "When she doesn't have an arcane torture trap attached to her side."

"You're blaming me for this?" he asks in disbelief.

I lift my chin. "Yes. It's cruel to kill mice that way. You should be ashamed of yourself."

"Unbelievable," he mutters, shaking his head. "Are you going to tell me whose cat just destroyed my pillow and scratched my arm? Because she sure as hell isn't yours."

"How *dare* you," I seethe, getting caught up in the lie.

"Just go," he says, swearing, then sweeps his fingers through his hair. I have a vivid memory of those strong hands tracing up my thighs and squeezing my hip. God, why do jerks have to be so capable with their hands?

"Gladly," I say as I take a step toward the cat. She hisses and bares her teeth at me. Shit, how am I supposed to get her out of here and to a vet?

"I might need a little—"

"Use the last can of food," he says, sounding exhausted. "She's obviously starving."

There's *definitely* an accusation in his tone this time.

"I told you, she went on a walkabout." For some reason I really don't want him to think I'd mistreat an animal in my care. I assure myself it has nothing to do with him, personally, I'd feel the same way about anyone.

I retrieve the food from under the sink, take the cover off, and sure enough, Professor X comes to me, mewing with discontent before she takes another swipe at the glue trap. I can't Pied Piper her all the way to a vet, though, can I?

I guess I don't need to—just out to Nicole's car.

Presuming Nicole lets me bring a stray cat into her car...and agrees to take us to the vet.

Honestly, it doesn't seem like something she'd do willingly— she's not the bleeding heart type—but maybe I can use this story as leverage. She'll think it's funny, obviously, and want every grue-some detail.

"Well, I guess I'll see you around," I say to Jake, throwing a wave at him as if I wasn't trying to suck his beautiful lips off his sexy face twenty minutes ago. He looks like he has whiplash, but I refuse to be sorry for giving it to him—I'll bet Cleo had whiplash when her gorgeous, sexy faced boyfriend cheated on her and then stole her necklace.

But he recovers quickly and calls out, "Hopefully not," as I shut the door behind me.

Well, screw him.

I wish I could see his face when he opens that necklace case and finds it empty, but I'll have to settle for knowing that I ruined his night.

A couple of people are standing directly in front of the stair-way, talking, and one of them is wearing a lanyard and badge that suggests she might work here. She could take offense to seeing a cat in this no-pets-allowed building, so I quickly veer in the other direction. I hurry down the hall with the can of cat food extended like a lure, and I'm almost at the stairs at the opposite end when I bump into an older woman with a kindly face and a mass of blonde and white hair loosely gathered at the nape of her neck. She looks like a model GMO companies would put on boxes of cereal bars so they can fool people into thinking they're healthy.

"Oh, dear," she says. "You wouldn't happen to be Elaine, would you?"

I nearly drop the cat food but settle for nodding.

"This is for you, dear. I used to get some very aggressive menses too." She holds out a little packet of tea…and I take it with my free hand and stuff it into my pocket with the necklace.

The part of my brain that is not currently occupied with the worst getaway attempt in human history registers that Jake actually asked around about tampons for me. So he's a tool, but at least he's not afraid of Aunt Flow, unlike ninety percent of the men I've ever met.

"You know…" she adds. "I thought I knew everyone in this building, but I've never met you before." She glances down at Professor X and does a doubletake. I'm sure I'm about to get lectured about the building rules, but she looks down the hallway before asking in an undertone, "You found Trixie?"

"Her name is Trixie?"

"Yes." She stoops as if to pet the cat, but Trixie hisses at her.

If the older woman minds, she doesn't let it show. Shaking her head, she says, "She belonged to the man who lived in 2D, but he left her behind when they moved. No one knew, so she was in there for days." She shakes her head, then adds, "But that was months ago, before your friend moved in."

"How could someone do that?" I ask, affronted. From what I can tell, this cat has two personality modes: overly clingy and raging, but maybe that's because the person she loved tried to destroy her.

"I never liked him," she says conspiratorially. "He said my rooibos tea gave him diarrhea."

Note to self: discard the menses tea.

"Well, thank you. I know we're not allowed to have cats in this building, but I found her outside, and I'm not going to abandon her again. I'll move if I have to."

I only said that to help explain why Joy will never, ever see me again, but she beams at me, and guilt skitters across my skin like a spider. I don't like lying to nice people, like Marjorie Eccles or Joy. Lies should be reserved for other liars. For the kind of people who use words like weapons, to hurt and destroy and trick.

For people like me and Jake.

Then Joy's eyes narrow on the cat formerly known as Trixie—because there's no way I'm going to let the man who abandoned her have the privilege of giving her a name, particularly not a name with so little dignity. She's a professor, dammit. I just promoted her.

"What's that on her side?" Joy asks, squinting.

I don't feel like getting into an explanation about the glue trap, particularly not since Jake is probably even now combing through the mess in his bedroom. Any minute now, he'll open that drawer...

Then a car horn beeps outside the building. Nicole's car horn?

"Thanks for the tea," I call out and run toward the stairwell, the open food can extended. Professor X runs after me, thank God, and vaults down the stairs like an Olympic gymnast.

CHAPTER SIX

LAINEY

It's Friday afternoon, four days after the emergency vet had to fully sedate Professor X to remove the glue trap, which cost more than what Cleo had paid me to recover the necklace. But the cat seemed grateful for it, and she's warming up more toward me every day. She only hissed at me twice this morning—once when I failed to produce her food in a timely manner, and again when I made the mistake of touching the shorn spot where she got glue-trapped. Now, I'm at my day job, assisting Mrs. Rosings of Smith House— the largest estate in Marshall, an enormous airy mansion that still manages to feel stuffy. It's the largest private residence in Marshall, which would be more impressive if most of the houses weren't one-story bungalows.

I left the necklace with Nicole, and she and I have arranged to meet Cleo in our office at the cabin after work to hand over the goods. It's hard to be patient, because I'd rather be there, not here. My heart's not in this well-paid, poorly defined job—and from the way Mrs. Rosings is glaring at me from across the table in her velvet-encrusted drawing room, she knows it.

This is another opportunity I fell into. Claire got her bakery, and I got her former job as Mrs. Rosings's personal assistant. Mrs. Rosings has made it very clear that she doesn't think much of me, but at least our resentment is mutual.

Claire likes the older woman a lot and thinks she's just lonely and bored, with a sharp brain that's underutilized.

Of course, Claire likes almost everyone.

Mrs. Rosings looks and smells like money—from her overpriced kaftans to the perfect white of her hair, made that way by dye, not age, since her natural color would be salt and pepper, heavy on the salt. I know because last month, she had to wait an extra week to get it touched up since her hair stylist had the flu.

When I look at her, it's like someone pressed fast forward on my life, and I'm seeing what I would have become if I'd gone through with the engagement and married Todd.

Proud.

Bored.

Lonely.

Manipulative as fuck.

She's been planning her son Anthony's engagement party and wedding to a woman she hates—doing a terrible job on purpose in the hopes of splitting them up.

While I would normally resent this sort of interference in another woman's love life, I can tell she's one hundred percent right about the future Mrs. Smith. Takes one to know one, after all. I can see it in the glint in Nina's eye—like she's won something and will turn into a feral cat if someone tries to take it away. Hear it in the proprietary way she calls Anthony her fiancé but never says his name. Intuit it from the fact that she has allowed Mrs. Rosings to do all of the planning for her wedding. She hasn't even offered an opinion about anything other than one crucial point—the wedding has to happen on New Year's, and it has to be at Smith House. Other than that, she's passively agreed to every microaggression and outright insult. Maybe she does it because she knows she's driving Mrs. Rosings crazy, her attitude underscoring that it's not the wedding or even the marriage she wants: it's Smith House and all its glory. Whatever the case, she's in it to win it, and nothing Mrs. Rosings has done so far has chipped at her façade.

Maybe Mrs. Rosings doesn't like me because she understands that I'm not helping her for her sake, but for Nina's. Marrying someone for money and status is a mistake. Anthony seems fine, I guess, if you enjoy hanging stuffed shirts in your closet, and he's handsome enough, but Nina has no love for him. It's as obvious to me as it is to Mrs. Rosings, and his inability to see that truth makes me dislike him a little. It suggests he's the kind of man who believes everyone loves him, so *of course* she means what she says.

Nina may think she's won something now—she may look at this house and dream of it being hers someday—but what will be left of her by the time that happens? Will she have become the future mother-in-law she hates?

Maybe she'll be so far gone she won't even be able to regret what she's done.

I don't know Nina well, but I've worn her expensive shoes, so I've felt the pinch. I know what it feels like to pretend to be someone else, day and night, like a hand was wrapped around my neck from morning until night, never releasing me. To feel the truth slipping away like it was covered in greasy film. To think I was in control of the situation, only to become owned by it.

I *know*.

So in my mind, I'm helping Nina, not Mrs. Rosings...not that I expect either of them to thank me.

The engagement party will be a buffet of horrors. There will be a petting zoo. Yes, a petting zoo for adults who were told to dress in black tie optional. The meal will be seven courses of Anthony's favorite childhood foods...from when he was five—chicken fingers and French fries, served up by hired help, while Mrs. Rosings gives a twenty minute speech about nothing. The fancy fast food will be followed up by an hour-long slide show of Anthony's childhood pictures, accompanied by multiple versions of "The Power of Love." Then there will be dancing, with an assortment of music selected to annoy, played on a sound system tweaked to emit a horrible sound every five to seven minutes, unpredictably. At the end of the night, each guest will get a cookie, made by Claire, that bears the likeness of the happy couple.

"You'll be there, of course," Mrs. Rosings says grumpily. "To make sure everything goes according to plan."

Which is to say everything goes badly. At least I'll have someone at the party to gripe to, because Claire's boyfriend's sister is one of the waitstaff. Rosie works with Claire at the bakery but gets bored easily and is constantly taking one-off jobs. She's done some work for Nicole and me for the Love Fixers—delivering the *fuck you very much* cookies and a bouquet of penis balloons with smiley faces for a "real dickhead."

"Does this count as my invitation?" I ask.

Mrs. Rosings makes a disagreeable sound. "As if you should need to be invited to do a job you're being fairly compensated for."

"Mrs. Rosings," I say, tsking. "A girl likes to be romanced a little. Do you want me to ask Claire to come too? I think she and Declan have plans, but they could be persuaded."

She shakes her head tersely. "No, let's let them have a night out. I don't think they'd enjoy themselves at the party." A wicked smile crosses her face. "In fact, I think we'll be the only ones who enjoy ourselves."

"Has Emma given her final RSVP?" I ask, referring to Mrs. Rosings's elusive daughter. I've worked for the older woman for a couple of months now, and I've still never met her. Mrs. Rosings tells me she stays busy with work, although it's less clear what she actually does for a living. In my mind, she's one of those professional rich people, who sips lemonade on verandas and complains about where she's seated even when she's the one who picked the table. But maybe that's just my own prejudice working—that and her name, Emma Rosings Smith.

Mrs. Rosings's mouth puckers. "No, but my daughter loves to keep us all in suspense." She taps her finger on the table, then says, "Speaking of RSVPs, Anthony said he's bringing someone else. A young man. So we'll need another place setting for him, at the very least."

Hopefully, it's not a business contact, because whoever this guy is, he's about to see a photo montage of Anthony in diapers.

"Should we warn Anthony?"

Her lips upturn slightly. "He must know I have something special planned. If I know my son, this new guest is supposed to 'talk sense into me.' Well, let him try. I hope he enjoys petting zoos. I'm told one of the goats is incontinent."

I mime tipping an imaginary hat at her.

She sighs and tells me to leave.

"I'll be here tomorrow at five to help get the petting zoo set up."

She seems deep in thought, and when she rouses, she says, "Can you ask Claire to add 'Eat me,' to the bottom of each of the cookies?"

Damn, this woman is vicious. She's also nervous. I can tell that beneath all of her machinations she actually loves her son. She's running out of time, and she can feel the next several weeks drifting through her fingers.

Anthony and Nina are having a New Year's wedding, and Halloween is next Thursday. Mrs. Rosings only has a couple of months left to convince her son he's making a mistake—which means I only have a couple of months left to convince Nina of the same.

"Will do, boss." I salute her and turn to leave.

"Wait!" Mrs. Rosings calls out.

I turn to look at her, and she says, "I'll need you to come in early. I've decided I want to put a few of my jewels on display in the drawing room. There are some cases we can use in the basement. Anthony needs to witness the hungry look in Nina's eye when she sees the Heart of the Mountain. Then he'll understand what he's doing."

I don't know what the hell she's talking about, and if Anthony hasn't seen the writing on the wall now, he's not going to see it if it's underlined and in neon lights, but I nod my agreement anyway.

"Did you see the documentary that the Discovery Channel released a couple of months ago?" she asks.

This is where most people would politely inform her that they have no idea what the fuck she's talking about, but I refuse. She already thinks I'm ignorant, why give her fodder for the fire?

"Which one are you talking about?" I ask, as if there are dozens of documentaries about obscure necklaces, and I've enjoyed watching all of them.

She rolls her eyes, probably thinking something along the lines of *stubborn girl, why did I have to lose the nice one?* Then says, "I'm surprised you didn't do your research. You're an enterprising girl too."

"I didn't think I'd be working here for this long," I admit.

I'd hoped that The Love Fixers would be bringing in more money by now, but we've been held back by our location in Marshall, the steep learning curve of Facebook ads—which has prevented me from successfully putting any up—and how long it took for us to put the LLC paperwork through. It probably doesn't help that I blew the income from our biggest gig on paying for a cat to be put under sedation.

Mrs. Rosings snorts. "That makes two of us."

There's a strange kind of camaraderie that's developed between us as a result of our mutual disdain. "If I were bored enough to look for this documentary, how would I find it? And, follow-up question, should we air it in its entirety after the hour-long slide show?"

She grins at me, showing all of her teeth. "Now, there's a thought. It's forty-five minutes long, dull as dust, and they don't talk about the Heart of the Mountain until the last five minutes."

I get a flash of Todd, talking about that Yankees bat until the people in front of him had fight-or-flight coming off them in their sweat, beaded at their brows. At least Mrs. Rosings has an objective other than pissing people off just because she can, I guess. I have to admit that if I had a son, I probably wouldn't want him marrying Nina either. Her intentions are, at a guess, not to love and cherish Anthony until the day he dies.

"Would you like to see the necklace?" she asks, something flashing in her eyes.

I wonder if she's only offering because she wants to see a greedy look in *my* eyes—confirming everything she suspects about *me*.

If so, she'll be disappointed. I have plenty of jewels and gems from Todd, which I've been slowly but surely selling on eBay.

"Sure," I say. "Are you going to pull an old woman in Titanic move and throw it into the mountains at midnight or something?"

"Maybe," she says, lifting her chin. "It would certainly create a stir."

And I find myself smiling at her—genuinely smiling. "Yes, I'd like to see it."

I watch as she rises from her chair, wearing one of her signature kaftans. They're the kind of clothes people wear for the same reason they tell long, pointless stories and subject other people to boring documentaries. Because they can. Because their status has given them power, and they want you to know it.

I grit my teeth, then my mouth falls open. Mrs. Rosings is approaching the fireplace, where, beneath portraits of her two children, is arranged a row of urns on top of the fireplace mantel. One for every husband she's buried—three of them—along with a special bequest from Claire's biological father, whose death resulted in us moving here.

A gasp escapes me when she opens the second urn. My grandparents were buried in plots economically purchased decades before they died, so my knowledge about them is limited, but I'm pretty sure it's against urn etiquette to *open* them.

"Oh, relax," she says with a smile that seems genuine. "I poured out Adrien's ashes underneath the apple tree *decades* ago. It seemed only appropriate since he died picking from it."

It's not the most lovelorn thing a person could say. Then again, Mrs. Rosings admitted to Claire that she married the man because she was a gold digger, just like the town suspects. She also told her that Adrien Smith was not the hero he's venerated for being. While Mrs. Rosings is a piece of work, I believe her.

Todd is universally beloved too—forgiven for his "quirks," like the boring-as-fuck story about the Yankees bat, or his inability to lose at anything, even Pretty Princess, which his niece insisted on playing at Thanksgiving last year. Todd pouted for half the afternoon because he didn't get the crown. But the people who flit through his life don't see the man he really is—the one behind the smile his parents bought him at the orthodontist.

Cold, withholding, punishing, cruel.

The kind of man who'd adopt a kitten and leave her behind in his apartment because she was too much work.

My mind flashes to Jake Jeffries, who'd gone up and down his apartment hallway asking for a tampon for me. Even though he's a bad apple, too, I can't help but smile at the thought. Todd would never have done that.

"It's something, isn't it?" Mrs. Rosings asks, jolting me to awareness, and then I gasp, my mouth falling open. The large blue, heart-shaped gem is surrounded by a starburst of white gold spikes embedded with diamonds, the chain an intricate and unusual pattern of white and yellow gold I've only seen once before.

The necklace she pulled out of her husband's empty urn is the exact replica of the one I retrieved from Jake Jeffries's room.

Or, I'm guessing, the necklace I stole from him is an exact replica of this one.

CHAPTER SEVEN

LAINEY

"Yup," Nicole says, leaning back in her chair in our makeshift Love Fixers office. I'm sitting next to her, and the necklace I took from Jake is spread out on the surface of the desk in front of us, the jewel glittering in the overhead light. The desk is parked several feet away from the wall, with our chairs behind it and two guest chairs in front of it. Above us is a window that beams in light from the outside world. "It's a fake. A good fake, mind you—the Mona Lisa of fakes—but a fake nonetheless."

I sigh and bury my face in my hands. "You already went to the pawn shop?"

"Didn't need to. Damien knows what to look for."

Damien being her husband. They own their private investigator business together, and the Love Fixers is a side project for her. One she probably won't be willing to spend much more time on, all things considered. This was my first big gig beyond fun but petty revenge pranks, and I blew it in a dozen different ways.

"This is..."

I feel a sinking sensation in my stomach. Professor X, who's been lovingly stalking me since I got home, mews loudly and leaps up into my lap. I carefully pet her, avoiding the glue trap spot, because I don't want to bring out her Mr. Hyde.

Sighing, I admit, "It's all my..."

Nicole's gaze meets mine in a no-bullshit kind of way. "This just became *way* more interesting. Before, it was about some boo-hoo boy toy stealing his woman's necklace out of spite. I mean, sucks for her, and she deserves it back, but who really cares, in the scheme of things? Now, though..."

A knock lands on the front door, but it's much too early for Cleo, and seconds later it opens without anyone getting up to unlock it. So it's either someone we know or the kind of home invader who knocks.

Claire steps into the room a few seconds later, holding a paper bag that smells delicious and beaming at us—and just like that something in my chest loosens. She's one of the only people I can completely be myself around. Nicole, I want to impress; Mrs. Rosings, I have the strange urge to piss off. With Claire, I can be myself. Mostly. Because I still need her to love me.

"What'd I miss?" she asks.

"Oh, nothing," Nicole says. "Just the moment when everything became interesting."

Claire sits down in the chair that will be occupied by Cleo in twenty minutes. Fifteen, if she's five minutes early like she was for our first meeting. "More interesting than Rosie telling a bunch of bros who came in that we eat Bronuts like them for breakfast?"

Nicole smiles for half a second before saying, "Yes."

"Can I get a recap?"

"The necklace I took is fake," I say woodenly, stroking the cat. Claire already knows about the disaster that unfolded in Jake's apartment—and has met the cat formerly known as Trixie.

Nicole strokes her chin like she's a kingpin. "There are hundreds of replicas available online, although this one's better than most.

Maybe Clover figured it was real and decided to send Lainey in to snatch it. All the risk would be on Lainey's side." Nicole grabs a Bronut from the bag, then rocks back in her chair. "Why she thought a therapist who lives in a shitty apartment building in North Asheville would have a multimillion dollar necklace lying around is anyone's guess. I'm thinking Clover's probably not the sharpest crayon in the box."

"You know that's not her name," Claire says. "You always remember when it's a client."

Nicole lets a smile flicker across her face. "This woman intentionally lied to Lainey. We can't do her the honor of remembering her name." She takes a bite of her Bronut and releases a satisfied hum under her breath. That's the power of Claire's baking, so good it makes even Nicole go soft for half a second. Professor X pads to the edge of my lap, watching Nicole's food with predatory interest.

"Don't even think about it," she says, and the cat, possibly recognizing a fellow apex predator, sits.

Lifting her gaze to me, Nicole adds, "The more interesting question is why the dude had it hidden inside that book."

"Maybe he planned on giving it to Cleo, and she jumped the gun," I say. "Or it could have been a gift for his mother or something." I did a background search on Jake Jeffries, too, and nothing interesting popped. Two parent home, check. College degree, check. Professional website, check.

She grunts and nods.

I try not to feel the guilty ache in my chest.

I might have wrecked the apartment of an innocent man. I guess that makes *me* the asshole.

"Have you guys watched the clip from the documentary yet?" Claire asks. I texted them both to let them know what I'd learned about the necklace—Nicole because she's my business partner, and Claire because she's the person I tell everything to.

Almost everything.

I haven't told either of them that I climbed into Jake Jeffries's lap or ground against his hard cock while he gripped my hips and hair and held me against him—a memory that sends a wash of heat through me. If I'm being honest, I've thought about that moment several times over the last few days and occasionally touched myself to get some relief.

Clearing my throat, I say, "No. I got home five minutes ago. Mrs. Rosings decided at the last minute that she wanted to do the whole necklace presentation thing at her party, so we had to unearth a few display cases from the basement. She also has an extremely ugly broach she's going to present to Nina. She plans on asking her to wear it to the wedding as her something borrowed."

Claire shakes her head fondly. "She'll stop at nothing."

"I have to get Nina out," I insist.

Claire gives me a sad, knowing look. "Lainey...I think Mrs. Rosings is right about her."

I snort. "I know she is. She needs to be saved from herself."

"Some women are just assholes," Nicole says through a mouthful of Bronut. "No silent crying on the inside. No regret. No empathy. I know this from personal experience."

"You mean from your own experience of being one of those women." I don't actually mean it—Nicole is tough as hell, but only someone who doesn't know her would accuse her of not having a conscience.

"Nina hasn't exactly been kind to you," Claire puts in, which is Claire-speak for *she's been a raging bitch, Lainey.* And I suppose it's true. While Nina has been sweet as saccharine mixed with simple syrup to Mrs. Rosings, she's treated me like I'm something the cat's dragged in. She negs me. She sighs dramatically every time I say anything in Anthony's presence, acting as if I'm too stupid to live. And she asks me to do things for her like I'm her own personal footman.

Because she can.

That doesn't speak of a stellar personality, but maybe she's just desperate. Desperation can do strange things to a person. I once purchased three collared shirts and a string of expensive pearls that looked like plastic balls.

"She's a tiger, caught in a trap," I argue. "She's lashing out."

"She's the one who made the trap," Claire says sadly.

"And she'll probably scratch out the eyes of the person who's dumb enough to let her out," Nicole says tipping the rest of her Bronut at me. "You know, you went to the trouble of telling us that long, mostly disinteresting story about your mother, but you missed the point, Mata Hari. The real takeaway is that you should take no one at their word. Especially people who seem to be above suspicion."

Her words seep into me.

She's right, dammit.

I'm guessing she doubted Cleo's story all along. Maybe I would have, too, if I didn't feel so raw over what happened with Todd. So like a tiger who wanted to bite back and prove to the world—and myself—that I couldn't be contained again, by anyone.

"You knew I was messing up and you let me do it anyway," I say, running a hand over Professor X's little ears for comfort. She swats me with her paw.

"You're like a baby bird learning to fly," Nicole replies with a grin. "How are you going to learn if I don't let you fall a few times? Besides, I figured the risk was pretty low."

"For *robbery*?" Claire asks.

Nicole laughs. "For nabbing a necklace from a therapist? This woman is a badass. You saw that bat she took from her fiancé. There's no way Toodles doesn't know she has it."

"He knows," I say tightly.

"See!" Nicole says, waving a hand at me. "That super rich dude knows she has his precious bat, and he hasn't tried to get it back." She nods as if agreeing with herself. "And that's because he knows better than to try. I wasn't worried about her."

That makes me feel slightly better, but then I get a flash of Jake's face when he told me to leave. *Shit.* I didn't care what he thought of me when I was sure he was a cheating, lying, stealing so-and-so, but now...

Maybe he's still all of those things. Maybe Cleo will be able to explain everything.

But I feel like that ten-year-old girl again, standing in the lobby of Marjorie Eccles's building.

Maybe we can never really learn from the past. Maybe we're destined to make the same mistakes over and over again, because the framework for them is built into us.

"Let's just watch the clip," I say with a sigh, grabbing my laptop and opening it.

Claire comes closer, and we all crowd in to watch, even Professor X. Nicole gives Claire a suspicious sniff, which makes her burst out laughing.

Claire wore Chanel No. 5 for years because her old boss backed her into it. Nicole told her it made her smell elderly. So Claire occasionally wears it under her bakery smell just to screw with her—and test her sense of smell.

"You're both unhinged," I tell them.

Nicole smiles at me. "Says the woman who asked a strange man to find her a super plus tampon after climbing into his lap like he was Santa and she wanted all the toys." She shrugs. "Not that I blame you. He's got this hot slacker thing working for him."

I startle. "How do you—"

She rolls her eyes. "You don't think I had eyes on you? For all we knew, he was a psychopath pervert who wanted to wear your skin as a hat. I'm not going to let him do that to one of my girls."

It's nice that she cared, I guess, but it also feels a little intrusive. Which is incredibly hypocritical of me since I did just go through Jake Jeffries's underwear drawer before strewing around his boxer briefs like they were confetti. I just...

Thought I could keep that moment for myself.

Why did you want to, you weirdo?

But I don't have time for self-reflection. Claire has turned to me, her eyes as wide as when I told her I'd begun my work as Robin Hood and stolen some of my mother's MLM Tupperware, filled it with food, and given it out to homeless people.

"Wait...you climbed into his lap?" she asks. She knows about my weird sex hang ups—how I struggle to let go. She's in a position to realize the possible significance of this information.

"I did what I had to," I say, avoiding her gaze as I turn on the video.

I feel her still watching me, though, so I send her a best friends look that I hope she can interpret—*we'll discuss my raging libido later.*

We spend the next five minutes listening to a very boring account of the Heart of the Mountain. It's described as a priceless relic five seconds before the narrator puts a price tag on it.

Nine point five million.

When it's over, Nicole whistles, her eyes shining, and rewinds to the place where we began. "I should have known. The uglier the jewelry, the more it's worth."

"I knew Mrs. Rosings was rich, obviously," Claire says, "but I didn't think she was *that* rich."

"She had that thing hidden in an empty urn without any security," I say, numb.

Nicole purses her lips to the side. "You know, that might be the best place for something like that. Who's going to open an urn?"

She has a point.

"Is she hiring security for the event?" she continues, sitting up straighter in her chair.

"Not enough. There'll be a guard at the gate to check everyone in. And there's an alarm attached to the actual display case."

"She's setting a trap for your tiger," Nicole says approvingly. "Vicious."

"But why would Nina try to steal it? If she marries Anthony, she doesn't need the necklace. I'm pretty sure he's got some kind of trust fund from his father."

"Sure, but if Nina takes the necklace, she doesn't have to marry him," Nicole says. "She can fleece it and be done with the whole thing." She taps her chin. "She'd be *free*, so maybe you should let her take it if that's your game."

Her words funnel into me and then ping around, as though they're unsure of where to go. I don't really like Mrs. Rosings—she's too hard, too conniving—and yet...

To let Nina take the necklace would be wrong.

To help her, even worse.

Besides, if it *is* a trap, then Mrs. Rosings thinks she has the ability to spring it.

Claire scratches her head. "I'd better warn Rosie about all of this. She can keep an eye out too. But how do Cleo and Jake fit in?"

"Great question. Let's ask her." Nicole pops the rest of the Bronut into her mouth. "Do we have the thumb screws ready?"

"Very funny," I say.

Nicole's gaze lifts above my head, to the clock mounted over the office door. "The moment of truth is upon us."

"Should I go hide somewhere?" Claire asks, glancing around the office, empty other than the desk and chairs and a couple of bookcases aligned with the opposite wall.

"So you can pop out and freak her out?" Nicole says, weighing the possibility. "That might be cool."

"Just stay," I tell Claire with a sigh. "You can play good cop."

"Oh," she says, seeming excited by this. She tucks her hair behind her ear, straightens her shirt. "I think I can do that. Kill her with kindness."

"Look at you," Nicole puts in with a grin.

There's a knock on the front door, and Claire's eyes widen.

"Go get her, good cop," Nicole says, cracking her knuckles.

I watch as Claire leaves the room, then shift my gaze to Nicole, who grins at me. "Watch and learn, baby bird."

I smile back, even though it feels like someone's been playing with my nerves with a rusted-out switchblade.

"Come in," I hear Claire say, followed by the sounds of footsteps. The door closing. "Can I get you anything? Some coffee, maybe a Bronut? Oh, sorry, I've gotten used to the name. They're a cross between brownies and donuts. I know the name's a little... well, but they're actually really good—"

"No thanks," Cleo says, her voice tight.

More footsteps.

Then, right before they turn into the room, Nicole swivels my laptop so it's facing the door and presses play. The computer starts booming on about the majestic Heart of the Mountain just as Cleo steps into the room, turning milk white. She swivels to leave, but Claire bars her path.

Nicole picks up the fake necklace and lets it dangle through the air, and Professor X leaps up in my lap to take a swipe at it.

Cleo's eyes widen as she turns back around.

"Seems to me you have some explaining to do," Nicole says, lifting the necklace higher to torment Professor X and possibly Cleo. "Because this isn't a family heirloom, and I'm guessing that fine-ass man didn't break *your* heart of the mountain."

CHAPTER EIGHT

JAKE

It's Saturday afternoon.

I no longer have the replica Roark gave me, which probably cost thousands to make, but I *did* express order a shitty copy of the Heart of the Mountain off Etsy. It's displayed on the coffee table right now. It's...imperfect, but it would be worse to take the necklace without leaving any kind of replacement.

I glance again at the shitty copy and run a hand through my hair.

Oh, who the fuck am I kidding. It looks like it came out of a gumball machine in the 1980s. The "gem" might as well be a hunk of children's slime dried out in the sun.

The only thing I've got going for me now is that Anthony's mother is at least seventy, and her eyesight is probably not what it once was.

Things I do not have going for me?

Two people now know about the expensive replica: Chloe, the woman I brought back here two weeks ago, when I was drunk off my ass and too fucked up and sad to remember why I shouldn't do that. I was also too messed up to recall anything about her other than her name and general appearance.

I went to the bathroom and came out to find her staring down at the necklace, which I'd left out on my dresser, her finger tracing the gem. Maybe she recognized it from the documentary; maybe she didn't. Either way, I could tell she wanted to pocket it and run, so I told her I had to call it a night.

She left, and the only people I've spoken to since are Roark, my neighbors in this building, and Anthony Rosings Smith. I've been going out of my head, but at least I was being careful—doing what needed to be done to get Ryan out of this shit.

And then I went and invited Elaine inside...

She doesn't live in this building.

I went up and down the hall after she left, hitting up the apartments of all the people I haven't met, pretending I was selling Girl Scout cookies for my non-existent niece. Then I went downstairs and did it all again. I got enough cookie orders that if I stick around long enough I'll have to hit up eBay or some shit because apparently the Girl Scouts aren't up to their cookie mojo until spring.

Unless someone had Elaine and the cat hidden in a closet—and I doubt any closet would contain them—she doesn't fucking live here. She lied to me.

It's not often I get hoodwinked.

It's...alarming.

Why did she choose me as her target?

I'd like to think she wanted to ride my dick because it felt ridiculously good when she practiced—but she spilled a whole beer on herself *and* pretended to have her period, so I have to be realistic.

She didn't want me. She wanted what she thought I might have.

Which leaves me with the question of why she thought Jake Jeffries, therapist and renter of a mediocre apartment, had anything worth taking. I guess it's possible she has a regular routine with her cat. She could go from building to building, suckering lonely men into letting her inside so she can mow through their shit, the way she did mine, and steal anything worth keeping.

A more alarming possibility is that she's friendly with Chloe, who thought the necklace might be the real deal and sent in a pal to check it out.

But that still doesn't explain the cat.

If it was some sort of a con, it wasn't a very good one.

Except it worked, a voice in my head insists. *She got you good, and you don't want to admit it.*

I checked out Nextdoor—a website that's much more useful for thieves and con artists than people probably realize—and also Reddit and Craigslist, but no one was talking about a hot chick with a cat sidekick or two women pulling off cons together.

Of course, that doesn't mean no one else has been fleeced. A lot of men would rather die than admit they've been taken in by a woman. Or women, as the case may be.

This morning, I told myself it was time to stop looking for Elaine, especially since I don't know what I'd do if I found her. I can't turn her into the cops for stealing the necklace.

But it's *really* not good if it ends up in some pawn shop.

No doubt about it, Jake Jeffries is on life support, and I'm going to have to pull the plug soon if I don't want Jake Langston to catch his disease.

So I have to finish this, and finish it quickly.

I have to finish it *tonight*.

I've never pulled off a job so quickly—usually, there's a planning period after I scope out the territory. But at this point, Ryan's life isn't the only one hanging in the balance.

If the wrong people make the right connections...

I swear as I slump onto the couch, running my fingers up through my hair.

This job started out bad, poisoned, because of the way I'd been made to do it, and now it feels wrong all the way through.

I'd step away if I could.

But...

My burner starts vibrating on the table next to the shitty necklace, and I know it's Roark.

I answer, and he doesn't bother with a greeting. He just says, "I'm getting tired of waiting for you, Jake. *Your brother's* getting tired of waiting for you. I think I'll let him play eenie, meenie, miny, mo to decide which hand I'll take. Seems only fair, don't you think?"

"Very menacing," I say with a sigh. "I know. I'm going to the house tonight. This'll be over soon."

It'll be over tonight.

But he knows I'm usually more cautious. If he finds out I'm planning to throw caution to the wind, he'll ask why. No way am I going to tell him about Elaine.

I may resent the woman, and she definitely screwed me over, but I won't shove her into the sights of a potentially dangerous man. The thought makes me bristle inside.

"See that it is," he says, with the sigh of a man who's been deeply disappointed by me more than once. "I'm giving you two more weeks. Any longer than that, and I'll know you've lost your ability."

"Can I talk to Ryan?" I put in quickly.

There's a very good chance shit's going to go FUBAR tonight, and I figure I'd better warn him that he might need to fumble his own way out of this one.

"Does this look like a Club Med?" he asks, sounding pissed, and the line goes dead.

So he's *really* angry with Ryan, as if I didn't already know.

I get dressed in my black tie optional suit, then pick up a couple of bouquets for the bride-to-be and Mrs. Rosings. Jake

Jeffries, therapist, is the kind of man who buys women flowers they probably don't want or have nowhere to put.

Anthony told me he put me on the "list," and I should meet him and his fiancée at Smith House, so I head over there next. A guard at the gate instructs me to park outside and then allows me entry on foot.

One guard. He's fifty or maybe sixty, unarmed, and about as threatening as a warm glass of milk someone's mother made them. He pats down my pocket, takes a look at my wallet and Jake Jeffries's ID, and sends me in on my merry way.

The house is old, ugly, and stinks of money. It looks like a gingerbread house left too long in the oven, or a comparatively small, less impressive copy of the Biltmore—kind of like the necklace in my shoe looks like the Heart of the Mountain. I've seen the house before, of course. I've studied the blueprints and done drive-bys. I've watched the full, dry-as-dust documentary about the treasures of the Eastern shore, which discusses the Heart of the Mountain from minutes 45 to 50. I've studied Anthony's family history and possibly know more about it than he does. I could write a five paragraph essay about the Smith family, but I don't need to do that. All I need to do is steal that necklace and get the fuck out. Easy.

But I'm not as good without Ryan, and I know it.

I've lost my edge, and I know that too.

I need for those things not to matter.

An animal brays so loudly it makes me flinch, followed by a woman swearing. Is that from…the yard?

I glance around the side of the building, but whatever's back there is hidden by shrubberies so thick a man could hide inside of them. Duly noted.

When I get to the door, I have to smile. A large photo of Anthony and Nina is arranged beside it, displayed on an intricate gold stand.

Damn, Anthony's mother is savage. It's a fine enough photo...
other than the fact that one of Nina's eyes is half closed.

I knock, and the door is opened by a woman wearing what
looks like a Red Lobster uniform—black pants, black shirt, red tie.
"Welcome to Anthony and Nina's happily ever after," she says
with a fixed smile that reminds me of a painted doll.

Yikes.

I plaster on a fixed smile of my own. "Thanks."

Her eyes widen when she notices the flowers in my hand.

"I'll take those for you, sir."

"They're gifts for Nina and Mrs. Rosings," I say.

"And I'm sure they'll be *cherished*," she responds. I don't need
to be good at reading people to know they'll be in the trash within
the next five minutes. Wasteful as hell, but fine by me. It would
just mean the gesture is being accepted in the spirit in which it was
made.

I hand them over, and she directs me to the "drawing room" for
cocktails and "light" conversation.

The contrarian in me wants to ask if I'll be thrown out if I tell
everyone I'm suffering from an existential dilemma, but I'm here to
do a job, and so is she. I shut the fuck up.

So I enter that room, wearing Jake Jeffries as much as the suit.
The first person I see is Anthony, who's probably only been in his
childhood home for a matter of minutes and is already rocking a
flop sweat in his grey suit. His choice of clothing is a micro-rebel-
lion, probably, against black tie optional. He lights up the instant
he spots me, which would make me feel guiltier if I hadn't already
drawn devil horns on him in my head. He leans in toward the
pretty, dark-haired woman standing next to him and says something. When they step forward together, Anthony's hand pressed
to her lower back, revealed by a dip in her silver sequined dress, I
see it. Behind her is a four-foot-high clear display case—and nestled

inside is the very fucking necklace I came here to steal—the Heart of the Mountain, out and proud.

Well, goddamn, I think as a genuine smile stretches across my face.

This is the first piece of luck I've had in weeks.

CHAPTER NINE

JAKE

"Nina, this is my friend Jake," Anthony says, stepping up to me.

The dark-haired woman nods and smiles. She looks lovely in her silver dress, which was obviously chosen with care and precision, much like the updo of her perfectly styled dark hair, but her eyes are cold and dark. Calculating. "I've heard so much about you."

"All good things, I hope," I say with a return smile, falling into the familiar rhythm of "light" conversation.

Her fake laugh sounds like a fork beaten against a champagne glass. My teeth want to grind together against the assault of it. "*Of course...*" She asks me questions about my therapy practice, which I answer with as much genuine interest as it was asked. I can't find it in myself to pay attention. My heart is beating too fast.

I want to go check out the necklace *now*, but Jake Jeffries, therapist extraordinaire and dopey nice guy, would probably never have heard about the Heart of the Mountain. That being said, it would be strange if I ignored the elephant in the room. It's not fucking normal to put out display cases in the middle of a party—because now I can see there's more than one—and if I failed to comment on them, that might also be noticed.

I make a couple of casual remarks about the beauty of the estate and the lady's dress before finally letting my eyes rest on the box.

If Ryan were here, he'd probably lean into my ear and say, "My precious," in his best Gollum voice, and I'd make a joke about getting into a rich lady's box. The thought makes me want to smile, right up until I remember my brother is in Roark's not-a-Club-Med and that I haven't talked to him for the better part of a year.

"What's this?" I ask, nodding toward it with casual interest.

Anthony swears under his breath, and for an instant, I see something real pass over Nina's face.

"My mother's idea of a joke," Anthony finally says in a tight voice, his gaze flitting across the room to an older woman who's shorter than half the people in the room but has the bearing of someone who's much taller. Her hair is snow white, slicked back into a perfect bun, and she's wearing a kaftan-style white dress threaded through with gold. She's talking to a couple of people.

Something tells me she's aware that white is supposed to be reserved for the bride-to-be at these things. After all, I know from my research that she's been married three times. Imagine that— wanting to shackle yourself not once but three times.

I've got nothing against relationships. Sure, I've never been in one that's lasted more than a few months, but blame the job for that. There aren't many women willing to understand if you disappear for several weeks or months at a time and can't tell them where you went. I've been accused of everything from having a secret family (false) to being an emotionally stunted man child (probably true). I walked away from that life last fall, but I still haven't gotten close to anyone. Part of it is that I can't tell anyone how I've spent the last seventeen years of my life. Add on to that that I also don't have much I'm willing to say about the thirteen years before that, and there's not much left to talk about.

Anthony's looking at me expectantly, and I realize Jake

Jeffries's sympathetic side needs to be rolled out. "Oh?" I say with interest, tilting my head.

Nina gives us a constipated look, then says, "I'll let you boys talk," as if we're a couple of schoolboys in uniforms. Then she takes off, probably to sneak a cigarette outside or go shout *fuck* into a fancy pillow. I can't say I'd blame her.

Anthony shakes his head slightly, then walks toward the display case. I walk beside him, trying not to act too eager. When we reach it, I peer down at it for half a second, taking in the blinking red light of the censor attached to the box.

I expected some kind of alarm, so that's not a surprise. Not really a problem either. If there's no auxiliary power, I turn off the breakers in the basement and take out two birds with one stone—giving myself an opening to take the necklace and making it possible to do so. Of course, that's assuming we're not going to be stuck in this room for the rest of the evening like a tin of sardines.

"This is the Heart of the Mountain," Anthony tells me. "Have you heard of it?"

I look back up at him, going for a quizzical expression. "No, should I have?"

He quickly explains what I already know. A Smith family heirloom, check. Worth a shit ton of money, check. Subject of a documentary, check.

"You said it was your mother's idea of a joke?"

His mouth tightens, then he sighs, glancing at the older woman across the room again. This time she catches his eye and offers a little wave, her eyes bright. He does not return the gesture.

"Nina asked to wear it as her something borrowed for the wedding. Mom declined. She said putting it out tonight is a compromise, but she's doing it to taunt Nina. Same thing with the uniforms." He angles his head at a woman with bright blonde hair, a purple streak weaving through it. Like the other servers and employees, she's dressed in a black button down with a red tie and black pants.

"Oh?" I ask, tilting my head.

"Nina used to work at Red Lobster."

A smile crests across my face. The old woman's savage, and I can't help but admire someone who's not afraid to play dirty.

A strange strangled sound escapes Anthony, and I glance at him in genuine shock. His face is a rictus of held-back...

Before I can think better of it, I ask, "Are you...laughing?"

He instantly turns his back on his mother—

"No," he says, although he's still struggling to keep it together.

Interesting. Maybe there's more to him, and this situation, than I thought.

"Look," he says, trying to get control of himself. "I don't want you to think I'm a dick—"

Too late for that.

"—I don't give a shit that Nina worked at Red Lobster. Who cares. It's just...my mother's shameless, and she'll stop at nothing... It's kind of..."

"Funny," I agree. "But you'd rather die than let her know."

He nods slightly, his lips tipped upward. "Precisely."

For the first time since our meet cute, I actually like the guy. Figures that it happens just before it's time to screw him over.

"So, what's the plan for the evening?" I ask, clearing my throat.

He rolls his eyes and silently pulls a brochure from his jacket pocket and hands it to me. Silently, I'm guessing, because he looks like he's swallowing down laughter again. I glance at the program.

> 6:30 *Cocktails and light conversation*
> 7:00 *Petting zoo – Anthony's childhood favorite!*
> 7:30 *Seven-course meal*
> 9:00 *Games*

> *9:30 Slideshow, followed by dancing*
> *11:00 Farewell toast*

"Petting zoo?" I ask, remembering the animal cry I'd heard outside. This could work for me. While everyone's outside, busy with the inane distraction, I could sneak back into the house, cut the power, and make a run for the necklace.

"I'm not participating, obviously," he says dryly. "Nina has informed me she'd rather die."

"But it's your childhood favorite," I object with a grin.

He shakes his head, a small smile on his lips. "No...it's not. It's another example of my mother amusing herself. We went to a petting zoo once when I was a kid. I got bitten by a donkey, then fell in a pile of manure. My father told me I wasn't much of a man. Good memory." He sighs, running a hand across his chin, probably to piss his mother off. "She doesn't know about that part—he made sure to take me aside for my dressing down—but she knows the rest."

"Your mother's vicious," I say.

His father, too, but I know he passed away when Anthony was young, and most people won't talk badly of the dead. I've never understood that—the way people are sainted just by the act of dying.

"Would you mind going with them?" he asks, his gaze shifting to the door behind my back. "It might be a good chance for you to talk some sense into my mother."

There goes the petting zoo plan, but it was probably dead in the water anyway if Anthony and Nina aren't going.

I'll do it during dinner, I decide.

I can excuse myself and cut the power while everyone's getting into their salad course or whatever. They'll freak out. They'll flail around like slugs in salt, and by the time they get their shit together, I'll have grabbed the necklace and replaced it with the gumball fake in my pocket.

Except...

Sitting here in a backlit case, the switch will be as obvious as if I'd swapped a real duck with a rubber ducky.

Frustration burns a hole in my gut. This is *her* fault. Elaine's. If she hadn't nabbed my good replica, I'd be golden. I could have replaced the necklace, flipped the breaker back on, and pretended I'd lost my way back from the bathroom in the dark.

The fake-as-shit replacement might have worked if the necklace had been hidden somewhere else within the estate, where it wouldn't be seen immediately. But now...

How do I pull this shit off without them immediately knowing that I, out of all the guests, was the one who did it?

I'm still chewing on that little chestnut when soft footfalls announce a new entry into the room. Then a woman clears her voice and announces, "The petting zoo is open. Please form a line by the door, and I'll see you to it."

That voice is smooth and familiar, and it feels like someone just strummed a chord inside of me...

I turn around and drop the brochure Anthony gave me, because it's her. It's the woman who fucked me over, and she's wearing a uniform that looks like it came from the Red Lobster catalog.

She works here.

CHAPTER TEN

LAINEY

When I was outside, a goat pooped on my foot, a chicken pecked my leg as if it were covered in seeds, and a donkey snapped its teeth in my general direction. But none of those things threw me much. I mean, *of course* Mrs. Rosings picked a shitty petting zoo to set up shop for the party. This, though...

The man I stole from is standing directly across from me in Mrs. Rosings's sitting room, standing next to Anthony as if they're best buds. Wearing a black suit as easily as he did jeans and a T-shirt, although his wavy, curly adjacent hair is as messy as it was the other night.

My first reaction is a hot, needy feeling, because damn, can this man fill out a suit. It's cut perfectly to his body—or maybe it's his body that's the true star of the show.

My second?

Fuckkkkk.

Yesterday afternoon, Cleo admitted the necklace had been Jake's all along. He'd brought her home from a bar, and she'd seen it laid out on his dresser.

So he's not a cheater. Not a thief. Just a guy with a suspiciously good fake necklace and bad taste in women.

On the one hand that's good news: I hated myself for being turned on by a dirty cheater. On the other...well, I'll have to figure out a way to return the necklace—ideally one that wouldn't end with me getting arrested.

But now he's here palling around with Anthony...

Is it possible he bought that replica necklace *for* Mrs. Rosings's son? Maybe it was supposed to be a gift for Nina since she won't get the real deal unless she plucks it off Mrs. Rosings's cold, dead neck?

It's also possible Anthony wants to pass it off as the real deal to Nina...or steal the real deal and swap it out with the convincing fake.

My brain feels like an overbaked pretzel.

From the intense way Jake's staring at me, he definitely recognizes me. His sour expression suggests he hasn't forgiven me for kissing him, grinding against his dick, and then stealing his necklace.

Or maybe it's the menses tea he resents me for.

Is he going to make a scene? I'm not worried he'll ruin Anthony and Nina's big party, because Mrs. Rosings and I already saw to that, but he could cause serious trouble for me.

"Lainey," a familiar voice says from beside me, and I turn to see Rosie, dressed in the same hideous outfit as me. "Are you checking out that guy?" she asks with a grin. "Don't think I didn't notice."

"No," I say tightly, watching as the various nicely dressed people gather at the door to visit a petting zoo full of animal shit and animals with an attitude problem. "But I want *you* to keep an eye on him. And Anthony and Nina."

She grins, a twinkle lighting up her eyes. "Abso-fucking-lutely." She's not whispering, not really, and a couple of the guests give her pearl-clutching looks. "Claire told me everything. This is the most exciting thing that's happened to me in Marshall since the trash guy came on the wrong day that one week."

I have to laugh, even though my nerves are prickling, the short hairs at the nape of my neck standing on end. "Marshall's not doing it for you?"

She sighs and jostles her tray, nearly upending the punch glasses filled with what smells like High-C and vodka. Knowing Mrs. Rosings's devotion to the bit, it probably is. "I have to move out, man. Living with my brother and Claire is..." She makes a face. "I'm really happy for them and all, but it's like living with two people on their honeymoon. The sounds they made last night were unreal. I had to bang on the wall."

Laughter bursts out of me. "Go, Claire. Why don't you come stay with me?"

My eyes find Jake again. He's watching me, his gaze hard, and when our eyes meet, he very deliberately joins the back of the line. Something tells me it's not because he has a burning desire to check out the petting zoo.

"No offense," Rosie says, "but you're still too close. I think I'll find a place with some other girls in Asheville."

I nod, barely listening to her now. My gaze is on Jake, and the look he's giving me leaves little doubt that we're about to have a conversation. He's decided not to carry on that conversation in front of everyone, which is good news, but I suspect it won't be pleasant.

Anthony doesn't join the line, not that I'm surprised. He's here, but he's not pleased to be. He's not the only one. I saw Nina outside just now, hiding out by the side of the house with a cigarette. Shaking her head every five seconds.

In my peripheral vision, I see Rosie smirking at me. "I'm going to have questions about this later, you know. Probably a lot of them."

"I'd expect nothing less."

I walk away from Rosie to spread the good word about the petting zoo to the guests who might not have heard me in the cavernous room. Or were trying to politely ignore me. I'm guessing that was most of them because no one seems particularly happy to see me coming, and one woman makes for the door, grabs a glass of champagne from Rosie, and downs it on her way out of the room to parts unknown.

"Aren't you going to join your friend, darling?" I hear Mrs. Rosings ask Anthony, who's standing by the fireplace, looking up at the urns as he sips from his cup. It hits me that it must have been strange for him, growing up beneath the shadow of his father's urn.

I pause in rounding up the stragglers. I have to wonder what Adrien Smith was like...what any of Mrs. Rosings's husbands were like. She's such a strong, independent woman, it's hard to imagine her tied to anyone *until death do us part*. The people in this town have taken to calling her the black widow, because she's been celestially parted with three of her husbands. Of course, it goes without saying that the people who say that are dicks.

"No thanks," Anthony says. "I'd rather stand here by myself and slowly get drunk. But it looks like you've convinced plenty of other people to go along with your plan."

Mrs. Rosings smiles as if she's won something. She's always trying to entice some sort of reaction out of Anthony. She's like one of those kids who doesn't care if it's good attention or bad so long as its hers.

"Emma's not coming to the party, I take it?" he asks flatly.

"She told me maybe."

He laughs humorlessly and tightens his hand around his drink. "Which we both know means no."

His mother sniffs. "She's exactly the sort of person who will show up the moment people start making assumptions."

"You mean she's exactly like you," he says, his tone making it perfectly obvious he doesn't mean it as a compliment to either of them.

This is interesting. I'd either love or hate to meet a mini Mrs. Rosings, but—

Mrs. Rosings gives me a significant look and nods toward the line of people at the door. The guests seem to be getting impatient, shifting their weight from foot to foot and murmuring to each other like kids waiting to leave for a school field trip.

Duly noted.

I head to the door before turning around and facing the group. "Let's go, friends. An animal adventure awaits you." It's a mark of skill that I manage to say it with a straight face.

I start to lead the circuitous way to the front door, deeply aware of the group following me. Especially aware of one person. I glance over my shoulder, not surprised to see Jake has made his way toward the front of the group.

He's conducting small talk with one of Mrs. Rosings's relatives, but I can feel his eyes burning into me. I turn back around, but I'm still aware of him in a primal way, from the short hairs along the slope of my neck to the tips of my toes. I can picture him in that suit, his fox on fire tattoo completely hidden by a button-down shirt and jacket. But *I* know it's there. I can feel him. It's as if a hot, stalking predator is breathing down my neck, and a strong hand might at any point wrap around my hip and pull me back against him, pinning me to him, and—

There is something deeply wrong with you, Lainey. This man is a therapist. The most he'd do is talk you to death.

Mrs. Rosings falls into step beside me, perfectly unaware that the man who's several feet behind us wants to rip my world apart. She's silent as we leave the house, pausing only to give Nina, still stationed in front of the shrubberies with a cigarette, such a scathing look it should burn her.

Could I have warned Nina that we were about to come past her?

Obviously, but she really seemed to need that cigarette.

Finally, we circle the last side of the mammoth house and reach the playpen set up in the backyard, overseen by a woman with wild white and blonde hair and a cane. "Ah, they're here!" she says, presumably to the animals. The goat who pooped on my shoe earlier, requiring an extensive clean-up operation in the bathroom, lifts its head hopefully.

Mrs. Rosings leans in toward me and says, "A word, Elaine."

Then she turns to face the guests, giving them an enigmatic smile. "We have half an hour to enjoy the petting zoo. Please try to contain your excitement. I'm told the donkey bites."

With that, she tugs me aside, toward the thick, almost impenetrable shrubberies lining all four sides of Smith House. Casting a quick glance back at the guests, most of whom are gathered outside of the playpen, perfunctorily patting goat heads and tittering nervously under their breath, she says in an undertone, "I need you to talk to Anthony's friend. Find out why he invited him at the last minute."

"You hadn't met him before?" I ask, angling my head to better study her. She's in one of her kaftans with her white hair curled at the ends. Her makeup is so expert it looks like she's not wearing any.

"No," she replies, her lips pressing into a flat, disapproving line. "Anthony stopped bringing his friends around when he was a teenager, after I caught them smoking marijuana and forced them to weed the grounds."

My first thought is goddamn, this place has at least ten acres.

My second is that it doesn't necessarily mean anything that Mrs. Rosings has never met him. I'm guessing Anthony doesn't like parading around his pals. She's probably just asking me to talk to him because she's one of the most suspicious women I've ever met.

Suits me. I have to talk to him anyway.

"I'll do it," I say bravely, as if I'm taking one for the team.

I take a couple of steps toward the playpen. It looks like Jake was the only person brave enough to step inside of it, and he's cuddling a baby goat in his arms as if it's a newborn. Another glance confirms that every woman present, from Mrs. Rosings's cousin Jennifer to an awkward teenager, someone's niece or cousin twice-removed, is staring at him with heart eyes.

I don't blame them—it's sexy as hell—but it doesn't do it for me, because there's no question he purposefully did it for the attention.

I shouldn't be disappointed. This man hates me and is possibly involved in a scheme against my boss. We were never going to be friends, but showboating is one quality I absolutely can't stand in a man. It instantly takes me back to Todd, who never did anything without considering what kind of reaction it would get.

"Jake," I say from the front of the makeshift pen.

He gives me an incredulous look—like he can't believe I have the *cajones* to approach him after I lied to him and stole his necklace.

I figure I should make some sort of public excuse for pulling him aside, even if Mrs. Rosings herself ordered me to do it, so I clear my throat and say, "Your car's going to get towed unless you move it."

He sets down the baby goat to a chorus of sickening coos.

I smile at the enraptured women as Jake picks his way out of the pen—and feel a little smug when he steps in a pile of shit left by one of the adorable little creatures.

He shuts the pen behind him, rubs his shoe aggressively against the grass, and then starts walking toward the front of the house. I fall in beside him, easily keeping pace. He doesn't say anything until we round the corner of the house. Then my breath leaves my lungs when his big, warm hand envelops my wrist, and he tugs me past the thick, leafy bushes—his grip insistent but not punishing—and backs me into the stone siding, planting a hand on either side of my body and leaning down toward me.

"Who the fuck are you?" he asks gruffly, his gaze fixed on me. His hazel eyes are galaxies of brown, green, and gold, surrounded by long lashes, presided over by dark, serious eyebrows. His fingers are so close to my arms, they're brushing my flesh, his body essentially pinning me to the stone. There's less than an inch between me and his hot, hard chest.

My breath is coming out in ragged puffs, but not because I'm scared. I *should* be scared. I don't know this man. I don't think I even like this man. But the truth is, I'm deeply, deeply turned on. I can feel his breath against my face, his hair brushing my forehead as he bends over me. And I can remember what it felt like to have his tongue in my mouth, one hand lost in my hair and the other wrapped around my hip like he had a right to it. His hard dick captured against me—a feeling so delicious, I rocked into it again and again even though I thought he was a cheater, a man who'd broken Cleo's heart.

Clearly, the vibrator's not cutting it anymore.

I swallow those unwelcome reactions down and take a moment to consider what I should tell him, deciding to go with the truth. Mostly.

"I'm Mrs. Rosings's assistant," I say, keeping my voice strong though quiet, for his ears only.

"Why did you come to my apartment?" he asks, leaning in closer, his heat burning me. "I know you don't live in the building."

"How?" I ask with interest, and to my surprise he actually answers.

"I went door to door saying I was selling Girl Scout cookies for my niece."

"But it's October. They usually sell their cookies in January."

"So you can imagine how hard it will be for me to fulfill their orders," he says flatly, with no sign of amusement. Just his body, leaning into mine, those hands so close they're touching but not holding me. My space, his. My breath, his. "Who. Are. You?"

I swallow. I could lie to him, but if I do, he'll be able to find out the truth. He knows who I work for, and from there it would be easy enough to track down the rest of the truth. Better for it to come from me. "In my free time I run a business called the Love Fixers. We help people who've been screwed over in love. Deleting photos from social media, sending glitter bombs, that kind of thing."

"So you're a woman with a grudge." My mouth falls open in indignation, but before I can deliver a scathing remark, he says, "What does this have to do with me?"

"Cleo," I say quickly.

"Who's Cleo?"

I raise my eyebrows. "You bring so many women home you don't even remember their names?"

I'm not saying he deserves to be stolen from or to have his apartment ransacked, but honestly.

He swears and dips his head again, his hair brushing a path on my skin—ticklish and tempting. "You must be talking about Chloe."

"No, her name's *definitely* Cleo."

"I was drunk," he says, his tone defensive, his hand flexing against the wall.

"You brought a drunk woman home with you?"

"I said *I* was drunk...she seemed sober. It was... I was having a bad night, and I overdid it."

Well, that does put a spin on things. Again, I'm thrown by how thoroughly Cleo reeled me in. I've been taught how to twist people's impressions to my advantage my entire life, and still I was hoodwinked by the need to believe what I wanted to believe—that she was an innocent who'd been taken advantage of by a man.

Because I might not be an innocent, but I *was* taken advantage of, and it still hurts. It's a splinter I carry around in my heart, and I've started to think it'll always be there, as much a part of me as my hair.

"Sorry," I say, pausing, then add, "Anyway...she told me she'd broken up with you because you were a cheater, but you kept her heirloom necklace. She hired me to look for it. Showed me a photo of you and everything. I didn't realize it was a copy of the Heart of the Mountain, honest to God. I didn't even know what the Heart of the Mountain was until yesterday."

"I don't let people take photos of me."

"You looked pretty hammered. Maybe you don't remember."

He gives me a flat look. "You expect me to believe that bullshit story?"

"It's *not* bullshit," I insist. "I did a background check on her *and* you before I accepted. I had no reason to think she was lying. She is who she said she was... I had no way of knowing she was using us to steal from you."

"A legitimate business wouldn't steal anything."

"You're not wrong."

He sighs, his hand brushing the wall as if he can't not move. "Why didn't you recognize the necklace? Didn't you see it here?" He nods to the stone wall behind us, his hair brushing me again. Each time it does, it sends little bursts of sensation across my skin.

"No," I admit. "Mrs. Rosings only decided to put it on display yesterday. I guess Nina's been asking about it, but to be totally honest, I only listen to about half of the things Mrs. Rosings says." Silence hangs between us for a moment, and I add, "I'm sorry. My business partner said this was like a training wheels mission for me, but I overstepped."

He swears and lets one of his hands drop. Takes a step back so he's no longer pinning me.

Something is seriously wrong with me, because I'm disappointed.

Then his gaze narrows on me again. "What about the cat? Did you really pick up someone else's cat?"

"She wasn't mine," I admit. "That was a ruse to meet you, but she's mine now. Your neighbor with the menses tea recognized her. I guess some dickhead abandoned her in the apartment building after he moved, and she's been a stray ever since." I wince. "Sorry about your pillow...and all the clothes I threw around."

He nods slowly. "It could have been worse. At least I didn't walk in and find everything covered in blood."

Surprised laugher escapes me before I manage to put a lid on it. Shrugging, I say, "Men and periods. Besides, I really did have my period, so it wasn't entirely a lie."

"Did the menses tea help?"

My eyebrows lift. "I didn't try it. It was from a stranger. I don't trust strangers."

If he sees irony in this, he doesn't say so. His mouth just lifts slightly at the corner—a half smile. "I'm starting to see things your way. Did you get the glue trap off the cat?"

I nod. "They had to fully sedate her."

His lips twitch up at both corners this time. "I'll bet. She's a hellcat just like you. Do you have the necklace?"

The tension has leaked out of him and he's less angry now. He seems almost relieved. So maybe it's time for me to ask some questions of my own. I won't give him the necklace before I do.

"Why did you have it?" I ask, studying him. "You're friends with Anthony. This isn't a coincidence."

"It's not," he agrees. "It's a gift for Nina. Anthony knew his mother would never give her the real necklace, and I know a guy who's good at making copies of famous jewelry. He asked me to get it for him, but I'd appreciate it if you don't tell Nina or Mrs. Rosings yet. It's supposed to be a surprise."

It's a reasonable explanation, delivered in a believable way. I'd thought of the possibility myself in the seconds after I first saw him in the drawing room. But something feels off. It's too clean, too neat. And I find myself asking, "How'd you meet Anthony?"

"I found his wallet outside of the gym," he says, giving me his nice-guy look. "I returned it, and he said he'd buy me a drink. We clicked."

My brain is probably broken, but I can't shake the thought that there's another layer to what's going on, one I'm not seeing. It says he's lying.

Maybe I just don't want to believe that I wronged a completely nice, normal guy. I narrow my gaze at him. "Why would a therapist know a guy who makes replica necklaces?"

He raises his eyebrows. "We went to college together. Duke. Want to see my diploma?"

I already did a background search on him, as he knows, so I know that's where he went to college. But I nod, because yes, I *do* actually want to see Jake Jeffries's diploma.

My gut insists on it.

"*You're* questioning *me*?" he asks, his voice turning gruff and a bit husky, like he maybe gets off on that even if he doesn't think much of me.

"Yes," I say, that thought giving me the strength to push his other hand away from my body. "Yes. You have to admit the whole thing's a little...convenient."

"You stole from me," he says tightly. "Doesn't seem very convenient for me."

"And now you know who I am and where I work. Feel free to turn me in."

I'm bluffing. If he turns me in, I'd be in trouble. *Nicole* would be in trouble. But my gut won't shut up. With the necklace displayed in that case, protected only by a motion sensor and an elderly guard who's not even in the house, I don't feel good about handing over the fake tonight. Obviously, I'll give it back—it's his, and Nicole thinks it's worth something, but...not tonight.

Not until the Heart of the Mountain is tucked away safely, and not just in Adrien Smith's urn.

My heart beating fast, I step away from the side of the house and say, "If you want me to give it back, all you have to do is show me that diploma."

"Cute," he says, his tone suggesting I'm anything but. He's closed down again. "Do you know how easy it is to falsify that kind of documentation? You should, if you've decided to fuck around in people's lives. Then again, I guess it doesn't matter, since you've been robbing people based on hearsay."

"You'll be comforted to know you're the first. But you can have it back as soon as you show me that diploma."

"What does where I went to college have to do with anything?" he asks, his voice shifting to a *let's be reasonable* tone. He's right— I'm *not* being reasonable. But I'm not going to relent either. Not until I know the real necklace is safe.

"Call me a college snob," I say, stopping at the edge of the closest shrub.

"Elaine," he says, his voice throbbing with intent, and the sound of my own name shakes through me in a way that frankly stuns me.

I glance back, and he shakes his head, his mouth lifted in that half smile, and says, "Is that even your name?"

"Yes, but my friends call me Lainey."

"You need to return what you took from me, *Elaine*. This isn't a game." He gives me a fake-as-hell smile. "The games don't start until after dinner."

Maybe it's not a game, but it shouldn't be urgent, either. The look on his face, though—it suggests the necklace is a matter of life or death. Why?

Is this about impressing Anthony?

That might make sense if he were some kind of business

contact, but Jake's supposedly a therapist. His business and the real estate business shouldn't intersect.

That's why I can't give him the necklace tonight. There are too many unanswered questions.

I'm still mulling everything over when footsteps approach us from the house. I have no reason to conceal myself, but instead of leaving, I retreat toward him, slipping back behind the shrubbery.

CHAPTER ELEVEN

JAKE

One second she's walking away from me, the next she practically flings herself at me.

Fuck me.

This woman is a menace.

A sexy menace. A hellcat.

But I'm not about to listen to the appreciative voice in my head —my dumb impulses are what got me here to begin with.

If I hadn't gotten loaded and brought Chloe—*Cleo* home, then she wouldn't have seen the necklace. If she hadn't seen the necklace, she wouldn't have hired someone to steal it. If she hadn't called up Elaine and asked to be part of her sour grapes project, then I wouldn't be in this fix.

I don't even know why I'm so intent on getting the real replica back. She knows about it now, so I couldn't leave it in the display case even if I had it. And all the lies that have spilled out of me over the last five minutes have given Jake Jeffries an even shorter shelf life. How long will it be before she tells someone else about the replica necklace?

All it would take is a word to Anthony...

Then there's another consideration: when the necklace disappears now, Elaine will know exactly who took it. No amount of playing with baby goats is going to make me above suspicion.

This needs to end tonight. You need to scrub Jake Jeffries from existence and lie low for a while. Ryan too, once he's released.

Everything in me is focused on that goal. Well, almost everything...

Because I still notice Elaine, huddled up next to me, her soft arm brushing mine as she uses the bushes for concealment, her eyes bright as she watches for whoever might be beyond them—catching the patches of color and making a person out of them.

Hellcat, my mind repeats.

Shameless about it too. She knows I know she's spying, yet it's not stopping her.

A voice speaks up, announcing that one of the flashes of white beyond the bushes is Nina. "This wasn't part of our agreement," she says, sounding pissed. It's nothing like the saccharine sweet voice she used earlier. This, I'm guessing, is the real Nina.

"Are you having second thoughts?" Anthony asks, identifying himself as the other blur.

Both of them pause a few feet beyond us, on the other side of that wall of green. I feel Elaine's skin against me—soft, hot—I hear her breathing hitch. I'm guessing she's excited to be listening in. From what I've gathered, she enjoys being naughty—pretending to be someone she's not, listening in on people who don't know she's there. Taking things that aren't hers, so long as she thinks she's doing it for justice. Getting pinned to walls...

My dick enjoys the thought.

"Are *you*?" Nina presses.

There's a thirty second pause, which is probably longer than a man in love would wait. Then he says, "Of course not." He swears under his breath and takes her hand—or at least that's how I interpret the glimpses I get between the leaves. "Of course not. Let's get everyone inside so we can get this fucking nightmare over with. But

I'm telling you right now, I'm flipping a few breakers before the slideshow. Give us an early night. No way do I want to pretend to reminisce over my childhood."

My heart starts racing, and I fight the urge to grin.

This is a lucky break. Beyond lucky. Not lucky enough to erase the whole mess with Elaine, but success is the only thing that matters.

If Anthony shuts the electricity off, then I won't have to assume the risk of doing it myself. I just have to be ready to react when it happens—to take the necklace and get out, and then go scorched earth on my Jake Jeffries identity.

Nina laughs and then says, "I asked for this ridiculous engagement party for *you*, you know. It's important for you to be seen as the heir to this estate. You can't let your mother run the show forever. That's why we need to have the wedding here too."

"Sure, yeah," Anthony says. "I know. My friend Jake's going to talk to her."

"You expect him to resolve this? You've only known him for three weeks."

"He's a good guy," he replies, defensive.

"We'll see about that."

If I were really his buddy, I'd tell him to run.

They walk off, and Elaine turns to me. Something flickers in her gaze. Then she swallows, and I can practically see her hardening herself. It would be fascinating if I weren't worried about what she's going to say next.

Studying me and finding me wanting, she says, "Why didn't you announce yourself since you two are such good friends?"

"Jesus, you weren't lying. You really do have trust issues."

Hurt flickers in her eyes, surprising me and making me feel bad for half a second. Then I remind myself that she took my necklace, with almost zero remorse. She's the one person who can absolutely wreck everything for both Ryan and me.

"You don't talk like any therapist I've ever met," she says pointedly.

"And you don't seem like much of a personal assistant."

Her eyes narrow. Shit, this isn't going well.

"I was giving them a moment alone," I say, trying to appease her. "I know Anthony's mother's resistance to the engagement has been a source of stress. He asked me to help smooth things over. You heard him say that." I cut off the *for fuck's sake*.

She tips her head up toward me, her expression defiant, and despite everything, I feel my body reacting to her. I only had a little taste of her, but I remember the needy way she ground against me, the pull of her teeth on my lip. And even though it was mostly an act, my ego wants to believe it wasn't *all* an act. I want to believe she felt the bizarre electric pull between us as much as I did.

She leans in toward me, maybe to intimidate me, but all it does is light a fire under my skin. "Three weeks isn't a very long time to know someone."

I laugh bitterly, leaning in too. I tell myself it's because two can play that game—not because I feel an unhinged need to be closer. "It took me less than three hours to know I wanted to stay away from you."

"Is this what you call staying away from someone?" she asks, lifting her eyebrows. Her voice is breathy, contemptuous.

Hot.

Her lips are inches from mine.

Stand down, stand down. Ryan's life might depend on it.

I gulp down air, then take a step back. I stop being an idiot, temporarily. "I'll see you at dinner, *Elaine*. Will you be serving me lobster?"

"No," she says with a feline smile. "But my friend Rosie will be. The one with the purple streak in her hair. She'll make sure your food is *extra* delicious."

And, because it's obvious this conversation isn't going anywhere good for me, I step away from her.

THE SEVEN-COURSE DINNER might as well have been pulled from a kids' menu at a two-star restaurant.

Most of the guests seem confused.

Anthony looks like he's going to blow an eye vessel, but then again he's sitting between his mother and his fiancée. He has a few friends here, but none of them have tried to intervene. One of them, a blond guy, looks noticeably amused by the whole thing.

The food looks pretty good to me, actually, and my stomach grumbles in complaint, but I'm not going to eat any of it. Because the woman with the purple streak in her hair served it to me, and when she caught me studying her, she winked.

"Not to your taste either, young man?" Mrs. Rosings says, from across the table. The "either" is because Nina hasn't eaten anything except for a piece of parsley that came as garnish—something she did dramatically, as if hoping every eye in the room would watch her lift it to her lips.

Anthony perks up, like he thinks I'm going to solve his life for him.

Honestly, and I'm not saying this to be a dick, but this guy needs a real therapist. Maybe I'll leave a note telling him so after I blow town with his mother's multimillion-dollar necklace.

"The food looks great," I tell her with a smile. "But I'm on a cleanse."

She makes a sound that suggests she thinks as much of people who do cleanses as she does Red Lobster waitresses. "What a delight. Why don't you tell us all about it?"

I make up a bunch of shit about resetting the limbic system with a diet of leafy greens, kale shakes, and protein powder. Half the table seems bored to tears; Elaine's friend looks like she's barely bothering to hold back laughter; and Anthony looks relieved that neither his fiancée nor his mother are currently talking to him. So at least I'm staying on his good side.

My eyes are on the clock over the door, ticking away the minutes before the "games." Will Anthony flip the breakers then, or after the start of the slideshow? How much time should I give him before I resort to doing it myself?

Truthfully, I'd prefer to miss the "games"—Elaine and her friend are both probably watching me, even though I haven't seen a glimpse of the former since our talk in the bushes. But I should try to mold my plan to Anthony's.

When dessert—individual cups of dirt and worms pudding—is cleared away, Mrs. Rosings claps her hands and gets to her feet. Elaine, who was apparently waiting for her summons, returns to the room from who-knows-where. She's carrying what looks like a custom-made wooden prize wheel. It's double-sided, so even though Mrs. Rosings is sitting across from me, I can see the different options.

Tag
Charades
Truth or dare?
Duck, duck, goose
Hide and seek

There's tittering laughter from the other guests, but Mrs. Rosings has a cunning look on her face that makes me feel like we're the group of people at the beginning of a horror movie in which almost everyone gets slaughtered. Something tells me Elaine Whatever-Her-Last-Name-Is would be the final girl.

"The moment of truth, my friends," Mrs. Rosings says, glancing at Anthony, whose jaw is so tight he's probably going to need dental work after this evening. Then she puts a little muscle into her arm and gets the wheel turning. I watch as the wheel slows.

For a moment it looks like thirty adults will be playing *duck, duck, goose*, but then the stylus clicks over to *hide and seek*.

A feeling of anticipation fills my gut, especially when I see Anthony give his fiancée a significant look, followed by a slight nod. He's going to cut the power now, before the slideshow. That means I'm about to make my move.

There's nowhere to hide in the drawing room. No closets, no human-sized ottomans. Just a table with chairs, pushed to the side for this event, a couch with legs and no fabric concealing the floor beneath it, a few armchairs that equally lack cover, and those display cases, of course.

No one with any sense will try to hide there.

Admittedly, I'm not getting a very sensible vibe from this crew, but I'm pretty desperate to finish my mission and get out of here. It's a go.

I feel eyes boring into me, and my gaze flicks up from the wheel to Elaine, standing behind Mrs. Rosings. Her friend is gone, probably back in the kitchen.

There's a scowl on Elaine's face as she watches me, her eyes that honeyed whiskey color, her lips lush and cherry red. I don't usually get off on women disliking me, but that look incites something in me. It makes me want to hear her scream my name.

I'll bet she's not the kind of woman who loses control often—not because she's type A but because she's tough as hell. I'd like to know what made her that way, but like so many of the people whose lives I've brushed against but never really touched, she'll have to stay a mystery. It's a bittersweet thought I don't have time to chew on right now...although something tells me it'll keep me up in the weeks and months to come.

Jobs do that sometimes.

They raise questions that'll never be answered, make you like people you're going to have to fuck over. Make you wonder what would have happened if everything were different.

There's a reason I turned away from this life before Ryan went and pulled me back in.

"Well, how fun," Mrs. Rosings says with a tight smile. "You'll have five minutes to hide, and then Anthony and Nina will come find you. The only place that's off limits to you is Adrien's old study."

God bless Mrs. Rosings. I'm guessing she just made all of us want to go in there, myself included, but I won't be giving in to temptation. I have to follow Anthony down to the basement to make sure he flips all of the breakers—especially the one connected to the drawing room—then I need to hustle up, grab the necklace, and disappear into the night.

Forever.

Roark will let Ryan go, and after this fuckup, I'm ready to move on from what my brother did to me last year. Maybe I can convince him to go legit with me. This whole mess can be left behind in our dust.

The only part of that scenario that disappoints me is that I won't be able to see the look on Elaine's face when she discovers I took the necklace.

Something tells me this is the one time a woman won't get off on being right.

CHAPTER TWELVE

LAINEY

I trail Jake, who's trailing Anthony, like we're playing a game of Assassins. Adrenaline pumps through my veins, filling me with its sweet, seductive thrill. With each soft footstep I take, I feel the beat of *something is happening*. I've wanted to be a part of something bigger than myself for my whole life, and this is my chance. I could stop a real crime from happening.

Considering what we overheard earlier, I'm guessing Anthony's going down there to cut the power, which I already warned Rosie about.

So why is Jake following him? Why isn't he walking down there with him?

Sure, he may be trying to jump-scare him. There are people who find that sort of thing funny, and it wouldn't shock me if Jake has a juvenile sense of humor, but it's still strange.

Anthony glances both ways when he reaches the door that leads down to the cavernous, half-finished basement—a place childhood nightmares are made of. His gaze completely misses Jake, who stepped behind a hideous statue of some long-deceased Smith, and me, tucked behind the corner of a skinny hall that leads to a room so useless Mrs. Rosings uses it to stow boxes from her online deliveries.

Jake watches as Anthony creeps down the stairs, his focus almost predatory. He waits. He listens. He looks. And then he follows him down the stairs, moving so carefully I can't even hear the scuff of his shoes against the stone—a bold maneuver, although there are *plenty* of places to hide down there.

Jake can't be a therapist. There's no way. He's much too good on his feet, too fit, to be a man who sits on a couch all day. And I absolutely cannot picture him spending all day asking people, "And how did that make you feel?"

He's not empathetic enough, and he'd go out of his mind with boredom. I *know* he would. There's a...wildness in him, for lack of a better word.

Of course, there are plenty of people who aren't good at their jobs. Maybe he's one of them, and he's feeding his need for excitement by going all in with hide and seek. Following the man who's supposed to find everyone might be his strategy. It's feasible he'd have one. I absolutely believe he's a man who likes playing games—and dominating in them.

Heat flashes through my body, lighting me up, as I remember being pressed up against the side of the house, hidden by the shrubbery.

I crush down the thoughts and consider the wisdom of following Anthony and Jake.

Not yet. I decide to wait for a solid minute before making a move, tracking the time by counting in my head. But before the minute's up, there's a clicking sound. The lights cut out, leaving me in a pitch black hall.

Adrenaline floods my system as a few shouts go up from various locations in the cavernous, three-stories-tall house. The guests have spread out far and wide—I can tell based on the distance of some of the voices. One person shouts, barely audible, "The lights just went off!"

As if this could possibly be news to anyone.

The other guests will start filtering their way downstairs, of course. But most of them aren't accustomed to maneuvering in the dark, let alone in a house this big and cumbersome. It'll take several minutes, maybe even half an hour, for everyone to converge.

"Everyone meet me in the front room," Anthony bellows from the basement stairs.

I knew this was going to happen; *Jake* knew it was going to happen.

The question is what he plans to do about it.

My mind whirrs over everything—

The fake necklace, the three-week friendship with Anthony, following Anthony now...

It all goes back to the Heart of the Mountain.

Jake said he got the fake made for Anthony so he could give it to Nina as a present, but how long would it take for someone to acquire a fake that good?

At least a few days, and it seems doubtful the jewelry genius who made it lives in Asheville. So add on at least a day or two for shipping.

I'm guessing Anthony wouldn't ask a man he'd met only once to make a fake necklace for him, so the request would have come recently—too recent for Cleo to have seen the necklace on Jake's dresser *last week.*

It all clicks, finally, and I see it clear as day, the epiphany filling me with vindication.

Jake Jeffries didn't just "find" Anthony's wallet—he pickpocketed him and then gave it back, like me bringing Marjorie her hand bag.

Jake Jeffries is a con artist like my parents, like *me,* and he wants to steal the Heart of the Mountain.

This is the key to every strange circumstance that's unfolded over the past week.

The universe is giving me a chance to stop him and redeem myself.

The logical thing to do would be to call the police, or at least alert Mrs. Rosings to my suspicion, but I don't have any proof. And I know in my heart, my soul, that this is his big chance. If I leave him unsupervised, he'll take that necklace, and he'll disappear in the wind—as surely gone as the asshat who abandoned Professor X.

Only I'm not going to let that happen.

My heart pounding, my body lit up like it's filled with liquid gold, I lie in wait.

Anthony's dark, shadowed figure comes up first. It's too dark for me to see his features well, but my eyes have adjusted enough that I can make out the slight smile on his face. He foiled his mother. Maybe that would sound like a minor accomplishment to some people, but I know Mrs. Rosings pretty well by now; it's not. He heads toward the front room with purpose.

I don't budge. I wait until another figure creeps out of the stairwell. My heart is pounding so hard, I hear it in my ears. The tips of my fingers are buzzing. Because I've become the predator, the hunter.

Jake pads slowly down the hall, moving quickly but paying attention to his surroundings. When there's a sound of quick, awkward footsteps moving toward us, he easily sidesteps into a doorway and goes still, and a suited man who's muttering unflattering things about Mrs. Rosings passes him without a glance. Passes me too.

Seconds after the ungraceful man turns toward the front room, Jake starts moving again. Right past me. He misses me, too, because I'm as frozen as that statue, although from the way he's glancing around he *feels* me. So I wait until he's well past me to make my move. I know where he's going, anyway.

Sure enough, I watch him sneak around the corner of the hall that leads to the drawing room.

Toeing off my high heels, I pad after him as quietly as Professor X. I don't know why—maybe it's the perverse part of me that likes winning, but I want to catch him in the act. To prove to myself that I may have gotten plenty of things wrong over the last week, but I was right about him.

I know he's unarmed—the guard at the gate may be mostly useless, but he checked everyone for weapons. Everyone other than me, that is. I had pepper spray already stowed in the house, and I pocketed it after coming in. I'll use it liberally if I need to.

My heart pounds a little harder as I turn the corner into the final hallway leading to the drawing room.

Behind me, I can hear someone thumping on a door, two people talking, but my ears are still buzzing, my senses all fixed on Jake. On the room ahead.

The door was left a whisper open, probably because closing it would have made sound.

I peer through it, and there he is, standing in front of a display case, dark now, the backlighting cut off along with everything else. But I know which case the necklace was kept in—I assigned it to memory, the same way he clearly did.

Not on my watch.

Without pausing to think, I run toward him and leap onto his strong, muscular back, wrapping my forearms around his neck. I expected him to cry out when I landed on him, or to try to try to fling me off. But the only sound he makes is a slight grunt, while my rapid breathing is almost deafening to my own ears. His hands don't rise to fight me at all.

I hike my legs around his waist for leverage, trying not to notice what it feels like to have the hard heat of his body pressed against me, my face up against his soft, slightly curly hair. His ear.

The adrenaline filling my body becomes slightly syrupy a

second before I get a better look at the darkened display case in front of him. My eyes have adjusted enough to the near dark, brightened only by scant light filtering in from the gaps in the curtains, for me to see that the case is empty.

So he already took the necklace. He works faster than I could have imagined, but I tell myself that's okay. I caught him in the act. The necklace will be on his person somewhere, and everyone will know he was the one who took it. In fact...

My bare foot is pressed near his pants pocket—and I can feel that there's something hard inside.

For a half a second, I wonder if he's just happy to see me, but it feels cold through the fabric, not hot. The necklace.

It's time for me to shout for help, to bring this whole shitty engagement party into the room running, but for some reason I don't. I'm not...ready. Maybe it's because he's not trying to shake me off or hurt me.

He attempts to say something, but my arms are too tightly wrapped around his throat for the words to be audible. He reaches up and wrenches one of them away—his grip firm but not punishing.

"Surprised to have been caught in the act, *doctor?*" I ask into his ear. It's an intimate thing to do, and we're in an intimate position, as closely pressed together as we were the other day, when I was cradled in his lap. My body pulses. It aches. It wants him without bothering to consider if it's a sensible ask.

My body is a horny idiot, but at least my mind is functional.

"You're too late," he says, his voice resigned. Almost...broken. "The necklace is already gone."

"Because you took it," I accuse. "I can feel it in your pocket."

He glances up at me with a half-smile, shaking his head slightly. In the dark, his eyes look black, his hair dark grey. "You're some hellcat, you know."

"What I know is that I've got you. I caught you in the act. Now, remove the necklace from your pocket," I say, my voice shaking slightly, but not because I'm afraid. Because...

Well, it doesn't matter.

"Sure," he says, "why not."

There's an undercurrent beneath his words, assuring me there are some surprises in store, and I'm probably not going to like them. But he doesn't buck me off or try to hit me. He reaches into his pocket and tugs out the necklace, lifting it up to me in the dark.

For a second, I think it'll be just that easy—he'll hand me the necklace, I'll turn him in, and life can go back to being...

Boring.

I bury the thought as I reach for the Heart of the Mountain, taking the pendant in my hand. And the instant my fist closes around it, I know. The jewel feels all wrong.

"This is another fake," I hiss, squeezing my legs around him reflexively.

He lets out a low sound, then says, "You should get a job working for a jeweler if the old lady fires you. You've got a real eye."

"You were going to replace it with *this*?" I ask skeptically. Because if I can tell it's fake in the pitch-black room, it's not passing any quality control tests. "Everyone would know instantly."

"You took the other one," he says tightly, not without resentment. "I didn't have to fool them forever. Just for long enough..."

"For you to disappear. What a good pal you are to Anthony, huh?"

"Get off my back, would you?" he says, and it's obvious he means it both ways.

"No," I say, stuffing the fake into my empty pocket. "I'm keeping this."

"Forming a collection?" he asks with a sigh. I'm still riding his back, one forearm pressed against his throat, but he surprises me by stepping away from the case and then lowering into the closest armchair. If I don't release him, I'm about to be crushed by a two hundred pound man, so I do—and quickly get out my pepper spray as he pulls away.

"If you so much as touch my pinky finger, I swear to God," I say in a heated undertone. "I will spray you in the face and then the nuts."

"You'd have to pull my pants down to get to them," he says, giving me a flat look. He's standing in front of me, but just inches away—too close for me to stand up unless I want to be pressed against the wall of him.

"I'd do it."

"I believe you," he says. "But I'm not going to try to hurt you. I'd *never* do that."

I shouldn't buy it, but I do.

He's physically powerful, but he's never come off as threatening. He doesn't have the air of banked violence some men do.

A bitter laugh escapes him. "You know, I've fucked over enough people that I shouldn't be surprised karma's coming for me. I guess I just didn't think it would look like this."

"That you'd be foiled by a woman who's smarter than you?"

"If that's how you want to put it. Are you going to call in the hounds?" His voice is resigned. Sad.

It doesn't take a genius to guess why.

The authorities will assume he's behind this. They'll poke into his background, doing a much less cursory check than I did, and they'll find it full of holes and fake necklaces. And then there's me...

If I tell them what I know, they'll arrest him tonight. He'll be in a world of shit, and he didn't even get to do the thing he obviously came here to do.

But why the fuck should I care if this man sinks or swims? He's lied to all of us. And, yes, I *did* lie to him too, but given everything that's come to light, he probably deserved it. It's like I've given him a taste of his own poison.

He didn't take it, a voice says in my head. *He didn't take it, but someone else did.*

And there's a part of me that wants to find out. That *needs* it. Six months ago, I was a desperate almost-housewife, who wanted to chew my own leg off to escape, and now...

Now, I'm in the middle of something exciting. Something life-changing. Something *dangerous*.

"Why this necklace?" I ask, letting my mind chew over that thought. "Did you see the documentary?"

There's murmuring from the direction of the hall. Maybe someone's coming to check on us, or maybe they were deep within the house and are still on their way to the front room. When they pass the drawing room, I can summon them. I can tell them what happened. I can—

"Not me," Jake says, peering down at me. He glances off, then meets my eyes, his expression more serious than I've ever seen it. Even though the room is dark, I can feel his gaze in every pore in my body. I'm glad its power is blunted by the dark because this is a man who knows how to act, and he's like a prisoner on death row, making a final plea for his life. "Look, hellcat, you were right about me. I'm not a therapist, God knows, and I introduced myself to Anthony with bad intentions. That mess with Cleo was the result of my own poor decision-making. But you have my brother's life in your hands. He pissed off the wrong person, and I was given the chance to make amends and save him. By taking this necklace. If I don't get the necklace, Ryan's going to lose his hand. Maybe worse."

"Is he the other boy in your sketchbook?" I ask, and his flinch confirms it before his words do. He didn't want me to see inside of that book because it was personal. Special. It was a peek at the real Jake—if that's even his name. And it contained the likeness of someone he's protective of, someone he would prefer to keep to himself.

"Yeah," he says slowly. "Yeah, he is. And he can be a dumb asshole, but he's the only thing I've got."

I wasn't prepared to believe him, but the truth rumbles in his voice. It's there in the desperation in his eyes. And I understand. I know what it is to only have one person you love unconditionally—one person with whom you can unreservedly be yourself. One person who makes you human.

Claire is that person for me, and I ask myself: would I have done it for her?

When I have my answer, I stand from the chair.

CHAPTER THIRTEEN

JAKE

Elaine gets to her feet—her bare feet, which were pressed about four inches away from my dick a few minutes ago—and I know I'm sunk. Why the fuck would she believe me? And, if she does, why would she care? Ryan's problems are his and mine, not hers. Besides, I've just admitted I was hoping to steal a multimillion-dollar necklace from her boss.

Even if she doesn't much like her boss, she seems like a woman who believes in doing a job thoroughly.

Hell, I know she is. She adopted a damn cat to get into my apartment. A voice in my head suggests that she took pity on an abandoned cat, and I could use that to my advantage. Maybe that's true, but I'd rather spend the rest of my life in jail than play the pity card. If she's decided to turn me in, there's nothing I can do about it. I'll lie, obviously, but the truth will come out in the end. Ryan will get hurt, my nightmare of being contained will come true, and that will be that. Maybe it's how it was always going to end for us—Ryan hurt and me in jail. He'll feel guilty, and I'll have to carry that too. And...

"Will you *please* get out of the way?" Elaine says tightly, and I realize I'm still standing directly in front of her, our legs touching, my head tipped down to her, the same way we were outside this house a couple of miserable hours ago.

Back when I thought I had a chance at ending this thing tonight.

"Sorry, by all means," I say, "let me clear your path so you can ruin my life."

"You ruined your own life." She gives me an annoyed look and shoves my arm, her hand leaving a soul imprint on my flesh, and I step aside, watching as she walks away from me.

My mind's barely functional, and even though I know I should be thinking of a way to talk her around, the only thought that's surfacing is that she has a truly spectacular ass—the kind of ass some dead British guy would have written a sonnet about, only he'd have pretended he was talking about a grapefruit. And what the fuck is the matter with me?

I need to convince her to help. I—

I take a step toward her. "You remember the Suicide Squad from the DC comics?"

She glances over her shoulder at me, clearly caught off guard. "Uh, yeah. You think now is a good time to discuss comic books, Jake?" Her brow furrows. "What's your real name, anyway?"

"Jake."

Her expression shutters. "Sure."

"It is," I blurt, needing her to believe me. "Just like you're really Elaine. It's easier to react naturally if people are calling you by your real name, or something close."

"Okay, *Jake*," she says, turning a little toward me. "Do you have a point?"

"The reason the government formed the Suicide Squad is because they needed people who have superpowers to fight people who have superpowers."

"And for some reason Superman wasn't enough," she scoffs.

A solid point, but I don't actually want to get into a discussion of comic books. Not when the seconds are ticking out on my chance to turn this thing around.

"My point is that you need a thief to find a thief," I say with emphasis. "Someone stole the necklace, and it wasn't me, and I'm more motivated to get it back than any officer of the law would be."

She raises her eyebrows. "But you wouldn't want to give it back to Mrs. Rosings."

"Maybe not," I admit, feeling my plan sink in on itself. "But couldn't we work that part out later? Maybe there's a compromise."

There's not, not with Roark. Especially not with Roark when he's this pissed.

"We'll see," she says in a voice designed to remind me that she has all the power in this situation and I'm vapor. She keeps walking. I take another step toward her, hoping I can convince her that she needs me. That she can't do this without me, and the cops wouldn't be able to do it at all.

"What if it was Anthony or Nina?" I ask. "Do you really think Mrs. Rosings would want you to unleash the police on them?"

Even as I say it, I realize that, yes, Mrs. Rosings would absolutely fucking love to see Nina behind bars for the rest of her life. She'd probably visit her in prison just to see her handiwork. Her precious son, though? I'm guessing she cares a lot about him, in her screwed up way, if she went through this whole charade to convince him he was marrying the wrong woman.

Elaine pauses and then continues walking again, unswayed. Completely unintimidated by me.

Then it hits me that she's not heading for the door, or opening her mouth to shout *Thief, thief*.

No, she's approaching the now-empty display case. I watch in disbelief as she stops in front of it. Then she untucks her button-up black shirt and pulls it up, flashing her tanned, taut abdomen, instantly making my mouth dry, and opens the case. I watch in disbelief as she pulls the fake necklace out of her pants pocket and wipes it down.

"You were right," I comment through a dry mouth. "It won't fool anyone. It looks like it came out of a shitty gumball machine."

Her lips tip up slightly, but she arranges the necklace in the case, careful not to leave prints anywhere. In the process, she shows me more of that tanned torso and a glimpse of her bra—red, lacy—and—

This is not the fucking time to get hard over a woman who hates you, Jake, for fuck's sake.

"It's the one from your apartment," she says as she closes the case, then gives me a pointed look. "It's pretty good, you know. Suspiciously good."

"You had it in your pocket the whole time?" I ask, torn between being impressed and sort of pissed. Very aware that she neither cares whether I'm impressed nor believes I have any excuse to be pissed.

"You should've guessed," she says, a challenge in her eyes.

"I should have," I agree. I pause, staring at her in the dark, taking in the soft features and hard eyes of this hellcat of a woman. She's a mystery to me. An enigma wrapped in a fucking riddle. If I were another kind of man, a man who knew how to get close to people instead of just swimming at the surface, I'd want to unspool her mysteries to see what lies beneath.

"Why are you helping me?" I ask, my voice quavering in a way I don't at all like.

Never show weakness, especially not to a mark.

She's not a mark, but she's something more dangerous—a woman who could destroy me with a word.

"I understand what it's like...to have just one person."

I can see in her eyes that she does understand, and I feel a pulse of connection. *Real* connection.

"I'm sorry," I say, barely aware of what I'm apologizing for. Trying to steal from her boss?

Pinning her to a wall earlier?

She looks me dead in the eye and says, "You should be."

There are footfalls just beyond the door. Close. I should have heard them earlier, but I've been wrapped up in our stand-off. Whoever it is will be in here within seconds...

We have every right to be in this room, but it seems like a bad idea to be caught standing directly in front of the case. If we're seen there, someone might get the idea to take a closer look at the necklace, and even if the fake is good, I'm not convinced it's *that* good.

There's barely time to think—definitely no time to say anything—so I just lift Elaine up by the waist and take the three big steps back toward that chair from earlier before setting her back down on her feet. Her pretty red lips open, probably to swear at me. But before any words or disgruntled sounds can escape, I lean down and capture her mouth with mine, my hand still wrapped around the sexy curve of her hip as I coax her to open for me, to put on a good show for our guest.

To give in to this strange, senseless pull...

Understanding registers in her eyes as the sound of the creaking door reaches us, but she still sinks her teeth into my lip, making me laugh into her mouth and flex my fingers on her hip.

"Oh shit," Anthony says, and I pull away, making a show of being surprised and then embarrassed.

"Sorry, man," I say, not letting go of Elaine, because that wouldn't be the gentlemanly thing to do. Jake Jeffries, who just got pulled off the execution block seconds before the cleaver came down, is most certainly a gentleman. "We got a little carried away."

Elaine layers her hand over mine on her waist, digging her fingernails in even as she makes a show of leaning into me.

He smiles slightly—a *good job, buddy* kind of smile—then says, "We're calling the evening short." He rubs a hand over his jaw. "I was hoping you'd be able to talk to my mom, but things got a little chaotic."

No shit. They started that way and stayed it.

"We'll do it another time," I say with an insincere smile.

Only...it occurs to me that maybe we really will have to do it another time. If Jake Jeffries isn't dead, then he'll have to make himself useful, and my top two suspects for snatching the necklace are Anthony and Nina. He couldn't have taken it personally unless he moves at the speed of light, but she could have been lying in wait. Clearing my throat, I add, "Maybe we could do a family therapy session."

He looks interested for half a second before his face lifts in a self-deprecating smile. "My mother would never agree to that. She'd sooner kill me."

"You're right," Elaine agrees, tugging my hand away like it's a snail that's left a trail of slime on her shirt. "So you'd have to act like it's something else. Why not invite her over for tea? She loves her high tea."

I don't know what the fuck a high tea entails, but I've befriended Joy at the apartment complex, so maybe she can tell me.

"There's an idea," he says, brightening again. His gaze shifts between the two of us. "Did you two just meet tonight?"

I smile at Elaine. "Yeah, blame it on the hide and seek and the power failure. It set a certain...atmosphere."

He laughs and runs his hand over his jaw again. Is that a nervous tic? And, if so, is it because he's worried we'll guess he cut the power, or because he has the real Heart of the Mountain tucked into his pocket?

I watch him to see if his gaze strays to the display case. It's possible he came in here to make a big show of finding it empty, because the person who sends out the alert is less likely to be accused of having committed the crime. But he doesn't seem to take notice of the display case or care about what's inside.

"At least my mother's games did something for somebody." He nods, and this time his gaze does stray to the case. I watch for any surprise or suspicion, but there's none on his face. Of course, it's dark in here, and he may have better acting skills than I've realized.

Sighing, Anthony says, "Well, I have to go find the other stragglers."

"I'll come with you," I say, stepping forward. It seems like a good plan to re-establish our rapport, especially since I failed to do the one thing he asked of me tonight, but Elaine grabs my hand.

"You offered to see me home, *honey*," she says pointedly.

I give Anthony an *aw shucks* grin. "Sorry," I say. "I did. I'll talk to you soon, man, and we'll get that tea set up."

He smiles back at me. "Thank you. I think my mother's already taken to you. She asked you all about your—" He waves a hand as if he can't think of the word cleanse or maybe just doesn't want to say it.

His mother definitely didn't ask because she was interested, but if he's an unsuspicious person, all the better.

"I think it's gonna work out just fine," I say—and then watch his back as he leaves the room. My gaze finds Elaine. I'm jumpy to leave now. She saved my ass, and I'm grateful, but I need to regroup. Learn some radio therapy so I can pull off this group session and hopefully score a solo invite to Anthony's house, too.

"You lose your car or something?" I ask her. "Because you don't seem like the kind of woman who needs help getting home. I feel sorry for the person who tries to carjack you."

She gives me an unamused look. "Well, make sure it's not yourself you have to feel sorry for, then. No one likes someone who always feels sorry for themselves. And this should be obvious, but I'm not letting you go off by yourself to cause trouble. You're coming with me. My friends will decide what to do with you."

"What, that blonde woman?"

"No, she already told me she'll have to be here late. Mrs. Rosings asked her and the other staff to stay to clean."

"You have more than one friend?"

She gives me a withering look as she pulls out her phone and sends a couple of texts. Truth is, humor has always been my coping mechanism, and I definitely feel the need for it now. Because however much I'd like to believe she's talking about the cat, or a group of women wearing bikinis who want to tickle me with feather dusters, something tells me she's not.

With my luck, she probably lives with seven bikers.

"You'll see," she says with a small smile.

I guess I will, because I'm good and stuck.

I don't have the necklace, and she knows my game, so my choice is to either work with her or give up and run. Knocking her out wouldn't help, not that I'd try.

"If you're good enough, you'll never have to hurt anyone," Roark said to me years ago, and he was right.

Today, I wasn't good enough.

But I'd never hurt her, and I can't give up on Ryan either.

So I follow her like I'm that damn cat.

When we get to the front room, Mrs. Rosings is sitting in a high-backed chair, watching by candlelight as the guests leave. There's a platter of individually wrapped cookies on the table beside her, the candlelight just strong enough for me to read the Eat Me scrawled beneath the likeness of Anthony and Nina.

You know what? Maybe I'm lucky not to have a mother.

She mustn't have planned the electricity outage, but she doesn't seem upset about it.

Maybe she's in on it, whispers the suspicious-as-fuck voice in my head. *Maybe this is about claiming insurance money.*

It feels notable that there's no sign of Nina. Why? She wasn't with Anthony. Maybe she's in the bathroom or Mrs. Rosings drove her to drink straight from a bottle of champagne in the kitchen. Regardless, it's interesting that she's not here.

"Does this happen often?" I ask, hoping to figure out a polite way to ask about the whereabouts of the future daughter-in-law she hates.

"No," Mrs. Rosings says. "But every time it does, it seems to be in the middle of a dinner party. Who knows why."

The look on her face suggests she knows perfectly well, however.

"Well, I have to leave, Mrs. Rosings," Elaine says. "It's an emergency."

Mrs. Rosings's gaze flicks up to my face, pausing there, before returning to Elaine. "Oh, it may *feel* like an emergency, Elaine, but it never is. Still, you can go. I find I'm rather tired."

"Have you seen Nina?" I ask. "Anthony was looking for her."

A lie, sure, but if she mentioned it to Anthony, he'd think nothing of it.

"Oh, I've seen her all right," Mrs. Rosings says with a sniff. "She made a big fuss about the power outage, not that I'm surprised."

That could be the behavior of an innocent woman, or a guilty one wanting to be considered above suspicion.

"Goodnight," Elaine says. "I'll check in tomorrow to see if you need anything."

Mrs. Rosings response is to laugh. "If you're going to make bad decisions, *dear*, make sure you give yourself time to enjoy them."

She's obviously making insinuations about what's going to happen tonight. Elaine must have decided it's best to play along with the pretense, given both her boss and my best buddy Anthony believe it, because she takes my hand and hustles me out of the foyer. She's still barefoot—and the gravel has to hurt, but she walks out as if she's the Queen of England. Once we're outside in the cool night air, she drops my hand like it burned her.

"What do we think, did she do it herself?" I ask in an undertone.

She doesn't respond, just leads me out of the gate and down the block, then around a corner, stopping in front of a shitty Ford Fiesta.

"I figured you'd have something sporty."

She spears me with a look as she unlocks the car with her fob. "I can't afford a sports car."

She says it with plenty of attitude, and I can't help myself. I ask, "How much did you get paid for stealing my necklace?"

"You're seriously getting on *my* case about stealing?" she asks, lifting her eyebrows.

"Just wondering how much I'm worth."

"I had to blow it all on getting Professor X anesthesia. Do *you* have a sporty car?"

"I don't have a car at all," I say, taking this in. Elaine is a woman who would assume risk for a stranger and wrack up debt for a cat someone else abandoned. That should make her an easy mark, but it would be a mistake to take her for one. I already know Elaine has a backbone of steel. "Jake Jeffries has a shitty sedan I paid cash for at one of those lots where they screw everyone over."

"Are you talking this much because you're nervous?" She tucks her inky hair behind her ear, and I remember the brush of it against my neck when she jumped onto my back. A pulse of heat shoots down to my dick at the thought of her hot weight pressed to my back, her foot near my dick. Her red-painted lips at my ear...

"Should I be?" I ask pointedly, pushing the thoughts away. "Are you just a vigilante when it comes to other people's shitty boyfriends, or do you take offense to thieves too?"

"I take offense," she says tightly. "But no, I'm not going to hurt you. My friends won't hurt you either."

"I guess I'll have to take your word for that," I say, preparing to climb into the passenger side of the vehicle.

"*Stop*," she tells me.

I look at her in confusion.

"I have to pat you down before we get in the car," she says. "I need to make sure you don't have it."

Heat washes through me as she prowls around the front of the car and stops in front of me.

"Hands up," she says, her voice low and throaty.

"What if someone from the party sees us?"

"They'll assume it's some kind of kink," she says carelessly, as if she doesn't realize how much blood she's sending to my dick. But she does. She absolutely does. It's there in the glimmer of her eyes, like she enjoys tormenting me. And I'll be damned if that doesn't make her more interesting. "Jacket off."

Eyes pinned to hers, I take it off and hand it to her.

She briskly examines it before slinging it over the hood of the car, and then I slowly lift my hands. "Have your way with me, *Mistress*."

She rolls her eyes, but I don't miss the way her fingers tremble slightly as they quickly sweep up and down my arms, spreading heat in their wake, and then glide over my chest. I'm not sure whether I'm imagining it, but it feels like they pause a couple of times over my pecs. Then they move around to my back, her body inches from mine, her heat seeping into me as her touch brushes across my upper back before dipping into my belt line.

I'm looking into her eyes when she finds something, her eyes widening.

She pulls out the bottom of my collared shirt and then tugs at the strap of my money belt. When the strap doesn't give, she runs her fingers around my waist, her bare fingers against my skin—a whisper of flesh against flesh that sears me—until they reach the clasp. She undoes the money belt, then pulls it out, eyes grazing over the tools inside.

"Disappointed?" I ask, lifting my brows, my heart beating

faster than it was thirty seconds ago. It was the brush of her fingers —so soft but forceful. Thorough.

A huff escapes her. "Your mother should be."

"My mother's not exactly in a position to be disappointed by anyone."

I didn't mean to tell her something that could be used against me. I definitely don't want to sound like Anthony—a grown-ass man complaining about his mommy. But I'm on edge. Nothing's gone as it should have tonight, and I suspect that trend is not about to reverse itself.

She watches me, emotions dancing through her eyes—there, gone—as she opens the passenger door and throws the tool belt inside before closing it again.

"You know I can't believe anything you say, right?" she asks finally, pausing.

"You believed me about my brother," I point out.

She doesn't respond. She just glances at me one more time, her honey brown eyes hiding more than they show, and then her hand pats lightly right the fuck over my half-hard dick before sliding in between my legs and then over my ass.

A hiss escapes me, but I don't flinch from her touch—and I definitely don't push her up against the car the way I'd like. I just stand there, a man made of stone, as she lowers to her knees in front of me. She looks like she's about to take me out and suck, and even though I know she's more likely to spray my dick with pepper spray than show it some love, it pulses harder as her hands dance quickly and efficiently down my legs.

She meets my gaze again—her stare challenging. I give back as good as I'm getting, neither looking away nor blinking.

"Take off your shoes," she finally says, her voice hoarse.

"Do you know how painful it would be to carry a necklace like that in your shoe?"

"You sound like you have experience with that," she says, accurately. "Shoes off."

So I slip them off, one after another, and bear the indignity of this woman running her fingers up my arches, the sensation rippling through me.

Finally, she pronounces me clean of any contraband or stolen necklaces, and I'm allowed to slide my shoes back on, reclaim my jacket, and get into the car.

I almost immediately start drumming my fingers against the dash, needing the release for the adrenaline and lust pounding through my body. But I turn toward Elaine as she gets into the driver's seat, her eyes settling on me.

What does she see when she looks at me? A liar. A thief. A man who pretended to be someone's friend so I could steal his family's prized possession. A man who gets hard-ons for a woman who doesn't have the least bit of genuine interest in him. She doesn't like what she sees, and I don't blame her.

After a second, she asks, "Who *are* you?"

"Damned if I know."

CHAPTER FOURTEEN

LAINEY

I can still feel his dick through his pants. See the way his eyes burned into me as I peered up into them, the breeze playing with his mussed hair. His muscular arms lifted overhead.

I can't like Jake, but I do want him—in a purely carnal, animal lust sort of way that I've never let myself experience before. In the past, lust has been a studied thing for me—what to wear to make him beg or drop to his knees. What sounds to make and when. Which angles complement me best.

This feels *nothing* like that. He makes me want to squirm. To make *him* squirm and beg.

Which is exactly how I don't want to feel about a man who's a man who embodies every one of my worst impulses.

Now, after a tense drive back to the cabin, Jake and I are sitting in the living room with Nicole and Damien. My bare feet are covered in the worst dirt and who-knows-what-else Marshall, NC has to offer, and I'm anxious to take a shower, but I have a feeling we'll be in here for a while.

Claire and Declan are still out on their date, and Rosie hasn't gotten back from Smith House, although she's texted, and she insists she wants a full and thorough update the *instant* she gets home. Honestly, I'm glad they're not here yet. This is the sort of situation that's best kept small.

Damien, Nicole, and I are sitting on the couch, and Jake's in the hot seat in front of us. The hot seat being a dining room chair, because Nicole insisted we shouldn't let him get too comfortable. Professor X, damn her, is curled up in Jake's lap.

I've just finished telling my friends everything that happened tonight, from finding Jake in front of that empty display case to deciding to help him.

Nicole glances at me. "And I hope you searched him?"

"*Thoroughly*," Jake says with plenty of insinuation. His hand smooths over Professor X's back, and I have the obscene thought that I'd like it to glide over my thighs like that and dip between them.

My brain has been poisoned by this man.

Nicole bursts out laughing, which Jake clearly wasn't expecting, and gives him a once-over. "I'll bet she did."

"Who's threatening your brother?" Damien asks, one of the first things he's said all night. He's like that sometimes—a sponge, soaking everything in—before he makes a pronouncement. He has a bit of a threatening glower going on right now, but Jake hasn't shown any tells of being nervous. Then again, he's an actor. A cipher. Who knows if anything he does is real. I've always had the curiosity of a cat with nine lives, and I can't deny that I want to know more about him. But the more I know, the more human he'll be—the more relatable. It's safer to see him as other. As the enemy.

We're only working together right now because the enemy of my enemy is my friend.

"I'd rather not say," Jake tells him.

"We're private investigators," Damien tells him, and for a second Jake's reaction is genuine: surprise. Alarm. "We're going to find out, but you might as well save us some tedious legwork and be straightforward."

"Not my strong suit."

"Suit yourself," Damien says, leaning back.

Jake eyes him as he pets Professor X's fur again. "You won't get far without my last name."

"Don't need it," Damien says with a lazy smile. "We know Jake Jeffries is fake, and somewhere along the way of making him, I'm sure you made a mistake. Everyone always does, no matter how careful they think they are. We'll find you, and then we'll find your brother, and given he's a hostage to some sort of gangster, I'm guessing he's not as careful as you are. What's his name, anyway?"

Jake rolls his eyes. "You think I'd tell you my brother's name if I wouldn't tell you who has him?"

"He said his name is Ryan," I tell them. I'm lucky looks can't kill, because Jake not-Jeffries would have just sliced my head clean off. There's betrayal in his gaze, and I understand why. He told me something vulnerable in a moment of desperation, and he thinks I just stabbed him in the back with it. I know Nicole and Damien, though. They have their own version of right and wrong, and they're not particularly worried about anyone else's. They'll care more about helping Ryan escape this kidnapper than nailing him for past thefts.

"I lied," Jake insists, his eyes boring into me.

"He didn't."

His mouth closes in a firm, displeased line, then he regroups and says, "Look, you're all focusing on the wrong thing. I don't have the necklace, but someone else does. I'm gonna guess it's Anthony and Nina. Hell, maybe it was even Mrs. Rosings."

"You think Mrs. Rosings stole her own necklace?" I say with interest.

"She could have," he says, his jaw flexing. "Or Anthony and Nina, like I said. I'll set up that tea with Anthony. We can get everyone into one place. That should help me narrow it down."

"Oh-ho," Nicole says, leaning forward, her elbows propped on her knees, "you're not doing anything on your own, Flynn Rider, not until this situation is resolved."

This is the first I've heard that Nicole watches Disney musicals, but my surprise barely registers before I realize what she must mean. "No," I say. "Absolutely not."

"Say hello to our new roommate," she says with a grin, leaning against Damien. "We're going to be staying here too, obviously." Shifting her face back toward Jake, she says, "Lainey may have temporarily saved your sorry ass, but you're on house arrest. You don't go anywhere, or do anything, without one of us."

"Then how the fuck am I supposed to get the necklace back?" Jake asks, his expression closing down fast. Gone is the penitent man who let me run my hands all over him to search for a necklace he knew he didn't have. He looks like a rat caught in a glue trap. Maybe that's why Professor X is being so sweet to him—empathy is a powerful drug.

Nicole grins at him. "Sounds to me like you and Lainey already figured out how to handle that. You and Lainey are a couple now. You'll do your group therapy session with the happy couple and the old bird, which I would honestly kill to see. And since there are two of you, one of you can keep the others distracted while the other looks for the necklace. Divide and conquer. Boom. It's perfect."

"I don't think it's perfect," Jake objects.

"Then it's a good thing your opinion doesn't matter," Damien says pointedly, resting his elbow on the arm of the couch.

"I can't stay here." Jake glances at the front door as if he's contemplating making a run for it.

"Are you stupid?" Nicole asks him pointedly.

"Maybe. I just got caught by a woman in a knockoff Red Lobster uniform."

I shoot him a glare.

"Yeah, you did," Nicole says, holding his gaze. "And Lainey's *definitely* stupid, because she cares enough about saving your brother's ass to have risked her own freedom. She could have gotten caught putting the fake in that case. She could still get caught. You may not be happy to be here, but you're damn lucky."

Something passes through his gaze, but I can't read him. I remember what he said in the car earlier.

Damned if I know who I am.

As if he's spent so long pretending he no longer understands what's real—something I relate to more than I'd like.

"What happens once we get the necklace?"

"That's above your pay grade, Flynn Rider," Nicole says. "But my husband and I will work out a plan for getting your brother released and getting the old lady back her Heart of the Mountain."

"I don't trust you," he says starkly.

She laughs. "And I sure as hell don't trust you. Which is why I'm also going to point out that after we had an intruder last summer, we shored this place up like it's Alcatraz. Damien and my sister's boyfriend, the really big guy who lives right next door, had a nice talk with the local police officers about what it means to serve and protect. If an alarm goes off in this place, they'll be shitting their pants trying to be the first to get here. You break out, they'll grab you."

He swallows, looks away before glancing back. "I don't do well in confinement."

Nicole gets up, stretches, then says, "You're a therapist, surely you appreciate the possible benefits of exposure therapy."

"I need my clothes. My things from the apartment."

I think of his sketchbooks, tucked carefully away, the comics of him and Ryan. I feel a pulse of unwanted sympathy for him.

"Damien has clothes. You'll wear his things. We can get you a phone charger, and there are extra toothbrushes and deodorant in the closet. Consider this your Club Med."

A half smile passes over his face right before he sags in his chair, and I know he's only pretending the fight's gone out of him. He's not going to let this go. He won't leave a piece of himself behind like that—not when it sounds like he has so few of them left.

"Fine, whatever," Jake says. "I have to pick up my car. Anthony's going to get suspicious if I'm parked outside of his old lady's place for days."

"This is a full-service prison," Damien says. "We'll pick it up for you."

Jake swears under his breath, but he plucks his keys out of his pocket and throws them to Damien.

"It's the red Corolla."

"Wait," I say, glancing between my friends in disbelief. "You're leaving me here with him?"

"He'll be locked in his room, and the window is alarmed," Nicole says. "You can handle him."

Here she goes again, trusting me to get it right, even though I've gotten it wrong every step of the way since the beginning of this thing. Maybe it was stupid of me to try to level up the Love Fixers. Maybe I'm only capable of glitter bombs and potshots on social media.

Nicole gets to her feet and claps her hands. "Okay, this has been fun and all, but nothing else is going to happen tonight. We need to give this a few hours to marinate, see if the fake is spotted." Nodding to Jake, she says, "Sleeping Beauty, your bedchamber awaits."

"Goody," he replies, lowering Professor X to the ground—earning a yowl and a paw swipe—and then getting to his feet.

I follow them upstairs to the guest bedroom. Jake glances inside before shrugging and stepping in. He turns to say something, and Nicole shuts the door...then pulls out a key ring and locks it.

"Keep prisoners here often?" he asks from the other side.

"When needed," she says.

It's bluster—we've never needed it—but they must have had the door retrofitted so it could be locked from the outside.

Leave it to Damien and Nicole to do that.

"This is completely unnecessary," Jake says from beyond the door. "As you've pointed out, I'm fucked. I need that necklace to save my brother, and if I don't stay on Elaine's good side, she'll tell Anthony everything. Hurting her would hurt me, and if I'd planned on doing it anyway, I would have already done it."

There's an edge of panic in his voice, and I remember what he said about not liking confinement.

Rat in a glue trap.

Nicole snorts at him. "I'm not worried about you hurting her. I've seen her with a Yankees bat."

"We'll unlock the door once we're back," Damien says.

Then Nicole turns to me. "Don't do anything I would do. And, for the love of God, take a damn shower."

CHAPTER FIFTEEN

JAKE

Panic wraps around me, my pulse jumping around wildly like someone sent a rabbit leaping through my bloodstream.

Fuck, fuck, FUCK.

I pace around the room, feeling like it's already closing in around me—a mouth, ready to chew and swallow. I roll up my sleeves and ditch the jacket, but it doesn't help. My skin itches; my head hurts. My stomach feels like it's eating itself. I need that door to be unlocked. I need it to happen *now.*

"Elaine?" I call out, but she doesn't answer. There's no sound at all other than the scuff of my feet on the floor and the creaking of the old boards.

I think of those sketchbooks, tucked away at the apartment, and the little bag under the floorboards. The things I carry with me from place to place are my anchor, my way of reminding myself that Jake Langston exists. I need them. If I don't have them, it feels like the particles of who I am will drift away into the night. All I'll have left is this body—anchored here. Caught.

"Elaine?" I call out a second time, not liking the shrill note in my voice.

I have to get the fuck out of this room. When I do, I guess I'll need to find a ride or borrow hers. Coming back is a must, unfortunately—they *do* have me cornered—but I have to get my things. If I have them, I might be able to calm down, to suck in enough air.

"Unlock the door," I call out, my voice ragged. "*Please.*"

Nothing.

I know it will do jack shit, but I pound a fist against the wood, then a jagged sound escapes me as I knock my forehead into it.

I need to focus. I need to think. I can pick the lock. It won't be easy, because they had a deadbolt put in, and I'm guessing they didn't leave any potential tools in here.

Ryan's better at picking locks than I am. When we work together, I'm usually the one who turns on the charm; he's the one who sneaks in through the back door. But I can figure it out. As long as I can get enough air.

The lock squeaks, the door opens, and I tumble out into the hall—into Elaine, who's wearing sweatpants and a short-sleeved red shirt, her hair wet around her shoulders.

She has a can of pepper spray in one hand.

"I can't be inside this room with the door locked," I say, ashamed by the way my voice breaks. "I *can't.*" It would obviously be overdramatic to say it would kill me, but that's what it feels like. It feels like it's *already* killing me.

She peers at me with suspicious eyes that soften from whatever she sees in my face. Fantastic. Roark always says, *never show them your weakness,* and here I am, flashing mine like it's an American Express Black. And not for the first time. I gave her Ryan's name. I told her about Roark, even if I didn't drop any details about him.

She knows more than she should.

She layers a hand on my arm, over the place bared by my rolled-up sleeves, her fingers moving over my flesh in a soothing gesture, soft and mesmerizing. I enjoy it for half a second before realizing the woman who caught me is now trying to comfort me, which makes me feel even weaker.

Never show them your weakness.

I pull away.

"I'm sorry," she says, her gaze holding mine. Earnest. "I could tell you were upset, but I didn't realize... You can come out or keep the door open. I don't mind." Her expression hardens. "Just—"

"Don't try anything or you'll put my nuts in a vise. Got it. And it was nothing. A lot of people don't like being in a locked room. No big deal."

She watches me, her eyes seeing more than I'd like. "Sure, but you think you'd be more used to the idea given what you do."

Given that I'm a thief, she means, and am probably heading toward a locked room one day, like it or not. It's nothing I haven't thought of a thousand times.

"If only people only wanted what was good for them."

"True enough." She looks like she's about to walk away, but she lingers, her eyes on my face. "I'll get your things later. After Damien and Nicole get back. I've already been seen at your place, so no one will think it's weird."

Unless they saw her leading that cat out of my apartment with the glue trap attached to its side. But I don't say so. After all, I don't have much room to talk. I went door to door selling Girl Scout cookies in October.

I run a hand over my face, my mind working fast.

If I let her do that, I'd have to trust her with my things.

No, no can do. She may have saved my ass, but she also gave up Ryan's name.

"It's okay," I lie. "I didn't leave anything important behind."

Her expression is doubtful. "I know you did. I saw the expression on your face earlier."

"Maybe I looked that way because you've imprisoned me."

She cuts me with a glare. "Leave if you want. Find your own way to the apartment."

"But if I take off, you'll keep Jake Jeffries's shitty car, and you'll tell Anthony everything. Got it."

"I'm glad we're clear on that. But if you're uncomfortable leaving your drawings at the apartment and you want your own clothes, I can…"

"I'm *definitely* uncomfortable with you going through my things again," I snap, feeling cornered. Stuck. The only person I've shown my sketchbooks to is Ryan. They're my way of making sense of the past. Of hanging on to myself. They're *mine*.

"How do you think the people you steal from feel?" she asks, her eyes blazing now.

She probably doesn't realize it, but her words aren't without impact.

"Just forget it." I start to turn back into the room, then rethink it. I can't be in there right now. I don't want to be stuck in my memories.

Elaine takes a step toward me. "You don't trust me because I gave them your brother's first name, but it was important. If anyone can help, it's Nicole and Damien. They're good at uncovering information."

My mouth hitches up. "Well, fucking fantastic, Elaine. Like your friend down there said, my brother's not as good at covering his tracks as I am. So excuse me if the last thing I want is to spoon-feed him to people who can find evidence to put him away."

"They want to help you, you idiot," she says hotly, and the cat yowls from somewhere and slinks up from parts unknown to stand beside her. Both of them stand there, staring at me with flashing eyes. It would be cute if I weren't here at Elaine's mercy, in this shitty cabin, hundreds of miles away from my brother.

"Why? I'm not a stray cat, *Elaine*. I'm a thief. My brother and I aren't good people. You were right about me. I befriended Anthony so I could steal from him, and it wouldn't be the first time. If you want to know the truth, most of the time I don't even feel that bad about it. So, no, I don't expect any of you to stick your necks out for me and my dumbass brother, because there'd be no benefit to you."

She looks a little taken aback, but she's not a hellcat for nothing. "Are you done?"

An amused sound escapes me before I start making my way down the stairs.

"You can't leave," she says as she follows me, her presence a phantom at my back, bringing back flashes of earlier, when she was literally hanging off of me.

"I know. If I try, you'll pepper spray my junk." Truthfully, there's a good chance I could disarm her first, but I'd be left with the question of what comes next. I meant what I said. I'd never hurt her. "Do you have any food?"

"You just had a seven-course dinner."

I laugh, turning toward her in the foyer at the bottom of the stairs. "You think I was going to eat anything after you made your little threat?"

"Rosie didn't mess with your food," she says, rolling her eyes.

I press a hand to my chest. "I missed seven courses of junk food for nothing?"

"Guess so." She nods toward the back of the house. "Kitchen is back there. You're in luck, because my best friend runs a bakery in town."

Once we're in the kitchen, I watch as Elaine reaches on her tiptoes for a Tupperware container stored on top of the refrigerator, her ass pressing against her sweatpants as she lifts up. A better man would probably look away—or get up to help her—but I've had a shitty day, and this is the best thing I've seen. Seconds later, she sets the Tupperware in front of me. I open the top and find myself looking down at half a dozen individually wrapped cookies. All of them have *Fuck you very much* inscribed on them in the kind of cursive that's usually reserved for rich people's invitations. The designs differ, and some but not all have an exclamation point at the end.

I give her a sidelong glance. The red lipstick washed off in the shower, but her lips look just as delicious bare, that bottom one begging for someone to suck on it.

"You trying to tell me something, hellcat? Because all you need to do is ask for it. Seemed like you enjoyed what I had to offer the other day. You were hungry for it."

I'm being an asshole on purpose.

Her scowl is not the turnoff she probably thinks it is. It puts a pretty little crease between her eyebrows that I'd like to lick. "You're not the only one who knows how to act. My friend Claire makes them for the Love Fixers. It's one of our services, delivering these to people who deserve them. But she made a few extra because she was experimenting with punctuation. I prefer it with the exclamation point. I think it adds something extra."

I give her another sidelong glance as I select a cookie and unwrap it. I can't seem to help it. This woman has drawn me into a world of shit, but I have a strange fascination with her. It's probably because she turned my game around on me. No one's ever done that before. No one's ever seen me so well after knowing me so little. She dislikes me, maybe even hates me, but I strangely appreciate that. Because at least it's real.

I take a big bite of the cookie and find it delicious. "So who fucked you over so bad you decided to get into the revenge business?"

"It's better if we don't share anything personal."

I shrug, trying not to feel disappointed. "Suit yourself."

Her gaze lingers on me as she takes out one of the cookies for herself. Hers, I notice, has an exclamation point. Seems fitting. She's the kind of woman who'd give you the middle finger with a smile on her face. Or trash your apartment after dry-humping you on your couch. "It's not just about me personally," she says as I take another bite. "There are a lot of women who get stomped on and used. They need someone to give them back their power, their dignity."

"And a cookie's supposed to do that?"

She rolls her eyes. "The cookies are just for fun, but yes, there's something empowering in telling someone to fuck themselves by cookie. I'm not surprised you don't understand."

"I might understand better if you'd tell me about what inspired you to start this whole thing." I'm fishing, and we both know it, but this isn't just about gathering information. I'm genuinely interested in her answer.

She studies me for a moment, capturing that lower lip between her teeth, then says, "All right. A piece of information for a piece of information."

My eyebrows lift. "What do *you* want to know?"

"Who you did feel bad about stealing from."

"You're asking for more than you'd be giving."

She shifts her head, her black hair falling to her shoulder. "I'm a woman who likes a bargain."

"You won't be getting one tonight."

"What about the man who has your brother...how do you know him?"

"How do you figure I know him?" I ask, surprised.

"He asked you to get the necklace for him. That suggests he knows you could."

I nod slowly—and decide I might as well tell her something. I've given them no reason to help us, but I probably should.

"He's a thief too. You could say he mentored us."

"But he's not so fond of you anymore."

I trace the fox on my forearm. "No. I suppose not. I made a decision he didn't care for, and Ryan tried to steal something from him."

I hold back the *for me*, because truthfully it doesn't matter. I didn't ask him to do it, and even if he'd tried to steal from Roark simply for the thrill of it, I still would have risked my neck to save him. Despite our recent disagreement, that's what we do for each other; who we are to each other.

"Why would he do that?" she asks. "Seems like there'd be a pretty high chance of getting caught."

"Like I said, he can be an idiot."

"And this guy's solution was to have you steal something else entirely?"

She sounds doubtful, and I feel my usual ability to talk anyone into anything slipping away.

I look up at her. "I'd quit. That was the decision he didn't like. We had a...kind of profit-sharing agreement going. Heavily in his favor. This is his way of getting us both to fall back into line. I don't know why he chose the necklace other than that he probably knew it would be a challenge."

She studies me, her eyes fixed on mine, her regard sliding over me—hot and prodding, the way her hands were earlier—and I feel something change inside of me. I couldn't say what or why or what it means, but I *feel* it.

"I want to know why you quit," she comments.

"I know you do. I'd like to know who screwed you over."

She takes out another cookie and slides it to me, which is the first I realize that I've already finished eating one. This one is shaped like a giant hand, middle finger extended. I unwrap it and bite.

"It certainly sends a message," I say with a half-smile.

"I started the Love Fixers because my fiancée and I broke up after he started sleeping with his childhood sweetheart."

"Did you beat him with a bat?" I ask hopefully, remembering what Nicole said. I don't like thinking of any man pulling one over on the woman who's bested me. She's a worthy adversary and deserves the respect of one.

"I got out," she says. "That was enough. I was grateful it happened, because it gave me a reason to leave."

Something ugly stirs in my gut. There's an implication behind those words. An implication that makes me want to plant a boot in this guy's face. Even without her saying anything else, I know a *fuck you* cookie would be much too good for him for this piece of shit.

"He hit you?"

She lifts her eyebrows. "You think I would have let her stay with him if he had?"

No, actually, I don't.

Elaine might be my jailer, but she's a woman who cares about people and animals. Who wants to do what's right. If she'd thought that woman was in danger, she probably would have kidnapped her for her own good, same as she's done with me.

I'm not beneath admiring that sort of thing, even if it's not working out to my advantage right now.

I take a deep breath, let it out between my teeth. "I quit because the last job I took was to steal something from an old man. A pocket watch worth a lot of money. I had to get to know him as part of the job, but I got...fond of him, and I couldn't go through with it. The man who has my brother...he got someone else to do the job. I couldn't forgive him for it."

There's more to it, but that's enough for now, and more than I should have said. It's just...

She gave me something raw, and I couldn't repay it with nothing.

I pause, considering, then say, "I'd very much appreciate it if you could grab my things for me tonight. Thank you for offering earlier. There's a package hidden under one of the floorboards in the bedroom." I take another deep breath, then say, "the one under the top right foot of the bed."

Her expression darkens. "Is it drugs? Something stolen?"

"No. It's…personal. I'm the only person it would matter to. I'm just not comfortable leaving it there. I was going to sneak out later, but I don't want to piss off your friends."

Curiosity ripples across her face. She might not want to be interested in what's under the floorboards, but she is. Which means…

"I'd prefer it if you didn't look at it. I know that's a big ask."

"Is that because you're lying to me about what's in there?"

I lift my hands. "I guess there's no way I can convince you I'm being truthful unless you look. You can look if you need to. I'd just appreciate it if you didn't."

"You're trusting me," she says, leaning in a little. I wonder if she's aware of it. I wonder if she feels my presence next to her like I feel hers next to me. I'd like to believe the charged feelings I have whenever she touches me are nothing more than the adrenaline I get each time I steal something. But I know better. Elaine is the least convenient woman for me to be attracted to, but there's no denying I am. One of my foster mothers once told me that I'd cut off my nose to spite my face, and I suppose she had a point.

"Don't get used to it."

CHAPTER SIXTEEN

JAKE

Elaine studies me while I finish eating the cookie, making me feel like a slide under a fucking microscope. "What?"

"I'm trying to decide if you were being honest."

I laugh. "And what's the verdict?"

"Undecided, but you *are* surprising."

"So are you. It's not every day I get tackled and patted down by a woman half my size."

She snorts. "I'm hardly half your size. You're probably only 5'11"."

"You sure know how to stroke a man's ego."

Her smile changes, shifting to something less amused, more brittle. "I do, actually. I spent years doing that. I'm sick of it."

"Would you like to stroke something else instead?" I ask, then lift up my hands. "Joking."

"No, you're not," she says, her voice somewhere between seductive and threatening.

"What, because all men are assholes who only want one thing?"

"No," she snaps, contempt flashing in her eyes, "because you were hard when I patted you down."

I tap my fingers on the table. "Can you blame me? You rubbed your hands all over me. The TSA would have been proud. And you climbed into my lap the other day. You didn't have to. You could have fast-forwarded straight to spilling that beer all over yourself. It felt good for you too, didn't it?"

Her eyes widen. She didn't expect me to go there, and I like that I caught her off guard. It's like I just earned a point in whatever fucked-up game we're playing. Will she deny it?

She licks her lips slowly, something that's obviously for my benefit...and torment. "It's been a while for me. It would have felt good if I'd kissed a mannequin."

I ignore the obvious lie and ask, "Did it feel that good when your ex-fiancé kissed you?"

"Did it feel that good when Cleo kissed you?" she rebuts hotly.

"What do you think? I couldn't even remember her name."

The look on her face says she's unimpressed. Fair enough. I don't feel the need to tell her that I was nearly out of my mind the night I met Cleo—full of guilt, because Ryan had risked himself for me, and if I'd been a stronger man he wouldn't have felt he needed to do it.

"Charming," Elaine snaps, getting to her feet lithely.

"She tried to steal from me," I say. "I doubt she's losing sleep over me forgetting her name. You know, you didn't answer my question about your fiancé."

But she doesn't have to. She's a hellcat, a woman of fire, and even without knowing the first thing about him, I'm not surprised he couldn't keep up.

I take a half step toward her and stop, wanting to see if she'll move toward me.

She doesn't.

"I abhor what you do," she says, still holding my gaze, her chin held high. "It's despicable."

It's nothing that hasn't been said to me before. By multiple people. Which isn't to say it doesn't affect me. I meet her gaze—one stare-off champion taking on another—and say, "I agree. That's why I wanted to quit. But you have to admit...whether or not someone is despicable has nothing to do with physical attraction."

I want to ask if she thought about me in her shower—if she slid her hand between her legs under the driving water and touched herself with my name on her lips.

I'm losing what few brain cells I have left. It's just...

I've never met a woman I can be wholly honest with. A woman who knows my secrets. It's surprisingly addictive, and that adrenaline from earlier is still pounding through me, asking for release.

Then she takes a step toward me—the sight sending my blood from a simmer to a boil, because she's tipping her head up to me, revealing the long slope of her neck. Fuck me, I want to kiss it. To bite it. To lose myself in her and forget everything except for how damn good it feels.

"No," she says. "I suppose it doesn't." She leans in closer, her voice the purr of an undomesticated cat. "I have to admit I am a little curious about what better uses you can make of that mouth."

A near feral sound escapes me, and I pull her to me and then back her into the counter, my mouth already on her. Her lips open to me, and she tastes like *fuck you very much* cookies, and I'm already so hard it hurts.

It's the adrenaline, I tell myself again. Adrenaline has always made me feel more alive. And, God knows, this woman has driven me to distraction since Tuesday. I can tell the same is true for her. She hunted me earlier; she caught me. And now we both get to claim the prize.

Our teeth clash, and then she sucks in my bottom lip and bites. Her hands tug my shirt out of my pants. They trail up against my flesh again, to the same places they branded when she gave me her pat down earlier.

I pull back, needing to see the look in her eyes—intent on

burning and destroying. "You liked feeling me up earlier, huh? You want more, hellcat?"

"Shut up," she says, then pulls me to her by the bottom of my shirt, not being at all gentle. I'm not going to complain. Right now, the only thought in my head is to take as much as she's willing to give me.

I kiss her again, pushing her into the counter as if it's that wall from earlier—because this is what I wanted then and also what I want now. I'm possessed by a pressing need I couldn't even hope to put into words, beyond this... Her, *now*. Her, *here*.

I kiss down her chin, her neck, I push down the front of her shirt to kiss the tops of her tits, captured in a sports bra that tries to hold them back, and her hand reaches down to feel my hard dick through my pants. It's straining to get closer to her.

I swear into her mouth as her hand works me. Then I push at the band of her sweatpants, desperate to get them down. I want to find her wet for me. I need it. I need to know I'm affecting her the same way she's affecting me, because I don't think I've ever felt this desperate to have a woman before. To touch her. To make her moan and lose control. Maybe it's because she's the only woman who's ever shared this part of my life with me. It figures that she thinks I'm contemptible, but I'll take her desire as the best consolation prize I've ever been given.

She reaches for the band of her pants too, and for a second I think she's going to pull them back up—party over—but she helps me get my hand inside. The feeling of her, slick and wet and so fucking ready for me, nearly makes my eyes roll back in my head.

The sound she makes as I rub her clit, my fingers exploring, is unreal. Her hand stalls on my dick, hot through the fabric of my Jake Jeffries pants, and the other one spears into my hair, gripping it until I'm looking at her—our eyes meeting and holding as I fuck her with my fingers.

"Do you like that, Elaine?" I say, my voice someone else's. *Out of control. Out of control.* And does it ever feel good. "Do you like being finger-fucked by the thief you caught?"

"Shut up." Her pupils are dilated, and I can feel her flexing against the fingers I have inside of her—her pussy so deliciously wet, so ready, and I know she's going to come for me. She's going to come for me, and then I'm going to lick my fingers and suck her down.

I hope to God there's no karmic justice in this world, because if there is, there's no way she's going to give me what I want and tell me to fuck her. I want to take her right here in this kitchen, even though those P.I. friends of hers could come home any minute, and should have been home an hour ago.

I want to bend her over that counter, and have her that way. I want her to sit in my lap and ride my dick. I want to fuck her against the wall of Mrs. Rosings's house.

I want—

She tugs me to her by my shirt again, not gentle at all, and her mouth works against mine while her pussy squeezes my fingers, and I know I'm going to feel her come around them. She's going to moan into my mouth. The expectation has me so hard, I'm in danger of coming in my pants. Then she makes a little sound in the back of her throat, and I know the moment is nearly here...

That's it, hellcat, that's it.

Except it isn't. Because she abruptly pushes me away, her eyes wide, a surprised exhalation escaping her.

"What just happened?" I ask, totally thrown. "Did I...did I hurt you or something?"

The thought's a poisonous one, because I wanted to show her a good time. Still want it.

"No," she says with a hoarse laugh, tucking her hair behind her ear, the action almost prim. "Not even a little...I just... That was getting a bit out of hand, don't you think?"

"No," I admit. "I liked what my hand was doing. But if you think it was too much, that's what matters."

Her hands sweep over her lips. I can see myself all over her now—her swollen lips, her mussed hair, the way her shirt dips down lower—and it only makes me harder. "You almost came," I say, my voice a low whisper, nearly a growl.

"I almost came," she says, with something like wonder. "That's what I mean. This is...I need some time to think about this."

"You don't like being out of control," I guess.

"No," she admits, although I think the opposite is true. She was, by her own admission, liking it quite a bit. It's more that she's not used to it, a thought that is frankly stunning. If she were mine, I'd try to coax her into losing control three times a day. No, three times before breakfast. Hell, I'd still like to do that. I can think of no better way to spend my captivity.

Watching her, I lift my hand up and make a show of sucking my fingers. I'm probably tormenting myself more than her. The taste of her creates an instant addiction—one that probably won't be satisfied. "Delicious. You think all you want," I say once I've gathered myself enough to speak. "But if you decide you want to stop thinking and start acting, you know exactly where I'll be." I manage a smirk. "Because I'm your prisoner, Elaine. You might as well make the most of it. I think we could have some fun being out of control together."

"You're impossible."

"And yet, here I am. Standing in front of you. So I guess it's your lucky day."

She studies me for a second, standing just a few inches from me, before swallowing and saying, "I'm not interested."

A lie, and I wouldn't need to be a man schooled in them to call it. It's there in her shaking voice and dilated pupils. In the way her hands have fisted, like she wants to touch but won't. "Sure, you're not."

"*I'm not.*"

"Shall I go back up to my room since you have no more need of me, *boss?*"

"Yes," she says through her teeth. "I think that would be best."

"You want to lock me in?"

It hurts to think about listening to the key rasp in the lock, even though I now know that she won't keep me in there forever. She doesn't think much of me, but she's not cruel.

"No," she says. "I'll talk my friends into leaving the door unlocked, but if you try to leave—"

"I'll be drawn and quartered. Roger that."

She narrows her gaze at me, but then her eyes soften. "And I'll get your things tonight. I'll grab the keys after Damien puts them away."

Her hair is hanging loose at her chin, her eyes almost luminescent. She's like a rare wildcat of a woman.

I can't help myself, I put a hand on her arm, the softness of her skin making me instantly want to touch more of it. All of it. She lets me stroke her skin, her lips parting. "Thank you, Elaine."

Then I get up and hurry over to the stairs. Up them. When I'm in the threshold of my prison cell, I turn around, and she's still down there looking up at me—the expression on her face suggesting she's as surprised by how this day has worked out as I am.

I feel a strange lurching sensation in my chest. The feeling that everything has changed, and it will keep right on changing, and soon I won't recognize anything. Including the person I see in the mirror.

CHAPTER SEVENTEEN

LAINEY

Something is wrong with me.

Because Jake is a self-admitted criminal, a thief and a con artist, and I rocked against his hand with as little self-consciousness as if it were made of purple silicon. All it took was him touching me like that, his talented hand strumming me, invading me, his lips and teeth on me, and I nearly fell apart. Right here in the kitchen.

Years and years of no orgasms with a partner almost ended with him, and he barely even did anything.

Maybe it's because I don't care what he thinks of me.

With Todd, I felt like I had to constantly assess myself. To try to see myself through his critical gaze. But it's not like that with Jake. I know he's not someone I should be with, and that means I don't really give a shit if he thinks I drink sexy or walk sexy or eat sexy.

So maybe I should have enjoyed myself without considering the consequences—but a voice in my head had objected, loudly. Because I'd *never* been so out of control with a man. Truthfully, I've barely ever been out of control with a man, other than a few wild days in college. And if I fell apart around his fingers, I probably would have had sex with him. My logical side insists it would be colossally poor decision-making to sleep with the thief who's a sort-of prisoner in my home. And, yes, dangerous things are inherently exciting, but the Jake situation has expanded beyond myself. Other people are involved, like Nicole and Damien. Even Claire and Declan and Rosie, living right next door.

When Nicole and Damien come in, Nicole shouts, "Honey, we're home!" They act like it's no big deal that they went off on an errand that should have taken twenty minutes, tops, and were gone for well over an hour. Then again, it's hardly the first time this has happened. They're not people who like to be bound by rules and schedules.

Neither are you, a voice deep inside of me whispers.

They lock Jake's keys into a drawer to which I possess the key and then get settled on the couch, Nicole practically in Damien's lap. I explain my decision to leave Jake's door unlocked, and why. I do not, obviously, admit that he finger-fucked me in the kitchen. Nicole's mouth quirks with obvious amusement.

"You don't think that sexy son of a bitch is playing you like a fiddle? You have a habit of lying to each other."

Is it possible? He did somehow turn things around from being locked in his room to finger-fucking me in the kitchen. My mind rewinds to the way Jake reacted to being in the locked room, to the absolute desperation in his voice, the *rat in a glue trap* expression in his eyes.

That was real. Or at least I think it was. One of the legacies my parents gave me is that I can never know for sure.

"No, I don't think he was pretending. There must be some—" *Trauma*, I think but don't say. Pretend therapist or not, I don't think he'd like me talking about him like that. "History there."

"Maybe he's been arrested previously," Nicole says, looking way too happy about the potential arrest record of our house guest. "That would make it easier for us to find him and the brother."

"Maybe," I agree, but I don't really believe it. Being locked up would make anyone's skin itch, but this was different. This was primal. "Either way, I don't think it's necessary for us to keep it locked. We want him to cooperate, and he seems willing." I clear my throat. "He told me a little more about his history."

My mouth feels dry as I share what he told me about his brother's kidnapper and the old man with the watch. It feels wrong to share his story, but he must have known I'd tell them, right?

Also, I can tell from the way Nicole and Damien are eyeing each other that they don't buy it. It's a good reminder that he might have been lying to make himself look better. For all I know, he's a very active thief who doesn't even have a brother

"His name is Jake, and his brother's name is Ryan," Nicole says, holding my gaze.

"That's what he told me," I agree.

"Jake Ryan," she muses. "That's the name of the fuck boy in that eighties movie. What's it called? *Pretty in Pink?*"

"*Sixteen Candles*," Damien says with the sigh of a man who's been forced to watch eighties' movies and apparently retains them better than the one who did the forcing.

"You think he made it up," I say, my gut churning, my body still aching from the almost orgasm.

"Eh, maybe," Damien says with a shrug. "It's not the most obvious cultural touchstone for a thirty-something man."

Nicole snort-laughs, nudging him with her shoulder. "You loved it."

"No, I did not," he says, smiling back at her. "But I do love you."

I sigh loudly, depressed by their love and devotion, even though it proves that it *is* possible for a person to meet their match. That not every relationship is about one person controlling the other, or both people pretending to be someone they're not. "So, basically we have no way to be certain whether any of this is true until you find something. Or don't find something."

"Sounds about right," Damien says.

I think again of that look Jake gave me when I opened his door, so desperate, like he was on the cusp of a panic attack—a wolf who'd bite off its own paw—and say, "I still want to leave his door unlocked. We'll let him come and go, but we'll keep an eye on him."

Nicole and Damien exchange another look, and he gives Nicole a slight nod. She shifts her gaze to me and sits forward on the couch. "He's your prisoner, Lainey. You can do whatever you like with him. You can sneak into his room and watch him sleep like that pervy vampire for all we care."

Damien tousles her hair, his expression amused. "Let's get you to bed before you piss Lainey off."

"Too late," I joke. Then, as they get up, I add, "You think you guys can find information about Jake and his brother?" What I really want to ask is whether they think his brother even exists, but I don't want to admit to having doubt. "Will the watch thing help?"

"Maybe," Damien puts in.

Eyes shining, Nicole adds, "We'll find them, all right. We'll find everything this guy has been trying to tuck away."

I think of his request, of the package tucked beneath the floorboards in his bedroom.

I'd intended to tell them what I was doing, but Nicole will insist on looking at whatever's inside that bag—and I *know* it's precious to him. Those sketchbooks too. He wouldn't want her flipping through them like they didn't matter.

I shouldn't care, but I understand. When I lived with Todd, I kept a little shoebox on the top shelf of my closet. He would have thought the things in that box were trash—an old hat with a feather in it that Claire had gotten me at a secondhand store one year because it reminded her of Robin Hood, a perfectly smooth stone I'd found at the beach, and that fifty dollar bill that Marjorie Eccles had given me. Never spent. That box had been my touchstone. It had been the only piece of my soul that was mine, mostly untouched by him.

"I have to go to the store," I say. "Do you need anything?"

Nicole turns and gives me a scrutinizing look. "You'd have to drive to Asheville to find a grocery still open this late."

"Jake needs laxatives. He says he has a chronic problem."

Might as well throw him under the bus.

The look on Nicole's face suggests she doesn't believe me but is amused by the lie.

"By all means. There will be no intestinal blockages on our watch. Still...if you get it into your head to make a pit stop and do something potentially dangerous, I'd suggest bringing a friend. Claire and Declan aren't back yet, but I saw the Jeep next door."

The car Rosie's been using.

"Maybe I'll see if Rosie wants to come," I agree. "I could ask her if anything else happened at Smith House."

Nicole grins at me and taps her temple. "Great minds."

She obviously knows I'm up to something, and is letting it lie. Which reminds me again of what she said the other day. *I trust you.*

Guilt claws at my throat. "I—"

"Goodnight, Lainey," Nicole says with a *shut the fuck up* look.

Damien nods to me too, and with that, they're climbing the stairs; they're gone.

And I'm left in the foyer with my thoughts twisted into another pretzel. Why didn't she want me to tell her what I was doing? Nicole is usually as nosy as I am.

Shaking it off, I collect a handful of black trash bags from the kitchen, grab the keys from the drawer, and go next door to collect Rosie.

The Jeep is there, as advertised, but it takes Rosie several minutes to come to the door after I ring the bell. Finally, she flings it open, her skin flushed, her hair loose around her shoulders. She still hasn't changed out of the Red Lobster-esque uniform. "You're here!"

"Uh, yeah," I say, wondering if I interrupted something. "You're all…" I gesture to her pink skin, the film of sweat on her brow. "Did you smuggle a guy in because Claire and Declan are out?"

She makes a dismissive sound. "Please. Anthony's friends are all stuffed suits. I was just cleaning."

At eleven p.m. on a Saturday?

From what Claire has told me, she's not a fastidious roommate when it comes to that sort of thing.

Something's up with her, but I don't call her on it. She obviously doesn't want to be straight with me, and I keep too many secrets to resent hers

"That was some game of hide and seek, huh?" Rosie continues. "It got pretty scandalous. One of the dudes got caught with another dude's wife, getting it on in a closet, and this other guy tripped and twisted his ankle. He seemed pretty salty about it until Mrs. Rosings said she'd 'personally handle any medical bills.' I know a payoff when I smell one. And Mrs. Rosings's daughter actually showed up after all that fuss, or at least I think she did. I saw someone who looks like her photo behind the house."

"What, seriously?" I ask, feeling mental whiplash. "When?"

Rosie's face scrunches up. "It happened sometime after the lights went off."

My mind latches onto that detail. *After*. But that doesn't mean she didn't arrive before that and keep herself hidden away. Someone could probably hide in Smith House for twenty years without anyone realizing it. At the same time, I know Anthony was the one who cut the lights. So if Emma took the necklace, were they in on it together?

Rosie shoves my arm. "I heard you went home with the hot therapist." Her eyes avert to my house, to the light gleaming in the guest bedroom. "Or did *he* go home with *you? Is he there now?*" Her gaze finds the trash bags stuffed into my purse. "Please tell me you're not here because you killed him and need help dismembering his body. I've been on my feet all evening."

A laugh escapes me. "That's not why I'm here. But I did want to talk to you about him."

Her gaze narrows. "I have to say you don't look like a woman who had her world rocked."

"I'm not." But I could have been. I almost was, and my core aches painfully from the orgasm that wasn't—the need pulsing through me on repeat, like a song that won't leave your head. His offer has been spiraling through my mind too. *If you decide to stop thinking and start acting, you know where I'll be.* "I'll fill you in on the way."

I'll fill her in on some stuff, at least. I have no intention of telling her that I wanted to climb Jake Not-Jeffries like a tree and refuse to come down until the fire department showed up. While I like Rosie a lot, it would be a betrayal of the laws of best-friendship to tell her any of that before I tell Claire.

"Where are we going?" she asks, already stepping out of the doorway. This is something I enjoy about Rosie—she's always up for anything, no questions asked.

A delivery of penis balloons?

Abso-fucking-lutely.

A late night trip to a stranger's apartment?

Whose car are we taking?

"We're going to collect a thief's belongings," I answer.

"UH...YOU neglected to tell me these apartments are dope," Rosie says, glancing around Jake's front room, taking in the open kitchen.

"Are you scoping this place out for yourself?" I ask, feeling on the edge of laughing. Just on the edge, though, because I'm self-conscious about having brought her here. Jake said he'd prefer it if I didn't look at whatever's under the floorboards. It goes without saying he was hoping no one else would look at it either.

Rosie can keep a secret, but she isn't exactly...discreet.

Or interested in listening to directions.

Still, I'm glad I asked her to come. It felt good to talk to someone else about everything that had gone down at Smith House —and Rosie was appropriately shocked by the episode with the necklace. She asked how much it's worth, and all the color drained out of her face when I told her.

I'm inclined to agree with Jake—the biggest suspects are Anthony, Nina, and Mrs. Rosings herself. Emma too, if she was really at the house.

"I mean...Jake's not coming back here, right?" Rosie asks, flipping her hair over her shoulder.

I laugh. "I regret to inform you it's an Airbnb."

"Bummer. But there was a sign on the bulletin board in the hallway. Someone named Joy's looking for a roommate. Maybe we can stop by on our way out."

I stifle another laugh at the thought of whirlwind-made-human Rosie moving in with Joy. "I met Joy when I was here on Monday. She's an elderly woman who makes tea."

She shrugs and heads into the kitchen. "I like old people. If she brings the tea, I'll make the crumpets. Plus, I'm guessing there's a lower probability she'll have loud animal sex in her room."

"Don't be ageist."

"Fair point. But I'm guessing I'd mind less if the loud animal sex didn't involve my brother."

"Fair point," I say with a laugh. "Still, I'm guessing she wouldn't want visitors at 11:30 p.m. on a Saturday."

Rosie thinks about this, then nods, pulling the purple streak in her hair. "I'll call her tomorrow." She tugs open the refrigerator door and glances inside. "Do you want a beer? I think I need one."

"Nope," I say, though I'm grateful she's distracted. "I'm going to go grab Jake's clothes. Why don't you take a look around the kitchen? See if it passes muster."

She might not need to bake the way Claire does—as an extension of her neuroses—but she enjoys it.

She doesn't fight me on the idea, so I head into Jake's bedroom, feeling a strong case of déjà-vu.

First, I stop at the drawer on the bottom left and gather up the sketchbooks, including the hollowed-out one, which has a different weight. I avoid the temptation to look through them, my heart thumping as I listen to Rosie padding around in the kitchen.

Then I head over to the bed and lift the upper half, finding the loose board. I wrench it up away from the others, making a squeaking sound.

I glance out the doorway to check on Rosie, but there's no sign of her. So I reach in and quickly grab what's inside, tugging it out before I let the board and the bed back down.

My heart's still thumping fast, my mind frozen in indecision. The bag is lighter than I thought it would be, and if there's a weapon inside, it's an incredibly subtle one. No metal. Actually, whatever's inside is soft, like a balled-up sweater, and light.

But why would he care this much about rescuing a sweater or a pair of socks or whatever?

Personal, he'd said.

Nicole would tell me I'm an idiot for not making sure that it's not a soft case containing stolen jewelry—or maybe drugs. Hell, even Claire might side with her, and Claire is the kindest, most understanding person I know.

But here's the problem.

I want to look, which means Jake is interesting to me in a way that goes beyond his cocky smile and nicely defined arms and abs. I want to sit in this apartment for hours and search through his sketches and this bag. To try to log in to the laptop I saw sitting on the coffee table in the living room.

I want to know if he really did quit stealing things before this current situation, and why.

Maybe that's the real reason I brought Rosie. So I wouldn't be able to do that. So I'd have someone in the next room, holding me accountable.

I stuff the bag into the trash bag and return to the dresser, where I start packing up Jake's clothes. Did he bring his own, or did he go to the extent of purchasing a whole wardrobe for Jake Jeffries? Where does his character end and he begin? I find myself running my fingers over some of the shirts, imagining him buying them in a secondhand store while working on his persona.

I've done that.

I've shopped for a person I wanted to appear to be rather than the person I am.

I've thought, *He'd like this.* Or, *This will impress him.* Not stopping to ask if I liked it too.

When I leave the bedroom, Rosie's staring into the trash can. "Looks like he threw all the glue traps away. I wonder if this building has a serious rodent problem."

He threw them away.

I think of the look on his face when he was locked in the room earlier and, before that, when he saw that thing stuck to Professor X's side.

I know in the way that I sometimes intuit things that he threw them out because he didn't want anyone to be stuck like that—to be ended like that. He did it because somewhere in his chest, Jake Not-Jeffries has a heart. A soul that doesn't want to be contained or boxed up, and he has empathy for other creatures who are the same way. I feel this knowledge change me.

"I don't like the look on your face," Rosie tells me. "What didn't you want me to see in there?"

I sigh and say, "He had some personal things in his room. He told me where they were but asked me not to look at them."

Her eyebrows wing up, and her mouth lifts into a smirk. "And how will he ever know if you do?"

I sigh again, hating the answer even as I make it: "I'll know."

Rosie whistles, her eyes glued to my face. "*Lainey*."

"Are you going to tell Claire about all of this?" I ask.

"No, but you should."

I nod, because she's right, even though I know Claire will realize what I do: this is significant.

It also means that I should stay away from Jake Not-Jeffries. Because fucking a thief who's basically in house prison with you is one thing. Fucking a thief you find interesting, a thief you would like to sympathize with, is entirely another.

CHAPTER EIGHTEEN

JAKE

I call Roark to tell him I've seen the necklace. And I pace in my assigned room while we talk because my heart's thumping fast and hard.

"You actually had eyes on it?" he asks in a low rumble.

"That's what I said."

"And you met the owner?"

"I did." I swallow. "She's...interesting."

"And you still don't have it?"

In my mind's eye, he's in his apartment in New York, a place I've been before. But that's not where he is right now. If he were, then I'd be putting my efforts toward busting my brother out, not stealing this necklace I don't want. But Roark's smarter than that. He's bunking out in his secret location, the one he never revealed to us.

Ryan might know where it is now, a thought that makes my heart thump even faster. Because if he knows what he's not supposed to, he might lose more than a hand.

"I'm not angling to get arrested," I say tightly, not wanting to give him even the slightest hint about what actually went down tonight. "These things take time. You're the one who told me that."

He makes a harsh sound that's not even nearly a laugh. "If it takes longer than two weeks, your brother's going to pay. I figure it's a hand for stealing, and then we have room and board to settle."

"Don't forget your goons. I'm sure they don't come cheap."

"You being cute?"

"I can hardly help it," I say, trying to get him to laugh or at least tone down the aggression. I usually can. One might even say it's a talent of mine, but he's been on edge lately, pumped up—as if Ryan has thrown him for a loop. Maybe he senses he's losing us, his dream team, and he's ready to go to desperate measures to keep that from happening. Even if he has to destroy us in the process.

He takes a ragged breath, then says, "What kind of security did the owner have?"

Someone knocks lightly on my door. I back away from it, because I definitely don't want him knowing I'm around other people. Especially since I'm pretty damn sure it's Lainey knocking on that door.

"An alarm. A lock box," I say calmly, trying to sound bored. "It shouldn't be a problem, but I need to figure out an easy path in and out."

He snorts. "Do it. Two weeks."

He hangs up, and I throw the phone onto the bed, giving it the finger. It does nothing for me, unfortunately. When I open the door, two full trash bags are sitting there, but there's no sign of Lainey.

I pull the bags inside and go through them like a mad man, heart thumping, sorting through my Jake Jeffries laptop and all the clothes—a mixture of mine and the man I made—before I find them. My sketchbooks. My pencils. And the bag from beneath the floorboards, tucked into the bottom. There's no knowing whether she looked.

So I tuck the little bag away and start stuffing my things into the drawers of the old dresser in the room.

Maybe I'm losing my mind, because my things smell like Elaine. Like spicy jasmine. And I don't mind. I *like* breathing her in.

I lie in my bed for fifteen or maybe twenty minutes, but I can't settle. It's that door, closed but not locked. It's Elaine, tucked into her own room farther down the hall.

Did she look in the bag from beneath the floorboards?

If so, does she think I'm some kind of weirdo?

I nearly laugh aloud at that thought—she already thinks the worst of me. What could it possibly matter?

Finally, I heave a *fuck it* sigh and get up, testing the door as if it might have magically locked itself after the last time I shut it. A sigh of relief gusts from me when it opens easily, without even a creak of the hinges.

I head for the stairs, figuring maybe I'll get another of those cookies or...

But I hear the TV, the volume on low, and when I reach the top of the steps, I can see Elaine nestled on the couch, the cat curled into her chest.

It's a pretty picture. Peaceful. And I feel a twist inside of my chest—until she jolts into an upright position, her eyes pinned on me. The displaced cat yowls and shoots each of us a look of death.

But as I make my way down the steps, it's Elaine's eyes I feel on me.

"Were you thinking you'd escape?" she asks in an undertone when I reach the bottom.

"Wouldn't have asked you to grab that stuff if it didn't mean something to me," I say, showing her my empty hands. "I can't sleep."

She pauses, as if deciding something, then says, "Me neither," and nods to the screen. "You can stay and watch *Matchmaking Small Town America* with me, but no smartass comments. I enjoy dating shows. There's nothing wrong with enjoying dating shows."

I lower down next to her. "No, but I live for smartass comments."

To my amusement, she plants a large pillow between us. "And no touching."

"I told you I won't touch you unless you ask for it."

A huff of air escapes her. "Then you'll *never* touch me again."

"If you say so," I tell her easily, even if I'm hoping she's lying. "Now, who's boning who?"

She smiles for a split second, then shoves my shoulder with hers over the pillow.

"Hey, easy with the touching, hellcat."

She shakes her head and tells me a bit about the show, and we fall into companionable silence as we watch—Lainey breaking her rule about smartass comments as much as I do.

I don't know who falls asleep first, but I wake up at some point in the night with the TV still humming and her sweet-smelling head tipped against mine. The pillow that was wedged between us has fallen to the floor, and her head is resting on my shoulder, her nose buried in my neck. The scent of spicy jasmine hangs in the air. For a second, I can only look down at her in disbelief, because this tornado of a woman looks so small and soft in sleep.

I carefully reach for the remote on the coffee table, not wanting to displace her, then turn off the TV and pull a blanket that was slung over the back of the old couch over her. She makes a little sound in the back of her throat and snuggles in deeper. A strange feeling crawls over me, and instead of going upstairs to my much-more comfortable bed, I stay put on my insufficient piece of the couch. When I wake up, I'm alone, the blanket is folded and stowed, and the sun is low in the sky.

There's a feeling of...disappointment, maybe. But I go upstairs and find my phone, figuring I'll text Anthony. Maybe we can get the tea arranged for this afternoon, and I'll be able to grab the necklace from his lady and blow town tomorrow. It should be a more pleasant fantasy—but another fantasy has supplanted it.

I want to make Elaine come.

Shaking my head at my folly, I send off a text asking when they're all free for "tea," then lie down for a few minutes to see if he answers quickly. When my phone stubbornly refuses to buzz, I pocket it and head out into the upstairs hallway. It's quiet, so I use the bathroom and then head down to the kitchen. I find Nicole in there, alone, putting jam on toast with a massive kitchen knife that's probably meant for chopping vegetables or cleaving meat off the bone. She's wearing boxer shorts and a long-sleeved shirt that says *It's not resting bitch face. I DO dislike you.*

I mime stepping backward, and she snorts. "Cute." She waves the knife at me. "How'd those laxatives work for you?"

"Excuse me?"

"Lainey claims she left the house last night to buy you laxatives," she says slowly. "I'm being polite and asking how they worked out."

Surprised laughter almost escapes me. Damn, Elaine didn't like lying to her friend for me, so she made me pay for it—and then didn't mention a single word about it after delivering the trash bags.

"They worked out great," I tell her with a grin, "never shit better in my life. Speaking of Elaine—"

"She's not here," Nicole says pointedly.

"And you're not inclined to tell me where she is."

"So you're smarter than you look," she says with a smirk. "Good for you."

I lift my eyebrows, think about swiping her toast, and think again. I like my fingers too much. "What's on the docket for today if Anthony can't meet up?"

"Feel free to waste your time however you'd like. You could take up knitting. There are *several* instructional videos on

YouTube. You could make a tube sock. A scarf. The possibilities are endless."

"I'd rather die." I pause, thinking about Lainey, off on some unspecified task. Is she doing something for the Love Fixers?

That thought skydives into another one. She kissed me when she was on a job for the Love Fixers. What if whatever revenge plot she's working on requires her to do that again? Even now, she could be making out with some douchebag.

I clear my throat. "Maybe I could help Elaine?"

She sets the sharp knife into the sink. "Yes, I've been wondering about that. What, exactly, would you like to help her with?"

Her tone suggests she's noticed there's something between us. I'm tempted to ask her if this place is covered in cameras, but if I did, I'd be giving something away.

Considering my options, I go for a partial truth. "She could have turned me in, and she didn't. You were right last night—she risked herself for me."

I haven't let myself dwell on that much—or make it into something it's not. She made it very clear what she thinks of me on a personal level, but she's a woman who won't let her opinion get in the way of her drive to help someone in need.

"She *should* have turned you in," Nicole insists. "But you're a handsome devil, so I'm sure you know how to use your wiles." She waves her jam-covered toast at me. My stomach growls. "Help yourself," she says, waving at a loaf of bread on the counter. "You may be a hamster in a wheel, but you can't expect to get fed like one."

"Thanks," I say, grabbing some bread from the bag and popping it into the toaster.

"I have to admit, though," Nicole says, "I'm glad she didn't call the authorities last night. This is more interesting than anything that's happened since Lainey stole that therapist's necklace."

"Still me," I say.

My phone buzzes, and I take it out. There's a message from Roark—13 *days*—and a longer one from Anthony.

Pulse picking up, I check my "buddy's" message.

> Thank you, Jake. My mother says next Sunday at my place for the tea. But would you be available to talk before that?

It's probably too much to hope that he'll confess to a near-stranger that he conspired with Nina to steal his mother's prize jewelry, but who knows? Stranger things have happened, and if I've learned one thing about Anthony from the past few weeks, it's that he's desperate for someone to talk to.

I type out a quick reply.

> Of course, man. My afternoons are wide open. What works for you?

> Would Friday be okay? Nina's going to a Halloween party with her friends.

But he's not going with her. Is this a further sign of trouble, or is he too WASPy to put on a mask?

Possibly both.

I confirm that I'm good for a Halloween meetup and show the phone to Nicole.

She nods. I feel the enormity of having to hang out in this house until at least Friday. Probably Saturday. It should make my skin crawl. But instead I'm almost...excited.

Elaine will be here. *I* will be here. For days.

Will she agree to make good use of it?

Nicole laughs. "Are you going to dress up?"

"Yes," I say. "As Jake Jeffries."

Again, I'm surprised by how refreshing it feels to talk openly about this sort of thing. To be straightforward about who I am and who I've been.

Nicole makes an amused sound, then says, "Friday's several days away."

I pointedly grab a butter knife from the drawer and add jam to my toast. "Elaine works for the old woman. Maybe she can figure out a way to get Anthony and Nina out of their house. If I know they've cleared out, I can get in and take a look around. See if I can find anything."

"*They* wouldn't leave something like that lying around," she says.

"Mine was a fake," I say, immediately feeling like a petulant child. "And it wasn't exactly lying around."

Or at least it wasn't lying around the second time.

She stares at me for a few seconds before saying, "Lainey's friend thinks she saw Mrs. Rosings's daughter at the house. She's another possible suspect."

"So we'll look into her too."

"Correction: Damien and I will look into her. She lives in Charlotte, and you, my thieving friend, are not taking any field trips."

Frustration ripples through me. I want to be able to do what I want, when I want. But I also don't want to trigger the doomsday clock. I don't want to convince her to turn me in.

"Tormenting our guest?" Damien says, coming down the stairs. When he reaches the kitchen, he wraps his arm around Nicole, who smiles up at him.

"Doing what I do best."

He shifts his gaze to me as I bite into my toast. "So you didn't try to run. I'd wondered if we were going to get woken up by sirens."

"Your wife made a compelling case for sticking around." Or at least I assume they're married. They have matching tattoos on their ring fingers, and Elaine doesn't seem to have much use for cheaters.

He nods. "She's good at that. You decide to make things easy for us yet and let us know who has your brother?"

I consider it, but only for a second. I trust Elaine to do what she thinks is right. I don't trust them at all. Not yet. I'll stay here for a few days, get the lay of the land, and maybe then, if they prove themselves...

Only...

Even if I make the leap and decide to trust them, I don't believe they can bring Roark down. He's been stealing high-end jewelry and tchotchkes since long before he found us—his golden geese—to be his helpers. He's made plenty of enemies along the way, people who'd like to make him pay in blood for what he's taken, and no one's been able to stick the landing. Sure, he's getting older, maybe losing his edge, but he's still sharp enough to cut, and his paid help is well-compensated and very dangerous.

Why would they succeed where everyone else has failed?

"It's not my habit to make things easy for anyone," I finally say.

Damien shakes his head with a small smile on his face, as if he didn't expect any different.

"You don't seem surprised," I comment.

"Takes one to know one. You think Nicole and I are the kind of people who give up easily?"

"The only two things I know about you are that you're P.I.s and you like imprisoning people in your house."

He studies me for a moment. "Lainey said you don't like being locked in."

"Who would?" I ask, feeling a squirming sensation in my gut that I try to shut down with another bite of toast. It doesn't work.

He grunts, studying me, then says, "Like I said, I don't blame you for not trusting us. We don't trust you. But maybe we can see about changing that? Do you plan on spending the next few days idly, or are you a man who likes to keep busy?"

"Busy," I say through another mouthful of toast. The thought of sitting here for days, doing nothing but programming websites makes me twitchy. At home, I spread the work out throughout the day because I need to be moving. Running. Walking. At the gym. And sure, sometimes I break into places just because I have the itch. The zoo in Central Park. An abandoned house. Not to take anything. But to wander around undetected, knowing I'm not supposed to be there. A real therapist would probably have something to say about that.

But I've found my own ways to cope. That sketchpad is one of them.

He nods slowly. "It just so happens that we can make use of a man who knows how to get in and out of places undetected."

Nicole snorts. "But Lainey might not. Sounds like a recipe for disappointment."

I ignore her, my attention on Damien's insinuation.

"You want me to break into places for you? Aren't private investigators bound to the same laws as the rest of us?"

"We prefer to think of the law as a fluid concept," Damien says with a smile. "How about you?"

"I don't really do that kind of thing anymore," I admit.

They both give me incredulous looks.

"Lainey didn't tell you?"

"She told us," Nicole says. "She seemed to believe you."

"You can believe me or not, but it's true. This is a one-off thing, because of my brother." Or so I hope. I know Roark doesn't want to let me go.

I set down the second piece of toast, half-eaten.

"What about using your...talent to help people who need it?" Damien asks. "People who deserve help?"

"Elaine took that necklace from me because she thought I was someone's cheating boyfriend. She got it wrong."

"She's new at this," Nicole says, leaning back against the counter. "I believe in on-the-job training and letting people make their own mistakes. But you can bet your ass I was keeping an eye on both of you."

I consider this a moment, my heart thumping faster because I feel like I'm on the cusp of something. "I might be interested in something like that."

CHAPTER NINETEEN

LAINEY

"Do you think Rosie is really going to move?" Claire asks. "She's been acting jumpy about it. About everything, actually. And she asked me to cut her hours at the bakery this week." It's late afternoon on Sunday, and we're sitting on her back porch, drinking wine on the side-by-side deck chairs as we check out the view of the rolling blue mountains under the bright, nearly cloudless sky. The leaves have started to change, and the air is deliciously crisp. Declan and Rosie are at Jake's old building, checking out Joy's spare bedroom.

I laugh. "Considering she told me about all of the animal sex sounds you've been making all around the house, yes, I do."

Claire cradles her head in her hands, her blonde hair splaying out around them, but she honestly doesn't look too embarrassed. Then again, maybe she's proud. Jake nearly made me lose myself yesterday, and it's the only thing I can think about. Would I want to shout it from the top of one of those mountains if I actually let him make me come? If, for the first time in seven years, I let someone else rock my world?

My gaze travels to the house next door. The thought of his nearness makes my skin prickle.

When I woke up this morning, I was basically plastered all over him on the couch. There's no way he's not going to need an Advil given I was lying on top of him, and he was essentially sleeping sitting up, his arm wrapped around me. In a weird way, it felt more intimate than what he'd done to me the night before, so I figured it would be best to leave and do some thinking. Not that I've gotten very far in said thinking.

Nicole and Damien promised to keep an eye on him so I could do my unspecified chores. But what has he been doing all day? Sketching in his book?

Looking at whatever was tucked into that bag?

I've stayed away all day on purpose. First, by going to the pet store to buy more shit Professor X probably doesn't need. Secondly, by helping Claire out at the bakery, which is only open from eight to twelve on Sundays. Then, I invited myself over for a late lunch.

I feel a little bad about leaving Jake at Nicole and Damien's mercy all day, but I can't go over there right now. Not until I get my head screwed on straight. Telling Claire about everything that happened last night has been part of that attempt.

"Okay, that's fair," Claire finally says, looking back up. She catches me staring at the cabin next door and says, "It's not like you to practice avoidance."

I sigh. "Is this your way of trying to get rid of me?"

"You know I want you to be with me forever and ever. Today's no different. It's just...maybe it wouldn't be so bad if you enjoyed yourself. You know, blew off some steam. You've been so angry since you and Todd broke up."

I nearly drop my wine. "Seriously? I thought you were going to talk sense into me. This man is literally a thief."

She shrugs. "He's still probably better than Todd."

Laughter bursts out of me. "Tell me how you really feel."

She shrugs a second time, her expression guilty. "I should have told you before, but I was deep into my people-pleasing era. And you hear about people getting shut out of their friends' lives for being too honest about their partners, and I couldn't take losing you. Not for anything."

"You couldn't get rid of me if you tried," I say, reaching out to squeeze her shoulders. "And it goes both ways. I should have been more proactive about getting you to quit your shitty job. You were there for as long as I was with Todd."

"But it was different with him," she says, pausing. "He was... He didn't want you to have anything of your own, and he got off on making you feel small. I hated him for that. I still hate him."

"Me too," I say, holding my wine glass out for a cheers, then lifting it to the sky after we clink. "May his big dick wither and fall off. May he get gonorrhea of the ear."

"Amen," Claire says with a smile.

"It was my fault, though," I add bitterly. "I'm like my parents. I let my head get turned by all the things he had. By all the things I'd have if I married him. I let myself care about that."

"So what? Who wouldn't want unnecessary kitchen appliances?"

I shrug. "But I don't need to resort to sleeping with a thief to get over it. For all I know, everything Jake's said to me is a lie."

But I don't really believe that. As with most people, there's more to Jake Not-Jeffries than there appears to be. He's a thief and a practiced liar...but he's also a brother. An artist. The first man to almost make me come in years.

Dangerous.

"I'm definitely not encouraging you to marry this guy," Claire adds. "You could just enjoy yourself. You *should* be enjoying yourself. You were with that jerk for seven years."

"Nicole's rubbed off on you."

"Is that such a bad thing?"

I think of the Claire that was...

Back in New York, she was the personal assistant to a lifestyle guru who enjoyed making life miserable for her. Here, she's in love with a man who worships the ground she walks on, and she runs her own bakery—a dream she's had since she was old enough to have dreams.

Nicole helped her with that. Nicole's helped her more than I ever did.

Here's another truth I wouldn't admit to either of them—I'm jealous of Nicole, because she's Claire's sister by blood, and I never will be. Because she gave Claire her dreams, and all I ever did was stand by her side being miserable with her, both of us caught in cages we'd made ourselves—her, tied to that job. Me, tied to the man I'd tricked into being my fiancé. A man who truly did get off on making me feel miserable and small.

It's a selfish feeling, one I wish were beneath me, because Nicole has been nothing but good to me in her prickly way. She's changing my life for the better too.

"No," I admit to Claire, tapping my glass lightly against hers. "It's not a bad thing at all."

She holds my gaze, her expression earnest. "I'm glad you're here, Lainey. It feels like this is where you're supposed to be, same as me. And maybe this is your opportunity to have some fun. You need that after Todd. It's like...you're the most lively person I've ever met, but you forgot how to enjoy yourself for a while."

I nod slowly, but I can tell she's not done. So I'm not surprised when she continues, "Maybe this is your chance to learn how to be yourself with a guy again. Look. I know this is going to bite me in the ass, but I brought that Tarot deck you bought me out here."

"You did?" I ask, shocked. My own Tarot deck was given to me by someone at the boutique I worked at in Brooklyn—my throw-away job, as Todd had described it, because he'd been of the mind that no wife of his needed to work outside of the home.

I'd decided the unexpected gift was a sign, and for a few weeks, I'd thought I could become a psychic on Coney Island or something. Until I realized it took a lot of training to read Tarot professionally—and also that I lacked the attention span to learn how to do it. Which didn't stop me from messing around with them for a few months. There's something seductive about lies, after all—and the belief that you can read the future with a card is wishful thinking, lying, at its best. Because almost every card can be interpreted in your favor.

Which is why I stopped using them a couple of weeks ago. I've lied to enough people, so I figured it was time to stop lying to myself. I want to be a person who always seeks out the truth even if it's not pretty. I'm already failing. I failed miserably with Cleo, and now I find myself wanting to make excuses for Jake. For all I know, he's a compulsive liar who thinks *Sixteen Candles* is the height of good cinema. But that doesn't mean I should stop trying to find that bedrock of truth.

I clear my throat. "I think I've decided I don't really believe in the Tarot."

Claire takes the cards out from the drawer of the little table sitting between us and removes them from their box, the silvered corners catching the light. "So I'll have to believe enough for both of us."

"Do you know what you're doing?" I ask with a smile as she shuffles the cards.

"Nope, but neither did you the eleventy billion times you took yours out, so I think we'll get along okay."

"This is completely unnecessary."

"I disagree, although I'll probably feel like a real jerk if you get a bad card."

"There are no bad cards," I say before I can stop myself.

"Which is exactly what you said to me when I kept pulling the DEATH card before I moved out here."

"It seemed to work out just fine for you," I say, indicating the house with its view of rolling blue mountains. It's only after I say the words that I realize I'm doing it again—acting like the card she pulled had anything to do with how her life turned out. Like truth is a thing that can be forged rather than something immovable.

"I don't know how to do a spread, so you're going to just pick one, Lainey. Pick the one you feel drawn to."

So I do...and then turn it over on the face of the table between our chairs.

It's the three of swords—a bloody heart pierced by three swords—and my own heart, broken less by Todd than myself, feels a pulse of recognition.

"Yeah, I don't think we like that one," Claire says. "Let's try again."

I could tell her that, like it or not, it's accurate. Scarily accurate, but instead I pick another card and turn it over.

Seven of Wands.

"Well, I'll admit I have no idea what that means," she says. "But it has a lack of bleeding hearts, which I like, and Google was invented for a reason."

"Probably several," I agree as she sets down the rest of the deck and retrieves her phone from her pocket. My heart is still quailing over the other card—the bloody heart with three wounds.

Three. I have two. Is Jake supposed to be the third? If so, I'd do better to stay away from him.

"Ooh," Claire says, lifting a finger. "This one's good. It's about standing your ground and defending the progress you've made." Her eyes dart up to meet mine. "It's for a person who stands against a multitude but perseveres. That's you, Lainey. You persevere."

A chill runs down my spine, because that doesn't sound like me at all. When it comes down to it, I'm a woman who runs. I found out Todd cheated, and I left. My best friend moved, and I didn't even try to stick it out without her. *I left.*

I say as much, and she shakes her head. "Bullshit. You're

stronger than you think. I just want you to love yourself like I love you."

I smile at her. "I'm trying."

"So go home and try harder. I say that with all the love in my heart, of course."

"Of course," I say, smiling wider. "Are you going to give me some Bronuts to go?"

"That depends, are you going to ask the hot thief to eat them off of you?"

Finding her dreams has emboldened her, and I'm grateful for that, even though I feel the ache of wanting to live my purpose too. "To be determined."

She gives me a bag of Bronuts, of course, because she's Claire, and even though she's found herself, she'll still always want to give the people she loves the things they want.

Five minutes later, I walk through the front door of the cabin. *Home.* Nicole glances up from the couch, where she's sitting with a snifter of something and a phone, and Professor X slinks out of the kitchen, chewing on God only knows what.

"So she's back," Nicole says. She nods to the bag I'm still holding. "You get the goods from Claire?"

"Obviously." I glance around, trying not to appear like I'm looking for him. Also, definitely looking for him, but I can already feel that he's not here. The house feels too...settled. Too quiet.

Nicole gives me a knowing glance. "If you give me one, I'll tell you where the thief is."

My heart beating faster, I sit on the couch next to her and present the bag. She takes it without ceremony as Professor X rubs against my feet and legs. "He's off doing P.I. shit with Damien. I think Damien's trying to butter him up for information by making him feel useful. You know, the thing they always tell you to do with children."

"You spend time with children?" I ask, both fascinated and maybe a little horrified.

She snorts. "I'll have you know, I'm going to be the best aunt that ever aunted when Claire and Declan decide to procreate. I'm going to let that little fucker do whatever he or she wants."

"I'm sure that'll bring a lot of comfort to Claire," I say.

She makes a flippant gesture. "You can be the good aunt."

I feel something warm in my chest. Aunt. She's accepting me as Claire's sister. As hers.

But the feeling blackens, like a marshmallow left over fire for too long. Because what could I possibly have to give to a child? Only poisoned lessons taught by poisonous people.

CHAPTER TWENTY

LAINEY

I stay in my room, curled up with Professor X, even though I hear Damien's car come back. I don't check my phone when it beeps. I'm raw without fully understanding why, my mind running through what Claire said over and over again.

I just want you to love yourself like I love you.

I also keep thinking about those Tarot cards and what happened last night—tackling Jake at Mrs. Rosings's house, helping him, letting him touch me.

Pulling away from him.

Why?

Why couldn't I let myself have that one moment of release?

I'd like to think it's because of him. He's so completely inappropriate, the last person I should be kissing or touching, but my patchwork heart knows better.

It's not him, it's *me*.

I don't trust myself.

The sun goes down, and I still haven't moved. Finally, there's a knock on my door.

"Don't come in."

It's Jake, dressed in a black T-shirt and jeans from the bag I packed for him. His fox on fire is fully exposed, flames curling off its face and tail. Professor X, the traitor, leaps down from the bed and does figure eights around his legs.

"I said don't come in," I hiss, glowering, even though something inside of me lifts at the sight of him. I realize that I'm relieved to see him. Part of me had expected him to give Damien the slip.

"I've always been told I'm bad at listening to directions," he says with a smile. "You're the type of jailer who'd let your prisoner starve, aren't you? I thought it was customary to offer a captive stale bread and water."

I sit up, watching him. My stupid heart speeds up. "I was reasonably sure they'd let you eat. Nicole told me you were helping Damien with something."

He gives me a half smile. "I doubt you'd approve. We broke into a guy's house to find proof that he's been hiding resources from his ex-wife. I know how you feel about breaking and entering."

I shrug. "I've realized I was being hypocritical yesterday. Maybe it's myself I hate more than you."

He raises his eyebrows, scrutinizing me, and I have the feeling he sees it all—the self-doubt and hatred. The hot, pulsing need I've tried to rein into submission.

I swallow. "Did you find anything?"

A wicked smile stretches across his face. "We did. Damien'll have to backtrack the information to its source, but it's a start." His eyes blaze into me. "What have you stolen other than my fake necklace?"

"Lots of things."

"I'm gonna need more to go on than that."

I glance out the window at the front yard, taking in the little squat car parked there. "My not-a-sports car."

This is something I haven't told anyone else. Not Claire, not Nicole, not anyone. It's absurd to tell him, but again, I feel a certain freedom with Jake. He won't be staying, and he's in no position to judge me. Maybe I needed to confess the truth to someone, and he's the best choice.

Jake grimaces. "You stole *that* car? There's a world of cars out there, and that's the one you looked at and said, 'Screw law and order. This has to be mine?'"

I throw my pillow at him, feeling laughter bubble up. "It's not like I took it from a used car lot, you ass. It was my parents' car."

Emotion flashes across his face, not lingering long enough for me to name it, and then he whistles. "What did they pull to get a girl like you to do a thing like that?"

I stand up for the first time in hours, putting a hand on my hip. "What do you mean a girl like me?"

He shrugs, walking over to my desk and picking up the small glass bird Claire gave me for my birthday last year—maybe her too-subtle way of telling me I was in a cage and should get out while I could. I take it from his hand, feeling the immediate sizzle of touching him, and throw it back down, nearly breaking its wings.

His mouth twitches as he gives me a sidelong look. "I wasn't saying it to offend you. You don't strike me as the kind of person who'd steal something from someone unless they deserve it."

"You think some people deserve to be robbed?" I ask, feeling a roiling of self-righteous fury, although it's more directed at myself than him. After all, I do too. I'm the child who wanted to be Robin Hood, the self-righteous woman who stole his necklace without really understanding what she was doing.

He's less than a foot away, close enough that I feel the heat roiling off of him. I wonder whether he felt a rush of adrenaline when he broke into that man's house tonight, of vindication when he found the information they needed. Both of those things are fuel to me, and it's so hard to come by them honestly.

"I really do." Then he lifts his hands to face me, palms out. "Which is not me saying that I haven't taken things from people who didn't deserve it, but that's me, and we're talking about you." He watches me. "So what did they do?"

I shrug. "They wanted me to get married."

"To the cheater? See, I told you, assholes."

I smile and shake my head. There's no reason to say anything else, but I find myself continuing, "He was rich and *important.* That's what they cared about. When he broke off the engagement, they accused me of not trying hard enough. Of ruining everything for all of us. That was supposed to be my job, you know. Marrying a wealthy, connected man. They'd been pushing me toward it for years." A laugh gushes from me. "You know...he got engaged almost immediately to the other woman, and when I went over to my parents' apartment to ask if I could borrow the car to come here, my mom threw Todd's engagement announcement at me. I'm guessing she thought it would be this powerful gesture, but it kind of just fluttered through the air and fell halfway between us. It was funny."

He doesn't say anything, his expression as readable as a brick wall. "So you took the car without asking."

I shrug. "Seemed only right."

"I'm glad you took their car, but you might have picked the wrong lesson to teach them. You should have taken whatever they value most."

I huff a little laugh. "Then I would have had to take *them*, and no thank you. Still, you're right about the car. They probably don't care. They haven't bothered to report it stolen. They didn't even call me to bitch about it. I'm guessing they're waiting for me to *apologize.*"

It probably goes without saying they'll be waiting forever.

"Maybe they don't want to get you in trouble," he says, but his expression is slightly sympathetic now. Fantastic. The thief I've captured feels *sorry* for me.

I shake my head slightly, looking down at the car again before I meet his gaze. "I doubt they care. Maybe they're happy I'm gone. I didn't do my part. I was supposed to marry a rich man. A man with connections."

His eyes beating into me, he says, "It wasn't your only chance. Maybe Nina will run off with the necklace, and you can have a go at Anthony."

"Is that your way of asking me if that's my angle?" I ask, horrified.

"Nothing personal." He straightens a framed photo on the wall, as if he's incapable of keeping still, and I barely repress the urge to slap his hand away and to hiss for him to leave my things—and me—alone. "I need to know."

"It's not my angle," I snap, pissed off even though it makes sense for him to question me. "I'm trying to save Nina from the worst mistake she's ever made. It's a mistake I'll never make again."

His gaze finding mine again, he inclines his head slightly, barely a nod. "Did you take anything from *him*?"

"His name's Todd."

He snorts. "Of course it is. And what did you take from dear Todd?"

Rolling my eyes, I nod toward the very expensive Yankees bat propped in the corner of my room.

Jake walks over, obviously grateful for the excuse to touch another one of my things. Picking it up, he turns it to study it from different angles. Whistles in appreciation. "They all signed it."

"Yankees fan?"

He watches me for a second before setting the bat down, then says, "I've been trained to recognize valuable things. Rare things. You're a rare thing, hellcat."

I feel raw and exposed, like a bug that's been hiding under a rock turned over by a child.

"You said he didn't hit you," he presses. "But I can tell he hurt you. What did he do?"

He sounds like he actually gives a shit about the answer, although he has no reason to. Maybe that's why I respond. Or perhaps it's because he's not going to judge me, the way Claire might, the way even Nicole could. "It wasn't all his fault."

"Oh?"

"You stole Anthony's wallet so you could get to know him."

He shakes his head slightly, walking over a couple of steps so he can run his fingers over the carved knob at the right foot of my bed. "So we're shifting the subject back to me again. I'm flattered."

"No," I say, capturing his hand on top of the knob. "Do you always have to touch something?"

His eyes are amused as they meet mine, his hand stilling beneath my touch. It's his right hand, I register. The hand that nearly made me come last night. The fingers I watched him lick as if he'd just had a gourmet meal. There's a needy ache between my legs that I resent. "Yes. Would you prefer for me to touch *you?*"

I pull away as if he'd burned me. Clearing my throat, I say "My point was that I did something similar with Todd..."

"You stole his wallet?"

"No...but I pretended to trip in front of him, and I let him help me up. He liked being seen as the good guy. The hero."

He doesn't comment, probably because he knows as well as I do that the best way to get someone to talk is to wait on them.

"So it was a lie from the beginning. I knew who he was. I studied the way his friends and their girlfriends dressed and talked. Their interests. I took *notes*. I paid attention to what he liked and disliked. And then I changed what I wore. Which classes I took. Which activities I pursued outside of class. I became exactly what he wanted." I pause, swallowing. Not quite sure why I'm telling him all of this, but needing to, anyway.

He runs his fingers over my arm without saying anything, his eyes on mine. Waiting. Somehow he knows I need to say the words, and he's silently telling me he's here to listen.

"But after we got engaged...I...I thought I loved him, and I wanted him to know the real me. But every time I tried to express myself—me, not the person I'd created for him—he'd try to snuff it out. He'd say I was being impulsive, or foolish, or classless." I shrug. "If I bought something he didn't like, he'd throw it away. If I got a drink with my friend Claire, he'd retaliate by getting one with a childhood girlfriend. If he got mad, he'd make me get down on my knees and beg for forgiveness. He didn't like it when I did anything by myself. We had this huge apartment, but it felt like a cage. It was suffocating."

"And he never made you come," he says, his voice rough, and I almost laugh, because of course that's where his mind went.

"No, but that was partly my fault. I had trouble letting go with him. I overthought everything I did." I pause. "I was really good at faking it."

"He should have known. A real man would have known." His gaze is penetrating, and I look out the window again, down at that car sitting there in the dark like an accusation.

"Maybe he did know. Maybe he didn't care." A sigh gusts out of me. "It was my own fault, though. I tricked him... So if I was unhappy, I have no one to blame but myself. And maybe my parents, for convincing me that the only way I could be someone was by marrying a rich man. They didn't care how he treated me."

He doesn't say anything for a long moment, his regard is a living thing, breathing down my neck, caressing my spine, whispering in my ear, and then finally he says, "Sounds to me like *Todd* got everything he wanted, and you got none of what you wanted. Are you sure you're the one who tricked him?"

Emotion suddenly gushes through me. Raw and consuming. Maybe this is what I've been dancing around for months. For *years*. I wanted to think I had the power all along—that I was fooling him and letting him do those things to me for my own purposes. Because I was getting what I'd aimed to get. But all along, he'd been taking, and I'd kept giving him exactly what he wanted, when he wanted it, and how he wanted it. Adding a little cherry on top for good luck. I'd folded all of the stuff that was important to me inward, hiding it from him—and from myself too. And I'd let it go on for years. The only thing that had saved me was that I'd found out he was cheating.

He'd used me and then spat me out, and my parents had set me up for it. They'd set me up, period. My mother's constant whispering in my ear.

Lainey, he just needs a little push and he'll propose.

Lainey, it'll all be worth it.

Lainey, you were born with that wildness inside of you, but you'd better swallow it up if you want to keep him.

Tears prick at my eyes, but I'm angry too. My whole body is on fire with it. Todd's lucky he's in New York. So are my parents. They're *lucky.*

"I...think I'd like to be alone now," I tell Jake numbly, only then realizing he still hasn't moved his hand off my arm. His fingers are curled around it, his head bowed down toward mine. A different feeling surges beneath the anger, but I tackle it and muzzle it.

He doesn't argue.

He doesn't try to talk me around.

He just nods and says, again, "You know where to find me."

CHAPTER TWENTY-ONE

JAKE

I watch, fascinated, as Elaine steps out of her room with the baseball bat white-knuckled in her hands. I'm standing behind my own door, cracked open to give me a view of the hallway, because I could tell she wasn't just going to lie down for a good cry. Maybe the cat knows it too. She slunk out of the other bedroom after me and is hunkered at my feet.

Elaine had the truth written all over her face, her light brown eyes full of the kind of rage that can lead a person to do something impulsive and potentially dangerous.

None of my business, and yet...

I've never been this drawn to a woman.

I'm fascinated by her. I'm smitten. I'm her prisoner in more ways than one, and I hope hell exists, even if I'm doomed to spend eternity there, just so her parents and that piece of shit Todd can be forced to suffer too.

Stupid. It's stupid of me to let these people become human for me, but it's too late. Elaine has had a hold on me since the night she showed up at my apartment door, and Damien and Nicole are already growing on me.

I know Damien had a purpose for taking me out with him this

afternoon. Sure, unpaid labor is the best kind you can get, but he was also sussing me out—and giving me a chance to suss him out. I appreciate that. It also felt good to do something that got the adrenaline pumping but didn't make me feel guilty.

Elaine slips past my door, her footfalls nearly silent, and I wonder if she learned to walk that way while she lived with him—to make less of an imprint, the way Ryan and I did when we lived in foster care. Rage fills my cup too.

I wait, listening to the slight creak of the stairs, listening to the beep of the alarm system being disengaged. Knowing that I could get away.

I could leave.

I could break into Anthony and Nina's house and question them. If I threatened them with my knife, I know Anthony would fold and tell me everything. If one of them has it, I'd be able to grab it and go. I could get in Jake Jeffries's car and drive until I'm far enough to ditch it and go to the airport. But the thought leaves a sour taste in my mouth.

I'd hate myself again if I did that.

All of the progress I've made over the last year would take its last gasping breath, and I'd be the Jake of before, who ended each night lonely, no matter who was around.

I tell myself that's the entire reason why I don't leave, not because Elaine both stuck her neck out for me and confided in me, and abandoning her would be a shitty repayment.

And when I follow her downstairs in the dark, Professor X padding behind me, I tell myself I'm only checking on her because if she does something stupid, I could be drawn into the aftermath, not because I want to make sure she's okay.

When I approach the front door, I see her through the window beside it, advancing on that shitty little car with the Yankees bat poised to strike.

"Fuck," I say conversationally to the cat at my feet.

She meows her agreement.

I don't wait to see what Elaine does next, because her intent is pretty obvious. Instead, I open the door.

She turns to look at me, her eyes gleaming like the cat's in the dark.

"You're going to stop me, aren't you?" she asks, her voice a jagged thing.

It makes me want to put my arms around her, to offer her the kind of comfort no one's ever offered me. But here's the thing—neither of us were raised on hugs and soft words; after our talk today, I understand that she's like me. Forged from harder things.

She needs this. She needs to prove to herself that she's not broken but is instead someone who's capable of breaking things.

"No...but do you need the car? Maybe you'd be better off beating the bat against a rock or—"

She swears, and taps the bat against the pavement at her feet. I see some of the fight going out of her, and I'd do anything to keep it from happening, to keep her mad instead of desolate.

"Just beat up the back of it," I say quickly. "It should still drive fine, and if it doesn't, you can have my Jake Jeffries car." I run a hand back through my hair. "If I don't have to burn the identity, no one's going to come looking for it. It's clean."

She watches me through the dark for a moment, the cat sitting its butt down on my bare foot. "You'd do that for me after... everything?"

"Sure. I can't take it with me."

Maybe my words downplay the gesture, but they're meant to. Because I'd like to believe that I don't have anything personal riding on the outcome of this moment.

Her eyes shutter, but she nods. "Thank you."

Then she hefts the bat up in a position that would do Babe Ruth proud, and she brings it down hard on the backend of the car.

A dog starts barking in the house next door as Elaine brings the bat down again, putting a dent in the back passenger side door this time, then again, and again.

I don't know for sure, but I think I see tears tracking down her cheeks. It feels wrong to stand here and watch her instead of helping, so I glance inside the front door and find a broken pink umbrella in a stand by the door. I grab it and then heft Professor X into the house, shutting her in and earning a paw swipe and some scratch marks on my arm.

I stride up next to Elaine as she swings again, splinters flying off the bat, already half-ruined. I wail on the dented car with the broken umbrella, making her laugh as she swings again, this time cracking the rear passenger window, the glass spiderwebbing.

The door to the cabin bursts open. Damien's in the doorway, Nicole peering over his shoulder. The cat's standing with them, her eyes glowing in the dark.

"Oh, it's okay," Nicole says. "Lainey's finally processing her shit. Proceed with the destruction."

"She right about that?" Damien asks, glancing between both of us. "Everything okay?"

Elaine nods heavily. "It's going to be."

Damien nods to me once—an *I'm trusting you with this* nod—and then shuts the door. I feel like someone just cut me down at the knees.

It's not that people don't trust me: they do. Many of them. But no one's ever known what he knows, what Elaine knows, and still decided to trust me. No one other than Ryan.

I'm unworthy, and I know it.

Elaine glances at me, her eyes shining. Definitely tears.

"Are we going to disturb your friend?" I ask, nodding to the house next door. They said her friend's boyfriend is a big guy, and I'd rather not piss him off.

She shakes her head slightly. "They just had their windows replaced. The ones in this house are still old."

Then she hefts her bat again, her expression fierce, and says, "Ready?"

And the only possible answer is to smile at her and nod, because I can see all the way down to her steel backbone, and in this moment, I'm a little bit in love with her. This near-stranger. This fellow thief. This woman who's so much stronger than most people would give her credit for.

But she still needs this. So I raise that stupid umbrella, and I hit the hatchback, hurting my fingers and loving it. Loving the strength Elaine is putting into each of her blows, the wood splintering, the metal groaning. Both the bat and the car giving in to the sheer force of her will.

Finally, she drops the broken bat, and I follow suit, letting the shitty umbrella, now a twisted, broken mess, fall to the pavement.

"I think the car actually looks better now," I say, but I barely get the words out before she grabs me roughly by the front of my shirt, pulling me to her. Her bare lips lifted to me.

Maybe this is another part of her revenge. To destroy her parents' car with her ex's precious bat and then give herself to a thief on top of the ruin. Maybe I should have a problem with that, a feeling of being used, but I don't. All I care about is that she's mine tonight.

My hands are raw, but I wrap them into her hair, tugging her even closer as her hot mouth presses into me, her tongue finding mine while her hand slides under my shirt. It must be sweaty, but the hand continues gliding up, undaunted. Her touch is as demanding as her mouth. I sigh into her, feeling a moment of pure contentment with the broken things around me, so much better than the ones inside of me.

My mouth still on hers, I lift her by the hips and whirl her around, her bare feet flying in a circle, and she laughs into my mouth before stopping the twirl by cinching her legs around my waist and nipping my bottom lip. My arms circle around to hold her in place, cupping the curves of her butt as she tips her head to try my lips from a new angle.

When she feels my hardness, she lets out a gusty sound and pushes herself into it, immediately making my problem more pressing. And then she reaches down to caress me through the pants, her hand cupping me, rubbing. Raw, uncontrolled need floods me. I want to take her out here, against this ruined car, the destroyed bat under our feet. I want to slide into her—to feel her clench around me and beneath me, her body working with mine to bring her what she needs. But I remember what she confirmed for me. That asshole never made her come.

I don't have much to offer her, but I can right that wrong. I can do that for her. I *will*.

I can give this beautiful, smart, funny-as-hell woman something to remember.

Pulling my mouth back from her, I say, "You got the key to this thing?"

"You want to bring it for a test drive right *now*?" she asks, her tone disbelieving. "I honestly don't care if it works. I'd much rather continue what we're doing."

"I had something else in mind," I say, setting her down on her feet. Relief filters through me when she pulls the key out of her pocket. The back is dented to hell, like a high school kid in a minivan backed into her ten times before managing to turn, but it opens. And I back her into it until she's sitting.

"What happens next?" she asks, smiling up at me, and I can see the adrenaline rush in her eyes as she parts her legs.

Oh, hell yes. She's wearing a dress—grey, like she couldn't find it in her to wear red today—so I have the access I need.

I get onto my knees, splinters on the pavement digging into them, and spread her legs wider, running my fingers over her panties. Even through the fabric I can feel that she's wet.

"I'm greedy," I say, leaning down to kiss her thigh, then run my tongue over the territory my fingers just traced. She digs a hand into my hair, pulling. "I love your taste," I say, "and what I got yesterday wasn't nearly enough."

Her eyes are dark in the night. "They could look out of the window and see us. From either house."

"You said the windows were soundproofed next door, and I have a feeling Nicole and Damien are actually giving us some privacy. Besides..." I grin up at her. "Isn't the danger part of the fun?"

My answer is for her to close her legs...and then lift up and pull her panties off before opening to me again, offering herself to me in a way that makes me harder and also unleashes something intoxicating in my chest. Like I just took a bottle of honey bourbon and swigged down the whole damn thing.

I push them open wider, getting a gusty sigh from her, and I meet her gaze again. "Don't pretend, Elaine. I don't need a participation award for eating pussy. I want to earn it. I want to hear you scream my name and know it's because you can't help yourself. I want to know I drive you as crazy as you make me."

She nods, and I touch her first, needing to feel how wet she is for me. A hum of appreciation escapes me as I curl my finger up and in, the sweet slide of it confirming she's as turned on as I am. "You like being bad, don't you? I can feel it."

She lifts her hips toward me. "You can put your lips to better use than taunting me."

I'm not taunting her. I appreciate the wild spark in her that I noticed the first night I met her, when she was spreading chaos in Jake Jeffries's apartment, but I'm not going to waste this opportunity I've been given by being contrary, so I lean in and kiss up her thighs, the skin soft and hot, fragrant with her scent. And then, when I can't take it anymore, I hike her thighs over my shoulders, burying my face in her slick, sweet heat.

"Oh shit," she murmurs as she pushes into me, her hips

bucking as I lick and suck like the desperate man I am. I need to give her what he didn't—I *need* it. Those breathy cries, those desperate movements of her body. I crave them.

I'm barely aware of anything but her taste, her thighs flexing around my neck, and the feeling of her against my mouth and tongue. She spears a hand into my hair again and tugs, holding onto me as if I'm the only thing keeping her anchored to the earth—and also the reason she's floating. And it hits me that the only times I've felt anything approaching good in the last few months have been here in this house, where I'm a semi-prisoner. With this woman who sees right through me like I'm made of glass.

I feel her tightening, her body shaking slightly, and I look up at her, needing to see her lose herself to it. To *me*. But when I meet her gaze, something like fright passes through her eyes, and she starts to pull back.

I instantly do the same. "What's wrong?"

"I can't…" she says through breathless panting. "I can't…"

She *can*; she's so close. This isn't a physical problem, but I'm not about to force an orgasm on her. So I pull away, my dick a hard, persistent ache. She arranges her skirt and sits up straight, but there's no way she's going to be able to make herself look chaste right now. Her hair is mussed, her lips swollen from me, and she's so fucking beautiful like this that I almost take out my burner phone to snap a photo. Instead, I sit beside her on the back of the ruined hatchback. There's barely room for both of us, our thighs pressed together, the top of the hatchback digging into me. It's uncomfortable, but I want to be close to her enough that I'd bear worse.

She gives me a sidelong look, her expression sad. "I'm sorry."

"Jesus, Lainey," I say with a groan, "don't tell me you're sorry. *You* have nothing to be sorry for."

She nudges me with her shoulder. "You called me Lainey."

"I'm guessing we're friends now. We just ruined your car together, and I know how you taste."

Another nudge. "You're a pig."

"How am I a pig?" I ask, turning my head to face her. "You're gorgeous and smart, and you taste delicious, and you should own that. You should wear it on a fucking badge."

Something flashes across her face, her lips turning up slightly, but then they drop. "Maybe I'm broken." She gestures to the ruined bat and umbrella, the wreckage of the car. "This isn't normal."

Rage rips through me—not at her but at the lowly piece of shit who made her feel this way.

"It's not abnormal. Haven't you heard of rage rooms? You just made your own." I pause, studying her face in the dark. The firm set of her lips, the slight line between her brows. "And I don't like hearing you say you're broken. That douchebag didn't break you. He may have wanted that power, but he doesn't get to fucking have it. No one has that power unless you give it to them."

I think of other locked rooms. Of the contents of that bag from under the floorboards.

A sniff escapes her. "It looks like I have. I don't know how to take it back."

I lift a hand to her chin. I trace her lips. I press a light kiss to them. They're soft and pink, and it's as if they have a gravitational pull all their own. "Practice makes perfect."

She smiles again before shaking her head slightly. "We shouldn't do this. I barely know anything about you."

It hits me that our scales are off, the balance gone. She told me something big tonight, something true, and I've given her nothing. Usually I'm a bargain seeker, the way Elaine told me she is, but I feel compelled to give her something. More disturbingly, I want to.

"You gave me something by telling me about him. About your parents. You want a truth for a truth."

"*Yes.*"

I pause, thinking, then say, "My brother's in trouble because of me. You remember that pocket watch I told you about?"

She nods, her eyes glistening in the dark.

"Ryan's the one who took it. He thought he was helping me because I couldn't bring myself to finish the job, but I was really upset. I...we haven't talked for months after he took it. So he tried to steal it back, and he got caught. That's why he's in trouble."

"How's that your fault?" she asks, cocking her head.

"He's a hothead. If I'd been paying attention to what he was up to, it never would have happened. But I was pissed, so I shut him out."

"It's not your fault," she tells me, giving me those words I love hearing. "I'd like to know why you didn't want to take the watch."

I shrug, staring off into the night. It's dark out here, secluded, with the closest street light far enough away that it's no more than a wink in the night, almost like a distant star. It's surprisingly nice. Usually, I want to lose myself in the chaos of a city—the noise, the bodies, the people. But it feels good to be sitting out here, in the back of this car, with this woman. It feels soothing, like slipping naked into a cool lake, knowing you could get caught but doing it anyway.

I can feel her waiting, and I'm not sure why, but I decide I'd like to tell her. She's given me a deeper knowledge of her, and I want her to have the same for me. "The guy who trained us...he always told us to demonize the people we steal from, to think the worst of them. Because if you let yourself see them as people, it would feel wrong." I give her a half smile. "Because it *is* wrong. Anyway. This guy...he was an older man, and he was all alone in the world. He'd lost his son. So it was easy for me to befriend him, but the more time we spent together, the more I realized he was a good person. Lonely. And he told me about the watch. It wasn't some expensive toy, Elaine. It had been passed down in his family, from his great-grandfather, to his grandfather, to his father, to him. He'd wanted to pass it on to his son. It was registered with the Sons of the American Revolution." I take a deep breath before letting it gust out, the truth stabbing into me. It's a persistent pain I've carried around, the way hard lessons always are.

She surprises me by taking my hand, our thighs still pressed together, and in a strange way, it's more intimate than what I was doing to her five minutes ago, when I was crouched on the ground with her thighs around my shoulders.

"He wanted to *give* it to me."

She squeezes my hand. "And you said no."

"I said I didn't feel worthy of it. He told me to think it over, and I called the guy we were working with and said I was done. I'd been working on a freelance business. Designing websites. I had some money in the bank, and I figured I could try doing that full time." I shake my head. "But he didn't want to let me walk away. If Ryan hadn't taken the watch, he would have found another reason to pull me back in."

"How'd you get mixed up with him in the first place?"

My mouth hitches up. "Ryan. I told you he was an idiot. We were teenagers, living with our foster parents. We didn't have a pot to piss in, but at least the state kept us together. He started stealing so we could save up some money, maybe get ourselves emancipated, and he took something from the wrong person."

"The man who has him now," she says, catching on quickly, not that I'm surprised. Give her two and two, and she'll get four every time.

I nod. "He told Ryan he had to pay the price for stealing from him."

"I'm guessing it wasn't a hand in the beginning?"

I smile and shake my head. "No, we both had to learn from him, that was the price. So that's what we did."

She calls him names under her breath.

"Sure. He was a lowlife," I agree. "But it was also the only real attention we'd ever gotten from an adult. It felt pretty good at the time. The money did too."

Her expression hardens, and for a moment I think I've lost her. "He took advantage of you," she finally says. "My parents were like that too. I was a tool for them. A way they could get what they wanted for the price of their approval. That's not a real family."

I nod in agreement. I'd learned that lesson too. I'd learned it when I'd told Roark that I'd had a change of heart and I couldn't do it anymore. He'd looked me in the eye and told me to do what he'd sent me to do or someone else would.

And then he'd arranged for my own brother to do it to really twist the knife.

"Why won't you let Damien and Nicole help you?"

I shrug, feeling the weight of the situation. Even if I find the necklace, even if Lainey and her friends allow me to bring it to Roark instead of returning it to the old woman, is he really going to leave us alone? Ryan and I have been working together as a pair, earning him money since we were teenagers. Why would he give that up?

"Maybe," I demur, turning her palm over in my lap to trace my fingers over it. Which is when I notice it's bleeding. Concern rips through me, stronger than it should be over a couple of scrapes. "Shit, you've got splinters from the bat. We're going to have to treat that. My brother got a wicked infection from a bunch of splinters in his hand."

"How'd he get them, from scaling someone's fence?"

A laugh escapes me. "Please. We're more professional than that. It was from punching a tree."

"I'm guessing the tree won?"

"Hot tip, Elaine," I say, getting up and pulling her with me. "The tree always wins." I glance at the splintered bat on the ground. "Unless it's turned into a bat and beaten into splinters by a hellcat."

Her laughter fills me up, and the moment feels as near to perfect as I'm likely to get it.

Except that I didn't get her to come. Yet.

I'm going to, before I have to leave her.

I want that almost as bad as I want the necklace.

No, the truth is that I want it more, because this is something I want for myself.

CHAPTER TWENTY-TWO

LAINEY

"Do you need a distraction?" Jake asks after he pulls out the first one. From the look of his hooded eyes, he probably means a sexy distraction—and yes, I *really* want one.

"We can't do *that* again," I say, even though I want to. Out there, for a brief moment, I felt so deliciously powerful and strong. I felt the pleasure waiting for me, ready to wrap me up in its grasp, but I couldn't give myself over to it—to him—even though I wanted to. Now, I feel lost. Confused. Burned, even though I'm the one who was wielding the flame.

Jake's being good to me—so freaking good to me—and that's even more confusing. Now, I'm sitting on top of the closed toilet in the downstairs bathroom while he kneels in front of me and removes the splinters from my hand with a set of tweezers, the overhead lights beaming down on us.

"You don't have any more cars for us to beat into submission?" He plucks out another splinter while I'm distracted, then adds, "It's like I told you before. I'm not going to touch you unless you ask me for it."

I almost object that I didn't ask for it this time, or last. *But I did.*

He's putting the ball in my court, giving me the power. He knows I need it, and he cares about what I need.

"Thank you," I say quietly.

He doesn't respond other than to incline his head. Then he pulls out the rest of the splinters as he launches into a story about his brother bleaching his hair while he was asleep. Afterward, he cleans my hand with hydrogen peroxide and bandages the worst scrapes.

It should be time to say goodnight. It's late, and I know I have to report to Smith House in the morning, but I'm not ready. I still feel as raw and splintered as my hand did.

Jake must be able to tell, because he lifts my hand and kisses the back—a gesture that sends yet another wave of emotion slamming into me. "What do you say we do the responsible thing and stay up way too late watching TV?"

"I could be persuaded," I say, grappling with the feeling of my heart being lodged somewhere in my throat.

"But no *Matchmaking Small Town America*."

"You don't like watching men make idiots of themselves?"

His mouth lifts up at the corner. "You'd probably just tell me to look in the mirror."

"No," I say, swallowing. "Not you." And anyway, I need comfort right now. It hits me, and I ask, "Do you like *X-Men: The Animated Series*?"

"You mean the show my brother and I have watched from start to finish about a dozen times?"

So that's exactly what we do, snuggled up on the couch together like we've known each other for months. Because in a way it feels like we have. We talk over most of it, but after a while I start nodding off against his shoulder.

I wake with a start, my head nestled into his neck, breathing him in, and I feel a new wave of emotion—something softer and more disarming—so I sit up abruptly. He smooths a hand over my hand, his touch gentle, and I remember him wielding that umbrella next to me, living in my moment of chaos with me. I'm never going to forget that, not if I live to be a hundred and five.

"It's time for bed," I say, my voice a little hoarse.

I half expect him to make a quip, but instead he softly kisses the top of my head and walks me upstairs, lingering at my door like he thinks I might climb out of my window.

"Goodnight, Lainey," he finally says. But he's back five minutes later, cracking my door open, and a gasp escapes me when he brings Professor X inside and sets her down on my bed. It's like he knew I still needed someone but wasn't ready to invite him into my bed.

It was another thoughtful gesture, but I didn't sleep for hours. I kept going over what had happened again and again. Asking myself why I hadn't let myself have what I'd wanted out there, amidst the ruin I'd created.

The answer came to me in the early hours of the morning.

Releasing my rage was part of healing...but I'm not all the way there yet. I'm not ready to make myself fully vulnerable. Especially since Jake's no longer a stranger whose opinion I don't care about, but a man I'm starting to have feelings for.

"AREN'T you going to ask what happened to my car?" I ask Mrs. Rosings after I get out of my car on Monday morning. She's out on the porch of Smith House sipping tea. Sometimes I park outside to avoid having to be buzzed in, but I was too tired for much of a walk this morning.

"I assumed it always looked like that," she says, but the slightest of smiles peeks out at me. She's messing with me and enjoying it.

Maybe that would amuse me more if I hadn't gotten five hours of sleep the night before. Claire wakes up unreasonably early to go to the bakery, and this morning she came outside with her coffee to find my car caved in in places. Jake and I had cleaned up the bat, which I'd saved, and the umbrella, which we'd thrown away.

She beat on our front door with her fist until I came down, my shoulders and back so sore it felt like I'd spent all night moving cinderblocks. I told her about my rage room moment, but I didn't tell her the rest, even though she was the one who'd encouraged me to have fun with Jake. I'm not quite sure why.

Maybe because I was embarrassed that I'd held back, again.

Maybe because it would feel too intimate—almost like a betrayal—to tell anyone what Jake did to and for me.

I lower into the patio chair next to Mrs. Rosings, who gives me a long look. "You haven't been sleeping. Is it Anthony's *therapist* friend who's been keeping you awake?"

It takes my tired brain a beat to catch up. "Uh. Yeah," I say. "We're definitely dating." My mind conjures the moment last night when he lifted me and twirled me around, my feet flying. I felt like everything was as it should be, and everything was *okay*. I felt invincible. I clear my throat. "He really swept me off my feet."

She makes a sound that could either be pleased or displeased— it's anyone's guess with her. Judging from her general contempt for marriage after trying it three times, I'm guessing displeased.

"Anthony has twisted my arm into agreeing to attend a tea at his house with your young man. I suppose you'll be there?"

I nod, surprised that she actually wants me to come. "Yup." I pause for a moment and then ask, "Did Emma ever show up the other night?"

She shakes her head and lifts her tea for a sip before setting it down with a clatter. "No. She said something came up." A tired sigh rips from her. "Something always comes up when she's asked to spend time with Anthony. I regret that my children aren't closer. If I've done one thing wrong in my life, it's that I've failed at keeping them together."

I think of what Rosie told me, about seeing the dark-haired woman who looks like Mrs. Rosings outside of the mansion.

Maybe it was a coincidence.

Maybe Emma took one look at the party and decided she'd prefer to turn right back around. Who could blame her?

Or maybe she's the one who stole the necklace. I make a mental note to ask Nicole what her plan is about Emma. At this point, Nicole and Damien have just done a cursory search—where she lives: Charlotte. What she does: divorce attorney.

Mrs. Rosings studies me for a moment, her gaze sharp, and then says, "You have Band-Aids on your hand, and your car is even more of a wreck than usual. I hope the therapist had nothing to do with that?"

I straighten in my chair. "Why, Mrs. Rosings, if I didn't know any better, I'd think you were concerned for me."

She regards me shrewdly. "I am. There's never any reason to stay with a man who treats you poorly. I learned that the hard way, Elaine, and I don't mind passing along the lesson to any young woman who needs it."

She's talking about Jake, but it's Todd I think of.

Todd, sneering at me.

Todd asking me to get on my knees and beg for his forgiveness. He'd done that multiple times, sometimes for the slightest of grievances. He'd done it because he knew he could. And I still hate myself for having listened. For having wrestled the hellcat inside of me into submission so I could give him what he wanted, because I didn't know who I'd be if I wasn't going to become his wife after all.

Mrs. Rosings's concern wraps around me like an unexpected blanket. My own parents would have built a statue in my ex-fiancé's honor if he'd asked for it. They didn't give a shit about what he did to me, but Mrs. Rosings, who always tries to act so above everything, actually cares about me being treated well. I care about her too, dammit.

Which of her three husbands treated her poorly? Could it be Anthony and Emma's father? I want to ask. I want to kick the offender's gravestone. Mrs. Rosings might be a pill, but she's *my* pill.

"No," I finally manage in response to her intrusive stare. "No, *Jake* never touched me like that. I did that to the car myself, and I hurt my hand." Even as I'm saying it, I realize it's exactly what someone might say if they were lying to defend an abuser, so I add, "The bat was my ex-fiancé's prized possession. The car belonged to my parents."

Mrs. Rosings gives me a strained smile, shaking her head slightly, the breeze whipping a couple of strands of her hair from their usual perfection, making her—temporarily—more human. "Oh, Elaine. You haven't learned yet. When you take something from someone who's mistreated you, you'd do better to keep what you've earned and take the benefit of it for yourself."

She is a woman who knows how to make an entrance and an exit, and she's already lifting from her chair, leaving me baffled. Does she know the necklace is gone? Does she think *I* took it?

CHAPTER TWENTY-THREE

LAINEY

I sigh, feeling the press of all those lonely hearts needing someone to help them feel full again. Admittedly, Cleo wasn't so much a lonely heart as a scammer, but that doesn't mean the others are. They don't deserve to be ignored by yet another person.

Tonight, I promise myself. I'll look tonight.

I want to ask about Jake—if Damien has been making use of him today or if he's doing his own thing.

Websites, he said.

Imagine, being a thief who works on websites in his downtime.

Then it hits me...

Jake told me more about the old man and the watch last night. One detail in particular might be helpful to them. I hesitate for a long moment, tapping my finger against the side of my phone and leaning against the green wainscoting of the second sitting room. He wouldn't want me to tell them, and it feels like a betrayal to do it anyway. At the same time...he's in over his head, he needs help, and I can't just let him hand Mrs. Rosings's necklace over to his former boss. Something deep inside of me revolts against it, as if I'd be benefitting not just that awful man, but every narcissist who was ever brave enough to look at the world and ask, "But what if everything really is about me?"

No. He can't be allowed to have Mrs. Rosings's necklace. At the same time, I can't let anything happen to Jake's brother. To his person.

If Ryan even exists, whispers a cynical voice in my head.

But I believe Jake.

I believe the story he told me, and last night I could see the impact it had made on him.

The man who offered him that watch probably doesn't know it, but he completely transformed his life, his outlook, and his future.

I tighten my grip on the phone. I can't let the man who kidnapped Ryan pull Jake back into a life of crime, and while I will encourage him to share his full story with Nicole and Damien, I have a feeling they'll need time to look into everything and form a strategy.

That is, Damien will form a strategy. Nicole is more the type to break the door down first and ask questions later.

So I send a few more texts telling Nicole about the watch's history and how it's registered with the Sons of the American Revolution.

She sends back a thumbs up.

On it after the coffee kicks in.

I try to look around the house without appearing to, as I move from task to task—the list was waiting for me on the table beside the front door, as usual. At around noon, just before my usual lunch break, Mrs. Rosings asks me to join her in the drawing room, and she follows me in. The display cases with the jewelry have been left out, the fake Heart of the Mountain gleaming at me like an accusation.

To my eye, it looks no different from the necklace that was stolen, but it's also not *my* treasure. Maybe she's spent hours looking at it, wearing it. Maybe she knew the truth the instant she saw the case, and she's spent all morning toying with me.

It doesn't make me feel any better when she leads me directly over to it.

My palms are sweaty as I fold my arms over my chest, trying to look like I'm patiently waiting for directions from my boss, not like I'm waiting to be accused of grand larceny.

"Anthony is the one who cut off the power on Saturday night. The breakers were flipped off, and no one else knows where they are." Her lips thin; her chin lifts. "I expect Nina put him up to it." She gestures to the backlit jewelry case. "I thought *this* might be why, but if she'd intended to take the Heart of the Mountain or any of the other pieces we put on display, she did not." The corners of her eyes crinkle slightly. "Not even the brooch I specifically took out for her use."

My gaze follows hers to the gaudy bluebird broach in one of the other cases. It looks more like it's dead than about to launch into song. "Maybe she forgot it in the fuss," I comment. "We should bring it to her this weekend. Should we put all of these away?"

"Not yet." She doesn't say anything for a few seconds, but I can tell she's working her way toward something, and finally she admits, "I want to know what Nina wanted, and whether she got it."

I could point out that Anthony and Nina both probably wanted to escape the party, like everyone else in attendance, but I suspect she's right. Unless Emma took the necklace and blew town immediately afterward, they're our next best suspects. I've already mentally crossed Mrs. Rosings off my list. She wouldn't be going to all this trouble if she had it hidden in her underwear drawer.

"Why are you asking me?"

"You have a cunning mind," she says, straightening her back, "and I trust you."

I feel like she just plunged a ceremonial knife into my chest. Jeweled, of course. But I know what Nicole would tell me: if someone's handed you a gift, don't toss it back to them. Hell, Mrs. Rosings herself basically told me the same thing this morning.

She's asking me to look into her daughter-in-law, which is exactly what I need to do. She's also capable of getting both Anthony and Nina out of their house.

Still, I find myself saying, "I get the sense that Nina dislikes me."

She sniffs. "That's because you're young and pretty, and your car looks like a tin can that's gone through the garbage disposal. She dislikes anyone she sees as competition. She's eager for the Smith family fortune, and to her mind, every other young woman is out for the same thing."

I'm tempted to defend Nina, but that would be like lobbing that theoretical present at Mrs. Rosings's head, so instead I nod slowly. "I'll see if I can get her talking this weekend. Maybe she'll be more friendly now that I'm seeing someone. But...if you'd like...I could take a look around their house if there's a time you can be sure they won't be home."

Obviously, she could do that herself, but I know Mrs. Rosings would think such a thing beneath her.

She watches me for a solid thirty seconds, and I'm sure I've got sweat dripping down my back by the time she nods her agreement. "I'll inform you once I've made the arrangements. You can leave early today."

It's *very* early, but I'm not about to complain.

I want to go home.

I want to see *him*.

CHAPTER TWENTY-FOUR

JAKE

Elaine needs to be comfortable around me. She needs to know she can trust me.

That's the verdict I've made after spending half the morning pretending to work on websites on Jake Jeffries's laptop in my bedroom while reliving that moment in the back of the hatchback over and over again, her sweet taste still in my mouth.

She needs to realize she can trust me, and then she'll be able to come.

Because now I have another mission, in addition to obtaining the Heart of the Mountain—

That fuckhead, Todd, screwed with Elaine's head and her heart, and I'm going to help her throw off the last of him.

I've already decided I'm going to steal all of his other beloved belongings when I get back to New York. Not to resell them, but to break them, one by one, and ship the ruins to him.

I'm going to screw with *his* head, the way he screwed with hers. I'm going to break him.

Then maybe I'll beat the shit out of him for good measure.

Why I care so much would be quite the question if I were really a therapist. So it's a good thing I'm not.

After reaching this epiphany, I close up the work I wasn't really doing in the room that isn't really mine, and go downstairs to look for Nicole. I find her in the kitchen, drinking a cup of coffee the size of a child's head while she studies her phone with a frown. She has bedhead and a shirt reading *Looking will cost you.*

"What do you want?" she asks without glancing up. "I should warn you that it's much too early for bullshit."

"It's ten-thirty."

"Precisely."

Fair enough. I've never been much of a morning person myself. There's no sign of Damien, but I don't ask where he is. She has no reason to tell me.

"I'd like to do something for Lainey. Is there any work I can do for The Love Fixers?"

Her first reaction is to laugh, which isn't promising.

"Ask, and it shall be delivered," she says next, which doesn't clarify anything.

"Is that a yes or a no?"

"It's a halle-fucking-lujah that I don't have to do it myself. I was just looking at the answers to our Craigslist ad, and it's a whole lot of nope for me. So, yeah, if you want to help her, this is the ticket." She shoves her phone at me, and sure enough, there are at least twenty emails on the screen.

The subject lines are full of exclamation points and the word "fuck."

I whistle, suddenly doubtful. "You think a bunch of wronged women will be willing to deal with a man?"

Nicole snorts as she gives me an up-and-down appraisal. "Oh, you'll do just fine. They'll take one look at you and forget the guy's name. Besides, this will free me up so I can spend more time poking into your background."

"Fantastic," I say, rolling my eyes. I go to take the phone, and she waggles her finger back and forth.

"How am I supposed to do it if you won't let me look at the inbox?"

"Sign in on your phone."

I don't know how easy it would be for her to get a bead on my phone, but I figure it would be better not to risk it. I say so, and she heaves a bored sigh. "Fine. I have a drawer full of burners."

Fifteen minutes later, I'm signed into the Love Fixers account on a burner phone. Sitting in the Love Fixers office. *Lainey's* office. In her sleek leather chair, as if she's some hotshot New York CEO. There's another chair, similar in style but smaller, but I was drawn to this one. I wanted to sit where she sits.

I would have known this was Lainey's space even if Nicole hadn't told me. It smells like her. It feels like her, truthfully. Most people probably wouldn't understand that, but places do have a feeling, when someone cares about them. She clearly cares about this place, although it's only half decorated. The desk looks like an antique. It's L-shaped, with a little roll-top portion on one side and a flat portion on the other, with two guest chairs across from it. The bookcases against the back wall have an assortment of paperback and hardcover books and some framed photos of Lainey and a blonde woman who must be Claire.

In the corner there's a little cat bed shaped like a giant paw, obviously a recent purchase, and it comes as no surprise at all when Professor X, who's been lurking who-knows-where in the house, slinks in and settles onto it like it's a throne.

I get going with the emails, clicking through to the first.

I'd like a dozen of your fuck you very much cookies delivered to my husband on Tuesday at noon. At his office. During his presentation. It'll totally throw him off his game.

Or...is that mean?

I don't know how to feel.

> *Peter said he wanted a baby, and he acted so excited when I told him I was pregnant. He cried. We cried TOGETHER. But then he cheated on me. A lot. My hands are shaking while I write this. I still don't want to believe it, but I know it's true, because I walked in on him with his head between a woman's legs. He tried to pretend he was helping her look for a tick, but I'm not an idiot. And then I found the emails...*
> *Please help.*

My jaw flexes. I think of my own mother, left alone and pregnant at eighteen. Maybe she wouldn't have made the decisions she did if she'd had any support. Probably so, but I'll never know. I type my response.

> *No, Peter deserves 10x worse. In fact, the cookies are on me. Can I recommend an assortment of Fuck You Very Much and Peter, Peter Pussy Eater cookies? If you're ready to take the next step: a cookie reading "I want a divorce" would make a memorable centerpiece.*
> *If you need proof of his income for child support, let us know. We have P.I.s on staff. We can help you out, no problem.*

Then I put together a quick spreadsheet on my Jake Jeffries laptop, adding a note about the order, the method for delivery, and who'll be paying for it, and move on to respond to the next message, from a woman who wants to warn her ex-boyfriend's new girlfriend that he has herpes.

First off: does he actually have herpes? If not, I'm thinking there are liability issues. If the herpes is documented, then hell yeah, we can help you with that. Maybe we can even soften the message by sending a "He has a herpes" cake or cookie. We have a standing relationship with Rainy Day Bakery.

There, now I've put in a plug for Lainey's friend's bakery too. I got the name off the sticker sealing those cookies the other night.

I move on to the next email, surprised to realize that I'm enjoying myself, just like I was the other day when I broke into that house with Damien. There's something fulfilling in helping Lainey mete out justice—like she's a superhero, and I'm her trusty side-kick. Even if she doesn't know it yet.

I move on to the next message.

I need some help.

Can you pretend you're a man and send me some texts to make my boyfriend jealous? Or, like, emails from a dating app?

He cheated on me with my mother.

Well, goddamn. Someone who has worse mother issues than I do. I have a feeling Therapist Jake Jeffries could do more for her than any thirst trap messages would, but Jake Jeffries has the sad problem of not existing. I lean back in the chair, tapping my foot against the desk, then respond:

Who does that? We're sorry you're going through this.

Sure, I'd be happy to make him jealous if it makes you feel better (I'm Lainey's friend, and I am a guy), but you want my honest opinion, you'd be better off putting a "mother-fucker" banner on his front door, or maybe his car. This guy's not going to learn his lesson.

Then maybe you can take yourself on a nice shopping spree—with his credit card if you have it!—and post some photos of you having fun and not giving a shit on social media.

What do you think?

I click through to the next email and grimace at the photo that's front and center—a gorgeous blonde woman with her arms around a guy who, no shit, looks like a basset hound.

My fiancé broke my heart. I thought he loved me, but we went on vacation with his friend and his friend's fiancée in the Poconos, and all three of us walked in on him and the receptionist.

"Plot twist," I mutter to myself.

"What are you doing in my chair?" asks a familiar voice from the doorway.

I've been so intent on my work that I didn't even hear Elaine come through the front door down the hall.

I set the burner phone down, glancing at the door. It takes me a second to realize that what I'm feeling—my heart thumping faster, my palms sweaty—is excitement.

Elaine looks tired, not that I'm stupid enough to ever say that to a woman. She's nonetheless sexy, obviously. She'd probably be sexy even in a Nickelback T-shirt. Those Band-Aids from last night are still slathered over her hand, and despite waking up at an unreasonable hour to go to Smith House, she managed to put her short hair into some kind of bun. Her red sweater's different from the one she had on the night we met, but the color repetition suggests it's one of her favorites. It suits her, just like this room does. It's hardly an undercover color, but she's hardly an undercover woman. She draws the eye—making a man look twice, thrice, a thousand fucking times.

A voice in my head suggests I shouldn't be thinking about her like that, or this much...

"You're home early," I comment.

She sighs and sweeps into the room, pausing to give Professor X a quick pet before heading over to the chair I'm sitting in. She grabs the back as if she intends to unceremoniously dump me out. "And you're in my chair."

Laughing, I get up and turn to face her. "Nice to see you too, even if I get demoted to the sidekick chair."

She glances at the burner phone, then my laptop, sitting open on her desk. "Are you working on your website stuff?"

"No, it turns out that stuff's pretty boring. Who knew."

A half smile ghosts across her face. "So...?"

Her eyes drift to the screen of my computer again, her painted lips parting as she notices my spreadsheet. "Nicole bullied you into doing Love Fixers stuff?" she asks, seeming kind of amused by it. Not displeased, thank God, because it only occurs to me now that I probably should have asked first.

"No," I say quickly, lowering into the sidekick chair, and instantly swiveling. "I wanted to. You made it sound..."

Like it might be nice, doing something worthy, helping someone. And also like it could be fun.

"You wanted to?" she asks, her face brightening as she reads the spreadsheet. Shifting her head to look at me, a lock of hair escaping the pins, she says, "Jake, you don't need to spend your own money on this."

"I do," I say firmly. "He cheated on her while she was pregnant. She needs to know not everyone's like that."

Her smile spreads wider, meeting her eyes, and suddenly I feel self-conscious. I've pleased her, which is what I wanted to do, but I don't want to trick her into it. I want to earn it—just like I want to earn her release.

"I'm not doing it to be nice. It's personal. My father abandoned my mother when she was pregnant."

Her eyes widen, and I realize that I've told her too much. The truth keeps slipping out with her, probably because I *can* tell her the truth. She already knows my biggest secrets.

"Okay," she says, her eyes twinkling. "So you're a big bad tough guy thief who only sends out free *FU* cookies when the guy really deserves it." She settles back into the chair, still smiling at me. "This is why I still have to work for Mrs. Rosings, you know. I keep comping people because their stories get to me."

"Or because you accidentally adopt clumsy cats."

Professor X yowls and starts pacing on top of her throne, as if she's developed a sudden understanding of English. I wouldn't put it past her. After slicing me with a green-eyed stare, she settles back down, as calm as you please, and forms a little ball of fur. Christ. I'm starting to really like this cat.

Of course, that's nothing on what I feel for the woman beside me.

"Or that." Elaine watches me for a moment, and in her eyes, I can tell that she sees me, really sees me, and no longer dislikes what she sees. It feels like a vindication.

"How'd you think of the cookies anyway?" I ask, clearing my throat.

She shrugs. "It was this story Todd told me, about a peanut butter cup someone had at work."

"Go on," I say, thinking of Ryan and the way he balloons up when he so much as thinks the word peanut. I sit, and nod to her chair.

A smile flickers across her face as she lowers into it. "There was this big gourmet peanut butter cup set out on the counter in the break room, and he thought it was up for grabs, so he took a bite, didn't like it much, and threw it away. Except it turned out it was this specialty treat one of his co-workers had bought for himself, and he was really upset someone had taken it. So Todd told me he bought the guy a new one, they had a laugh about it, and all was well."

"I assume you're going somewhere with this."

She shakes her head slightly. "You're impatient. So I meet this guy at a party, and when he gives me his name, I say, 'Oh, Todd ate your peanut butter cup,' and he looks shocked. Because it turns out Todd hadn't copped to it at all. In fact, he'd made this big deal about it, pretending he was going to help the guy find out who the culprit was, when it was him all along."

"Sounds like a superhero villain," I say, feeling a pulse of hatred for Todd, the douchebag. Todd, the piece of shit who could get away with anything, by virtue of being rich and "important." Admittedly, I have *also* gotten away with lots of dumb shit, but I had to work for it.

"Anyway. That's how I thought of the cookies. An FU by sugar."

I start typing into the search bar of my laptop, but I give her a sidelong glance. "How long did you stay with him after that?"

A corner of her mouth lifts higher. "Three years." She shrugs. "What can I say? He was my peanut butter cup. I didn't like it much either, but I convinced myself I did because I'd already taken a bite."

She glances at the screen, *Peanut Butter Cuppies*, then bursts out laughing. "You're getting him a gift?"

"You did say he just got engaged. Why don't we really stir up some shit and say it's from the guy he stole it from?"

Her eyes gleam. "He'll think it's one hell of a grudge for him to do it after all these years."

"I think a monthly delivery would be best, don't you?"

She leans in a little, her smile in her eyes, and I feel a swell of something warmer and sweeter than attraction, like I just ate one of the one-pound peanut butter cups on my computer screen. It's intoxicating...and terrifying. "I think I like you after all, Jake Not-Jeffries."

That feeling wraps its arms around me and hugs. I swallow, I squirm, I try to shake it off. "Should I get my name legally changed? Not-Jeffries has a certain ring to it."

"Can't tell you without knowing what you'd be changing it from," she says pointedly.

She wants me to offer up my last name willingly to prove that I trust her. I do. To a point. But I know she'll tell Damien and Nicole for my own good. Part of me wants her to do that, but there's another part—the kid who's never left the room he was locked into —who doesn't want to trust another human being with my brother's life. That part of me thinks it needs to be just us, against the world, and no one else can fully be let in. I'm also uncomfortable with my own need for her. I've known her a week, and only really known her since finding out who she was at the party, and yet...

I care about her.

I'd gladly destroy Todd for her.

I want to make her smile, and moan, and I want so badly to take some of the heaviness off her shoulders.

That terrifies me.

So even though I'd like to tell her my last name, then kiss her, then lock the door to this office and spend the rest of the afternoon showing her what sex should be, I clear my throat and look at my computer screen. I select the biggest peanut butter cup on the page. Hurling it at someone's head might kill them, and while I doubt the delivery person will do such a thing, a man can hope. "Should I include a balloon?"

I dart a glance at her, worried she'll be upset, but if she is, it doesn't show. "Jake Not-Jeffries, you should *always* include a balloon."

As I make the order, I feel her eyes on me, lasering through me again as if she's a non-lethal Cyclops from X-Men. When I ask for the address, she gives it to me without flinching, and I'm glad for that. It was her address once, but she doesn't regret that she no longer lives there, even though I recognize where the building is located. It's nice. A whole hell of a lot nicer than this place with the sagging walls and blotchy paint.

We both laugh as I type in the note to Todd.

I'll never forget, with the name of his peanut-butter-loving co-worker.

Then, when it's done, Lainey tells me about her piece of luck with Mrs. Rosings. I'm glad for it, because it means waiting is our best strategy—why risk breaking in when they could be home if Mrs. Rosings is going to hand wrap an opportunity for us?

It means that I get more time with Lainey. I want that. I want it bad, even if I feel guilty that I'm not more proactively working on solving Ryan's problem.

I pull up the Love Fixers spreadsheet again and turn my chair toward hers. "I want to be your sidekick, Elaine."

She smiles at me, that one lock of hair still loose at the side of her face. Without meaning to, I lean in and tuck it behind her ear, my fingers feeling the soft skin of her neck and trailing down it like they don't know how to pull away. Her eyes dilate, but she doesn't touch me. Doesn't swat me away either.

"I already have Professor X," she says.

"She's your familiar. You need a sidekick too."

Her mouth lifts. "So I'm a superhero and a witch? What's my code name?"

"You'll be the Love Fixer, of course."

"And you?"

I think for a moment, then grin. "The Love Bandit."

"Of course," she says with a soft smile that activates that warm feeling in my chest again. Maybe that's her special power—dispensing sugar and retribution. Dazzling people with her witchy splendor enough that they'll do anything for one of her smiles. "Will you draw us, Jake?"

I think again of that moment last week, when I dropped the book and she flipped through it. "You didn't seem to think much of my scribbles," I say, lifting my eyebrows.

"I thought you were one of those guys," she says, nodding toward the spreadsheet. "A cheater. A thief—"

"Well, you were right about that last part."

She takes my hand, her touch sending a shockwave through me, because she did it purposefully, pointedly. Watching me, she weaves her fingers through mine and holds on tightly, telling me something without words. "I wasn't right about you at all. And I lied. Your illustrations are amazing. *Obviously*. I want to see all of them."

I think about the sketchbooks. It's my history with Ryan, or some form of it. It's our story, which doesn't actually have an ending. Yet.

"Someday," I agree, and I mean it. I'd like to show her someday, even if our time is limited.

Two weeks, Roark told me. And Roark is not the type of man who gives extensions. If I don't manage to locate the necklace within two weeks, I'll have to go back anyway. I'll have to beg him to spare Ryan's hand—even if it means accepting whatever price he sets.

Not for the first time, it occurs to me that he might have purposefully set me a task he didn't think I could fulfill, or at least not fulfill alone.

I lift her hand to my mouth and kiss it.

"Jake," she says, her tone urgent, her eyes holding mine. "I don't know—"

"I'm not going to do anything you don't want me to do. Ever." It's the type of promise a person probably can't fulfill, but I mean the words as they leave my mouth. I nod to the computer again. "But I want to do this with you. I want to help. Do you think you can take off some time tomorrow afternoon so we can give Peter, Peter, Pussy Eater a real *fuck you* he'll always remember?"

She feigns a cough. "I think I'm coming down with something."

"That's my girl."

CHAPTER TWENTY-FIVE

LAINEY

Jake and I spend the rest of the day answering emails on the Love Fixers account and then we work on erasing every last breadcrumb of "Droopy Dave"—Jake's nickname for him because of his resemblance to a basset hound—from his former fiancée's social media accounts.

I laugh and melt when I read the responses he wrote by himself that morning. He gets it. He understands. He enjoys doing this too.

And when I look at him, I feel a raw, aching want in my chest. I don't need anyone to tell me it's an unsafe feeling. Jake's not going to stay. He has one reason to be here: to steal a very expensive necklace that I can't let him keep. Once we acquire the necklace, he's going to leave, one way or another, and I'll never see him again.

I'll never see him again.

I swallow down the fear that rises up in the wake of that thought, telling myself I'm being ridiculous. I barely know Jake. And if I feel like he understands me better than most of the people I've known my entire life, maybe that's just a sign that I need to be more forthcoming.

Maybe it also means I should let myself enjoy him fully, for as long as I do have him.

"You look deep in thought," Jake says, nudging my shoulder from his chair as he pulls up another photo on Droopy Dave's fiancée's account. "Are you plotting someone's ruin?"

"Not at the moment," I hedge. "But that could change. Would you like to be ruined today?"

His lips tip up. "Maybe."

He's still sitting close, his proximity seeping into me, but I don't move. Neither does he. He doesn't look away either, and that fear creeps back in. I glance away, looking at the photo drawn up on his screen, and he averts his attention to it too.

"Hey, is that him?" he asks, pointing to a yawning dog in the corner.

"You're terrible," I say with a grin.

"Nah, *he's* terrible. His resemblance to a dog is the best thing about him."

I glance at him and find him staring at me, his gaze appreciative. He's smiling again. I know he's enjoying this—he's enjoying this thing I've made for myself—and I have the urge to lean in and kiss him. To show him I appreciate him too.

But Nicole strides into the room without knocking, a duffel bag slung over her shoulder. "What have you been doing in here all day?"

I glance out the window and am surprised to see the sun's going down. It passed in a blink.

"Kicking ass and submitting cookie orders," Jake says, making me laugh.

"We're keeping Claire busy," I confirm.

"Good. She needs someone to keep her in line."

"What's with the bag?"

"I'll be back in a couple of days." She gives us a salute and turns to go, clearly not intending to explain anything.

Before Nicole can stride off, I ask, "And where, pray tell, are you going?"

"I'm going to stalk Emma Rosings Smith," she says, turning back toward us. Then she points to each of us in turn. "Your job is to stalk Anthony and work the old lady angle." A sly smile crosses her face. "Work her hard."

"Sure," I say, ignoring the innuendo. I'm a little befuddled by this sudden change. She's leaving. Damien is God knows where. Will Jake and I be alone together?

Do I have the strength to stay here with him without pulling him into my bed?

Do I *want* to have that strength?

I clear my throat. "Where's Damien?"

"He's working on something else. He might be gone all week."

She's always appreciated the power of a good cryptic phrase, but I understand what she's not saying. He's following up on the watch, on Jake.

I feel a stab of guilt.

Here Jake is, giving me his time, and I've told some of his secrets to people who will use them to unearth more. He may have expected me to do it, but part of me feels like it was wrong.

You didn't look in the bag, I remind myself. *You could have, and you didn't.*

"I assume you don't need any help containing the prisoner?" she asks with a smirk. Her smile shifts to Jake. "You've seen what she can do to a bat, and she did that to her own car. You don't want to know what she'd do to someone who pisses her off."

"Send them baked goods," he says with a perfectly flat expression.

A delighted laugh escapes me, even though my heart is beating faster and my mind is a mess of thoughts. Most of them of tangled sheets and Jake's body.

"Pole-ax them with kindness," Nicole says, waggling her brows. Then she grins, salutes again, and is gone, leaving behind a house that's empty other than me, Professor X, and Jake.

But I didn't need to worry much, because before we've gotten through another half a dozen photos, a knock lands on the door.

I glance at him, and he shakes his head. "The people I know are more of the door kicking-in type. Plus I heard from Roark this morning. He's been texting me this daily countdown, like an advent calendar, except my brother's bloody hand will be in the last door."

I scrunch my nose. "We're not going to let that happen." He's got a dark, serious look, and I've learned humor is a tool for him, the same as it is for me, so I add, "I refuse to let you ruin advent calendars for me forever. Peanut butter cups have already been destroyed."

He smiles at me as the knock lands again, and I reach in my bag for the pepper spray I carry around everywhere. Just in case. I'm ninety percent sure it's Claire, and in all likelihood, everyone who lives in the house next door. Knowing Nicole, she told them to check on us the second she stepped out the door.

Nicole is protective, in her own way. She partially trusts Jake, but she also wants him to know that I'm not the only person he has to win over. There are people watching, and they may not all be equally sympathetic.

"Peanut butter cups were already destroyed for me too," Jake says, running his hand through his hair as he moves to get up. "My brother's one of those people who blows up if there's a peanut in a mile radius. Which is weird because we're—"

He cuts himself off, because the front door audibly cracks open. Relief twines through me when I hear Claire's cautious, "Hello?"

I'm relieved it's her and not some potentially dangerous lurker. I'm also relieved I'm not going to be alone with Jake right now, because I feel myself wanting something I know I can't have. Wanting more than the release I know he is more than capable of giving me.

I need to believe I'll be okay when he leaves—not like the world is dimmer and less exciting without him.

"Hi," I call out, jumping up from my chair. I reach for Jake's hand, and his eyes widen with surprise as he gives it to me and accepts the boost he obviously didn't need.

You're looking for reasons to touch him, a voice in my head informs me.

The voice is smugly correct, and I release his hand and lead the way into the wood-lined hall so I don't have to see the look on his face.

I might have been okay with him thinking cat-having, period-embracing Elaine was crazy, but I don't like the thought of him thinking *I'm* crazy.

Then again, he stood by my side while I destroyed my ex-fiancé's bat and damaged the car I'd stolen from my parents. If that didn't put him off, then maybe nothing would.

Claire, Declan, and Rosie are hovering by the front door in the living room. There's a big smile on Claire's face, and Declan is awkwardly holding an enormous, foil-wrapped tray of what smells like lasagna. Rosie has a salad in a glass bowl, and Claire, thank the lord, is double fisting two bottles of red wine. "We brought dinner!" she announces unnecessarily.

"You really shouldn't have," I say sunnily, but I'm not actually upset. We don't have to cook now.

And we won't be alone together yet.

"I'm going to go put this down," says Declan, but even though he's spent plenty of time in this house, he waits for my nod to do it. He's at least six foot four and broad, but he's not the kind of guy who'd impose on other people. So coming over to dinner uninvited —even though they've brought the food—would be well beyond his comfort zone. Still, he's already proven he'd do anything for Claire.

It's yet more proof that in addition to men like Peter, who

cheated on his pregnant wife, there are also good men. Faithful, devoted men.

I glance at Jake, thinking about last night. About how he's put the ball in my court, again and again. About how he's spent all day helping me, and he *enjoyed* it.

"Hi," Rosie tells him brightly, playing with the purple streak in her hair. She looks both tired and hyped up—like she hasn't been sleeping, but it hasn't put a damper on her personality. "We saw each other at the engagement party. Hope you're hungrier tonight than you were then."

He smiles at me before glancing back at her. "That depends. Did you tamper with the food?"

"Why does everyone always assume people are tampering with other people's food?" Claire says, shaking her head. "Am I the only one who takes food safety seriously?"

Declan returns from dropping off the lasagna and ignores the salad in Rosie's outstretched hands, instead taking the wine from Claire. "You're the one who takes it the most seriously," he says, kissing her forehead. Then he nods to Jake and says, "Hi, Jake, I'm Declan. My sister Rosie is the one who might or might not have spat on your food, and Claire is my beautiful girlfriend."

Rosie laughs at him, one hand on her hip, the other barely managing the salad. But Jake sees the writing on the wall, and he relieves her of it before it falls to the wooden floor to get investigated—and then inevitably rejected—by Professor X.

"What?" Declan asks. "Why are you laughing? That was a perfectly reasonable thing to say."

"It's just...*girlfriend*. It makes it sound like you're both twelve, and you spend all day holding each other's sweaty hands."

"Excuse you," Claire says. "Your brother never has sweaty hands, and I'm perfectly content to be known as his sweaty-handed girlfriend." She puts her arm around him but keeps her gaze fixed on Rosie. "I know what you're doing, by the way. You're trying to make us happy you're moving out."

"You're taking the apartment?" I ask, surprised but not. Yes, Joy may be in the octogenarian set, but I actually think Rosie will fit right into that building. I can see her and Joy making tea together. Maybe we can convince them to make some sort of empowering tea for our clients.

"I'm moving this week," Rosie says, glancing at Jake with open curiosity. "Into your old building. So I guess I have you to thank for that. I went with Lainey the other day when she went to grab your stuff."

"You did?" he says, his expression closing down, but it's a millisecond too late. I saw the look of betrayal that crossed his face.

Maybe Rosie saw it too, because she immediately follows up by saying, "She wouldn't let me look at any of it." Jake gives me a grateful look; she rolls her eyes. "For future reference, she's probably the least fun person to bring along on a break-in."

"You sure about that?" he says, his eyes dancing as he starts to lead the way down the hall toward the kitchen as if he lives here. I guess, for the next week and a half, that he does. "Because I have marks on my back from where she tackled me on Saturday."

"I was trying to prevent a robbery," I insist.

I give his back a shove, and he dramatically turns around, salad raised in his hands. "There she goes again. Honest to God, Lainey, I wasn't trying to take off with the salad, but if you want it, I'll give it to you."

I laugh and shake my head. "You're not going to get out of being a packhorse that easily. Declan already did the hard work."

"Caught me," he says, and winks. Then he carries the salad off in the direction of the kitchen, Declan close behind him, and I fall back with Claire and Rosie.

Claire gives me *the look*. "I haven't been holding out on you," I say as we slow down, then stop, no longer making any pretense of following them. "Much."

"Was he there when you beat the shit out of your car last night?" she asks in a pointed undertone.

I glance at Rosie, who doesn't pretend to even consider joining her brother in the kitchen.

Then again, she's our friend too, and maybe there's no point in being circumspect.

"Yes, as it happens. He helped me with your pink umbrella."

"Oh, I was looking for that." Claire glances around the foyer as if she'll find it propped up.

"Sorry, it was very much destroyed."

"And the bat? Can we send Todd the splinters?"

I smile. "It *would* add a twist ending to his thirty minute story about buying it at auction. Also. Way ahead of you. I saved the pieces, and I'm going to box them up tonight."

Rosie shakes her head. "I have no idea what you two are talking about, but what happened after you messed up your car? Claire told me about that, obviously, and with all that adrenaline pumping... Don't tell me *nothing* happened. I mean...this guy is so much hotter now that we know he's not a real therapist, and there's definitely something vibing between you. I saw it at Smith House the other night."

"What's wrong with therapists?" I hedge.

I can feel Claire staring at me. I can feel her *knowing*.

Rosie shrugs. "I have issues with men who understand me better than I understand myself."

I laugh—at myself—because I've never felt in danger of that happening...until now.

I take a step toward the kitchen, but Claire catches my arm. "Rosie asked you a question."

I shrug. "I like him, but he's not going to stay. So what does it matter?"

"The present is the only thing we're guaranteed." She squeezes my arm. "So it *does* matter."

"I'll keep that in mind," I say.

Part of me wants to fully confide in Claire about the way I keep pulling back at the last moment with Jake. But I'm not ready to get quite that forward with Rosie, and I'm too confused about what's going on in my own head to try sharing it.

"I'm in desperate need of wine," I add.

"Amen, sister," Rosie says, and this time we all head down the hall together, to find Jake and Declan talking as if they've known each other their whole lives. I roll my eyes at Jake, and when he grins in response, I feel a gush of warmth.

"Hey," he says, taking a step toward me. "Is your friend going to be able to fulfill all of those cookie orders?"

His obvious pride is—*sigh*—adorable.

I turn toward Claire. "We need to have them before two so we can mess up Peter's meeting and hopefully destroy his hopes and dreams. It's all Jake's fault."

She laughs, her eyes sparkling as she glances back and forth between the two of us, obviously making all kinds of conclusions. "Well, we wouldn't want Peter to find any kind of happiness and fulfillment."

"We may also need a cake that says, *He has herpes*," Jake says, his eyes twinkling. "Pending confirmation that it's true. I know Lainey likes to play fast and loose with the law, but I don't want to risk her getting sued."

I walk over and bump his shoulder with mine. "Thanks, sidekick."

He puts his arm around my waist, sending a gush of shock and *yes, yes, yes* through me—along with a healthy dose of fear.

Wine. I need wine.

Declan, bless him, must have poured us glasses of wine before they started talking, because there are three of them waiting on the table. I squeeze Jake's hand and pull away.

The five of us settle around the small table in the kitchen, Jake next to me on one side, Rosie on the other. We drink. We talk. We eat lasagna.

As the night progresses, the warm feeling in my stomach grows. Jake gets along with my friends. They like him, and he likes them. That feels stupidly good. My friends were never good enough for Todd, and my parents, who would have loved to worship the ground he walked on, were an embarrassment.

We're having another glass of wine after dinner when Claire asks for an update on the necklace.

It's a bit like being splashed with cold water, but I fill her in on everything, from Mrs. Rosings's request to the high tea scheduled for Sunday.

Rosie, who's had more wine than anyone else, smacks the round table with her open palm, making it wobble on its uneven supports. "You need to hire Joy to cater the tea. She's so great, *so* great, but she needs more confidence. I'll come along and help her. It'll be perfect."

"Um, Anthony is technically holding the tea," I say, caught off-guard. "Plus, Joy thinks Jake's a therapist."

Jake shrugs, his knee glancing off mine under the table, sending awareness shooting through me. My whole body feels attuned to him—like it's waiting for him to finish what I've kept him from doing.

"So does Anthony," he says. "If anything, it supports my cover, and I've always liked Joy. She loves giving out free medical advice. Following it would probably kill me, but I appreciate the effort." Nodding to Rosie, he says, "I'll text him about it."

She smiles. "You won't regret it."

I'm not so sure about that, but Rosie looks lighter than she has in days, so I let it go.

"You up for doing the dishes, Declan?" Jake asks. Claire looks at me from across the table and pats a hand over her heart.

My friends head out not long afterward, Claire promising she'll have the cookies ready in time to give Peter his terrible surprise.

And, just like that, Jake and I are alone together again.

After the front door closes behind them, he reaches up and tucks my hair behind my ear, the way he did earlier.

"Thank you," I say. "Thank you for being so great with them. It..." I feel choked up all of the sudden, emotion pushing up from the well of my stomach. "It means a lot to me."

"You don't have to thank me," he says, his hand cupping my jaw. His thumb moves softly over my skin. It feels deliciously good, and I want to scream at myself. Why did I stop him again last night? Why have I been torturing both of us? It may only have been a week since the first time I cut us off, but it feels like seven desert-dry months rather than days.

"I like them," he says. "And even if I hadn't, I would've kept it to myself because *you* like them."

"So maybe you were lying," I say, then immediately regret it when a hurt look crosses his face and he lowers his hand.

"I want you to trust me, but I know that's probably impossible because of who I am."

"I don't even know your last name."

He peers at me in the dim lighting of the foyer. "I don't know yours."

I laugh, amused by this—by how much has passed between us without even the most basic information changing hands. "Catlan."

His gaze narrows. "You're joking."

More laughter spills from me. "I'm not. And Professor X is the first pet I've ever had. My parents wouldn't let me get one because they thought animals were a bad investment."

"Charming."

"Right?" I pause, waiting for him to offer up his name.

He shakes his head. "Do you think you'd know me any better if I told you the last name of the mother who abandoned me?"

I suck in a breath and grab his bicep, feeling a soul-deep need to comfort him. To show him that I'm here, even if our lives are only destined to intersect for this strange, stolen blip in time. "I'm sorry. I guessed it was something like that, but I didn't really know."

"It doesn't matter," he insists. This time I can tell he's lying, but he shakes it off and adds, "It's like I said. I had Ryan, and we went to the same foster homes. It was fine."

"Still. I'll send her some cookies if you change your mind."

He laughs humorlessly. "I'm not sure even Nicole and Damien could find her."

"They can find anyone," I say, but the look in his eyes suggests he doesn't see this as good news.

"I wouldn't want them to."

He presses his hand over mine, still planted on his arm, and then he tugs it away, softening the sting by lifting it to his lips and kissing it. It's a soft kiss, his lips landing just below my knuckles, nothing like the fever that took hold of us last night, and there's something sad in his eyes.

"Goodnight, hellcat." He brushes his thumb over my knuckles and then releases me. "It was a good day. One of the best. Let's kick its ass with tomorrow."

If this were a cartoon, my mouth would probably drop open as I watch him turn and walk to—and then up—the stairs without turning around.

Disappointment threads through me, but maybe it's for the best if he's given up. Maybe there are only so many times a man will try to give a woman an orgasm before he decides it's not worth the effort.

CHAPTER TWENTY-SIX

LAINEY

I sleep horribly, full of an awful pulsing awareness that Jake's there, down the hall. He's there, and I'm...here.

I could go to his room. He did tell me that the next move is mine, but I feel incapable of going to him. He's right. I *don't* trust him. I definitely don't trust the urge I have to give him a break—how I've been telling myself that he had his reasons for becoming a thief, and anyway, he didn't take the watch when the old man offered it to him.

In the morning, I call Mrs. Rosings, who probably hasn't sent or received a text message in her life. She doesn't give me any grief about calling off from work. She just informs me that she hasn't secured a time for me to check out Anthony and Nina's house but is working on it.

I get ready for the day quickly and head downstairs, where I'm greeted by the delicious scent of life-giving coffee. I smile when I see that Jake has already set out a mug for me.

Don't speak to me until the cup is this empty, it reads, with a line drawn nearly at the bottom.

I pour myself some coffee and head to the office, gasping as I stop in front of the door. Taped to it is a hand-drawn picture of

Jake, me, and Professor X. I have on a scarlet cape and a matching face mask, Jake's mask and clothes are black, and Professor X is her usual petulant self, although there's a charm on her collar that looks suspiciously similar to the Heart of the Mountain.

The Love Fixer, The Love Bandit & Professor X.

Tears fill my eyes. I take a second to swallow them back, then breeze into the room, laughing when I see Jake has seated himself in his "sidekick" chair. He's wearing a grey T-shirt and jeans, his hair damp from the shower. My mind, the dirty traitor, immediately conjures images of him standing beneath the spray, his hair sopping wet, rivulets of water running down his abs.

"You could have gone for the other chair," I say. "I wasn't here to stop you."

He smiles at me. "I know my place, Prison Guard. Besides, I want you to trust me. Stealing your chair wouldn't be a good look."

The warm feeling from last night is back, pressing at me.

"Jake...I love the picture. It's..." Words fail me, and I feel heat pressing at my cheeks, so I finish with, "I love it. Thank you."

He gives me a slow, pleased smile, and I feel it in my chest, the pulse point at my neck, and the slight curl of my feet in my shoes. I want to bottle up that smile and keep it. "Good. I think I made Professor X look too regal."

"Never." Then, glancing at his screen, I add, "Any new messages?" I ask, my hand lifting to my neck.

His mouth lifts at one side. "Herpes guy *definitely* has herpes, and Motherfuckergate is on. She wants to do the banner. Any chance you know how to cross-stitch? I feel like that would add a little something extra."

I shake my head, fondness twining through me. "Sorry. You did good, Love Bandit." I feel the urge to touch him, to run my fingers through his hair and kiss his neck. But instead I sip some of the coffee and lower into my chair.

"You need a new website," he tells me, his brain obviously moving faster than mine. "And an advertising campaign that isn't Craigslist. I think we should use Facebook. There are a lot of pissed-off people on Facebook."

"I tried running an ad, but I mucked it up."

"We'll do it together. Tomorrow, maybe."

"You're going to help me?" I ask, wonder leaking into my voice. Because I can tell he's probably already thought of slogans. It's there in his energy—the way he's found a pen from God knows where since I can never find any and is tapping it against the desk.

He lets it fall onto the desktop. "Of course. Peter-Peter is just the beginning, Lainey."

I grin at him...and then steal his pen. "I'm going to take that as a promise."

His eyes holding mine, he grabs the pen. His lips lift—a little higher on one side, and I want to press my lips to that corner. I want to absorb it, so I can have this crooked smile—this moment— always.

He's going to leave.

He's going to leave, and that sign he drew will still be here. And I'll be remembering what it was like to be a part of a team instead of some lone, kicked-out-of-the-club X-Man. I'll still have Nicole obviously, but it won't be the same.

Staring into my eyes, he says, "I want you to take it as one."

———

SEVERAL HOURS LATER, after we make a satin banner for Motherfuckergate—Jake revealing an admirable skill for cursive— we're standing in downtown Asheville with a cookie basket. Claire really outdid herself with this one. There's an assortment of *Fuck*

You Very Much cookies shaped like oversized lips, along with an equal number of *Peter, Peter, Pussy Eater* cookies designed to look like cats. In the center is the pièce de résistance—a cracked heart cookie reading "I want a divorce." The whole thing is encased in black, translucent plastic, but we'll unveil it once we're inside the conference room.

We're standing on Church Street, in front of an old clapboard Victorian. The only indication it's an office is some scrawled cursive branding on the window of the front door, but that only bears the man's name—Peter Jenkins.

"Do you think it's significant that his office is on Church Street?" I ask, giving Jake a sidelong look. Church Street is so named because of the multiple churches lining it. Jake is the one holding the cookie basket, because he insisted he'd "look like an asshole" if he was seen empty-handed with a woman half a foot shorter carrying a huge basket.

I told him he already looked like an asshole, and he thanked me.

He gives me one of his crooked Jake Not-Jeffries grins. "I guess we're about to find out."

We enter the building and find a rosy-cheeked woman with pin curls sitting behind the broad reception desk. She has a big smile on her face as she takes us in.

"We're here for Peter," Jake says with an answering smile. "We have a gift from his lovely wife for his big presentation."

"Oh, how delightful," she says, smiling, her gaze flitting to the enormous cookie basket wrapped up in dark plastic.

"From a local bakery," he continues.

A look of consternation furrows her brow. "Peter doesn't like to be interrupted. He can get a little tetchy about it." She pauses. "But he *does* have a sweet tooth, and I think he just got started. Let me take you back."

"Thank you," Jake says warmly. "I'm sure it'll make his day."

I hold back laughter, barely, as she leads us to a closed door, the wood floor creaking beneath our feet. She knocks once on the door, behind which a voice is droning on, and seconds later a man with a narrow face and dark brown eyes opens it. "What is it?"

"Are you Peter?" Jake asks, already pushing his way into the room with the cookie basket. I follow him in.

"What's this all about?" asks the man I presume to be Peter. Inside, there's a long, broad conference table, newer-looking and out of place in this lovely old house. There are twelve people sitting around the table, and it takes me half a beat to realize they're all sitting in pairs. Couples, judging from the way a few of them are turned toward each other, one pair holding hands. As we enter, their attention averts from the white board at the front of the room to the wrapped cookie basket.

I glance at the whiteboard long enough to see the message:

Save Your Marriage Bootcamp

Jake meets my gaze, and I can feel the electric glee zapping between and through us. This man is a hypocrite. A jerk. A fraud. A terrible husband and a worse teacher. And we're about to ruin him with nothing more than a basket of cookies and an inconvenient truth. I brush Jake's free hand with mine, needing to touch him, to share this moment in every way.

"I hope you're hungry," I say with a wide smile as Jake sets the cookie basket down at the head of the table. "Peter's wife wanted to send in a present for his special presentation. The cookie in the middle is for him, but I'm sure he'll be willing to share the rest."

Something passes over Peter's gaze, but he smiles broadly at the couples, who are murmuring softly to each other. "My wife and I had a little argument," he tells them. "But what you need to remember is that arguments are natural. They'll happen to every-one, no matter how solid the marriage. But you can never let an argument fester. This is Mary's way of saying she's sorry for our misunderstanding."

It's obvious the narcissistic prick means it. He actually believes his poor pregnant wife sent him a cookie basket as an apology for walking in on him giving head to another woman. The audacity is staggering.

There's something malicious in Jake's smile as he withdraws a pair of scissors from his pocket and snips the ribbon securing the black plastic covering. It springs open, revealing the basket in all of its glory. The *I want a divorce* cookie is the size of a dinner plate, the text large and written out in red capital letters.

Peter stares at it in disbelief, his mouth falling open, his hand lifting to his tie. It's only then I register that it's covered in tiny wedding rings.

Plucking out the central cookie, Jake slaps it on the table in front of Peter, who seems frozen. It cracks in half, which is delightfully appropriate. Then Jake pushes the basket to the first couple seated at the table. "Let's pass that around. Make sure everyone gets one. Sharing is caring, people."

"Does that say—" chokes out the first man as he pushes up his small, rectangular glasses. His eyes squint at one of the cat cookies.

The woman sitting next to him, who has a profusion of salt and pepper hair and a simple beige dress, scoffs, "If you can't say it, let alone touch it without two layers of clothing between us, I don't see this working, Theo. No amount of work will help us overcome that."

"Mary wouldn't send that," Peter snaps, finally waking up from his fugue. He pulls his tie. "Who are you?"

"The Love Bandit," Jake says, winking at me. "And you know what?" He pats Peter on the back, hard. "Sometimes sorry's not enough, buddy. Tough break. But at least she told you in a nice way. She could have asked us to dose you with laxatives and remove all the toilets. We would have done it, too. Gladly."

Glancing around at the murmuring couples seated around the table, Jake adds, "You might want to remember that if you decide you want to fuck around on your pregnant wife. And if he screws up anyway, ladies, here's how you reach us."

He throws a bunch of business cards down on the conference room table.

My first thought is: we have business cards?

My second thought is that I'm falling for Jake—or maybe I've already fallen, so dizzyingly fast I'm going to break myself. At this moment, I want him more than I think I've ever wanted anything, other than to be allowed to be myself. Goosebumps rise on my skin, and my whole being is sensitized to him. To watching him hold court and stand up for Mary, acting as her vindictive guardian angel. He's doing this for her...and for me...and it's glorious.

I trust him.

I *want* him, even if it can only be for another week and a half.

He's like the last cookie, tucked away in the back of the cabinet —so much sweeter for the knowledge that its quantity is limited.

The basket has continued its voyage around the table, and one man grabs a cookie, shrugs, and takes a bite right out of the center of the cat.

Jake's lips twitch. "Here's a marriage tip. Be like that guy." He points to the man with the full mouth. "He's not afraid to put his mouth where it counts. Peter isn't either, of course, but he should have shown his appreciation to his pregnant wife. That's the ticket."

Everything happens very quickly after that. Peter forms a fist and takes a clumsy swing at Jake, which he effortlessly avoids, and all of the couples get to their feet, everyone talking at once.

One man says, "Well, this is exciting," while a woman pulls out her phone, possibly to film it.

Face blazing, breath coming in puffs, Peter takes another go at Jake, who again sidesteps him—only this time, the bespectacled man standing behind Jake gets the fist in his face. His glasses release an audible crack, or maybe his nose, and he screams.

Jake gives me a wide-eyed look, a wicked smile stealing across his face, and reaches for my hand. I give it to him, and we run out into the hall, ripping past the poor, formerly cheerful receptionist. She looks completely flabbergasted, her hand lifted to her mouth.

"Thank you, sorry!" I call. "Keep up the good work."

A few steps and we're in the lobby, and then the squeaking wooden porch, the boards so old they make music. We're laughing, our hands still clutched together as we race down the uneven steps and across the cobbled street to our getaway car—my beaten-up Ford Fiesta.

I'm gasping with laughter as Jake opens the door and hastens me in. I climb over the gear stick and tumble into my seat, and he starts the car as a sweaty Peter bursts out from the building, nearly tripping over an uneven board on the ramshackle porch as he jets into the road. There's blood on his lip and he's shouting obscenities. Then a husband spills out onto the cobbled sidewalk behind him and tugs him back by the collar of his jacket. Greeting him with a fist.

Jake pulls away from the curb, laughing, his smile cracking something open inside of me. I'm ridiculous, but I do up my seatbelt and then lean in to secure his, the car beeping its protests until I manage it. My fingers feel like sparklers as they glance over his abdomen, feeling a sweaty spot on his shirt and the hot, hard flesh underneath.

"Thanks, Mom," he says with a teasing smile.

"You're welcome, asshole."

"Do you think we can find out who took that video and get it for Mary?" he asks. "She deserves to see it."

"I hope so," I say, but I'm struggling to pay attention to anything but him. The look he's giving me is fond and intimate and his eyes are warm and lively. Everything about him is always so animated. He's always moving and thinking and planning. He's clever and funny and kind to the people who deserve it, and yes, he's done bad things, but *so have I*. The world isn't black and white, right or wrong—there are shades of grey and he's the king of them, and I want him. I want him for myself, not because he can do something for me, or I can do something for him, but because I feel a tug whenever he enters the room. I want him because whenever he touches me, I feel a burst of fire.

I want him all the way, and suddenly I can't wait.

"Go to Jake Jeffries's apartment," I tell him, my voice hoarse.

"Why?" he asks. "You already got everything important for me."

"That's not why," I say, giving him a sidelong look. He's alert now, something inside of him recognizing what I want, and I see his hand flex around the wheel as he takes a turn toward the apartment before he even gets my answer. "I need you, *now*, and it's at least fifteen minutes closer."

CHAPTER TWENTY-SEVEN

JAKE

I'm riding the high of Peter's professional demise, because there's no way whispers about this aren't going to pulse through Asheville, Buncombe County, and hopefully the rest of the state. The only marriage he'll be trying to save is his own, and I hope Mary refuses to take him back.

Sharing this crazy, adrenaline-soaked moment with Lainey made me feel like I was on top of the world, and I'm still up there, elevated and full of untapped energy. Adrenaline zipping through my bloodstream and making my skin extra sensitive, my heart tapping along faster than usual.

So it takes my brain a second to catch up with the gleam in her eyes and the intent lining her voice.

But only a second, and now it's hard to focus on the road, because she's next to me, wrapped up in a red sundress like a festive piece of candy. God help me, I want to sink my teeth into her. I want to lick my way to her center. I want to make her moan and scream my name until even Mr. Tim across the hall can hear it.

"You're going to give it to me, Elaine?" I ask slowly, the words grinding out of me. "You're going to come for me?"

"If you're good enough to earn it," she says with a sidelong glance.

"Oh, I'm good enough. I'll blow Peanut Butter Cup out of the water."

"You'd better." She laughs, her eyes shining, then runs her hand up my thigh and rubs it directly over my dick through my jeans.

I glance at her, feral need pounding into me, and then press on the gas pedal, prompting her to laugh, especially since I almost immediately need to brake. "Adrenaline gets you hot too," I comment, grinning. I'm on a high that can't just be explained by Peter, or by this beautiful woman's hand on my dick. It's more than that. It feels like I'm soaring over the city, hand in hand with her, and I know I'm going to find myself sketching that later—the Love Bandit and the Love Fixer taking to the skies.

"*You* get me hot," she says pointedly, her hand still on me. "I wanted you to bend me over the conference table. Especially when you gave them the business cards. When did you have those made?"

"I ordered them yesterday, overnight. They came this morning."

Something flickers in her eyes, and her hand rubs me, up and down. "That was really sweet of you."

"I didn't do it to be sweet," I say between my teeth.

"You didn't do it to get laid," she rebuts. "You already know I want you. You could have knocked on my door last night, and I would have gladly fucked you against it."

A swear tears out of me, because I'd spent half of the night restless, thinking about exactly that. The reason I didn't go to her was because I still wanted to prove myself and didn't feel that I'd done it. And because part of me worried it would change things, and I liked the way she looked at me, like she'd fooled herself into thinking I'm some kind of prize. Swallowing, I say, "I did it to please you."

"That doesn't mean it wasn't sweet."

I barely make it a few feet before I need to brake again. We're downtown, and the traffic is thick, the foot traffic thicker, and even though we've blown past Peter and his married gang, we still have a while to go. Too far.

Her hand reaches for the button of my jeans, unfastening it, and desperate need floods my veins, threatening to drown the last of my ability to think logically. I've never wanted to sink into a woman this much, to claim her. To drive in deep and stay. I've wanted her since the first night she came into my apartment, before I knew the real Lainey.

And she wanted me before she knew the real Jake.

Because there's something connecting us—some thread of understanding, of like recognizing like, and it scares the shit out of me even as it drives me insane. I've never been with a woman who understands me before.

I can feel her eyes on me as she slowly lowers the zipper of my jeans, my aching dick jutting out now.

I stop at a crosswalk, nodding to an old lady with a walker as she makes her way across—all while Lainey slides her hand over me, curling her fingers around to capture more of me. There's nothing soft or gentle about her. She's acting like she's greedy for me, and there's no way I could be more desperate for everything she's offering.

"You like to drive me crazy, don't you?" I ask, glancing at her.

Her eyes are bright with enjoyment and shiny with lust, and I'm *definitely* not going to make it to the apartment building. Maybe I'll just pull over on the side of the street. I'll take her in the car in the middle of downtown Asheville, and we'll probably get arrested, and it will be worth it because I'll have finally felt her clench around me. Because I'll know she decided I was worthy of bringing her over the edge.

"Yes," she says, her voice breathy, her hand working me as I glide down the road. "*Yes.*"

And then my heart nearly beats right the fuck out of my chest because as I get the car moving again—*just a few minutes, only a few minutes*—she tugs my dick up out of my underwear and leans down and—

"Shit, Lainey, I can't—"

But she can't answer because her lips are wrapped around the tip of my dick, her tongue swirling over it like it's a lollipop.

She's going to kill me. She's going to kill both of us, actually, because it's hard to pay attention to anything but the gorgeous woman with my dick in her mouth. She bobs up and down, and I swear prodigiously, my hand finding her soft hair.

"*Lainey,*" I hiss through my teeth. Her response is to run her teeth lightly over my dick on her next pass, and I white-knuckle the wheel, trying to think taming thoughts as I hit another red light. A car edges up next to me, and I move the Fiesta forward by several inches, crossing the line slightly so they won't get a view of her, bent over in that red dress, her head buried in my lap, and I'm really not going to make it. I'm not going to be able to fuck her, because she's going to make me lose myself in her mouth.

At the same time, I'm not going to tell her to stop sucking my dick, because this is the hottest thing that's ever happened to me.

So I think of the necklace and Roark. I think of locked doors and Ryan's hand. I think of the pocket watch and all the many ways I've failed, and I find the strength inside of myself to turn off on the correct roads. To pull into the small underground parking garage beneath the old-fashioned white apartment building. To find a corner under a non-functional lightbulb, dark and therefore abandoned by the other residents, and park the car in it.

It's about three o'clock, and the garage is empty, and I can't wait. *I can't wait.*

I've never unfastened my seatbelt quicker. I pull her up off my cock, and she smiles at me, her lips glistening, her eyes bright in this dark corner of the garage. Leaning in, I kiss her hard, thinking about what she said about wanting me to bend her over that conference table.

Pulling back, I say, "I can't wait. Take your panties off."

"But we don't have a condom," she objects, her eyes dilating more as she unfastens her seatbelt. I run a hand up her dress, slipping it between her thighs, which open for me, giving me the slick heat of her.

"Are you kidding me?" I ask into her ear. "You don't think I've been carrying one around for days in the hopes you'll ask me to use it?"

"You have?" She sounds pleased by my confession, not weirded out, thankfully.

I lean in and kiss her ear, the side of her face, her mouth, my hand still moving between her thighs, pressing into her. Worshipping her. "I want you here," I breathe into her neck. "I want to fuck you on the hood of the car."

I can tell from the look on her face that the thought of doing something slightly dangerous turns her on.

"Someone could see," she says, lifting into my touch, giving me room to slip past the thin fabric of her underwear and run my fingertips over her. She's so wet, my fingers sopping with her, and my dick gives another pulse of *now, you idiot.*

"They could," I agree. "It's not a busy time of day, and there's no one down here now, but someone could come. They could see me pushing into you, holding you down while I fuck you against the car we destroyed together. They *could* see that."

She swears under her breath.

"We'll keep our clothes on," I say, kissing below her ear again before softly biting the lobe. "And if they catch us, I'll tell them we're having engine trouble and we're trying to get the hood open."

"What if they offer to help?" she asks, lifting up, a little moan escaping her as I slide my fingers into her, curling them to find that spot that nearly sent her over the edge the other day, my palm pressing into her clit.

"I'll tell them that I don't fucking share," I say into her ear, a grumble that lights something in her eyes.

"Move your hand," she says, her voice a command. I do as she ordered, lifting my fingers to my lips again to suck off the familiar taste of her. I watch as she slides her damp panties down her legs—black lace, pretty but even prettier in the footwell—and then she's opening her door, peering coyly over her shoulder at me as she steps out of the car. I watch her slide around to the front, planting her hands on the hood near the windshield as she leans forward, giving me a perfect view of her tits as they press against the top of her bra, wanting to tumble out. I'm in agreement with them, because I'd like them to break free too.

Any words in my brain dry up and crumble to dust, and all that's left is my throbbing dick, still exposed, and the need to please her. It may be the only thing I have to give her, but I'm absolutely going to give it to her. Again and again, as many chances as I get. I get the condom out of my pocket, open it, and roll it on—all while she watches me through the windshield, her gaze so heated I'm surprised the glass doesn't crack. She makes a show of slowly licking her lips.

My pulse pounding, and all the blood in my body thrumming to a common location, I get out of the car and stalk around the hood. Lainey makes a little hum of pleasure as I flip up the bottom of her dress to palm the perfect curve of her ass. The garage is dark in this corner, but not that dark. There are cars on the other side, the stairwell is in front of us and to the right, and the single elevator hulks beside it. We'd have only a few seconds of warning if someone entered the garage that way, and a few seconds more if a car drove in.

"Are you having car trouble, ma'am?"

She steps back, attacking my foot with her heel. The move surprises a laugh out of me, even as I move my fingers over her, stroking, appreciating, in no hurry, even though there is a very real chance a stranger could come along. Part of me almost wants someone to, so they'll see this perplexing, maddening, deeply tempting woman is mine. Mine to kiss, mine to touch, mine to fuck.

You're losing it, a voice in my head whispers, but I'm too far gone to care. I lean in and kiss her neck, her ear, the side of her face, my hand gliding over her bare ass, her slick center. *Her.* There's a sense of wonder unfurling inside of me, because she's decided to fully give herself to me.

She trusts me. She has no reason to, and it's probably not the soundest decision she's ever made, but she does.

Her voice quavers when she looks over her shoulder and says, "You should know better than to call a woman 'ma'am.'"

"My mistake," I say, sliding one finger into her and then two, delighting in how she feels and the knowledge that I'm finally going to get to slide into her and feel her clench around me. She pushes up, rocking her hips a little so she gets my fingers where she wants them.

"It turns out I don't know shit about cars," I say through a hoarse throat. "Maybe I can fuck you against the hood as a consolation prize."

"That's very thoughtful of you," she says. "I like it deep and thorough. Maybe a little bit rough."

"You're going to kill me," I say into her ear, rubbing her with my hand. She's ready—she's beyond ready—but I want her to come hard. I want her to see stars. I want to give her everything *he* didn't.

When I'm gone, I want her to remember me fondly, and touch herself while she's doing it.

"No, I won't do that," she says, kissing the side of my mouth. "I need you to be very much alive for this. And I need your cock now. You're not supposed to keep a lady waiting."

I *can't* wait anymore. It's not in me to keep denying myself when she's been so clear about what she wants. So I grab her hip beneath her dress, lining myself up, hearing her gusty little inhale as she feels me behind her. And then I press in slowly—both because I need to get her used to me and if I don't pace myself I'll be in serious danger of plunging over the edge without taking her with me.

The sensation of her engulfing me is so exquisite I'm not sure I can keep my feet, and I bracket one hand next to hers on the hood of the ruined car.

"Oh. My. God," she murmurs, pushing back and taking more of me. She whispers it again as I reach around to touch her, rubbing the place where she needs me as I finally bottom out. My lips find her neck as I pull out and then press into heaven again. I find a jagged part of the hood with my hand and grip it tightly, needing the nip of pain, because I already feel the tingling at the base of my spine. I know, I damn well know, I won't last long this first time.

I slide out again, then dip only partway in. Then do it again. Again.

"What are you doing?" she hisses, trying to buck her hips and take in more of me. "I need you deeper. It felt so—"

This time, I slide my hand from between her legs to her hip and thrust in hard, pulling her hip to me to make it even deeper, and a surprised, pleased sound bursts from her. "*Yes.*"

Sliding my hand around her neck, I tuck my thumb under her chin to tilt her back toward me so I can kiss her. I'm nearly frantic. Not because she's making noise and someone might hear, but because she's close. I can feel the first waves of her pleasure lapping at me. Squeezing me.

But I won't get to see the look on her face, not fully.

I need to see her.

I need to experience this with her, all the way.

I need to feel her clutch around me, to see her face twist with pleasure and know that I was the lucky asshole who got to give it to her.

So I pull out and whirl her around so she's facing me. My jeans are down around my thighs, uncomfortable as hell, but I could give a shit about anything but being inside her. Her legs instantly splay open for me, and I stalk in between them, guiding her onto the hood, her back against the still-hot metal. She cinches her legs around my waist as I stroke in again, fast because I need to get back inside of her, then lean in to capture her mouth. Her arms wrap around me, her hands burying into my hair as she sucks on my lips. I press in again and again, barely aware of where we are—of anything but the feeling of her around me. It's blissful. It's...

"Jake," she whispers raggedly in my ear. "I'm going to come."

And I pull back a little as I stroke into her again, feeling the first pulses around me—the feeling almost painful because I need to come too, but I can't until she's all the way there. Her eyes close, her head tips back against the hood, and she's so beautiful, so beyond anything I've ever experienced before or will probably experience again that it almost brings me to my knees.

"That's it, hellcat. That's it," I murmur, continuing with the same rhythm that got her here, hard and deep. So deep inside of her.

Her eyes flutter open, and her hands grab my back, pulling me farther down onto the hood, her fingers clawing me like she's become her nickname. "*Jake.*"

I can't hold back anymore. As she clutches around me, pleasure rips through me, and I lean into her neck, biting her lightly as I fall over the edge into a kind of molten bliss I've never felt before in my whole life. A bliss that burns and scars, because I already know that after this I'm going to want only her.

Well, fuck.

CHAPTER TWENTY-EIGHT

LAINEY

My whole body is dizzy and liquid with pleasure, even though the car's hood is digging into me, and Jake is stretched out on top of me, his elbow planted on the metal to hold his weight. My mind is full of a million different things—so many of them that it would be impossible to fish just one thing to the surface—but I feel *good*. Jake made me feel good, and I let him, and I'm glad. He's looking down at me with the same kind of wonder I feel coursing through me.

"Wow," I finally say.

And he laughs, pinging his fingers against the hood, his dick still buried inside of me.

"Why are you laughing, you jerk?" I say, shoving his arm, but I'm laughing while I say it, because...well...*wow*.

He leans in and kisses me softly, his hair brushing my face, then pulls back a little and grins. "Because you really are a hellcat. I'm going to have scabs across my back."

"You're still inside of me," I say, my voice coming out breathy.

"I don't think I want to leave. I may want to stay in here for the rest of my life."

This time, I pull him in for a kiss—

And then I hear a distant tapping sound, followed by a—

I shove him away. From the look in his eyes, he heard it too—and he pulls out, groaning a little at the sensation, and then tugs on his pants. He barely manages to get them up by the time the door to the stairwell creaks open. I pushed my dress down, but I'm still sitting on the hood of the car while he's standing in front of me.

It'll look odd, although admittedly less odd than if he were buried inside of me.

Joy steps out of the stairwell door, smiling broadly when she sees us.

"Yoo-hoo," she says, lifting her hand in a jaunty wave.

Of course it's someone we know.

She walks over without hesitation. If she thinks it's odd that we're hanging out on the hood of my car under a light that's guttered out, it doesn't show.

Jake shoots me a glance, then reaches out to help me up as Joy gets close. I expect him to release my hand, but instead he weaves his fingers through mine. I'm undone by this small gesture.

Joy beams at him. "Oh, I could just tell there was something special blooming between you two. Rosie told me you've already moved in together in Marshall. Lovely place. Some people would say it's too fast, but when you know, you know. Why, I knew the second I saw my Mortimer. Bald as a cue ball, but his love line went clear across his palm. Oh, but he was a *beautiful* man. Not much to look at from the outside, I'll grant you, but he had the kind of beauty that really matters. We were soulmates. My good friend from the teashop told me so. Every time she read our leaves, she saw a heart. Every time."

Jake smiles at her, his hand still firmly wrapped around mine. "Did you have a nice celebration for his birthday the other day?"

I glance at him in disbelief. It's adorable that he remembers this about her. Even more so that he thought to ask. Each time I tell myself Jake Not-Jeffries can't possibly surprise me anymore, he one-ups himself.

"So kind of you to ask, sweetheart," she says, reaching out to pat his cheek. I know from experience what it feels like—the rasp of his five o'clock shadow, the strong line of his jaw. "Yes. He would have been eighty-five, God rest him. I made a pot of his favorite tea and brought it to the Arboretum." Smiling, she pats him again and steps back, "We liked to have a little fun in public places too. You know, my dear Mortimer spent so much of his seed there, I'm surprised a forest didn't spring up. Oh, to be young. You might want to zip up before you go upstairs, dear, the folks in 2C are prudes."

Laughter rips out of me as Jake lifts his brows and then pointedly fastens his zipper. The condom must still be attached to him, and I can't imagine it's comfortable, a thought that makes me laugh until I'm breathless and nearly doubled over with laughter.

"Yes, it's very funny, Lainey," Jake says, rubbing my back. Turning to Joy, he says, "We were fixing the car. Something was rattling in the engine. That's my story, and I'm sticking to it."

Laughing softly, she winks at him. "Thank you for connecting me with your friend last night. I'm looking forward to helping out at his tea. Is there any particular energy you'd like me to tap into?"

Jake grins at me and then her. "I don't know. Can you make the other guests confess their deepest secrets to us? That would be helpful."

I expect her to take it as a joke, but she tips her head. "I'm going to give that some thought."

WE GO UP to Jake's apartment to collect the rest of his belongings in trash bags so Jake Jeffries can officially check out of his rental—and so Jake can get rid of the condom that's been "strangling" his dick.

We take a shower that has very little to do with getting clean, and right before we're about to leave so we can drape our home-made banner across the motherfucker's Ducati, my phone rings with a call from Mrs. Rosings.

I show him the screen and then answer.

"Thursday evening," she says without any preliminaries. "Eight o'clock. We'll be attending the community theater together, so please make it worthwhile. It's a *Halloween* play, Elaine, and they encouraged the audience to 'dress up.' A woman my age shouldn't be forced to suffer through such an indignity."

"Do you have a key?" I ask, my heart racing in my chest.

"I do not," she says with a sniff. "Do you think they've ever deigned to entertain *me*? Perhaps those friends of yours could find a way in?"

She knows about Nicole and Damien.

"We'll figure it out," I agree.

"You sound different," she says suddenly, her tone sharp. "You're with that boy, aren't you? The charming one with the incredibly foolish diet."

"I am, and I *feel* different," I admit, glancing at Jake, who's sitting on the couch beside me, fiddling with his phone. His toe is tapping to some kind of internal rhythm. I put a hand on his thigh, and he smiles at me.

"I'll see you tomorrow, bright and early. In the meantime...be careful, Elaine," she says, then cuts off the call before I can ask what she means.

Only I think maybe I know. She told Claire that she never really loved any of the three husbands she lost, but maybe that's just a story she tells herself to make it easier. Or, at the very least, it's reductive. Because I can tell Mrs. Rosings is a person who's had her heart broken, and a heart can be broken without being fully given to someone. I know that firsthand.

Maybe she thinks I'm falling into a trap she bit her own leg off to escape from.

I wonder if it felt like this for her too—if excitement and ecstasy lined the path to hell.

"She found us an in to Anthony's house?" Jake asks.

I nod slowly, a feeling of unease creeping into me. "On Thursday night. What happens if we find the necklace?"

"Well," he says, pulling me onto his lap. "I'm glad you asked. We're going to steal it back, hellcat. Maybe we should leave Nina with the bubblegum machine necklace to add insult to injury."

I turn in his lap to face him. "You know that's not what I mean."

His throat bobs as he nods. "I do." There's a few seconds of silence, then he traces his fingers across my lips. "I've got to save my brother, Lainey. I'm all he's got."

"You mean *we're* all he's got," I correct, wrapping my hand around his jaw and turning his face so his eyes are boring into mine. "You're not alone in this anymore. *We're* going to save him. But you have to trust us so we can figure it all out together."

Something flashes in his eyes, and he leans in and kisses me. "I trust *you*."

But that's not good enough, because I can't help him fix this in a way that sees his brother to safety and gets Mrs. Rosings back what's hers. For that, we need Nicole and Damien. They're the ones who can make that kind of alchemy happen.

I trace the fox on fire on Jake's arm. "You drew this." His hands are always in motion, touching, tapping, *drawing*. I don't think he even realizes he's doing it half the time.

"Ryan has the same one," he comments, turning his arm so my finger can continue its winding path.

"Why?"

His lips lift slightly. "Foxes need to be crafty to survive. When we were kids, we made up this story about foster kids who could shift into a fox at night and got up to all sorts of crazy shit. Whenever we couldn't sleep, we'd continue the story."

"Is that what your graphic novel is about?" I ask.

He laughs self-consciously, running a hand back through his messy hair. "Yeah, but I wouldn't call it a graphic novel." He lifts his eyebrows, his mouth quirking. "Just some scribbles from when *I* can't sleep. I know one woman who was particularly unimpressed by them."

I'd like to ask what keeps him up at night. Or what happened to them after their mother left. I'd like to ask him a thousand questions, but with each one he answers I feel the connection between us deepening. And that's more terrifying than the seven years I spent in a cage.

Then, at least, I knew what to expect. I knew where the bars were, and I'd played a part in making them or propping them up.

Now, I don't know what the future holds, other than that it's almost certainly going to tear us apart.

CHAPTER TWENTY-NINE

LAINEY

CONVERSATION WITH NICOLE

I'm in with Emma.

We're gonna get shots together tomorrow tonight.

Does she know this?

She will.

What's up with you? Did you bang the thief yet?
Damien and I have a bet running.

Sometimes I dislike you.

Is that a yes or a no?

Mrs. Rosings got us an opening at Anthony's
house on Thursday night.

You're avoiding the question. Cold. You should
want me to win because if I come out ahead
we're BOTH winners.

Has Damien gotten anywhere?

A big fat nope. But he's working on an angle.

I stick my phone in my pocket and leave the bathroom in Jake Jeffries's old apartment, feeling unsettled by that.

He's working on an angle.

It suggests Damien's on the cusp of finding something. Possibly something complicated. But I shake it off as I step into the living room, where Jake's waiting for me with a grin. "You ready to make that motherfucker pay?"

We brought the banner with us when we left Marshall this morning, so we follow his former girlfriend's directions to where he keeps his very expensive motorcycle, and then string it around the bike, adding plenty of fancy bows for flair. Then we hide in the trees by the parking lot so we can watch while the motherfucker himself finds it.

We film his attempts to destroy it for his ex's social media, nearly pissing ourselves from holding in laughter when he trips over the banner, then tries to rip it in half five times without getting anywhere, and finally stomps on it before dropping his lighter onto it—at which point a cop rolls by and gives him a citation.

As we pick our way out of the trees, heading back toward my car, parked with the others in the lot, Jake glances at me, a smile on his face. I say, "You're going to tell a story about today, aren't you? With your drawings."

"Maybe so," he says as we approach the car, "but the garage won't be in it. That was just for us."

"Us...and Joy. Joy definitely saw your dick. It was a whole thing."

He laughs easily, his shoulders shaking with it, and then wraps an arm around me, and I feel...

I'm happy, but it's a happiness edged in teeth, because it's a happiness that can't stay.

We pick up a pizza and a tin of sardines for Professor X, and we go back to the house and change into comfy clothes and watch

Matchmaking Small Town America while we compete to come up with the best slogan for the Love Fixers.

Love got you down? Call the Love Fixers, and turn that frown upside down.

Want to see him cry? So do we.

We're barely paying attention to what's on the TV, but one of the guys on the show who was introduced as a New Yorker doesn't seem to know anything about the subway system—or to understand that the Statue of Liberty is on an island. Jake snorts and says, "He's not from New York City so much as he showed up on a bus six weeks ago for an audition and never left."

"*You're* from New York," I say in wonder, because I can tell. It's there in the way he's saying it. In the knowing roll of his eyes.

It's kind of magical to think he was there the whole time I was —that we were living our lives in parallel. Maybe going to the same bagel shops or bodegas.

Part of me feels like I would have noticed him, as if it would be impossible not to, but there are millions of people who live in New York, and his would have just been another attractive face in the crowd.

Jake studies me for a second before nodding and running a hand down my calf, settling it on my ankle. "Sure, but I'm telling you that. I'm not telling Nicole and Damien."

Which means I'm not supposed to tell them either.

"They'll find out," I warn. Then, thinking about what Nicole said earlier, I add, "They might already be finding out. It would be better to just tell them."

He thinks this through before saying, "Probably. But if I did the smart thing all the time, I definitely wouldn't have met *you*. So maybe I should keep being stupid and hope for the best."

Maybe this says something about the company I keep, but it's one of the best compliments I've ever gotten from a man.

"What do you miss most about the city?" I ask as New York Man mouths off on the TV.

His mouth lifts up. "I'd kill someone for a bagel, maybe. But right now? Nothing. I'm exactly where I want to be, when I want to be." He kisses my hair. "With the person I want to be with."

"That's a good thing," I say, trying not to show him how much his answer means to me. "Because you still can't leave."

Just past dusk, Claire and Declan stop by to ask about the cookie basket, and Jake tells them how it all went down in a way that has even Declan in hysterics. Storytelling is one of his talents, but a voice in my head whispers that it's convenient to be a good storyteller if you're also a liar. The two go hand in hand. But I shake the voice off like it's a wasp I'd rather not be stung by and suggest we all have a drink around the firepit.

Declan lights a fire, and we drink and laugh, our chairs turned to face the mountains in the distance—soft, rolling lines still visible as darker pieces of night. The weather's a little crisp again but not cold—the perfect weather for sitting outside and enjoying the mountain air—and as Jake gives me a look, I feel a different kind of want.

It could be like this. My whole life could be like this if he stayed.

But he's not going to, and I should be smarter than to want what's never going to be mine. I need to dig my feet into that bedrock of truth and live there.

"Can I check the closet in my old room?" Claire asks out of nowhere. "I think I left my comfiest shoes behind."

I admire the way she says this with a straight face, when both she and I know she's wearing her comfiest shoes—the one she always praises for at least five minutes whenever she has them on. Honestly, I would have wanted to get the goods from her too.

As soon as we get through the back door leading into the kitchen, she pushes it shut and turns to me, her eyes shining. "Something happened between you two, didn't it? I can tell. You decided to go for it."

I think about what Jake said about wanting the garage to be just for us.

I do too, but that doesn't mean I can't confirm something happened. Claire's my oldest friend, my person.

So I grin at her. "Maybe, but if you tell Nicole, you're dead to me. She has this bet going with Damien about…" I taper off because Claire has a guilty look on her face. "*No.*"

She covers her mouth with her hand, then speaks through her splayed fingers. "I'm sorry. I didn't…you know Nicole. It's really hard to say no to her, and we were both rooting for you to have some fun. Damien's more protective. He insisted we come out here every night to check on you, not that I wasn't one hundred percent planning on doing that anyway, and…" She sighs and lowers her hand, worrying at the pocket of her pants.

Laughter gushes out of me, and I push her arm. "Who are you, and what have you done to my best friend?"

"I'm sorry. My sister's been a bad influence. I'm ashamed of myself."

I wrap her into a hug, still laughing, and she hugs me back hard before I pull away. "I'm not mad. But I still don't want you to tell Nicole. Let's keep her on her toes. What's the prize for guessing correctly?"

"The winner has to wear a Bronuts costume of the loser's design and dance outside the bakery in it for an hour. Damien will basically be bankrolling my theoretical future child's education if he does it."

Because he'd be a hot man dressed up like a baked good. The tourists will show up in droves.

"But it would really torment Nicole if she had to do it," I put in.

Claire and I both laugh at the mental image, before she shakes her head. "It's too bad you had to go and sleep with him."

I laugh and give her arm another shove. "I regret nothing."

She jumps up and down on her feet and actually claps her hands, as if my sex life is a boy band concert. "Oh my God. You confirmed it! I want to know everything. Did you..." She moves her hand in a yada-yada gesture.

"*Yes*," I say, seeing movement through the glass in the door—Jake and Declan, coming back toward the house. "But seriously don't tell her," I continue in an undertone. "Let's let her sweat a little. She'd never admit it, but she's worried she'll be the one wearing those balls."

"Okay," Claire says, her eyes shining as she glances past me through the glass. She reaches out and squeezes my hand. "I'm glad you're having fun, Lainey. You deserve it."

She doesn't ask if it's more than fun, because Claire probably can't imagine I'd ever want more with a thief—a man who has made his living on the wrong side of the law. She's known me as the Lainey who zeroed in on the first rich, handsome, and connected man who crossed my path in college.

A part of me wishes she'd see what I haven't said, even if she'd only reach the same conclusion I have—that I can only live in the moment with him, because that's all we're ever going to get.

Claire and Declan head out to help Rosie pack, but they leave the fire blazing in the pit, so Jake and I stay out there until it's late, the sky painted entirely black.

We talk about the Love Fixers and *Matchmaking Small Town America*. We discuss our favorite Thai takeout places in New York, argue about the best place to get bagels, and have a stirring debate about which subway line is the least reliable.

We do not talk about Thursday, or what will happen if and when we locate the necklace.

We do not talk about the text messages he gets every morning from his brother's captor.

And when our words run out, he keeps looking at me, studying me by the warm light of the fire.

"Why are you staring at me?" I ask.

He smiles and shakes his head. "I can't seem to stop looking at you. You're gorgeous."

My breath catches, but I'm already feeling exposed in a way I'm not used to. With Todd, I was unhappy, but I never felt like he could truly break me—only bend me until I fit a different image. So I clear my throat and say, "If you tell me I look even better than the view, I'm going to throttle you."

"You can throttle me if you'd like," he says with a slow, lazy grin that stirs something in me. "In fact, I was just wondering if you'd ever had sex by a campfire before. That seems like the kind of thing that would do it for my little exhibitionist."

"My best friend lives next door."

His smile spreads wider. "You've assured me they have new windows, and they already did their nightly check-in for Nicole and Damien. So there's nothing holding us back."

"You knew?" I ask, laughing, getting up from my chair, pushed up next to his, and climbing into his lap. He slides his hand up the back of my long-sleeved shirt, his eyes softening once his flesh is pressed to mine—as if he needs this as much as I do.

"I don't blame them," he says, expertly unlatching my bra before sliding his hands around to the front to cup me. "I like that they're concerned for you. You should have someone out here who's worried about you."

I don't tell him that I'd like that someone to be him—I decide I'd prefer to show him.

It turns out sex outside *does* do it for me. Although I have a sinking suspicion that it's Jake Not-Jeffries who's the real secret to my sudden ability to orgasm on command.

He stays in my room that night. The three of us do—Jake, me, and Professor X, who falls asleep on top of Jake, not that I blame her.

To my surprise, he's awake before I am, sketching in his book at the kitchen table. When I come down to the kitchen, I glance over his shoulder and grin when I see that he's drawing the cookie bouquet. He and I are in the scene too, wearing the costumes from the picture he sketched for the door yesterday.

"You have a gift," I say, leaning down to press a kiss to his head. He drops the colored pencil and grabs my hand, pulling me into his lap.

"A gift for making you come."

I'm laughing as he kisses me, his hand lifting into my hair to cup the back of my head. He pulls away slightly, smiling at me. "I made some precious, precious coffee."

"Oh, thank God," I say, in no hurry to get up. I look into his eyes, taking in the layering of colors, like in one of his pictures. He's achingly beautiful. Maybe that's why I decide to ask, "Are you ready for Thursday night?"

A corner of his mouth lifts. "You know me. I live for breaking and entering." Then he shrugs and wraps an arm around my waist, pulling me closer. "My brother's better at picking locks. That's kind of his thing. If lock-picking were a class, I'd probably get a B-. Maybe a C+. But we'll muddle through."

I'm confused by this. Surely, a professional thief should be able to get through a lock, any lock. I pull back a little, turning to look him in the eye again. "Maybe you picked the wrong career plan."

He gives me an inscrutable look, his hand flexing around my

hip. "If you make them like you enough, they'll open the door for you."

From the way he says it, it's meant as a warning. But if so, it's been delivered too late. I've opened the door for him—I've propped it with a metal anchor.

We eat breakfast; I leave for my day job.

When I come home, he's waiting for me, his pen tapping against my desk. Professor X is curled up on his lap. "Are you ready, Love Fixer?" he asks with a grin. "We've got some work to do."

And my heart gives a funny little lurch as I grin at him and say, "Thank God. I figured I'd just come home and rest like a normal person. It's a good thing I have you to save me from being boring."

"I knew you'd see things my way," he says, picking up Professor X and setting her down gently. Then he lifts me up by the waist and swings me around before kissing me, and my heart gives another sickening lurch.

We help a woman pack up her things while her crappy, cheater of an ex is at a concert. We make a cookie delivery. We call up a woman's ex, and Jake pretends to be her new boyfriend and tells him in no uncertain terms to back off.

It is *exhilarating*.

And five minutes after we pull into the driveway of the cabin, Claire and Declan come over with dessert.

Jake grins at me. "Look, honey, your friends just happened to come over again. Who would have thought?"

But he doesn't act like he minds, and I definitely don't mind. It feels strangely right to have them here. Like this might become a habit I'll depend upon if I'm not careful.

By mutual silent agreement, he sleeps in my room again that night.

When Jake's phone buzzes the next morning, I groan and bury my face under my pillow. It's much too comfortable next to him for me to want to deal with the day yet. Still, I can't help glancing at him as he checks the message, his brow furrowed.

"Your girlfriend?" I joke. Or at least I'm mostly joking. There's still so much we don't know about each other's histories, so much we haven't said. In some ways, I feel closer to Jake than I've ever felt to a man, and in others...

I don't know his last name.

I don't know his last name.

"No, it's Roark," he says with a sigh, flashing me the screen. I see a few texts from a number coded ASSHOLE. Based on the text he just received, his brother has just over a week left before he faces his consequences. "He wants to keep me on my toes."

"Prick."

He nods, tapping the side of his phone, but there's something melancholy about him. "I guess he is. You know...I didn't used to think so. I used to think of him as...not a father, but close. It's been one of those hard truths."

There's something vulnerable and sweet about his expression, and my heart gives another of its lurches. I lean in and kiss him softly, marveling over the fact that he's here, in my bed. That I want him here. That my bed would have felt empty and cold if he'd left in the night.

At Smith House, Mrs. Rosings is practically humming with nervous energy. She spends the whole morning talking my ear off, and then sits beside me all afternoon while I package the wedding favors for a wedding she hopes will never happen. With favors like these—brown goat milk soap that smells like the inside of a barn and looks like excrement—I'm guessing the guests would prefer it that way too.

My phone rings at around three.

It's Damien's number, and my heart instantly starts racing.

He was looking into Jake's story, and he's found something. He *knows* something.

Part of me doesn't want to answer.

Part of me has been waiting for this like a child sitting by the Christmas tree at the end of November, waiting for Santa to come.

Mrs. Rosings glowers at me as the phone buzzes on the table beside the gargantuan stack of horrible gifts. "It's that boy, isn't it? He's already keeping tabs on you."

I shake my head. "It's my roommate."

She waves for me to go, and I answer Damien's call as I head toward the front door.

"It's about time," Nicole says as soon as I click on.

"Nicole?"

"I conferenced in both of you," Damien says. "I had an interesting morning."

"Where are you, anyway?" I ask.

"I'm in Connecticut. I found the old man with the watch. He never declared it stolen, but it's definitely him."

My pulse pounds faster as I step out into the crisp but sunny day. I make my way to one of the rocking chairs and lower into it.

"How'd you find him?" I say softly.

"Jake said it was registered with the Sons of the American Revolution. There were only a few possibilities, so I followed up on all of them. This guy recognized Jake's photo."

The same one Cleo showed me a few weeks ago—the one she must have taken while he was falling down drunk, a thought that makes me sick.

"You're killing it with the dramatic timing, hot stuff," Nicole says. "But it's way too early for this shit."

"It's nearly four o'clock," I say, the words dry in my mouth. Three hours. Jake and I have three hours until we're supposed to break into Anthony's house.

"Yeah, you try waking up at four after going shot for shot with that woman."

Damn. I've seen Nicole drink, so Emma Rosings Smith must

be some kind of machine. But I have to admit I don't really care about Emma Rosings Smith or her ability to drink Nicole under the table, or even what Nicole might have learned from her, because I have no doubt Damien called us for a reason.

Still, part of me doesn't want to hear it.

"Did you get anything from her?" I ask, my voice distant, as if it's someone else's.

She snorts. "No. Only that she doesn't want her brother to get married either. If they let people take objections at the ceremony, it'll be longer than one of your stories about your mother."

"Damien?" I ask.

"Jake told you the old man offered to give him the watch, and he turned him down."

"Yeah," I say, my heart thumping. "And then the guy who kidnapped his brother sent someone else to steal it."

"That didn't happen," he says, his tone regretful. "I'm sorry, Lainey, I liked the guy too, but he's been straight up lying to you."

"What did this older gentleman tell you?" I ask stiffly, trying to sound like all of the fears that have been chasing me haven't just bitten down and I'm not metaphorically bleeding out here on Mrs. Rosings's front porch.

Jake's a liar.

He's been lying to me from the start.

Chasing around those thoughts is another one: don't I deserve it? Isn't this exactly what I deserve for the lies I myself have told?

"Dale. His name's Dale. I showed him that photo of Jake," Damien says, "and he knew him as Jack Ryerson. He said he met Jack at an AA meeting—"

Shit, pretending to be an alcoholic to dupe an old man is bad. Really bad. The hits keep coming, slapping me in the face and telling me I've been a fool.

"And they got along great. Dale invited him over for lunch, thinking maybe he'd be his sponsor, and they got close. So he offered him the watch as a sign that he believed in him and his ability to get clean. I guess Jack said no the first time he offered, but a couple of days later, he came over and told him he'd given it some thought and it would be an insult to say no to a gesture like that. So he took the pocket watch and then disappeared. The guy never saw him again. He seemed pretty torn up about it, to be honest. He was worried about him. Thought maybe he'd done something self-destructive."

I feel pretty torn up inside too.

My mind rewinds through everything, pausing at what Jake said to me this morning: *if you make them like you enough, they'll open the door for you.*

From what Jake told me the other day, Dale's gesture had changed him. It made him realize that what he'd been doing was wrong—and decide that he couldn't do it anymore.

What else has he lied about?

Does he even have a brother?

Was there something stolen or dangerous in that bag I took for him?

My heart feels like it's chomping its way out of my chest—a Pac-Man heart—and I feel a sharper understanding than ever before of what it is to feel like a fool, a dupe, a patsy.

Worse: I should have known better.

I knew who he was: he'd told me. But I'd let myself think I was different—that I was the person he'd decided to be himself with. That thought was as seductive as the way he looked at me, the way he touched me...the way he made me feel like there was a special connection between us.

Of course he was good at making people feel special. He'd made Dale feel special too—right up until he'd taken his most prized and sentimental possession.

But then I think of those text messages from ASSHOLE. I think of the countdown. Whatever else he's lying about, I believe that Jake really is in trouble, and he'll be in deeper trouble if he doesn't get the necklace.

"Have you found out his last name?" I ask tightly, my whole body quaking.

"Not yet. The new cover name should help. I've got two names to follow—"

"He's from New York City," I say, my heart beating fast. Because even now I feel like I'm betraying him, sharing something he'd wanted me to keep to myself. "Although obviously that doesn't narrow it down. He told me his first name's definitely Jake, and that he either uses Jake or something close to it whenever he's on a job, which matches with him going by Jack in Connecticut."

"That *will* help," Damien says, "but Lainey, you shouldn't be alone with this guy, and you definitely shouldn't break into that house with him. Put him off. If he gets that necklace, he'll take it and run. We'll never see him again. You don't want to be on the hook for that if it comes out that you helped him."

Nicole groans, then says, "Fine. I'm coming back from Charlotte. I'll break into the suit's house with you, Lainey. We've got this. No problem."

"No," Damien says sharply. "Wait for me. I'm on a five o'clock flight. I'll be home this evening."

But not early enough to coincide with the Halloween play.

Maybe I'm a fool, a dupe, and a patsy, but I'm not going to lie down and let my friends solve this for me. I'm a woman who handles her own damn problems. I'm going to confront Jake Whatever-The-Fuck-His-Last-Name-Is. And I'm going to do it tonight.

I will find out what's real and what's not.

And until I know?

I'll be damned if I let him take that necklace.

CHAPTER THIRTY

JAKE

MESSAGE FROM ASSHOLE

Tick-tock.

The last few days have been a blur of working on my graphic novel, doing work for the Love Fixers, and preparing for tonight. I've done drive-bys of Anthony's two-story arts and crafts house in North Asheville—the swanky part, different from where the apartment building is located. The houses there have gone all out with decorating for Halloween, and one house has so many realistic skeletons and zombies in their yard it's obvious they dislike children and would love to give them nightmares. Anthony's house doesn't even have a single carved pumpkin on its stoop.

I've also studied the house on Google Maps so I can eye the layout and identify the best entry point—in the back, away from the neighbors' prying eyes—and the best place to leave our vehicle: the parking lot at a trailhead located behind their home.

Now, it's time to put that knowledge to use, even if I feel a little...hesitant.

I haven't taken anything that's not mine for months.

Staying at the cabin this last week, I've dared to think about what a different kind of life might be like. A life in which I can feed my need for adrenaline by helping people instead of harming them.

I pace until the floorboards creak beneath me. I'd fix them, but I don't know how. My whole life, no one's ever taught me to *fix* anything. Only how to take.

It's a thought that makes me pace harder, until I Google how to fix creaking floorboards and find an answer too complicated to wrap my restless brain around. Professor X is as twitchy as I am, pacing beside me, mewing enough that I feed her a second break-fast she doesn't touch.

I tell myself it's always like this before I steal something.

But I know the truth: part of me doesn't want to find the real Heart of the Mountain. Because once I do, this will all be over.

Elaine has told me multiple times that Damien and Nicole will help me, but I'm unconvinced. At the end of the day, she's their friend and Mrs. Rosings is her boss. They might convince her to do the right thing and return the necklace to the old lady. Still, I don't know if I have it in me to steal it out from under her and leave without a word.

A part of me also recognizes that stealing Mrs. Rosings's neck-lace is only a temporary solution to a much larger problem. I don't think Roark is just going to let us wander off into the good night and do our thing.

He doesn't want to let us go.

This whole mess is about him not accepting my choice.

We're important to him, although not for the reasons I let myself believe once.

Even if I'm able to convince Ryan that we have to both go legit, Roark's going to find a way to tug us back in. And, if I'm very unlucky, he might find out that I care about Elaine and decide he wants to use her against me too.

You're falling in love with her.

The thought passes through my mind like fluff from a blown

dandelion, catching and sticking, ready to sprout five hundred new dandelions like a pestilence. It should be impossible. A man shouldn't be able to fall in love with a woman he's known for two weeks.

Leave it to me to go my whole life without falling in love with a woman and then to leap into it like I'm cliff-jumping, without any sense of survival.

When my phone rings at around four with a call from Anthony Rosings Smith, it almost comes as a relief. I'm so desperate to talk to anyone that he'll do.

I nearly fumble the phone in my need to answer it.

"Hey, man, what's up?" I say, continuing to pace across the living room floor, the creaks and squeaks rising up in the same places with each pass.

"I was wondering if you could get a drink tonight instead of tomorrow." He sounds like I feel—hopped up on nerves and adrenaline, which stirs my curiosity. Did he find the necklace in his fiancée's things? If he did, would he tell a guy he'd known for three weeks?

Here's to hoping.

"What time?" I ask, my brow furrowing. Elaine and I are supposed to break into his house tonight. Does this mean he's cancelled his plan to attend that god-awful play with his mother and fiancée?

He swears under his breath. "There's somewhere I need to be at seven. I don't suppose..."

"I'm free," I say. Glancing at the wall clock—4 p.m.—I say, "My last client just left. Where do you want to go, the peanut bar?"

His laugh rumbles across the line. "You must think I'm absurd, choosing a place like that."

"Maybe you just have a thing for peanuts. I hear they're popular with jelly."

"I don't. It's... There's something I have to get off my chest, and I don't want to be overheard by anyone I know."

"So not a lot of peanut fans in your life, got it," I say.

He pauses, and I can practically hear his crank turning on the other side of the line. "You're still seeing my mother's assistant."

I nod, then realize he can't very well see me. "I am."

"Can you keep this—"

"You don't even need to say the words. I'm a therapist. Confidentiality is the name of the game."

I say it without a stutter, feeling like a real shithead as the words come out. But I need that necklace to save my brother, and no one in his family seems to actually care about it except as a belonging to put in a box—a show of power and money. Besides, I have every intention of giving him solid advice, or as solid as someone who's been a career criminal for most of their life can offer—unless he's about to ask me if he should bring the stolen necklace to the play and slip it into his mother's bag.

"Thank you. I mean it."

"I'll see you there in fifteen minutes, man."

"*Thank you*," he repeats, then ends the call.

My heart is thumping hard, because this could be it. This could be over tonight. I could be on a flight back to New York by midnight...

It could all be over.

Suddenly it feels like the ground's dropping from beneath my feet. *I don't want to leave.* I definitely don't want to leave and not come back, but that's the preferred method of leaving the scene of a crime.

I slump down, sitting where I was standing, and Professor X stalks up and then curls up in my lap. "I don't know what to do about any of this," I tell her.

She gives me the kind of unimpressed look I'm used to getting from her now-owner, then meows.

No one's ever thought to teach me cat, but a stopped clock is right twice a day, and I know what she's saying: *Yes, you do.*

I could trust Elaine and take Damien and Nicole into my confidence. I could tell them everything and let the chips fall as they may. I *could* do that.

But panic presses in on me again, because this isn't just about trusting them with my fate and Ryan's. If I tell them everything, they could throw it down with Roark, and they could lose.

If I tell them, I could be putting them—and especially her—in danger.

Only...based on what she said, she thinks there's a very strong possibility that Nicole and Damien will learn everything anyway. Wouldn't it be better to be the one to tell them myself? Maybe, if I do, they'll allow me a role in deciding what happens next.

Sucking in air slowly, I try to breathe steadily—in and out, in and out—and when I'm no longer dancing on the edge of panic, I text Elaine:

> Sounds like the play's still on, but Anthony asked to move drinks up to tonight. I'm guessing he's about to tell me something important and probably relevant. Meet you at the spot at 7?

We've already discussed the best strategic place to leave her car so we can get in and out of Anthony's house without being seen. Now, we'll leave both cars there.

I see a few dots ripple across the screen before disappearing. It happens again, then again, and finally her answer pops up.

> OK.

I glance at Professor X, who's pawing my shirt. "Got any insight into that?"

This time her meow is distinctly just a meow.

I tell myself it's nothing. Elaine is hopped up on nerves and adrenaline just like I am. But my gut doesn't like it.

I should probably decide what to do before I leave the house, but I don't. The only strategy I have is the one that's gotten me this far in my sorry life—jumping in the deep end and hoping like hell I remember how to swim.

———

WHEN I GET to the peanut bar, Anthony's already there, sitting in a booth with a couple of beers, which is a first. The last time we were here, he got white wine. I guess it was bad enough that he didn't want to go in for a second round, which isn't a shocker. Getting wine from a place like this is like going to a restaurant called Fried Freddies and ordering a salad. In a nod to the holiday, there are a couple of uncarved pumpkins sitting on top of the bar, plus circus peanuts sitting in a skeleton bowl on the counter. Judging from the height of the pile, no one's gone in for one, and I won't be the first.

I join Anthony, grinning. "Is one of those for me, or is the situation bad enough that you're double-fisting on a Thursday?"

His smile is barely a quirk of the lips as he pushes one of the beers across the table. I sit. I drink.

"What's on your mind?" I ask after he's silent for a solid thirty seconds.

"It's about Nina."

I try not to lean forward in my seat. "Oh? Are you two having problems?"

He glances around, confirms most of the people he knows wouldn't be caught dead here, and also that the bartender doesn't give a shit about anything but pounding down peanuts and whatever he's watching on his phone, and says, "My father never thought much of me. He…he died young, but he'd already made a will."

He pauses, takes a drink of the beer.

"I have a trust…a trust with a lot of money in it, but I don't gain full access to it until I'm thirty-four, the age my father was when he 'built his empire.' Everything was symbolic with him."

"You don't seem to be hurting financially," I point out.

"No," he says with a bitter smile. "I get an allowance from the trust. I'm a thirty-three-year-old man with *an allowance.*"

"What's the catch?" I ask, because if there wasn't one, we wouldn't be here.

He glances at the bored bartender again before saying, "I have to be married by the time I'm thirty-four. That's the only way I'll get full access. If I'm not married, I'll lose it—and the business deal I've been working on for six months goes down the drain."

I whistle. "Does your sister get the same deal?"

"No," he says tightly. "She had a smaller trust, but it's all hers. He thought I was weak and would need to tether myself to someone stronger to succeed. He gave my mother full veto power over my bride."

"Ah." Only…Mrs. Rosings has made it very fucking clear she doesn't want Anthony to marry Nina, so why hasn't she exercised this supposed veto power?

"I can see you're wondering why she hasn't said no," he says with a grunt. "After my father died, she promised me she'd never use that clause against me."

"You're worried she'll change her mind," I comment.

"No." He runs his finger over the condensation on his glass of beer. "I mean…maybe she will, but that's not what I'm really worried about. I'm worried she's right. Nina knows about my father's will. We started seeing each other right after Christmas, and it was casual. It was *fun.* We went to amusement parks and shitty restaurants and dive bars. She didn't know who I was, not really, and I didn't know much about her other than that she wasn't really career-driven. But we got drunk one night, and I told her about my father's will and my birthday coming up in January. Less than a year away. She's the one who said she'd marry me to help me gain the trust. So we got engaged, and all of this was set in motion, and she's *changed*."

"Do you have a prenup?" I ask.

A corner of his mouth lifts. "My mother's right. Nina's marrying me for the money, but I'm marrying her for the money too." He turns the glass around in his hand, takes a long pull before saying, "There's no prenup. There's no money if there's no wedding. That's something else we agreed on."

He must see the doubt on my face because he snorts and says, "It's not just the business deal that gets buried if I don't get the money. The company will die, and I'll go down in Marshall history as the Smith who lost it *all*."

"Where does the money go if it doesn't go to you?"

"Causes I don't particularly believe in. Insult to injury. He knew what he was doing."

"He knew what causes you supported as a twelve-year-old?" I ask doubtfully.

"He knew what causes my mother *didn't* support. Anything to drive a wedge between people."

I genuinely feel for him. I may not have ever known my father, but it's easier to guess that your old man's a dick who doesn't care about you than to spend your life in the shadow of that knowledge. Then again, the only semi-parent I had besides foster parents who came and went like the wind is currently holding my brother hostage.

"Well, shit," I say. "That's a hard pill to swallow."

"I don't know what to do," he admits, sitting back. "If I don't marry her, I'm fucked, but I'm starting to think that if I do marry her—"

"Damned if you do, damned if you don't," I agree.

Based on what he's told me, he definitely had motivation to steal that necklace, but I don't think he'd be sitting here with me if he had it.

It's still possible Nina has it.

This confirms she's definitely motivated by money. She probably doesn't want to marry him any more than he wants to marry her—and it's possible she took the necklace and is only sticking around because she's worried the person who replaced it might figure out it was her.

"But it's too late to find anyone else," he says, slumping back. My birthday's in two and half months."

"You could find someone else who'd do it for the money, but then you'd sort of be in the same fix. You said she's changed...*how* has she changed?"

He runs a hand across his mouth. "We used to have fun together, but that changed a couple of months after we got engaged. She stopped hanging out with her old friends, and the places we used to go weren't good enough anymore. It's all about the money now. What we're going to do with it. What house we're going to buy until we can move into Smith House. That kind of thing." He pauses. Swallows. "She's...her parents aren't in her life. She said it was her choice. I hoped planning the wedding would bring her and my mother closer together, but Nina's handed off everything to my mom, who's done her best to make it as awful as possible to get a reaction. Nina hates her, obviously, but she hasn't fought back. She doesn't really care about the wedding. She doesn't care about me either...all she wants is her piece, same as everyone else. She'll never love me, and I'm starting to think..." He pauses again. "I don't even *like* her anymore. She's jealous whenever I talk to another woman, but everything I do is wrong, and she *never* wants to touch me anymore." He laughs without the slightest bit of humor. "It's like my father hand-picked her for me, if you want to know the truth. He'd love the irony."

He looks really torn up, and even though I'd *also* like several million dollars, I feel bad for him. I've seen this before, with Dale—how being rich can be as isolating as being poor. I feel another surge of sympathy for him.

"Are you asking me what to do?" I ask.

His lips turn up again. "I don't know," he admits. "I guess I just needed to get it off my chest. I'm not sure there's much I can do, unless I'm willing to let the company fold. That's what my sister Emma thinks I should do. She's a divorce attorney, for fuck's sake, and she thinks I'm worse than an idiot for agreeing to no prenup. But I can't do it. I can't be the one who ruins everything. It's not just about the Smith family legacy—I've got hundreds of people working for me. They're counting on me to get it right."

"You could still find someone else to marry," I insist.

"Why bother?" he asks, his tone falling into bitterness. "Why exchange one gold digger for another?"

Some fanciful part of me, awakened by Lainey, wants to tell him it would be a fuck-ton better to marry a woman you could possibly love than to marry a woman you absolutely know you can't. But I sense logic will work better with him, so I say, "But you don't have to be in a relationship with the person you marry. You could hire someone to be your wife. Get your sister to pull together an ironclad prenup and pay the woman a set fee. There are plenty of women who'd be willing to do it."

He rubs his head as if this idea hadn't occurred to him. "What would people think if I got married so soon after ending an engagement?" he asks after a moment.

I shrug. "Probably that you're an asshole, but I'm going to be honest with you, plenty of people already think that."

Surprised laughter gusts from him, and he shakes his head

slightly as he smiles at me. "This is why I like you, Jake. You're willing to be honest with me. I can't say that about a lot of people."

It's my own bitter pill, and I swallow it.

"Think it through," I say. "I may know someone who can help you if that's the way you want to go. You've already got the wedding planned. All you'd need to do is sub out the bride."

Maybe this is a job for the Love Fixers. It's possible Lainey is only interested in helping women who've been wronged, but if we're going to screw this guy over by finding and taking the real Heart of the Mountain, the least we can do is soothe the scratch.

He nods slowly. "I will." Then he takes out his phone and sighs. "I've got to go. I'm going to the community theater with my mother and Nina."

"Thoughts and prayers," I say with a smile, then, "Hey, are we still on for Sunday?"

He nods miserably, as if he's agreeing to his execution. "I don't know what good will come of it, but yes. I'd appreciate your read on the situation. Thanks for connecting me to the woman who makes the tea."

He trusts me, and again, I feel a stab of unworthiness. I'm the asshole here. I've tried not to like him—to see him as a person unworthy of friendship and courtesy—but I'm not capable of doing that anymore.

Dale started my awakening by offering me that watch, but Lainey has continued it. Because she's shown me how different it feels to form a genuine connection with someone—to let them see glimpses of the ugliness inside of you without flinching away.

I don't blame Anthony for wanting something real for himself. And, more alarmingly, I want it for him. I definitely don't want him to be stuck marrying Nina.

Anthony swears to himself, then looks at me. It hits me that while he's normally clean-shaven, he has a heavy five-o'clock shadow. He's falling apart at the seams—driven to the point of breaking by a man who left his life almost a quarter of a century ago, a woman who doesn't love him, and a mother whose love is suffocating.

It's strange to think of the impact people can have on us even after they're gone—the crater they leave behind to be filled by other things. It's even stranger to think of creating such a crater.

I think about Dale often. I think about his busboy hats and broad white mustache, and the way he used to swear under his breath whenever anyone broke a traffic law but never swore otherwise. I think about the way he held out that box to me, his eyes full of warmth and pride—of belief in me, the stranger who was trying to pull one over.

I wonder if I caused him lasting harm, which leads me to wonder about the other people whose lives I've touched. Have I taught them to distrust? To hate? Do they know Ryan and I were the ones who stole from them?

Anthony shakes his head, then says, "I haven't asked you a single thing about yourself. How's it going with Elaine?"

"You know what, man? It's actually going great."

CHAPTER THIRTY-ONE

JAKE

Half an hour later, I pull into the parking lot at the trailhead behind Anthony and Nina's home in North Asheville, my agreed-upon meeting place with Elaine. Warmth floods me when I see her sitting in her car. I've become pretty fond of her car, even though it looks a little worse every time I see it—like maybe she's been using it for target practice whenever she's pissed off.

I pull in several spaces down from her, then walk over. She gets out to greet me, and I go in for a kiss, but she moves her head at the last second. My lips land on the bridge of her nose, so I make do and kiss her there, across a sprinkling of freckles. I expect her to laugh about it, but she doesn't, her mouth pressed into a stony line.

Alarm floods my gut, and I find myself remembering those three dots that Professor X didn't have much of an opinion on. Something happened.

Or, maybe she's realized she was making a mistake with me— that I'm not a man who could make her happy for the long haul.

"What did Anthony want?" she asks, her words clipped.

I nod to her car. "Let's sit in there, and I'll tell you."

"Won't it look suspicious?"

"I'll give you a quick rundown."

So we get in, and I tell her what I've learned about their engagement.

"So he knows," she says once I've finished.

"That she's marrying him for money? Yeah."

"At least *he* was honest with her."

I turn in my seat to more fully face her. "What are you talking about?"

I've been more truthful with Elaine than I should have been. More truthful than I've been with anyone else in my life.

"Why'd you turn down the guy who wanted to give you the watch, Jake?" she asks, studying me as if my answer might solve world hunger. "Why would you turn down someone who was offering you exactly what you wanted?"

It's obviously a trick question, but I don't hesitate to answer. "Because I didn't deserve it. The person he thought he was giving it to didn't exist. Taking it from him would have been wrong."

Anthony's grappling with similar truths, I guess. His situation hasn't instrumentally changed since he asked Nina to marry him, but now he's realizing that marrying for money feels like marrying for money.

"You *didn't* deserve it," she says, her tone harsh as she stares out the windshield. "You fooled him into offering it to you. An old man."

I can hear the accusation underlying her words. *You've fooled me into helping you too.* It's like she just swung a tire iron into my stomach, and the pain won't stop rippling through me.

I place my fingertips lightly under her chin, turning her head toward me, because I need her to look me in the eye right now. "What the fuck happened? Where is this coming from?"

But I already know what must have happened.

Damien and Nicole have both been gone.

One of them found Dale. They talked to him, and he told them that I came back for the watch. He must have told them that I'd accepted it and then turned my back on him. Disappeared.

The thought feels like an amoeba eating me up from the inside.

If I tell her...

"Damien had a very interesting conversation with the owner of that watch," she confirms, sweeping her hair out of her face as if it offended her.

"You think you know everything," I say, and in my voice I hear the same bitterness I heard from Anthony.

"What don't I know?" she challenges.

My heart races, and there's a voice inside that whispers I should tell her. Nicole and Damien are going to find out soon enough, so I might as well just say the words. But it hurts that she believed the worst, even though most thinking people would.

I'm not a man who should be trusted. I accept that. But I wanted *her* to trust me. I wanted it with every broken, jagged piece of my soul, and I thought we'd reached a place of trust and mutual regard. The past couple of nights, with Lainey curled up beside me, I felt like a new man. A man who suddenly had a lot to lose. But now it's gone as easily as if it had been made of smoke or mist.

"Do you even have a brother?" she asks, her voice hard, her eyes as cold as chocolate chips left in the freezer.

"Wow," I say, already getting out of the car. I need to move. I need to *go*. "*Wow*."

"What are you doing?" she hisses. Seconds later, she's clambering out of the driver's side after me.

"What I came here to do."

I'm furious with myself. I let myself forget why I was here. Despite those daily texts from Roark, I let myself forget that this whole thing is about saving Ryan—the one person who really *does* trust and rely on me. It was stupid of me to think otherwise, to let myself get pulled into these peoples' lives as if I could matter to them.

It was like that when I was a kid. Ryan and I would get used to a foster home, we'd come to rely on it. And then, once again, we'd be taken away and brought to a new one. The only person who lasted for him was me, and me for him.

It's better not to rely on other people, and smarter not to rely on them so quickly.

Still, those dandelion seeds are inside of me. I'm riddled with them. With sprouts of love for this woman who's staring at me, again, like I'm an accident that dared to dirty the bottom of her shoe.

So I look away and start to pick through the trees that'll eventually land me in Anthony Rosings Smith's backyard.

She's quiet, but I hear her moving right beside me, lithe and graceful as always, but angry. Really fucking angry.

Well, so am I. Mostly, I'm angry at myself, but I'm angry at her too. I'm angry that she'd think so little of me that I'd lie about Ryan, and lie a lot.

The two-story house looms in front of us through the trees, visible long before we reach the yard. No fence. No cameras, or at least Mrs. Rosings told Lainey there aren't any. Anthony wants to live a 'normal' life. The house is a dark blue that's vaguely depressing, as if it's somewhere light goes to die. The roof is metal and modern and probably makes it sound like popcorn is popping whenever it rains.

Elaine grabs my arm, her touch radiating through me. "They're gone. Mrs. Rosings just texted me."

"Fantastic," I say tightly, taking another step.

She tugs harder. "Jake, I'm not going to let you take that necklace if it's here."

"Try and stop me," I say, even though I'm pretty sure she fucking could. I'd die before hurting her, and if she got the jump on me, the way she did at Smith House, I might not be able to dislodge her without doing her harm.

I make my way to the back door, Elaine still gripping my arm. But when we reach it, she drops her hold. In mutual agreement, we creep around the side of the house to verify that there's only one car in the driveway before returning to our spot at the back door. She lets me take out my toolkit, but I can feel her watching me with disdain. With the bitter knowledge that I've done this before. It makes me feel like a stain on humanity, and even though it's not fair, I resent her for that.

For treating me like someone who deserved to be loved and then realizing what everyone else has: that a man who does bad things is, deep down, a bad man.

I get to work with my tools, and after a couple of minutes the lock clicks over.

"You sold yourself short," she says, her voice bitter. "I'd give you at least an A-."

I ignore her. I don't look at her. I can't.

I just swing the door wider and let her follow me in, hearing the slight creak as she closes it behind us, leaving us in the darkness of a living room. It's smaller than I would have thought, with a sedate but classy beige sofa, love seat, and chair set, an expensive-as-fuck-looking coffee table, and a flat screen TV. There's some framed art propped against the wall, as if Anthony and Nina couldn't agree about what to put up so decided on nothing—or maybe she took down what he already had up.

From what little he's told me, I'm guessing it's the latter.

"I'm not going to let you take it," Elaine reminds me.

"The way my day is going, it's probably not even in here." I sigh. "We should probably split up so we can get through the house quicker."

She laughs without any humor. "Yeah, right. You're not going anywhere without me."

"Okay, ball and chain," I say flatly. "Where do you suggest we start?"

"The bedroom."

"Too obvious," I say. "I'm guessing the kitchen."

A snort escapes her as she surveys the bland room, taking in the same details I noticed. "You think either of them cook?"

"No," I say pointedly. "That's why we're starting in there. She'd want to hide it somewhere he wouldn't easily find it."

We go through every cupboard, look inside every dusty glass and bowl. Nothing.

So I let Lainey decide where to look next. There's nothing in the bedroom, but it's worth noting that it doesn't look like two people have been sleeping in here. There's a king bed with slate gray covers and an amount of throw pillows that suggests a woman's touch. One nightstand has a glass of water, a *Southern Living* magazine with reading tabs, and an iPad. The other small table is completely empty.

I glance at Elaine, then try to turn on the iPad.

No one's more surprised than me when it opens for 0000, especially when I pull up the messaging app, and the first thing I see is the image of a man's hand wrapped around his dick.

"Ugh," I say. "I both really hope and really do not hope that's Anthony's dick."

Elaine glances at the screen, looking almost crestfallen. "It's not. This guy's blond. Look at the hair."

Well, shit, I'd rather not. I feel another round of sympathy for my pretend buddy.

Steeling myself, I minimize the dick pic and scroll through the other texts. There's nothing about the necklace, but plenty about what the unidentified sender would like to do with her with his blond dick.

I close the iPad, wipe it down, and return it to the table.

Both closets are full, one with his clothes, the other with hers. She has jewelry, but the Heart of the Mountain isn't sitting out and waiting for us.

"Where to next?" Lainey asks.

"I think he's been staying in the guest room."

"Or that very nice couch," she agrees.

"Let's check the bathroom?"

We search that next and find nothing except some vaginal itch cream I really wish I could unsee in a surprisingly messy medicine cabinet.

Next, we do a lightning quick check of the two guest bedrooms upstairs and find them disinteresting.

It's been about an hour. The play, presuming Mrs. Rosings can terrify Anthony and Nina into staying, is three.

"The basement," Elaine says next, so we head down there together. It's only a basement in the strictest sense of the word—there are wood floors, plush rugs, and an enormous black leather sectional couch, but there's also a huge walk-in closet. And when we open it and flick on the punishing overhead light, we see a stack of black leather luggage at the far end, under a shelf supporting a dozen or so games that look unopened.

Elaine and I exchange a glance.

"The bottom one," we say at the same time, and I almost smile. But I don't. Even though we've been working together, it's with the knowledge that she no longer trusts me. I lift the other bags off, and she pulls the bottom one out.

When she opens it, she immediately glances up at me. Because it's full of neatly folded clothing and a toiletries case.

"The toiletries case," I say hoarsely, and she unzips it, still kneeling beside the suitcase.

The Heart of the Mountain isn't in there. But there *are* five other very expensive pieces nestled inside.

"I'm pretty sure these are Mrs. Rosings's," Elaine says, giving me a sidelong look.

"Looks like Nina definitely changed her mind about the wedding." I swallow through my dry throat. "She doesn't have the necklace. If she had it, it would be here. Maybe she took these during the power outage instead. Easier access."

"Either that, or she's already in the process of selling the Heart of the Mountain to someone," Elaine says. "Or having it evaluated."

Which would still put it beyond my reach. I'm exactly where I started, only now I'm a little more broken. I stare woodenly down at the toiletries case, splayed open on top of the bag.

"They're worth a lot of money," Elaine comments, her eyes on the jewels. Then she looks up at me, a challenge simmering in her gaze. "You can take them and leave. Mrs. Rosings doesn't know they're here. No one will know it was you. I won't tell."

It's obviously a test, but it means she's not convinced I won't take her up on it. Part of her believes I'll take those necklaces and run. I probably deserve that kind of doubt, but it feels like my heart just got sprayed with acid.

"I need the Heart of the Mountain to save my brother," I grit out as she pushes to her feet. "I could give a shit about stealing your boss's jewelry, however much it's worth."

She holds my gaze, studying me, and whatever she sees there changes her. Her gaze softens; something inside of her seems to give. She spans the small distance between us, her nearness bringing her spicy jasmine scent to me. A stray dark hair tickles me as she tips her face up to me, her expression all hellcat. "Jake...why did the old man think you took his watch?"

Think.

That means she doesn't fully believe it.

Still, my feelings are sore, and I say, "You told me you know everything."

I go to step away, but she reaches for my shirt, grabbing fistfuls of it to keep me in place.

Her eyes boring into me in the low light, she asks, "*Why?*"

"I didn't take it," I say, my heart pounding, everything in me needing her to believe me. "I wouldn't. I *liked* him. He..." I search for words that will fully encompass what Dale's offer did to me. The way he held out something precious to him and told me to take it. *Me*. My voice is strangled as I add, "He changed my life."

"So why was he so sure you took it? Damien showed him a photo."

I don't say anything—*I can't*. My need for her to believe me, to trust me, has rendered me mute. I just stare back at her.

Something flashes in her eyes. "He thought it was you, but it wasn't."

I don't flinch, but I don't tell her. I wait.

"You're twins. You and Ryan are identical twins. He gave it to Ryan because he thought he was giving it to you."

An old ugliness is unleashed in my gut. I couldn't talk to Ryan after that, not for months, not until Roark called me to say he'd caught my brother trying to steal the watch back. Because I cared about Dale, and now he only remembers me as one more person who screwed him over.

"You thought the worst of me," I say, the words coming out harsh. "You *immediately* thought the worst of me. You're the one person who I thought understood me. Even more than Ryan..."

She pulls on her two fistfuls of shirt. For a second, I think she's about to slap me, but then her soft lips are pressing against mine. Maybe this is just her way of saying goodbye, but even if it is, I can't bring myself to say no.

I back her into an area of the wall empty of shelves, attacking her mouth, because I have a need for her that's feverish and probably not entirely sane. Her hand slips down to my pants, my button, my zipper, and I swear into her mouth. A fucking kickball falls from the shelf next to us, jostled free, and hits me in the head, but it doesn't stop me for more than the half a second it takes to swear.

We shouldn't be doing this here in their house. They could

come back, for one thing, for another, we'll be leaving behind plenty of DNA, not that we intend to steal anything. But it doesn't matter. I need her more than I need the air in my lungs and the ground at my feet. I fucking *need* her. And I need her to forgive me for the things I'm not sure I can forgive myself for.

She pushes down my pants and my underwear, her hand wrapping around me roughly. A hiss escapes me, captured by her lips, and she swallows it up, as greedy as I am.

I pull away enough to say, "I don't have anything with me."

"I don't care."

Jesus. "I can't risk..."

She's staring into my eyes, my dick in her hand, and I can tell from the flash of understanding in her eyes that she gets it. My mother, knocked up at seventeen. My mother, abandoning us.

She understands me. She really fucking does.

"I'm on the pill."

I tug her hand, earning an angry sound from her, but then I get down on my knees and flip up her dress. Capturing the side of her underwear in my teeth, I pull them down, glancing up at her. Watching her watch me, her eyes wide with lust. When her panties get past her knees, they fall the rest of the way. As she steps out of them, still in her shoes, I rise back up, pausing to lick and suck, my head fully buried under the bottom of her dress.

I meant to just go in for a quick taste, but I grip her hips and go in deeper, wanting more of her, wanting to show her what I can give her. What we are together. Wanting to bury myself inside of her and stay because when we're together I feel better than okay. I feel happy. I feel...hopeful. And when I'm tasting her and feeling her writhe against me, I'm a god among men.

Her hand weaves into my hair, keeping me in place and then pulling me up.

"I need you inside of me *right now*," she says, her eyes shiny, and fuck, is she crying? I didn't want to make her cry. I want her happy, joyful, and writhing with pleasure, but not crying.

I lift my hand, tracing through the wetness lingering on her bottom lashes.

"Right now, Jake," she repeats.

So I do what my woman has fucking asked. I lift her up, and she wraps her legs around me as I back her into the wall.

I flip up her dress, and in seconds I'm buried deep inside of her —the relief of it nearly enough to make my eyes roll back in my head. It's even better like this, with nothing between us. Every sensation is ten times brighter, sharper. She bites the lobe of my ear, arcing into me, encouraging me not so gently to get on with it.

"I don't want to leave you," I admit as I pull out and then stroke back in hard, her shoes digging into my back.

"So don't," she says, as if it's the simplest thing in the world and I'm an idiot for not having considered it. Maybe I am. I would be, if I gave away the best gift I've ever been given. Because something tells me that my only chance of making something of myself lies with this woman.

I lower my head, still moving inside her, and kiss the tops of her tits, her neck, her jaw, her lips—every bit of her that I can reach, while I claim what I'd like to be mine. Her body strains against me, meeting every thrust, one of her hands lowering to my ass so she can push me in deeper, the other one burying in my hair. Every bit of me is hers. She owns it if she wants it; and if she doesn't, it's her right to throw it away.

"Jake," she says on a gasp, "Jake, I'm coming."

Music to my ears. I feel her grip around me, and I fall over the edge with her, my lips on hers, my dick buried so deep that I see stars.

This, I think, is true happiness.

Love, a voice in my head whispers, and I can't find it in myself to call it an idiot.

CHAPTER THIRTY-TWO

LAINEY

I've never felt like this before.

That truth has been dancing around the edges of my brain all week, but now, with Jake buried inside of me in the closet of a home we've broken into...

I can't deny it anymore

He said he doesn't want to leave me, and I want to believe him. I want to believe that we can build something beautiful together.

I want to believe it so badly, the tears I've tried holding back threaten to track down my cheeks. Because I have something I don't want to lose, and I'm worried it will be taken away.

He leans his forehead down against mine and whispers my name, still inside of me. Like he really doesn't want to leave. "You think we're the first people to ever fuck in here?"

I shove his arm, laughing a little as he pulls out and sets me on my feet.

I feel the loss of him and of the moment.

He leans down and kisses me, then pauses and kisses me again, like he can't help himself. "We have to get out of here," he says. Then he nods at the open suitcase, which we left splayed on the ground. "You should take photos for your boss."

"You think I should tell her?" I ask, surprised.

"I don't want you to get in trouble because of me." He pauses, tucking himself away and zipping up his pants. "And Anthony's a good guy, mostly. He deserves a head's up...especially because of blond dick."

"You don't think Nina took the necklace," I confirm.

His lips firm, and he shakes his head. And I feel a burn of shame for having doubted for even a second that he has a brother. He wears his concern for Ryan like a cloak. "No," he says hoarsely. "Anthony either. Maybe Emma has it. Or Mrs. Rosings. Maybe she'll admit something's up if she sees that photo."

"Nicole's coming back from Charlotte," I say. "She can help us. She's good at this kind of thing. Plus we still have the tea this weekend. If anyone can make them talk, it's Joy."

"What if none of the Rosings Smiths have it?" he says. "We've been assuming they do, but it could have been any of the guests at that party."

"Then we'll find another way," I insist.

He smiles at me and bends to kiss my forehead. "Thank you."

"I'm sorry I thought the worst," I gush. "Bad habit. It's hard for me to—"

He weaves our hands together and lifts mine to kiss the back. It feels like his lips leave a tattoo—a mark I'll carry forever. "It's hard for me to trust people too. It was rational of you to question me." Then he drops my hand and pulls his phone out of his pocket. He pulls something up before handing it to me.

It's his text conversation with ASSHOLE. I scroll through it, my mouth dropping open, because there are a few proof-of-life photos of Ryan. His hair is slightly shorter than Jake's, but the lines of his face and the shape of his eyes are the same. His body has the same fluid grace, and even the fox on fire is in the same position on his arm.

"You look almost exactly alike," I say.

His mouth quirks up. "*Almost?*"

I study one of the photos, trying to put my finger on what makes Ryan look different to me. "It's the black tooth."

"Very funny," he says, reclaiming his phone.

I capture his hand. "It's the set of his jaw, the way he's sitting, and the little scar under his lip. It's a dozen different little things, but he's not you."

He smiles at me as if this pleases him, then nods again at the suitcase. I take out my phone to get the photos of the jewelry.

Afterward, we pack it back up the way it was, returning it to the bottom of the stack. The ball goes back in its place too, and we flick off the light. I use the bathroom to clean up, drying off the sink so it doesn't look like anyone used it, and we leave the way we came, Jake locking the door behind us.

We walk back toward the car hand in hand. I wait until we're in the woods to ask, "That's why he wanted you, isn't it? The man—"

"His name's Roark," Jake says.

My heart soars, because this means he's decided to accept our help, all the way. "Roark," I repeat. "He wanted you because you were twins. Because one of you could be talking to the mark while the other took whatever he wanted."

He gazes at me in the dark as we circle a tree. "Sure. It's the perfect alibi if no one finds out. But I didn't realize that when I was a kid. I thought he was just helping us. One abandoned kid to another. He told us he'd been a foster kid too. Of course, that was probably a bunch of bullshit, but I didn't figure it out until later."

"He used you," I say, fury beating into the words.

He squeezes my hand, a smile playing on his lips. "We might have been kids when we met him, but we haven't been kids for a long time. Still, I'll gladly accept your righteous fury on my behalf."

"I'm upset about Nina, too," I admit.

He tucks his arm around me. "I know. But maybe we don't just help women who've been heartbroken and used. Maybe we help anyone who deserves some vindication."

I glance up at him, surprised, and see his eyes glimmering in the night. "You want to help Anthony?"

"I do." He swallows, his Adam's apple bobbing attractively in his throat, my fingers wanting to capture it, my teeth to bite. "I think we should. He's a case for the Love Fixers if I've ever seen one."

He's talking about the future like it's something we're going to share. Hope blossoms in my chest, and with any luck it's not the kind of bloom that lasts for only one day—beautiful and then dead. I want to preserve it in glass.

We get to our cars, and Jake kisses me softly before opening my door for me. I get in behind my wheel and watch while he does the same. Seconds later, a hand snakes around from the back and grabs my shoulder.

"Jesus!" I scream as I turn around in my seat.

"I've been called worse," Nicole says, laughing. She's wearing a beanie, a black shirt, and leggings—robbery gear.

"Did you follow us to the house?"

"I did," she says with a grin, "and then back. I saw you canoodling with the thief, so air high five for winning my bet for me. I figured Damien had it in the bag when he found out about the old guy and the watch. He figured so too. He was gloating, but that won't last."

"There's something seriously wrong with you two," I say, my heart settling back into a more natural rhythm. "Are you riding home with me, or do you have your car here?"

"I took an Uber to the greenway," she says as she climbs into the front seat next to me.

Jake rolls down his window a few cars down. "You've got to stop picking up strays," he says. He's joking, but I hear a thread of worry in his voice. He's concerned she'll convince me not to trust him.

"It worked out okay for me last weekend," I tell him, rolling my window down to answer. The fall air comes seeping in, smelling of pine and crushed leaves. "I'll see you back at the house."

Turning forward, I say, "Buckle up, buttercup."

She rolls her eyes but does it, and I pull out of the lot a few beats after Jake.

"So, as happy as I am to have won my bet," Nicole says, "*why* were you canoodling with the watch thief? Do you have a secret fetish for the tears of old men?"

"He didn't do it," I say. "He has an identical twin."

She gives me a doubting look and scratches her head under the hat. "When a man tells you his identical twin did it, Lainey, you should absolutely punch him in the face."

"I saw photos of Ryan," I tell her, since 'I believe him,' won't wash. "He exists. That's why this guy doesn't want to lose them. They're the perfect thieves."

Her eyes light up. "Holy shit, seriously? Twins wig me out, but we need to get the other one and make a pair."

"We're not going to use them," I say tightly, moving slowly through the neighborhood. "They've already been used enough."

"No, no." She waves a hand, grimacing when someone outside the car waves back. "We're not going to use them. They're going to use other people for us. For a good cause, obviously."

I decide not to object. If this is the motivation she needs to find and help Ryan, I'm all for it.

I quickly tell her about what we found, from the blond guy's dick pic to the stash of Mrs. Rosings's jewels.

Nicole whistles, her eyes glimmering in the dark. "You still got a boner for saving Nina?"

I sigh. "Fine, I'll admit it, I was projecting. She's a jerk. Jake actually thinks we should help Anthony once this is all settled."

She laughs softly in the dark. "Well, all right. Hiring someone who's willing to marry a hot millionaire will probably be the easiest gig we can get."

"Famous last words," I say. "Did you get anything else out of Emma?"

She puckers her mouth. "She's a worthy adversary, but I don't think she has the necklace. She's got plenty of money, and when I brought up the documentary, she seemed annoyed. Didn't get a *my precious* vibe. But..." She shrugs. "Worthy adversary. It's possible. Right now, my money's on the old lady. Maybe she snatched it to set up Nina, and now she's wondering if dementia has set in because she's got an exact copy sitting in her case."

I nod, but I'm not convinced. There's still a chance Nina stole it and hid it somewhere other than the suitcase—or even gave it to blond dick guy.

When I pull up to the cabin, Jake's already parked in the driveway, next to Nicole's car. He's standing by the driver's side door, leaning against it as he watches us pull in, and relief travels through me as quickly as the growth cycle of an invasive plant. Part of me worried he wouldn't come back—that he'd freak out after telling me about Ryan and Roark, especially knowing that Nicole was in the car with me.

"Something's different between you," Nicole comments as I turn off the engine. "And it's not just the power of the peen."

I roll my eyes at her, and she shocks me by saying, "You know, the reason I didn't pull the trigger on Todd was because I knew you'd do it yourself when the time came."

"You did?"

She pats my arm. "My sister needed help getting revenge. You didn't." She pulls a face. "Then again, all you really did was ruin his most prized possession and send it back to him in splinters."

"You know about that?"

"You used the Love Fixers' mailing account."

I nod, because that was a rookie move, then tell her, "I'm sure it emotionally destroyed him. He cares about that bat more than he does about any living person."

She studies me in the dark. "And yet he let you take it."

"Who says he let me? I said he knew I had it. He may be a big man in the board room, or those parties he goes to, but I don't think anyone had ever stolen anything from him before. And when I found out he'd been cheating on me, I invited him to the park for a picnic and then set his expensive collared shirts on fire in front of him. I think he's afraid of me."

She grunts with amusement. "What about your parents?"

"I took away the one investment they put the most time and money into."

"Don't tell me you're talking about this hideous car."

I laugh. "No. Me. I think that's enough revenge."

She considers this for a second before nodding. "I'm not worried about you at all. You, Lainey Catlan, might have gotten lost for a while, but you know exactly who you are and what you're doing. Even your fuckup with the thief ended up okay."

In that moment, I believe her. I feel better than okay, actually. I feel like I'm on the cusp of actually being the person I'm supposed to be, living the life that suits me.

If I can prevent it all from tumbling down.

We get out of the car, and Nicole claps her hands. "So...time to get drunk?"

The question is loud and asked for both Jake and me. He scratches his head and looks at me, his eyes deep and dark in the night. Then he shifts his gaze to her. "Nah, not right now. Lainey tells me I can trust you."

"Yes, but you can't trust my memory. If you're about to spill your guts, we should wait until Damien gets here. He knew about your visit to Anthony's house but not about your twin brother, so

I'm guessing he's in a hurry. We might as well have a drink or five while we wait."

"Don't you have a hangover?" I ask her, crossing the few feet that separate me from Jake and taking his hand. I'm claiming him, I guess, and my heart flutters like a trapped butterfly when he squeezes my hand, accepting the claim.

"Oh, hell yeah, this is the king daddy of hangovers," she says with a whistle. "But when I meet my adversary again, I'm going to defeat her. I need to prepare for battle. Emma Rosings Smith will never outdrink me again, mark my words."

Jake squeezes my hand and shoots me a look. "These are the people who are going to save me?"

"Yeah," I say. "I think so. God help us both."

We make a fire in the backyard and start passing around a bottle of bourbon from the kitchen—Nicole's "good stuff." The fire has barely roared into existence by the time we hear a car pull up out front. Damien circles the corner of the house half a minute later, moving fast. A look of...relief crosses his face when he sees Jake sitting with us.

"I'm guessing there's a good reason he's not tied up in the basement?" Damien asks. "Or is he torturing you with a good time?"

Laughter escapes me, and Jake leans his shoulder against mine, while Nicole gets up and takes a running jump at Damien. When he catches her, she wraps her legs around his waist, laughing in his ear. "I think they only do that when we're not home. Speaking of which, you lost our bet, hot stuff."

He kisses her and sets her down, grumbling under his breath, and I lift the bottle of bourbon. "Need a drink, Bronuts?"

He laughs as he sits in Nicole's abandoned chair, pulling her onto his lap. "I'd apologize for the bet, but I'm obviously going to pay for it." Then he takes the bottle from me and slugs back a long sip.

I feel Jake watching us, soaking everything in. I meet his gaze, and I can feel how big this is for him—to share all the things he's kept hidden for most of his life. To trust not just me but the people I care about with the most important person in his life.

I reach for his hand, and my heart swells when he threads his fingers through mine, holding on to me like I'm his lifeline.

"So what was it?" Damien asks him, his gaze sharp. "Why'd you come back and take the watch from the old guy? Were you threatened?"

Jake tells him about Ryan, then shows the photos of his brother to both Damien and Nicole.

"And your last name?" Damien asks pointedly.

Jake sucks in a breath, decides—quite rightly—that they're going to find out anyway, and besides, he's come this far...

"Langston. Jake and Ryan Langston. Roark's first name is Ed."

We drink some more as Jake tells us everything he knows about Edmund Roark. Where his apartment in NYC is located, Tribeca. How long he's been stealing high-price items from rich people, over forty years. How old he is—sixty or maybe older, but fit. He does it partly for fun. Because he doesn't sell everything he takes or hires others to take. He has a fucking *museum* of stolen things.

"You've seen this with your own eyes?" Damien asks with interest.

"No. But he's the one who bragged about it. It's not in his apartment; I've looked. But he has other real estate."

I've never met this Roark guy, but I'm pretty sure I'd like to burn his fortress down to the ground, leaving only ash. He gets off on having power over people, from Jake and his brother to the owners of his stolen toys.

"Find the museum, we got him dead to rights," Damien observes.

"I don't want to ask for any trouble, especially not when he has Ryan."

"We'll get your brother out first," Damien says, seeming

pleased. He and Nicole exchange a glance, and it hits me that all four of us are adrenaline junkies—looking for our next fix and hoping it won't bury us.

"Ryan might know," Jake says, sounding tired. "The museum is where Roark would have kept the watch." He stares into the fire for a moment, then says, "He'll have proof that my brother and I worked for him."

Nicole gives him a not-so-patient smile. "The powers that be give much less of a shit about Oliver Twist than they do about the guy who told him what to snatch. But, sure, we're sympathetic to your point. And if they know you were involved, they'll probably want to keep an eye on you. If we can do this without involving the authorities, that might be best all around."

Jake picks up the bottle of bourbon and lifts it to the sky.

"I'll drink to that."

So he does, and I do too.

Damien seeks out Jake's gaze. "Dale seemed pretty torn up about thinking something might have happened to you. You might want to reach out to him."

Jake breaks their stare-off. "I can't do that. I'd be incriminating Ryan."

"Who did nothing but take a gift that was offered to him. No criminal charges would apply."

"Identity theft. Pretending to be someone else."

"I'm not going to try to talk you into it," Damien says with a shrug. "You make your own decisions, but if I've learned anything over the years, it's that your ghosts will keep haunting you unless you lay them to rest."

"He's still alive." Jake says it a little urgently. Like he's asking, not telling.

"For now," Damien agrees. "But none of us are getting any younger."

Jake nods but quickly changes the subject, asking for their read on whether I should tell Mrs. Rosings about the other stolen jewels.

Damien shrugs. "Might as well. Maybe she can scare Nina into coughing up the other one...if she has it. Of course, we'd have to go through the trouble of stealing it again, but at this point we just need to know where it is." He falls silent for a second, looking off into the distance, in the direction of the rolling mountains, barely illuminated by a sliver of moon. "What are the chances your boss will know if you give him the fake? Mrs. Rosings still hasn't figured it out."

"Presuming she's not the one who took it from the box in the first place," I put in, Damien acknowledging the point with a nod.

Jake swallows. "He'd know. Joe does other fakes for him. There's a...signature of sorts."

"Well, that's inconvenient," Nicole says with a sigh. "But we still have a week. We can manage this."

Later, Claire and Declan join us at the fire. I'm curious about where Rosie's been—she's not the sort of person to fade into the night—but I don't ask, and they don't say, and suddenly it's late, the dark nearly shifting into light. Claire and Declan go home. Nicole and Damien go upstairs, and Jake and I stay out later than any of them, even after the fire fades to embers. He douses it with sand, then gives me his hand. I let him pull me up from my chair.

"Thank you for believing in me," he says, when I'm standing inches from him, his hand resting on my hip.

"I didn't," I admit, feeling guilty about it.

"That's what it felt like to me earlier," he says, sweeping my hair away from my face. "But you did believe in me. If you'd genuinely thought I was lying about everything, you wouldn't have gone to that house with me. You would have thought of an excuse to put it off until Nicole or Damien got back. But you didn't. You went with me because you hoped I'd have an explanation."

I consider this, then nod in acknowledgment. I needed him to have an explanation, because what Damien had told me had broken something inside of me.

"There's something I need to show you."

He leads me inside and upstairs to his room—his *original* room —and removes something from the back of the closet. I instantly recognize it as the bag that I retrieved from his Airbnb. I've been thinking of that bag, wondering what it could contain.

"You didn't look at this," he says. "I know you didn't. But I want to show you." He grins at me, his eyes crinkling at the corners. "And if you tell anyone else, I'll claim you planted it."

"You're building this up to the point where anything will be a disappointment," I say.

He laughs, then nods to the bed, and we sit next to each other, our thighs pressed together. The bag is sitting next to us. It's not enough, though, so I turn toward him and climb onto his lap, facing him. He smiles at me, like he's not surprised but is very much pleased. "It's not a particularly funny story, hellcat."

"It's yours, and I want it. Not everything in life needs to be funny."

A corner of his mouth lifts. "But it helps if you can find humor in everything."

He upends the bag onto the mattress without ceremony. A small, worn teddy bear falls out, one of the eyes crusted-over plastic, like the bear has aged the way an actual bear might.

"Is there something inside of it?" I ask, thrown.

"No," he says, laughing. "It's not stuffed with cocaine or the codes to bank safes. It's exactly what it seems to be, and I can't bring myself to get rid of it. I know it's really fucking weird for a grown-ass man to carry around a teddy bear everywhere he goes. Especially one that looks like that. I'd feel more dignified if it were Paddington."

Something twists inside of me, and I remember a few of the things he's told me about his past—puzzle pieces thrown out with pretended carelessness. How his mother left them. How he and Ryan never knew their father...

He swallows. "This is..." He swallows again, and even though I already chose to believe him, any iota of doubt that might have been left in me is obliterated by the look on his face. "I don't like being locked in because when we were four, our mother locked us into a motel room by the beach in Jersey and left. We didn't know how to unlock the door. So we waited for her, and we ate the gummy bears and Goldfish she left with us, and the only thing we had left was this damn teddy bear, only one for the two of us. She told us not to make any noise, because it would get her into trouble, so we didn't."

"How long was she gone?" I ask, running a hand over his jaw and then the side of his face.

"Four days. She had up a Do Not Disturb sign, but she'd only reserved the room for four days, so when she didn't check out—" His hand slides down my back, settling on my hip. "Don't look at me like that, Elaine. I don't want you to feel sorry for me. We were better off without her. I don't carry it around for sentimental reasons. It's a reminder."

"Not to trust anyone?" I ask softly.

"That my brother and I can make it through anything if we stick together...and also that I never want to let myself get stuck like that again. It's the first thing I remember."

"Did she come back?"

He shakes his head. "No, but they found her. She'd met some guy. Said she'd lost track of time. She didn't fight it when they put us into foster care. I think it was a relief."

"I'm sorry," I say, kissing the side of his face and then his mouth. "Thank you for telling me."

"I need to get him back, Lainey. I *need* to."

I stare into his green-flecked eyes and make a promise I'm determined to keep. "We're going to."

And then I kiss him again, pouring into it all of the feelings I can't yet find words for.

I trust you.

I want you.

I'm falling in love with you.

"Do you want to hide the teddy bear's face?" I ask, sliding my hand under his shirt. "Because I'm about to do some bad, bad things to you."

"He's at least thirty," Jake says with a smirk. "It's about time he learns about the birds and the bees."

CHAPTER THIRTY-THREE

JAKE

Lainey tells Mrs. Rosings about the necklaces she found in Nina's bag, and as a reward, her boss says she doesn't have to report to work on Halloween. The tea is still a go, so I'm guessing it's going to be a doozy.

We dress up like the characters I created for us, because why the hell not, and spend Halloween handing out candy to kids at Claire's bakery since no kids would ever venture far enough to show up at the cabin.

The next couple of days slide past in the way that only really good days do, one spilling into the next without any regard for all the not-so-great shit on the horizon. I've always been the type of guy who'd prefer to live in the moment—the past wasn't exactly great, and the future is only a possibility, not a guarantee, and I've wanted to do that even more now. Because even though I don't want to leave Elaine, I have to be realistic—if shit goes south, life might do it for me.

I might get pulled back in by Roark, or worse, I might get taken in by the police. Put in a cell with no escape.

Anthony texted on Friday to say that Nina had actually invited him to her friends' party. I think he'd still like to be deluded about her, because he went.

Now, it's Sunday, D-Day. Or rather Tea-Day.

Joy has sent me several follow-up texts asking what "vibe" we want at Anthony's tea, so I don't know what the fuck to expect on the tea front. I suspect it will be memorable, although all Lainey and I care about is finding out if anyone in the house knows where we can find the necklace.

I'm worried about Ryan. In the check-in photo Roark sent this morning, his color looked off. He's been stuck at Roark's place for too long. Weeks. If I couldn't hack it for one night in that room in Lainey's place, then what must it feel like for him?

I'm itchy to end this thing. To end it, and hopefully start a new life.

Lainey watches me as I pack into the beat-up car beside her. Even though Jake Jeffries's piece-of-shit car is now in better shape than this one, we always take hers by some silent agreement, as if she's fond of it too.

"We'll get the necklace," she tells me.

I nod, but I'm not so sure I believe that anymore.

What the alternative is, I don't know, although I'm guessing it will be more dangerous for all of us, something that makes me doubly uncomfortable now that Elaine is officially involved.

I glance back at the house, and Damien and Nicole are standing in the doorway waving to us like they're proud parents.

"Is it just me," I mutter, "or do you feel like we're kids they're sending off to school?"

"I think that's exactly what they're doing," she says. "They're letting us handle this."

Or letting us think they are.

She starts driving, and my heart thumps an unnatural rhythm, like she's taking me to my doom rather than a tea with a dysfunctional family.

It's only then that I register that I've done zero additional research about which methods a therapist might use at a meeting like this. "Do you think it matters that I still don't know dick all about therapy?"

She laughs, a breezy sweet sound that helps settle me. A bit. "No, actually. I'm guessing none of them have been to therapy. And in this case, I don't think the best outcome is for them to suddenly get along and weave friendship bracelets together." Her lips press together. "Nina's got to go."

I nod, knowing both of us are thinking of blond dick. When Anthony told me he was going to Nina's friend's party the other night, I just barely kept myself from asking if the host was a blond guy. He deserves a warning. Mrs. Rosings knows about the stolen jewelry, though, and given the lengths she's gone to in order to prevent this marriage, I think we can count on her pulling through for us.

Too soon, Elaine pulls up to Anthony's house. She parks at the curb because there are already four cars in the driveway.

"Looks different from the front," I tell her, my mouth hitching up.

"Good," she says with an answering smile, "because we've never been here before."

"I absolutely didn't fuck you in their closet and get hit in the head by a kickball."

"Why do you think they even have a kickball? You think they take it out for some pick-up games with Mrs. Rosings?"

I lean in and kiss her, feeling a pulse of gratitude for this one thing in my life that's suddenly right, and then we pile out of the car.

When we get to the door, Nina answers it. She has a tight, ungenerous smile and is wearing a sweater set with pearls. "So glad you could make it," she says. "Your *friend* is already here."

She shows us into the living room we swept through two nights ago. It hasn't noticeably changed, although someone removed the framed pictures that were propped against the wall.

Mrs. Rosings is sitting in an overstuffed armchair, her back as straight as a queen's, and Anthony is sitting beside her on an adjacent loveseat, wearing an expensive dress shirt and slacks, like he's dressing for the job he has but not necessarily the one he wants. He smiles at me, but there's no real happiness in the expression. He's on edge, caught between two women he doesn't understand or necessarily like.

The only happy person in the room is Joy, who has already set up the tea service on the coffee table, complete with a two-tier snack tray, savory on the bottom and sweet up top. Elaine's friend Rosie is standing with her, but there's something off about her. She's chewing on the ends of her hair as if they'd been dipped in sugar.

"Oh good, you've deigned to bless us with your presence," Mrs. Rosings says without rising from her chair. "Do sit."

It's clearly an order, not a request, and even though my natural response to orders is to give them the middle finger and walk out, I do as I'm told and sit on the loveseat. Elaine settles onto the cushion beside me, and Rosie makes sure everyone has a cup of steaming tea that I don't have the slightest inclination to drink.

I hate tea. I've hated it ever since we stayed with our third foster family. The mother always plied everyone with tea, and if you didn't drink it, you were failing her.

It looks like everyone else has been sipping from their cups, though, and I don't want to insult Joy, so when Lainey lifts her cup for a sip, I pretend to do the same.

"Well, thank you all for coming," Nina says, joining us and reprising her place beside Anthony. She picks up a half-drunk cup of tea and takes another sip. "Can you tell us a bit about the tea you prepared for us, Joy? It's *delicious*."

Anthony wobbles a little in his seat, making me wonder if he has a flask on his person.

Joy smiles beatifically at Nina, then spreads her smile around as if she doesn't mind sharing. "It's a special blend with some ingredients that I grow myself. Very enlightening." She pointedly winks at me.

Everyone falls silent, and it hits me that they're all looking my way. If I were really Therapist Jake Jeffries, I'd have something to say about everyone getting along. Maybe lead a group round of "Kumbaya." If I were a different kind of guy, a careful one, I'm sure I would have spent the last few days buried in psychology books instead of buried in Lainey, but I have no regrets. On my tombstone, if anyone bothers to get one for me, it'll say: *At least he enjoyed himself.*

But we're here to get them talking, so get them talking I will.

"Why don't we play a little game?" I say, setting my tea cup and plate down on the coffee table.

"I'm not averse to playing games," Mrs. Rosings says, then shifts her head to study Nina. "Are you, dear?"

"Not at all," she says tightly, glancing at Anthony. "I *love* kickball."

What now?

I exchange a look with Lainey, who's got to be thinking what I am—did we leave something in the basement closet? But I shake it off and continue, "We're going to play a little game called Never Have I Ever. When it's your turn, you'll tell us something you've never done, and the people who have done it will need to drink tea."

Lainey snorts beside me, giving me a sidelong look that tells me I wouldn't make it far as a therapist. Fair enough.

"I'll go first," I say, deciding it would be best to break them in with something easy but potentially still informative. A soft ball of a question. "Never have I ever met Anthony's sister, Emma."

Mrs. Rosings, Nina, and Anthony all take a long sip of tea.

Lainey's sitting next to me, so it's her turn to go next. She clears her throat, then says, "Never have I ever tried on the Heart of the Mountain."

Mrs. Rosings immediately lifts the teacup to her lips. Nina glances at her, then drinks, which suggests she tried on the necklace with her mother-in-law's permission. Disappointing but not particularly surprising since Mrs. Rosings set it out as bait. It would be better bait if Nina knew she wanted it—if she'd felt its cool weight at her neck.

A beat passes, and then Anthony laughs a little and drinks as well.

Nina's eyes flick to him. "You didn't."

"I did. I was seven. I wanted to know how much it would weigh."

They both laugh, and it's almost a nice moment—or it would have been if I didn't feel the strange undercurrents between them.

We make it through a few rounds of the game without anything particularly interesting coming to light other than that Anthony hates tuna fish and has never met Nina's parents, Nina dislikes dogs, and Mrs. Rosings never plans on leaving Smith House. But there's a weird vibe developing in the room that I can't quite put my finger on.

Nina has commented on the pattern of the carpet three times, and Mrs. Rosings keeps calling Anthony by his father's name. Lainey has been staring at her hands as if they contain all the mysteries of the universe.

"It's your turn, Nina," I say, but she points at the carpet.

"Did you bring that snake with you?" she asks, accusatory. "I don't like snakes. *No one* likes snakes."

"What on earth are you talking about, you insipid girl?" Mrs. Rosings snaps. "There are no snakes here. This carpet is *beautiful*. One of a kind. It was handwoven by—"

"Children, probably," Anthony says bitterly, running a hand over his jaw before glancing over his shoulder again. "Father bought it, after all. Why do you keep calling me Adrien, mother?"

Something passes over Mrs. Rosings's face. "Because you look...in this light, why, you look exactly like him."

Anthony looks sickened by the thought. "You hated him."

"So did you."

I shift my gaze to Lainey, giving her a *what the fuck is happening* look, but her gaze is still fixed on her hands. She's moving her fingers slowly, her gaze riveted on the lines on her palm. I take her hand in mine, and she gasps and looks up at me, her pupils so dilated the brown is nearly swallowed by black.

My eyes fly wide, and I glance around at the others. They all have dilated pupils. This time, I dart a glance at Joy, who gives me a thumbs up from the periphery of the room. Rosie is standing next to her with a worried look on her face as she glances around at everyone.

Alarm pumps through my veins, and I look at my full teacup, sitting on the table, and all of the other cups, nearly empty. The conclusion is obvious: Joy dosed their tea with something, and they're all high as kites.

"Joy," I say, my voice unsteady. "Can I speak with you for a moment?"

"Of course, dear," she says, looking mildly alarmed.

I get up, handing Lainey back her hand, palm up, and tug Joy into the hallway leading to the bathroom and then the bedroom. "You said this tea is a special blend. What's in it?" I ask through my teeth, trying not to lose my temper. I *like* Joy, and if she just dosed everyone at the party, I'm guessing she thought she was being helpful.

"You told me you wanted everyone to be honest with each other, sweetheart," she says, sending a worried look back to the living room.

I hear the word "snakes" and "palm" from down the hall.

"I didn't want to resort to drugging them," I say flatly.

"There's nothing inorganic in there," she hedges, "just a bit of dried mushrooms from my garden, but I take small doses all the time. It helps me connect with Mortimer. I thought it would be exactly the thing to help everyone here connect with their greater truth."

If I weren't convinced this was about to fuck me over, I'd probably laugh. Because I'm pretty damn sure this is the first and only time Mrs. Dahlia Rosings has ever tried magic mushrooms, let alone Anthony and Nina.

"Joy," I say tightly. "You can't just give people psychedelics without telling them. That's something you could get arrested for."

"They're not drugs," she insists, her always pink cheeks getting pinker. "They're one hundred percent natural. *Mushrooms*. From a garden. Nothing you grow in soil can hurt you."

"What about cocaine? Hemlock? Fuck, what about *mushrooms*? Mushrooms kill people."

She averts her head to the side. "It's the quantity that can do the killing, and it was really the smallest dose, honey. They'll all be fine."

"They'd better be."

I'm slightly reassured that she looks more remorseful than concerned. But it fucking bothers me, a lot, that Lainey's under the influence of something without having chosen it. The others too.

"Is there anything we can give them to reverse the effects?" I ask, already knowing the answer.

Only time will do the trick.

Joy looks worried now, like she realizes she messed up, but it's too late for all of the people in there to undrink the tea. It hits me that I very much know how that feels—doing something stupid on impulse and then having to pay the price.

I reach out and squeeze her hand. "We'll deal with it. It's

okay. Just...Jesus...just promise me this is the last time you'll ever dose anyone with mushrooms or anything else they don't know about."

She nods several times, her hands messing with her sweater as she peers into the living room.

"We should go back," I say, needing to check on Lainey. Needing, also, to see if we can at least make use of this mess and get the information we need.

We return to the other room just as Nina rises unsteadily to her feet, her gaze fixed on the rug. Mrs. Rosings and Anthony don't appear to notice, because they're in the thick of arguing about something related to his father. I slide onto the couch next to Lainey, who's tracing a finger across her palm, murmuring under her breath. She's okay. She's going to be okay. I put an arm around her and lean in close. "Lainey, I don't want you to panic," I whisper, "but there was something in the tea. Mushrooms."

She glances at me sharply, her eyes wide. "*Mushrooms?*" she repeats in an undertone. No one's paying attention to us—Nina just climbed up onto the couch and shouted. "There're so many of them! They're hissing!"

"Is that what that noise is?" Anthony mutters.

Nodding to Lainey, I move my hand over her back in a slow caress.

"Oh. My. God," she whispers, her eyes shifting from Nina to Anthony, who's rubbing his forehead now, and then Mrs. Rosings. Her boss has a distant look on her face, as if she's not seeing what's in front of her but a different tableau, from another place and time. Her departed husband, maybe.

"I'm here with you," I say, rubbing Lainey's back in that same repetitive pattern, hoping it helps ground her.

"Anthony, I don't like snakes," Nina says, getting onto her tiptoes as if that can save her from the snakes in her head.

"Fooled me," Mrs. Rosings retorts with a snort and then clucks her tongue. "Get down from there. You look like you're auditioning to be an exotic dancer."

Anthony hesitates and then gets to his feet and steps onto the couch too, wrapping his arms around Nina. "It's okay, Nina, there are no snakes. There's just that strange sound. It's like my ears are buzzing. Are your ears buzzing? And the room looks different. It's...it's really dull in here. Where'd all the pictures go?"

"You're worrying about pictures at a time like this?" Nina snaps. "There are at least a dozen snakes in the carpet."

"There aren't any snakes," he repeats. "Why don't you sit down with me and drink some—"

"Water," I say sharply, nodding to Joy and Rosie, who's been watching everything with a wide-eyed look that suggests she wasn't in on the psychedelics plan. Good, because otherwise I'd fear for the world with the two of them living in the same apartment. "Can you get everyone some water?"

"I'll do it," Rosie agrees quickly, peeling off from the living room before I can tell her where the kitchen is.

"Someone's getting you water," Anthony says to Nina. "You're going to be okay. Let's sit down."

"I don't like snakes," Nina repeats in a lower voice, then glances back down at the floor, blinking rapidly.

The optical illusion must have eased temporarily, because she sits down with him as if none of it had happened and primly looks up at me. "Is it my turn? I lost track."

"Just a second," I say, figuring I should find Rosie and redirect her. "I need to use the restroom."

Lainey looks up at me. "It's down the hall and the last door on the left."

"Why do you know where our bathroom is?" Nina asks, gasping. "No one's gone back to use it yet."

Lainey swears under her breath, then starts laughing, burying her head into the arm I still have wrapped around her.

Nina's dilated eyes fix on her. "It was *you!* Those were *your* underwear in the downstairs closet."

Well, fuck.

Turning toward Anthony, still sitting next to her on the couch, Nina smacks him across the face with her open palm while he gapes at her. "How dare you screw your mother's assistant in our house! Never have I ever fucked someone in our closet. Honestly, *the closet?*"

She picks up the nearly empty teacup sitting in front of Anthony on the table and shoves it at his chest, splashing warm tea all over his collared shirt.

He continues to gape at her as if he doesn't understand what's going on, probably because he doesn't, and his mind is further muddled by the tea. I feel another wave of sympathy for him. He's in so far over his head he can no longer see anything but water.

"Oh dear," I hear Joy mutter from her position by the wall. She wanders off, presumably to help Rosie. Or maybe she's just appalled by her own handiwork.

"Are you accusing my son of infidelity?" Mrs. Rosings says, rising to her feet. "*You?* I saw you and Wilson canoodling, but I knew if I told Anthony he'd never believe me. He's too trusting."

Something flashes over Nina's face as the name clicks into place for me. Wilson is one of Anthony's friend's—his buddy from college or something like that. He's mentioned him a few times at our drink meetings.

"Is that blond dick?" Lainey asks, swatting at my arm. "You're talking about blond dick, aren't you? We saw the photos."

"What the fuck is going on?" Anthony snaps, pulling the now-empty teacup from Nina's hand and throwing it at the fireplace. It bounces off of the grate before landing right-side up on the carpet. He gapes at it, as if the cup's failure to break represents a deeper failure.

Mrs. Rosings clears her throat and grips the arm of her chair as if to steady herself. "The floor is..." She shakes her head and meets Anthony's gaze. "What's going on is that Nina has been unfaithful and is accusing *you* of being unfaithful. It's a classic ruse for people of despicable character. You can*not* marry her."

Anthony turns to Nina, his expression desperate. He looks like a man being torn in half. "Nina, is that true?"

"There were underwear in the closet, Anthony," she deflects, lifting her chin. "A woman's underwear. I'm surprised you weren't more discreet."

Screw it. Might as well come partially clean, since we've already been backed into a corner.

"Those *were* Lainey's underwear," I admit.

"I knew it," Nina practically shrieks, banging a fist against the tea spot on Anthony's chest. He flinches but doesn't try to push her away.

I shake my head, seeking out his gaze. "Your mother asked Lainey to come by the other night to look for proof that Nina was up to something, and I came as her lookout. We kind of got carried away in the closet. Sorry."

"Oops," Lainey says, laughing softly. "Oops-a-daisy."

Anthony looks like he got pole-axed and then run over by a car. Maybe it's a blessing that he's high on whatever Joy dosed everyone with. "You broke into my house and fucked your girlfriend in my closet?"

At my nod, he says, "I thought you were my friend."

I could object that I'd only done it to be a good boyfriend. That I'd thought I was helping him out too, but some kind of madness compels me to be honest. Maybe because I truly feel like I've wronged this man. Maybe because I've stumbled onto the need to make amends, and he's on my list. I take in a deep breath and say, "That's because I wanted you to think that."

"You're no different from the rest of them," he says. "Everyone wants something, and no one's honest about what they want." The look of accusation in his dilated eyes hammers into me.

He doesn't say anything else to me, or to Nina, who's busy glaring at Mrs. Rosings. He just lowers down onto the carpet, which has a pattern that does resemble a mass of snakes, pulls his knees up, and buries his head into his hands.

Fuck, this isn't good. None of this is good. There's a sick feeling in my chest, made worse by the sight of Anthony sitting on the floor. Seeing him like that makes me hate myself.

I was dishonest with him. I tried to make myself see him as a spoiled rich kid. An entitled asshole. But he's not, or he's not only those things. He's a person, and today, he's a person who got dosed with mushrooms and then found out his fiancée has been cheating on him and his new best buddy has been lying to him. I want to comfort him, but I'm the one who caused part of the damage, and there's nothing I can do except be sorry for it.

"Now, Nina," Mrs. Rosings says, still holding onto one of the arms of her chair for dear life. "This is your goodbye party, and I think we can all agree it would be better if it came to a close. Your bag is already packed, because *you* already packed it, and Lainey tells me there are five necklaces nestled inside. Very expensive necklaces."

Nina's eyes bulge. "I didn't—"

"Yes," Mrs. Rosings says flatly. "*You did.* It was clever of you not to take anything from my bedroom. I don't know how you got into the basement safe, but a thief has her ways. I'm only surprised you were clumsy enough to lose the Heart of the Mountain since you went to the trouble of getting such a fine replica made."

What's this now?

Lainey leans into me, her hair tickling my ear, and stage-whispers loudly enough for everyone to hear, "She's talking about the Heart of the Mountain."

She's adorable, and I might be about to get busted for any

number of things, so I take the opportunity to kiss the side of her face. "Yes, I picked up on that, hellcat."

"But I didn't do that," Nina says, and this time I can tell she means it. It's there in her tone and the honest confusion painted all over her face.

Rosie and Joy walk back in with a pitcher of water and five glasses, but when Rosie sees Anthony curled up on the floor next to the sofa, she sets the pitcher down on the coffee table with a resounding crack. Then she goes to him and wraps a hand around his shoulder before leaning in and whispering something into his ear.

He looks up, his expression as astonished as a man who's seen the face of God, and says, "Who *are* you?"

"I'm Rosie," she says simply, her hand still on his shoulder.

My attention shifts to Mrs. Rosings, whose hard gaze is on Nina. "You're trying to tell me that you didn't steal the Heart of the Mountain, replace it with a fake, and then hide the necklace in a bush? You must have been surprised when it wasn't still there when you went back for it." She huffs out a bitter laugh. "As if I wouldn't have a tracker on my most expensive piece of jewelry."

"I *didn't* take it," Nina huffs. "I wouldn't know how to sell something like that." She lifts her hand to her mouth as if she could stuff the words back in.

"I'm the one who took it," someone says in a small but forceful voice.

It's Rosie, her hand still on Anthony's shoulder. And as everyone turns to stare at her, she bursts into tears.

CHAPTER THIRTY-FOUR

JAKE

"See!" Nina shrills. "See! I told you it wasn't me." She takes a step toward Rosie, her gaze narrowing to where her hand is wrapped around Anthony's shoulder.

"That woman was after my fiancé—she—" She flinches, her gaze dropping to the writhing vines on the carpet as she nearly steps on one.

"*Snakes*," Lainey hisses out, her tone a bit vindictive. She squeezes my hand and gets to her feet, a bit wobbly. I watch as she goes to Rosie, wrapping her up in a hug. She's probably as thrown by Rosie's confession as I am, but she trusts her friend. She's giving her the benefit of the doubt.

Fuck.

Elaine Catlan is one hell of a woman, and *I don't want to lose her*. I'd do anything to stay with her, to hook my carriage to hers, but Mrs. Rosings has the necklace.

Nina, who doesn't give a shit about my internal crisis, is having a stare-off with her would-have-been mother-in-law.

"Leave," Mrs. Rosings commands, her voice hard as she stares Nina down. "Take your valise from the front closet and go. You may keep the necklaces, but if you ever try to contact my son or anyone in my family again, I will report them stolen, and I will ruin you so thoroughly you'll discover new meanings for the word."

Something flashes in Nina's eyes. Her gaze dips to Anthony again, but she only holds eye contact with him for half a second before turning wordlessly toward the front closet.

"Uh, she can't drive right now," I say. I don't want to tell them what Joy did. For all I know they'll insist she's thrown into jail for it, so if possible, I need to avoid telling them *why* Nina shouldn't drive. But I can't let any of them get behind the wheel of a car for hours.

Nina turns to look at me, hatred burning in her eyes like they're the coals at the bottom of a fire. "Just because *he* bought the BMW doesn't mean it's not rightfully mine."

"It's not yours," Mrs. Rosings insists. "Because I bought it for *him*. She can bring you to the airport." She nods toward Joy, who's even pinker in the face than before.

"Yes, of course," Joy offers quickly, probably recognizing the reprieve, same as I do. She hurries toward the door as Nina lugs her heavy suitcase from the closet where Mrs. Rosings stowed it.

Anthony gets to his feet and watches his former fiancée prepare to leave without so much as a goodbye. "That's it?" he says, sounding sober now, like whatever was in that tea has already started to wear off.

Nina glances back at him from the door, her expression hard. "Don't pretend you were in it for the right reasons either," she says with a shrug, as if all of it meant nothing, and then she steps out of the house and, presumably, out of his life.

Joy gives us an apologetic wave and hurries out after her, closing the door behind her with a snick of sound.

A sigh leaves Mrs. Rosings's lungs as the front door closes on Nina.

Anthony doesn't say anything, he just turns and leaves the room, staggering a little as he heads down the hallway. From where the door slams shut deeper into the house, I'm guessing he's in his bedroom.

Mrs. Rosings mutters something about Adrien, her mind probably still giving her his father's image when she looks at him.

"He'll be fine," Mrs. Rosings murmurs. Then, turning toward Lainey and Rosie, who's still quietly crying, she clucks her tongue and says, "There's no need for carrying on. Tears never did anything for a woman. You'll sit down and explain why I shouldn't have you arrested. *Now*."

Rosie shoots me a panicked look, and I know, I just fucking know, that her reason for taking the necklace involves me.

"And then you," Mrs. Rosings adds, skewering me with a look, "are going to tell me just who it is you are, and why everything in this room suddenly looks like it's alive. I enjoy playing games as much as the next person, but after a while, they grow tiresome."

"Jake's a therapist," Lainey says, straight-faced. She guides Rosie over to the vacated loveseat and then walks over to me, wrapping an arm around me as if she could protect me from the world.

She would, I think.

And I know that even though I'd destroy myself to save my brother, I'd do the same for her. I can't let her get in trouble, not for something I've done, not even for something she did, so I only have one move here.

"If he's a therapist, then I'm the Queen of England," Mrs. Rosings says imperially, reaching for her teacup.

"Don't drink that," I tell her, deciding I might as well start being truthful now since I've decided to try it on for size. "There's something in the tea blend that's a little...psychedelic."

She smiles at me, shaking her head, and then lifts the teacup to her lips anyway. "Good."

Turning to Rosie, she says, "Well?"

I sit back down, tugging Lainey with me because I have a feeling we're going to be here for a while. Rosie is giving us a desperate look. She's nearly red in the face, and I know she's agonizing over what she can say without pointing a finger at me.

"Tell her everything," I say to Rosie. "I'm going to do the same."

Lainey turns on her cushion to face me, her pupils still dilated and her eyes fearful. "*Jake.*"

Maybe she's remembering how well I did in a locked room for ten minutes, and drawing the obvious conclusion that I'd be fucking wrecked in jail. Maybe she's thinking what I am...that I want to continue the life the way we've lived it this past week—understood, cared for, supported. As a pair.

But the only way I can live that life with her, whatever it might look like, is by facing up to the man I've been. I never figured an old rich woman would be my judge and jury, but maybe it tracks. I've stolen from the rich, so it's probably only poetic justice that I find myself facing their judgement.

Even though I can feel Mrs. Rosings shamelessly staring at us while Rosie tries to pull it together, I lift a hand to Lainey's chin and trace my thumb over her bottom lip before kissing her. "This is how it has to be. I love you."

Her eyes widen. "You're not the third sword. You're my wand."

I have no idea what the fuck that means, but I kiss her again before holding her hand and nodding to Rosie.

Rosie clears her throat. "I'm so sorry. I..." She glances at us.

"Eyes over here," Mrs. Rosings says sharply.

Rosie looks at her. "I...I knew Lainey was worried about the necklace being taken."

By me, obviously, but I appreciate that she doesn't state the obvious.

"When the power went out," Rosie continues, "I figured it was purposeful, and whoever wanted the necklace was about to act. I'd headed straight to the drawing room once the game of Hide and Seek started, so I was already in there. So I just...I tried to open the case to see how good the lock was, but there was no lock. Anyone could have come in and grabbed it."

Mrs. Rosings laughs under her breath, as if she's patting her back and saying *good one*.

Rosie swallows, playing with the ends of her hair, then says, "It occurred to me that if I took it out of the case and hid it, I could put it back after the power came back on. So I took it and hid it beneath a bush at the back of the house, where I thought no one would find it..." More tears trail down her cheeks as she steals another glance at Lainey. "I know it's awful that I didn't say anything. I thought I'd lost it...and when you told me Jake didn't have it, I figured it must have been someone else. I...I moved away from my brother's house in such a hurry because I didn't want anyone to know what I was doing. I've spent every spare minute I have trying to figure out what happened to it and who could have taken it. You were looking into Anthony and Nina, so I've been following around other people from the party."

"And that's why you convinced us to suggest using Joy to cater the tea," Lainey says softly. It's obvious from the look on her face that she believes Rosie, and I do too. "You wanted your own chance to search the house."

Rosie nods softly. "Yeah. I poked around a bit when I went back to find water, but then everyone was acting so weird, because... Well..."

"Of the psychedelics in the tea. Yes," Mrs. Rosings says. She shifts her attention to me. "Do we have you to thank for that?"

"Indirectly," I say, clearing my throat. "We told Joy we'd love for everyone to be in an...honest mood. And she should have asked for more direction."

She holds my gaze. "You've lied to me, and you've lied to my boy." Her eyes drift to Lainey's hand, cradled in mine. "And despite that, you've managed to win over what is usually a very sensible young woman. How am I supposed to believe *you're* in an honest mood?"

I squeeze Lainey's hand lightly. "Because I love her," I say. "And I like Anthony. And I'm sick as hell of lying."

CHAPTER THIRTY-FIVE

LAINEY

My heart is pounding fast, so fast I can hear it, or maybe that's an auditory hallucination from the psychedelic tea. I didn't drink much of it, but I definitely still feel it. I feel it now, wrapping around Jake's confession—*I love you*—and surrounding it with curlicues and candy hearts. I feel it whenever I catch sight of my palm and the love line splashed across it. Or when I glance at the hardwood floor and get lost in the lines of it.

I don't know why I haven't said the words back to him yet. I do. I love him. It's not a rational feeling. You shouldn't be able to spend seven years with a man without truly loving him, only to fall in love in two weeks. But there's nothing rational about the way Jake makes me feel. He makes me feel like I can breathe. Like I can be myself, and that's good enough. Like I'm even more of myself because he wants me to be me.

I can't let something bad happen to him.

Yes, he has stolen things.

Yes, he fully intended to steal Mrs. Rosings's necklace.

But he's not a bad man, and he wants to be a better one.

If he'd had anyone in his life who'd given a shit before he met Dale, things would have turned out differently for him.

And maybe his brother's a real asshole—there's no telling—but he means a lot to Jake, so he means a lot to me. Which means I'm going to make damn sure he's okay too.

I will accept nothing less.

We'll figure out a way to help him without the necklace because we have to.

Still, I don't try to stop Jake from telling Mrs. Rosings his story. I just sit there as his witness, determined to step in if he doesn't include any of the things he *should* include. And if she tries to call the police?

Jake and I will be leaving this house, together, before they get here. I'm not going to let them lock him up. No way.

"I befriended Anthony because I wanted to steal your necklace," he says. Which is a little too honest.

I'm about to say so, when Mrs. Rosings laughs and slaps her knee like he's told her a real humdinger.

"Tell me, are you really on a diet for your limbic system?"

"No," he says, running his thumb across my palm, tracing my love line. The feeling sends sparks of pleasure through me, and right now, I can see them, pink and purple sparkles floating through the air. Combustible. "Lainey suspected I was up to something, and she implied she might ask Rosie to spit in my food."

Mrs. Rosings laughs again, probably more amused because of the mushrooms.

"I didn't," Rosie says quickly. "I swear. I've worked in multiple restaurants, and I've never spat in anyone's food."

Mrs. Rosings laughs harder. "I imagine that's taken some restraint."

Jake takes a deep breath, then says, "I'm not saying this to excuse myself, because I've indisputably done bad things. I've been stealing from people since I was a teenager. I could tell you sob stories about being abandoned by my mother and being in foster care, but I'm not going to. Because I've known for a long time now that what I was doing was wrong, and it took longer than it should have for me to stop. But something happened to me last year that finally made me. The man I was working for didn't want to let me quit, though. So when my brother made a mistake, he took him hostage, and he's going to cut his hand off if I don't bring him the Heart of the Mountain. I'd do anything for him. Lie to you. Your son. Anyone. He's..." He glances at me, his eyes warm. "He was the only thing I had, but not anymore."

She's watching him with fascination, and it hits me again that Mrs. Rosings is *bored*—deeply bored and lonely and in need of drama. So I add, apropos of nothing, "Jake and Ryan are identical twins."

Her eyes widen. "And I suppose you have reason to believe this man's story, Elaine?"

"I do," I say. "I can feel it's true in my love line." Then, realizing that's probably not a convincing argument, I add, "I've seen photos of his brother sent by the guy who kidnapped him. And Damien and Nicole are looking into him."

"Why does this man who has your brother wants my Heart of the Mountain?" she asks imperially.

"I don't know," Jake says. "I'm guessing he saw that documentary and figured it would be hard for me to get it. It was a challenge."

"Or a punishment," she insists. "Tell me more about this man."

So he does. He tells her Roark's name, and I interject and tell her a little more about what he did to Jake and Ryan. How he used them. She listens with an unreadable expression, her posture perfect.

Rosie sits and listens to it all, too, mostly silent.

I'm still in shock that my sweet friend is the one who stole the Heart of the Mountain. Sort of. But now that I think about it, there were signs. She's been more agitated and jumpy than normal, and everything happened so quickly with Joy.

Mrs. Rosings's lips purse as we finish our story.

It hits me that this woman whom I thought I didn't like, whom I've spent the last couple of months begrudgingly working for, has our fate in her hands. I should be more nervous about that, but if I've learned anything about Mrs. Rosings, it's that she operates by her own laws...and they're fair, more or less. I disliked the way she treated Nina, but now that I know why, I can't say I blame her.

Finally, Mrs. Rosings clears her throat and says, "*Well*, this afternoon has been exceedingly exciting. Has this Roark set a meeting place to make the exchange?"

"No," Jake says, his body tensing beside me. I squeeze his hand and lean in to him, because I've gotten to know her well enough that I can sense what she's dancing around. "I was supposed to get in touch with him once I acquired the necklace."

"Then you'd better get around to that, hadn't you? I'll be going with you, of course. The necklace doesn't leave my sight."

He stares at her, his mouth opening and then closing. "Mrs. Rosings..."

"Oh, not to worry. We'll get your brother out if he wants to be gotten."

"Roark's going to want to keep the necklace," Jake finally manages, running a hand back through his hair. His hand is trembling slightly, and I lay claim to it once he's done. I know he has to be thinking about Dale, the man with the watch. My own heart feels like a stranger, because Mrs. Rosings, the woman who's always looked at me and seemed to find me wanting, is being kinder to me and the man I love than my parents ever were.

Jake swallows, then adds, "He has this museum..."

"Does he?" she asks with interest. "Tell me about it."

He does, and Mrs. Rosings nods as if this confirms something for her. "It's not the necklace he really wants. It's revenge. Well...I think this *Roark* has caused quite enough of a fuss, don't you? We'll set him straight."

Jake is now openly gaping at her. Rosie too.

"Mrs. Rosings," I say, catching on. "This man is a dangerous criminal, and you're saying you're going to set him straight. Do you...do you *know* this man?"

"Yes," she says, smiling at me as if I'm a star student. "Yes, Elaine, I rather think I do."

"*How* do you know this man?" I ask in disbelief.

She sighs, picking at the arm of her chair as if she finds the beige fabric wanting. With a glance down the hall, she says, "Perhaps that's why I keep seeing Adrien today. I had an affair with Edmund about thirty years ago, and it would seem he's held a grudge. I'm guessing most of the people lucky enough to make it into his museum earned his ire in some way."

Jake makes a face that almost—*almost*—makes me laugh.

"*Mrs. Rosings*," I say with a gasp.

She smiles at me. "Does it shock you that I was young once? I tried to warn you about your young man, you know. After spending half an evening with him, I was quite sure he wasn't who he said he was."

More shock, chased by a healthy dose of respect runs through me. "No," I admit, my hand still wrapped around Jake's. "But he's who he said he was today. He's a good man," I say, my voice swelling with emotion. "And he's going to use the skills he acquired from doing...questionable things to help people from now on. We *both* are."

Jake turns on the couch and regards me with parted lips, his eyes warm and so full of love. "I fucking worship you," he says, his voice low, although everyone in the room can probably hear him. He doesn't seem embarrassed though. He *never* seems embarrassed. It's one of the things I love about him—he's unapologetically himself, which is not to say he's unapologetic. He regrets what he's done, and he'd like to atone for it, but he doesn't seem to hate himself.

I don't want to hate myself anymore. Before Todd and I broke up, I loathed looking in the mirror. The person I saw staring back at me never felt right. She was well-groomed but not happy. Definitely not fulfilled. But I'm on the road to feeling that way, and I'm enjoying the journey. Because he's seen me as I am—not some shined-up version of me—and he's made me feel special and loved. And that's a gift I'll always carry with me, no matter what happens next.

"Can we have a minute?" I ask Mrs. Rosings and Rosie.

Mrs. Rosings laughs as if I've cracked a joke. "This isn't your house, you know."

"It's not yours either."

She gives me one of her signature withering looks, but her lips are quirked slightly in amusement. She doesn't hate me. Maybe she never has, and I was just projecting because a part of me still hated myself. That's going to change. It's going to change now.

"Five minutes," she says. "I'll start gathering up Nina's things."

"I'm guessing you won't be returning them to her with a bow on the box," I say.

"No," she replies flatly, then nods to Rosie. "Come, you might as well make yourself useful. There are some boxes in the basement. I suppose you can build a box?"

Rosie gives her an *are you for real?* look, but it's obvious stealing this woman's multimillion dollar necklace has humbled her, because she just says, "Of course."

They leave the room, and I turn toward Jake, who's still studying me. His gaze is so deep, I could fall into it—fall in and stay. His whole being in his eyes, and they're fixed on me. He wraps his arms around me, leaning his head in close. "*Lainey.*"

"*I love you,*" I tell him, able to say it now. "And I want us both to be Love Fixers. We're going to run ads, do the website, all of it. *If you stay.* We haven't really talked about it, because we didn't know how all of this—" I wave at the house, "—would work out, but I want you to stay. I really, really want us to do this together. For this to be our life."

My heart is beating so fast, I'm afraid it'll burst like a squished grape. I'm *terrified* that he'll tell me no. That he'll say his existence is tethered to New York, and we can only be together if I go back to the place where I always felt like a prisoner in a glass cage.

"I just said I worship you, didn't I?" Jake says, tucking some of my errant hair behind my ear. "I'll stay for as long as you'll have me."

"That's good," I say with a laugh, feeling effervescent and good. "Because once I decide to keep someone, it's extremely hard to get rid of me. Ask Claire."

"Is that a promise, Elaine?" he asks, his voice hoarse. He's studying me in a way that makes me remember that he's someone who's felt abandoned and unwanted too. His mother walked out on him and his brother, and they never knew their father. The man he'd thought of as a father had betrayed him too.

"Yes."

And he leans in and kisses me, his lips making a promise of their own. His hand weaving into my hair to take it deeper.

A beleaguered sigh gusts from someone's chest. I break the kiss but don't back away from him. I can't right now. I need his arms around me. I need the reassurance that he's still here—that he'll continue to be here. When I look, Mrs. Rosings and Rosie are emerging from the stairwell to the basement, Rosie carrying four boxes, Mrs. Rosings carrying nothing.

My boss sighs, her lips pressed tightly together. "Does this mean I'm going to have to find another assistant?" She says this as if she doesn't have Rosie grappling with giant boxes for her for free.

"Do you really need one?"

Most of what I've done has been in service to her attempts to break up Anthony and Nina, and surely the wedding will be cancelled.

Her eyes widen, as if she's only just realized the import of what happened here today. "Perhaps not." Her gaze shifts to Jake. "I expect you'll find a way to make it up to my son."

The scene around me still looks different than it should. Sharper, brighter, and everything is too funny or not funny enough, but when I focus on him, it all seems all right anyway.

Clearing his throat, Jake says, "I'd like to. I...have a plan for doing that, if he'll let me."

She drills a hard look into Jake. "I don't want him marrying another gold digger."

He lifts his hands. "It wouldn't be like that if it were a business arrangement with a firmly established prenup—both of them get money, then they walk away after the one year separation period."

She considers this for a moment before nodding. "Good. I couldn't care less about the money. God knows, I have plenty of it to share with both of my children, but my boy needs to feel like it's really his. He won't take it otherwise. But we'll cross that bridge when we come to it. First, we have to put this nonsense at bay." A smile spreads across her face. "You know, I have to admit, it's been some time since I've had this much *fun*."

Anthony's not having a banger of a day, but I'm not going to point that out, since she's opted not to press charges against my friend or my boyfriend.

Boyfriend.

Rosie's right. It's such a stupid word, like we're children drawing in each other's notebooks. It doesn't encompass the way he's drawn me out and helped me process the past seven years of repression. But using it—even thinking it—puts a warm, soft glow in my chest.

And...is the carpet *moving*?

CHAPTER THIRTY-SIX

JAKE

My heart thumps fast and wild in my chest—a real fucking rabbit of a heart. Lainey's here but not here. She's in a car with Nicole and Damien a couple of blocks away. Backup, they say. Sitting ducks, I say. I didn't want her that close to Roark and everything he represents, but it's incredibly hard to tell my woman no. Usually, I wouldn't have it any other way, but today her proximity has me riding scared.

So does the multimillion dollar necklace riding shotgun in a little hinged box—and Mrs. Rosings, reclined in the backseat so she can't immediately be seen.

It's Saturday, a little less than a week after the tea. Over the past week, there's been plenty of drama, between the fallout from Rosie's secret to Anthony's broken engagement. Lainey and I have also been working on our plan for expanding the Love Fixers.

All of us drove to upstate New York yesterday to take this meeting, because no one wanted to fly with a multimillion dollar piece of jewelry. Mrs. Rosings rode with Lainey and me, and talked seemingly the whole time without really saying much. Which would be fine by me, normally. I enjoy talking. It's just...the plan is...

There is no fucking plan. Mrs. Rosings insists she can get Roark to release my brother *and* Dale's watch, although I have to wonder if that's just because she's so accustomed to bossing people around that she expects everyone to bend to her will. Truth be told, I can't imagine what she could have on Roark from thirty-some-odd years ago that would hold any sway now.

Nicole's guess was "dirty photos," Lainey's friend Claire thinks he might still love her, and Damien pointed out that it doesn't actually matter, since the only way we were getting the necklace to the meet-up was if she went with it.

So here we are, parked in the lot of a fast food restaurant that looks like it's been closed for the last decade, sandwiched between the dirty façade of the building and a bunch of trees gone to wild, waiting for Roark to show up with my brother. I'm sweating, my palms patting the wheel as if I'm trying to form a loaf of bread.

"Can't you sit still?" Mrs. Rosings asks from the back seat.

"Nope. Are you sure about this? He's not the kind of man who gives things away for free."

"I can't entirely be sure," she admits, lips pursed. "People change. But I do believe I have the right of it."

I glance back, taking her in. "Do you ever believe otherwise?"

She makes an incredulous sound. "Why on earth would I?"

Not much I can say to that.

Her eyes narrow. "That's part of the reason I knew you weren't a therapist. Therapists can sit still. Anthony would have figured it out too if he weren't so trusting."

"I expect he won't be as trusting anymore," I say, feeling the burn of having played a part in that.

"No, but at least he won't be married to a woman who'd make a fool of him morning, noon, and night."

She continues to watch me, and it's more fucking unnerving than it should be, but I'm not the kind of man who enjoys backing down either. I hold her gaze.

Finally, she nods, as if having established something. "You'll do."

"For what?"

"For your young woman. She's a spirited girl. She needs a man who can keep up with her, if she insists on having a man."

"You care about her," I say, stating the obvious. It's not as if it surprises me. Anyone with sense would care about Lainey and want things to go well for her, but it is something that twines us together, Mrs. Rosings and me. She cares about Lainey, and I'd burn the world down for my girl—or beat it really hard with a shitty umbrella.

"She reminds me of myself as a girl," Mrs. Rosings says after a moment. "Which is why I've been hard on her. You're too young to understand, but as you get older, you start to recognize patterns. You can see where someone's choices are likely to lead, and it's hard to sit in the backseat and watch without attempting to direct them."

My mouth hitches up. "And yet here you are in the backseat."

She smiles at me and gives the slightest nod of her head. "And yet here I am." She's quiet for a second, which is a real novelty for both of us, then says, "Will you really help my son?"

I slide my hands along the wheel. I toggle my foot. "I'd like to, but I'm far from sure he's interested in more 'help' from me."

Especially once he learns the full truth about who I am and why I sought him out. I've decided I'm going to tell him, which won't be a particularly fun conversation. But if I'm going to start living my truth, I need to break free of the lies that have piled onto me over the years—the luggage of people who do not exist.

I've also decided that I'm going to go talk to Dale, watch or no watch. Damien's words have stuck with me like the burrs from a burdock plant. I don't like the thought of Dale wasting his time worrying about me. It's fucked up that he should have to lose both his watch and his peace of mind.

Mrs. Rosings gusts out a slow sigh. "I'm afraid that boy needs all the help he can get. Not just to secure his trust fund. He needs a real friend. It's no easy legacy, being Adrien's son."

She's not wrong, and guilt plucks a familiar rhythm in my head. I'd like to be that friend, if he'll let me.

Then I hear a car pulling around the front of the abandoned restaurant, and my heart starts hammering. And all other thoughts vanish from my head.

I'm finally going to see my brother. He's going to be free, out of that locked room. *Out*.

A black van with tinted windows turns the corner, and after it parks, Roark climbs out of the front. He looks...old. His face is lined, and there are dark circles under his eyes. Maybe being in constant contact with my brother has drained him. Good for Ryan.

I expect one of Roark's goons to come out with him, but he appears to be alone, unless Ryan's tucked away in the backseat. Please let Ryan be in the backseat.

I pick up the necklace case and get out of the car.

"You got it?" Roark says, his countenance brightening. "I knew you could do it." He looks happy to see me, and some fucked up part of me still wants his approval—same as when he first trained us up. It pisses me off.

"Where's my brother?"

Something I don't like passes over his face. "Let me see the necklace."

"Not until I see Ryan."

"He's at the house," Roark says, but anger flickers across his face before he shuts it down. "Couldn't be bothered to get up."

Ryan's a lot of things, but he's not lazy. He'd be itching to leave Roark's place. It would be driving him nearly crazy by now—over a month in. He'd be here if he could be.

"Where's your muscle?" I ask.

His jaw flexes again, and I know. I just fucking know.

Ryan's gone.

Somehow he convinced Roark's goons to turn on him, because otherwise *they'd be here*, and they got him out.

A smile threatens to spread across my face, stopped only by the question of why Ryan hasn't reached out to me if he escaped.

The back door of the car opens, and Mrs. Rosings pops her head out. "Where's the boy?" she asks, delivered as coolly as a queen, and Roark suddenly looks like he's going to be pushed over the edge into cardiac arrest.

"Dahlia," he gasps. His gaze darts to me. "You got caught."

He sounds disappointed in me, and I'm relieved by the anger that pumps through my veins.

I grab his collar and shake him. "Does my brother still have both of his hands?"

"He won't if I get ahold of him again," he says tightly, every line in his face rigid as he removes my hand. "He won't have either of them."

Mrs. Rosings clucks her tongue and steps out of the car. "You taught the boys to steal. Who do you have to blame but yourself if they turned against you?"

"You shouldn't be here," Roark says, his voice hoarse. He's staring at her as if she's an apparition, a ghost, a *goddess*. I've never seen him look at anyone that way. Maybe the reason he sees her that way is because she's a person who's bested him. Surprised him. Beaten him.

I know a thing or two about that. It's hard not to fall all over yourself to impress a woman whose skills are superior to yours. But I have a feeling Mrs. Rosings is even less tolerant of bullshit than Lainey.

"No, I shouldn't be here," Mrs. Rosings says, "but you tried to steal my necklace. An interesting way of reaching out, but I confess I'm not interested in renewing our acquaintance. You will *not* be taking the Heart of the Mountain. Besides. We'd agreed to exchange the necklace for the boy, and it's clear you don't have the boy."

His gaze stuck on her, he says, "I can see you haven't changed."

"Neither have you." The expression on her face leaves little doubt that she considers that to be very bad news for him.

"Where's Ryan?" I ask again, needing the confirmation that he took off on his own and didn't get hurt.

Roark turns toward me, his expression bleak. "I treated you like sons."

The little boy I was would want to regain his approval, but he stopped feeling like a father the moment he sent my brother to do what my conscience had ordered me not to. "You threatened to cut my brother's hand off to force me to steal a multimillion dollar necklace," I say flatly. "You refused to let me quit when I told you I couldn't do it anymore. You wouldn't win father of the year unless your only competition was my actual father."

He watches me for a long moment, his eyes tired. His face looks like a deflated balloon, the extra material having nowhere to go. "He convinced the guards to help him. They cleaned out the museum. Your watch too, Jake. I'm guessing Ryan's not planning to give any of it back. He's not the sentimental type. He's trying to take over for me."

My heart feels like it's going to choke me.

He's not wrong about Ryan. A mark is a mark to him, and he's never let any of them slip under his walls and matter. But *I* matter to him, and he did this for me. So yes, I think he will return the watch.

Which is not to say he'll return everything from the museum. Because it may not be a popular opinion, but there are people who don't deserve sympathy. Like *motherfucker*, and Peter, Peter Pussy Eater of the cookie bouquet. Sometimes karma doesn't deliver unless it has a helping hand. Over the last few weeks, I've discovered how much I like being that helping hand.

"You don't know him. You don't know either of us."

"Did you know he's been gone for three days?" he asks pointedly.

The news rattles me, the way it's meant to. "Why would you still agree to the meet up?"

"Because I knew he wouldn't come to you."

Worry pricks at me. Ryan is gone, who knows where, and he hasn't reached out to me. He isn't involving me in his plans.

But I won't show my hand. "Goodbye, Roark."

He stops me with a hand on my arm. For a second, I'm brought back seventeen years to when I was little. He taught us to thieve, but we hadn't started with expensive jewels or one-of-a-kind pieces. We'd started small. Part of our training had involved hanging out in public places where it was easy to "part fools from their money." The zoo. The park. On those outings he used to silently signal to us like this—with a quick touch to the arm. Sometimes he'd direct our attention to a man whose wallet was practically asking to be liberated from his pocket, or a woman who kept setting her purse down to take photos. But other times he'd point out a monkey, hanging by its tail. A giraffe licking a little girl's hand.

Sometimes I pretended I was what I seemed to be—a kid hanging out with his dad.

I glance back and see he's holding a gun on me.

My stomach lurches.

Demonize your mark.

Maybe he thought of Ryan and me as sons once. Proteges at least. But now we're just drains. Ryan's his enemy, and I'm the wall blocking him from what he wants.

"Give me the necklace," he says.

"On second thought, you're worse than my actual father."

"No more bullshit," he sneers. "Give it to me." His gaze shifts from me to Mrs. Rosings, who's standing behind the decrepit fast food restaurant, staring at him like a queen from her throne. His expression shifts and then hardens.

"*No,*" she says. "I'm the one who suffered for it. It's mine, and one day it will belong to my daughter. Now, you can kill us in cold blood and take what's mine, but you should know there's a tracker on that necklace that's *very hard* to remove, and also that we have friends parked two blocks away who know where we are and who we were meeting. You will get caught, and this time you'll go to jail. Now, your pride has been injured, your museum of curiosities cleared out, but one would assume you still have your bank account. Why not do the world a favor and retire?"

He's staring at her now, his attention averted from me. They're still talking, but their words have become white fuzz. My heart beating in my ears, I try to gauge if I should go for it. His gun is aimed at me. If I jump him, there's a chance it'll go off, and I'll lose a lung or maybe my life. But if I don't, he could shoot both of us. The sound of the bullets might draw Nicole and Damien and Lainey, and then—

That's all it takes. The fear of him seeing her, of her being close enough for him to harm her in any way. I still think he wouldn't, but the possibility is unacceptable. My brother is safe, and Lainey must be kept safe too.

I jump.

CHAPTER THIRTY-SEVEN

LAINEY

The sound of a gunshot makes me jolt.

Fear axes into me, but I don't hesitate...

I open the car door.

"Lainey," Damien says urgently, turning back in the driver's seat, "I'll go in first. We need—"

But I'm already out of the car, running.

When I reach the edge of the shitty fast food restaurant, I glance around the side of the building, keeping my body covered—

Jake is on top of Roark, and he's pounding his arm against the concrete of the parking lot, the gun angled sideways in his grip. The necklace box is sitting on the concrete too. The gun skids away, toward Mrs. Rosings, who's standing there with the confidence of someone who's much more familiar with decrepit parking lots. I'm about to run in and grab it when she casually steps forward and does so instead.

I pull my pepper spray out of my pocket and run toward Jake, who's still struggling to immobilize Roark.

Jake sees me, his eyes rounding with panic, and I realize my mistake when Roark manages to get his hand free and punches my boyfriend in the face.

"No," I scream. Running forward, I bend down and spray Roark in the face just as Damien and Nicole come racing around the side of the building.

Mrs. Rosings announces like the baller she is, "I will shoot you if you make me, but I'd prefer not to deal with such a mess."

Roark roars, trying to lift his hands to his face, but Jake pins them. Jake's nose is dripping blood, and his face has pink spots on it, which means I must have gotten him with some of the spray. But he's okay. He wasn't shot. *He's okay*.

There are tears in my eyes. Because I'd thought...for a second, I'd thought I'd lost him, and it was as if someone had shut off all the lights and left me in darkness.

Suddenly Damien's taking over for Jake, and Jake's standing up. He runs his hands over me, as if he's worried that I might have spontaneously become injured in between running around the corner and macing his shitty ex-boss. I don't think, I just lift my sleeve to his nose and hold it there to stop the bleeding, my other hand gripping him because I don't want to let him go.

I lean in and kiss the side of his mouth, his chin, and his lips, and my face is burning too—the mace rubbing off—and I honestly couldn't care less.

"You're okay, you're okay."

He laughs, leaning back slightly, one of my sleeves still pressed to his nose.

"Let's not exaggerate," he says in a nasal voice. "Can you promise not to mace me the next time you get pissed off?"

"I wasn't pissed off today," I say, laughing. Crying a little too.

"That's what I'm afraid of." He kisses my cheek, layering his lips over a tear. "Ryan's not here, hellcat."

I glance around, only then registering that Roark must have come alone.

"Is he..."

He runs a hand through my hair, nestling me in close. "I think he's okay. He got out. He cleaned out the museum and left. Roark... he thinks Ryan's trying to take over where he left off."

"And you?" I ask, my heart thumping a faster beat. If Ryan's going off on his own, will Jake want to join him? Was his time in Marshall just a pit stop?

"I need to go to Connecticut."

I look up into his eyes, the hope in them nearly turns me to vapor on the spot. He wants to believe that Ryan brought the watch to Dale. He's hoping the person he'd pinned his world on before he met me won't let him down the way everyone else always has.

I'm hoping so too, because I want to like his brother, and if Ryan has screwed this up, I might just mace him on purpose.

"Will you go with me?" Jake asks.

"Of course."

"I love you," he whispers, kissing me beneath the ear, in a spot that instantly radiates the feeling throughout my body.

"I love you back," I say. "I was so scared something had happened to you." My voice is trembling, and he pulls back slightly to smile at me, leaving my shirt smeared with blood. It's stopped dripping from his nose, so hopefully it's not broken.

"I saw you," he says playfully. "You were pretty fucking scary, charging in with that mace. My life flashed before my eyes."

I know he's joking to defuse the moment, to soothe my fear, and more love for him floods me. "You didn't already know I was scary?"

"Oh, I knew you were scary after you trashed my apartment. Or before, when you were disrespecting Professor X with all of that baby talk."

"Good," I say, leaning in to kiss his jaw, the side of his face. "But what are we going to do about my shirt? It's covered in blood."

He pulls back slightly, then pulls his own shirt off and tugs it over my head.

"The bloody one's underneath," I hiss, before removing it and pulling it out of the top of his shirt. "And you're going to get hypothermia."

"It's barely cold enough for goosebumps, and I didn't want you to have to flash your old boss."

"Yes, thank you for that," Mrs. Rosings says dryly, reminding me that she's witnessed this whole mess of a scene. "However, now we're all getting an eyeful of *you*."

"Oh, come on, Mrs. Rosings," Nicole says, looking up from the trunk of the car, which is now open. I was so lost in Jake that everything around us had faded away, but the details are filling back in, like the shading in one of his drawings. "You can't possibly expect us to believe you object to Jake walking around shirtless." Still, she throws him a shirt from his bag in the trunk. "The things I do for the elderly."

I glance at Damien, who's tying Roark up with what looks like mud-brown ribbon.

"Is that...ribbon?"

"Yes," Mrs. Rosings says with a sniff. "I was going to ask you to use it to decorate the chairs for Anthony and Nina's wedding, but that's obviously moot. We'll have to cancel the plans, of course."

"Hang onto it," Jake says, his eyes on me. "And don't cancel everything just yet. The Love Fixers are going to find him a wife. After we go to Connecticut."

"We're going on a road trip?" Nicole asks. "Cool. But I get to choose the playlist. That's a hard rule."

"Be forewarned," Damien says, smiling at her as he finishes tying Roark's hands and feet with the ribbon. "She likes showtunes."

"Are you going to leave me tied up like this?" Roark roars. "It could take hours for someone to find me."

"Oh, I hope it takes way longer than that," Nicole says, approaching him and then wagging her finger in his face. "And I hope you'll think about this, *many times*, if you ever consider fucking any of us over. And remember...we could have ruined you, but we didn't. Even though you pulled a gun on our boy, we've enabled you to carry on with your sad little life. You're welcome. But guess what? If you so much as steal a stick of gum, I'm coming for you. You start shouting before the count of three hundred? That's not going to work out for you well either."

WE BRING the cars to an overlook off the highway so we can decide what comes next, picking a corner of the lot far away from the tourists exclaiming over the hazy view of the changing leaves.

Mrs. Rosings wants to go home to check on Anthony, and Nicole and Damien agree to go with her and leave their car with us. Which is to say, I convince them to leave, against their inclination, because I need to do this alone with Jake.

Before they pack into Mrs. Rosings's car to leave, Nicole points to both of her eyes, then swivels her fingers around to point at Jake. "You're bringing it back, lover boy. I like this car. The cushion has an imprint of my ass."

"Far be it from me to rob you of your ass imprint."

She cuffs him on the arm, grinning like the cat that ate the canary and then spat out its feathers. "You like me."

"You like me back."

"I liked you better before that guy made your nose look like a squashed tomato."

"So did I," I tease, wrapping my arm around his shoulders. I can't stop touching him, reminding myself that he's still here, that his body didn't get seriously hurt, even if what happened has messed with his mind. I know the sound of that bullet will stay with me for a long time.

"You'd better be careful," Nicole tells him, waggling her

eyebrows. "Lainey may decide to swap you for the bizarro version of you."

"Can we please leave?" Mrs. Rosings says with a groan. "I'm ready to sleep in my own bed tonight. That hotel we stayed in last night was *ghastly*."

Actually, at her insistence, it was a four star hotel with a bed more comfortable than the one I have at home, but Mrs. Rosings is nothing if not a woman with impossible standards.

"Are you going to talk the entire way back?" Nicole asks her with a sigh.

"Yes," Jake and I say at the same time.

Surprising me once again, Mrs. Rosings actually laughs and then adds, "But I do love a good showtune."

"That makes two out of three of us," Damien says as he slips in behind the wheel. Mrs. Rosings has made it clear that despite owning the car, she prefers never to drive. That job always falls to whatever paid employee, offspring, or unsuspecting soul happens to be around when she needs to go somewhere.

We watch as the others get in and they drive away.

Once they're gone, Jake turns toward me, wrapping both arms around me. He cleaned up in the bathroom at the overlook, but his nose is swollen, and it looks like he's going to have two black eyes. But he's alive, and he's *mine*. "I was thinking we could stop at my apartment in Manhattan to get my stuff. If that's okay with you."

"Of course," I say. "I want to snoop shamelessly. It seems only fair."

"Because you already snooped shamelessly when I was Jake Jeffries?" he asks, then leans in to kiss my forehead.

"Yes, I require a thorough snooping."

"What my woman wants, my woman gets."

"Have you tried to text your brother yet?"

His mouth lifts at the corner. "Only about a hundred times. And I called, not that he ever answers his phone. He wouldn't recognize this number. My regular cell phone's at the apartment. For all I know he's using a different number anyway."

"He'll get in touch with you," I say, wanting to believe it for him. Wanting to believe, too, that Ryan brought that watch back to Dale. If he didn't, I know it will hurt Jake, maybe even crack his heart a little—and I'm absolutely not okay with that.

A few hours later, after a forty-five minute struggle to find street parking, he leads me up to his third-floor walk-up with a railroad style layout, one room transitioning into the next in a row. His apartment is much bigger and nicer than the one Claire and I briefly shared in Brooklyn. The furniture looks like an assemblage of thrift store finds, with a mustard yellow table in the kitchen, and a black leather sofa and chair set with antique brass buttons in the living room. The walls are covered in art, but I don't get a chance to thoroughly snoop yet, because a note with Jake's name on it is sitting on the kitchen table.

I glance at Jake as we approach the table.

"It's in his handwriting," he says, his voice rough.

CHAPTER THIRTY-EIGHT

JAKE

I'm afraid I'm going to open that envelope and find something inside that'll make it hard to forgive my brother. Whatever happens, he's still my brother, but I want to believe he's had a change of heart, like me. I want to believe he took those things because he wants to give at least some of them back. I need to believe it. Lainey wraps her arms around me from behind, her hands clasping over my stomach.

"That's very close to where I'd like your hands to go."

Lainey being Lainey, she reaches down to give me a squeeze before saying, "Quit messing around and open it."

So I do, my breath ragged in my ears, Lainey's arms bolstering me to help me get through this. I lift the paper up so she can read it at the same time I do.

Jake—

By now, you know that I managed to persuade Roark's guards to let me go and leave with me. It wasn't easy, but you're not the only master manipulator. I'll be honest, it didn't hurt that we agreed to split the loot from the museum. I took the pocket watch and a few other things it felt important to return; I let them keep most of the stuff we lifted from assholes.

You were right. There, I said it. It was wrong of me to take the watch, and I've felt like a real piece of shit right up until I tried to steal it back. For the last month, I've just had itchy feet. But when I came up with my plan to get out—and executed it—I felt something more than that. I felt good for the first time in a long while.

I know Roark told you to take that necklace, but I hope you can turn around and give it back. I also hope he doesn't give you a hard time for what I did. He's been a real dick lately, and I don't want you to get strung up in that. I tried to call your phone, but given that I just found your phone in your apartment, I'm guessing you only have a burner with a number I don't know.

I'm on my way to bring that watch back to Dale, and then there's something else I need to return.

Roark had me snatch a holiday relic last Christmas, and I've felt like the fucking Grinch ever since. It's time to bring it back and make amends.

I guess you could say this is my Dale.

After I do that, I hope you'll be able to forgive me. I'll find you brother, wherever you are. Because we'll always find our way back to each other.

—Ryan

I only realize there are tears in my eyes when Lainey reaches up to trace them, same as I've done with her.

"He brought it back," I say, only then realizing how fucking worried I was that he wouldn't. That he really would decide to become Roark 2.0.

"Of course he did," she says, shifting me so I'm facing her. She wraps her hands around my neck. "And when he comes back to us, there'll be a place for him. There'll always be a place for him."

The tears are still silently tracking down my face, and I lean into her neck and kiss her there, where she's soft and slightly sweaty and smelling of spicy jasmine. Then I trail my mouth around to kiss her soft, sweet lips. They open for me, and I bless whatever twist of fate led me to her. Because it *was* a twist of fate. Everything else fits together, but one thing relied solely on fate—Cleo, seeing that necklace on my dresser and deciding to fool someone else into stealing it just in case it was the real deal.

I pull back slightly. "We should name our first kid Cleo."

She laughs, her eyes widening. "We're having kids?"

"Well, maybe we'll start with another cat. We should definitely get another cat. Professor X wants to be a tyrant, and it's hard to be a tyrant if you don't have any subjects to rule over. Maybe an orange cat. Everyone says they're pushovers."

She pushes my chest slightly. "It wasn't Cleo's doing. It was the Three of Hearts and the Seven of Wands. They put me in an emotional state."

"You think a couple of cards led you to me?" I ask, tracing her face. She told me about the Tarot cards Claire drew for her, and I made a vow to myself that I'd never be that third sword in her heart. "I'll draw a photo of the wand one and have it framed. I'll bow down before it."

She leans in close, a whisper between our lips. "I love you, you idiot."

"Thank God," I say, and lean in and kiss her again. And again. She tastes sweet, and I feel euphoria licking through me, threatening to engulf me. My brother's okay. Lainey's okay. She wants to be with me.

I taste more of her, wanting to remember this moment always, and then lift her up, her legs automatically cinching around my waist, and carry her into my bedroom. Even though I'm going away, and this won't be my place anymore, I'd like to make some final good memories here to chase away the bad ones. And I'd really be doing my neighbors a disservice if I didn't make some noise they could complain about.

"Can you be really loud about your appreciation?" I ask as I lay her down on my bed.

"I seem to remember you not wanting participation awards," she says, waggling her eyebrows.

"I didn't say I wasn't going to earn it," I tell her, then reach for the button of her jeans.

"I like the way you think," she says.

And I like the way she thinks, and smells, and tastes, and a few minutes later, when I have my face buried in her, her moans filling the air and probably aggravating the hell out of the bickerers next door, I feel like the luckiest man alive.

She tugs on my hair, hard, and pulls me up. "Your cock. Now."

So I bury myself in her, and it feels like a meeting of the world to have her here, in this place where I lived as Jake Langston. I kiss her as I thrust in deeper, her hand clutching my ass, because I want every part of me to be touching every part of her. Her soul has lit something within me, and I never want it to go out.

I kiss her more deeply, my eyes on hers as I take her slow and deep, bottoming out with each thrust, drinking up her little moans because they're for me, and I've earned them. When I feel her tightening around my dick—sweet torment—I thrust in one last time, slow and deep, my mouth still on hers, and the feeling of her clenching around me so tightly is enough to shove me off the cliff too, into a pleasure so encompassing and deep that I can't see the beginning or end of it.

This is love, I think. *This is what love feels like.*

"I love you," I whisper again, for probably the millionth time today. I'm still buried inside her because I don't want to leave. I never want to leave.

"I love you too," she says, her eyes on mine, her body under and around me, and I'm in that ocean beneath the cliff doing the backstroke.

Later, my body still wrapped around hers, I say, "What do you think about buying a rude welcome mat for Todd while we're in town?"

"I say yes," she says, her eyes dancing, but then she reaches up and lightly taps my injured nose. "But we're still going to Connecticut."

I consider telling her no, but it's incredibly hard to say no to my woman, and there's a part of me that needs to see Dale again. I'd like to know him as myself. To let him know that he had a more profound impact on me than he ever had on my alter ego. If he's open to it, I'd like to be his friend.

"We'll do it." I weave my hand through her hair, looking into her eyes. "We're going to have lots of adventures together, Elaine Catlan."

"And you're going to write about all of them in your comics?"

"*All* of them?" I ask, running my hand over her perfect, round ass and giving it a squeeze.

"Of course," she says with a smirk. "But those will be just for us."

***

IT'S A MONTH LATER, in early December, when Anthony Rosings Smith agrees to meet me at the peanut bar. I still haven't heard anything from my brother, but his note had made it sound like he might be gone through Christmas.

I'll keep hoping, and if he doesn't show up after the holidays, Nicole and Damien have offered to track him down. They both seem excited by the challenge it would offer.

I'm nervous about this meeting—almost as much as I was when Lainey and I arrived at Dale's place weeks ago, and I had to stop at a bar to knock back some liquid courage before I could find it in myself to ring his doorbell.

He was good to me, too good, and hearing what he'd done for me—how he'd convinced me to change my life—had made him cry.

So when he asked Lainey and me to stay a while, we did. For a whole damn week, and we've asked him to come visit us too. He feels like...family.

So does Mrs. Rosings, actually. We've fallen into the habit of having weekly teas with her—a tradition that started as soon as we returned from Connecticut. Claire usually comes, too, and occasionally we can twist Declan's arm and get him to join us. Joy supplies the tea, but Rosie has never accompanied her after the disastrous mushroom tea incident. She's embarrassed, I guess, even though everyone has forgiven her for her role in the mess with the necklace.

According to Mrs. Rosings, Anthony now knows who I am and why I came here. Her ability to keep secrets for thirty years is apparently selective, because she told him days after she returned from our trip to New York. I guess he wanted her to have me arrested initially, but he changed his mind.

When I arrive at the peanut bar, he's already there, two sweating beers waiting on his table.

His eyes are shuttered as I approach him, and two things hit me —he's grown a beard, which is surprising, and he's wearing a long-sleeve T-shirt and jeans.

I slide in across from him, shrugging off my coat, and he silently passes a beer to me.

"I'm hoping you didn't spit in it?" I ask.

He gives me a flat look. "Do I look like the kind of person who spits in drinks?"

Maybe. I'm not so sure that sort of personality has a look attached to it, but it would be the wrong thing to say, so I accept the beer with a nod and a thanks.

"My mother told me who you are," he says.

"I know, she mentioned that the other week." I let that linger for a moment and then add, "Mind telling me why you didn't try harder to get her to turn me in?"

"The police probably wouldn't have even arrested you," he says with a sigh, leaning back in his seat. "But that's not really why." He turns his beer around, his expression distant. "My mother told me about that guy...Roark. How he was like a father to you, and he screwed you over. I know what that kind of thing can do to a person. I guess I figured you deserve a chance at a do-over as much as anyone."

"I want more than a do-over," I tell him, leaning forward a little. "Lainey and me...we've been helping people, and we're scaling up." I tell him a bit about the Love Fixers. How we've started running ads and are going to have to bring on extra staff soon since Nicole and Damien are so often busy with their own agency.

"I sense you're going somewhere with this," Anthony says after a couple of minutes.

"You only have a few weeks left, man. Let me help you."

He's already shaking his head, and he looks like he's ready to leave without even taking a sip of his beer.

"I need this," I say, my voice shaking a little with the force of it. "I *need* to do this for you."

"I forgive you," he tells me. "I..." He swallows. "In a fucked up way, you helped me. So I forgive you. There's no need for all of this." He waves his hand around.

"There's always a need for peanuts," I joke. "Unless you're my brother, and then they'd kill you. Look, let me do this for you. If you make an ironclad prenup, there's no reason why this will blow up in your face. It's not really a marriage, it's a...workaround."

"And you're in the business of workarounds, I take it," Anthony says with a grunt that doesn't sound particularly impressed.

"You might say it's my specialty."

He sighs and sags back again, plucking at the hem of his shirt as if he too is puzzled by why he's wearing it. "I don't know if I have it in me anymore. I...it was a lot, with Nina leaving. She...I might not have loved her anymore, but she was a big part of my life. Now, that's just...gone."

I pause, wondering if I should say this next bit, or if it will push him over the edge of his early mid-life crisis. Fuck it, I've never been the careful sort.

"Your mother hasn't cancelled the arrangements for the wedding yet. It's all prepared for someone else to step in. You can still inherit the money."

His mouth drops open, then he swears liberally and takes a swig of beer. "But everyone knows. Fuck. Nina's dating Wilson openly now."

My mind automatically substitutes 'blond dick' for Wilson, but I don't say so. I'm hanging by my fingernails here—if I push him in the wrong direction, I'm gone.

"So wouldn't it be funny to get married to someone else using the wedding that was planned for her? Hell, you should *invite them*. That'd be a trip."

"She'll know it's fake," he says, his mouth a flat line.

I shrug. "She'll suspect. But she'll still be jealous. Hell, she was jealous when Rosie touched your shoulder last month. There's no one more jealous than a cheater."

"Rosie," he repeats, a spark in his eyes. "The woman who took the necklace."

I nod. "But it was a misunderstanding."

He's quiet for a second, then he takes another gulp of his drink and nods. "Let's do it."

EPILOGUE
LAINEY

Christmas

Professor X has snatched approximately ten ornaments since we put the Christmas tree up late last month. It's become a game, getting ornaments only for her to destroy them.

Her Christmas present, which we brought home early a few days ago, caught her by surprise—a big, lazy orange cat named Jeffrie. Because I firmly insist that Jake Jeffries is what got Jake and me together, not Cleo.

Jeffrie is completely unrattled by her antics, and it obviously drives her crazy. But she loves it too—when she thinks no one's looking she'll groom him, and last night, Jake and I found them curled around each other like a yin and yang.

Now, it's Christmas morning, and Jake and I are sitting beside the tree with cups of coffee. Later, we'll go over to celebrate with Claire and Declan. Nicole and Damien will be coming over with their own brand of chaos, and in the afternoon we've been invited to a tea at Smith House, probably so Mrs. Rosings can interrogate us as to whether we've found a wife for Anthony yet.

No, because he keeps saying no to all of them, but he has less than a week left, and Jake remains persistently positive, insisting that he'll pick someone before the wedding bells ring on January first.

I'm less sure, but far be it from me to dampen his light, which is one of the things I love best about him.

This is another: he looks like a kid let loose in a candy store as he shakes and rattles and squeezes the wrapped gifts I set out for him.

"Just open them," I say, nudging his shoulder.

He shrugs. "Then the anticipation will be gone, and I'll be left with..." He eyes me with as much mischief as that fox on his arm. "A mug. Not much you can do with a mug."

"You're currently drinking coffee out of one." I point to one of the gifts. "Open that one. It's more of a present for both of us."

He snorts, then motions to my small pile of presents. "What about you?"

"We'll take turns," I say.

He looks up at me, then rips into the present like he's a Tyrannosaurus Rex.

I'd make fun of him, if I weren't so eager to see what he'll think. It's a swag pack for The Love Fixers—a bag bearing the logo he designed, plus redesigned business cards that we've decided to leave in Free Libraries around Asheville, Marshall, and the surrounding towns. We'd also discussed matchbooks, but we figured it would be best not to tacitly encourage people to set things on fire.

He looks up at me with wide eyes, then leans in and gives me a kiss. "I love it." He looks just as excited as he did two minutes ago, when he nods to one of my packages. "Open one of yours. The one that's book shaped."

A laugh gusts out of me as I open it, then all the air gusts out of me entirely.

It's a bound book—his bound book. Not the story about the fire fox brothers, but our story—The Love Bandits.

He shrugs when I look at him. "I figured we should be the Love Bandits for this first one. Because of the necklace and all."

I flip through it, mesmerized, taking in the carefully drawn pictures of us, Mrs. Rosings, and Professor X, laughing to myself when I get to the cookie bouquet. Then looking up at him and whistling when I get to the scene in the car parking lot. "I take it this is the book that's just for us?" I say, setting it down and climbing into his lap. Nearly toppling him over as I do it.

"Yes," he says into my ear and kisses just beneath it. "And you nearly knocked my totally useless mug over."

"This is the best thing anyone's ever given me," I say, leaning into him.

He buries his face into my neck. "Then Professor X is going to be really disappointed."

"What are you talking about?" I ask, craning my head to get a look at his face.

"Here, get up for a minute, but please be prepared to return to that position at a moment's notice."

I give him a salute and watch, fascinated, as he pulls some heretofore never seen cat treats out of the cabinet sitting by the sagging sofa.

The cats come running, and sure enough, there's a little gift affixed to the top of Professor X's collar.

I give Jake a curious look, feeling very concerned that he's won Christmas. In addition to the swag, I got him art supplies, a shirt that says *Don't make me use my therapist voice*, and a framed, blown-up Seven of Wands card. I couldn't bring myself to look at a bleeding heart all day, so I refrained from getting him both.

But the book, and now this...

"Go on," Jake says with a slow smile. I detach the gift box from Professor X's collar, glancing up at Jake.

"Open it," he says, practically jumping. "But before you do, I really can't emphasize enough that I didn't steal it. It's a regifting because I'm nowhere near wealthy enough to afford something like this, but it's not stolen. One hundred percent not stolen."

"I don't think that's as reassuring as you think it is," I say, but my heart is thumping wildly now. Because it's a little box. The kind that holds...

"Jake," I say, worried now. Because I love him, more than I'd thought I could possibly love anyone, but I just ended an engagement that made me feel small and alone, and I'm not—

"It's not what you're thinking right now," he says, his voice low and reassuring, his hand on my chin, lifting it up so my eyes meet his, so warm and full of love. "But not because I'm not ready. I'm fucking ready. And when *you're* ready, I'm going to race you down the aisle to the closest Elvis lookalike we can find. But I still want to worship you the way you deserve to be worshipped, and we're lucky enough to have an elderly friend with way more jewelry than she can wear or give away in a lifetime. She agreed you need to have these."

"I'm blown away by you," I say, my voice shaking. I feel so deeply understood. So loved.

"Just wait until you open the box," he says with a cocky grin.

So I do, and I laugh with glee at the sight—a pair of earrings that match the design of the Heart of the Mountain necklace. My gaze lifts to meet his. "These must be..."

"Very expensive, but they were made afterward. Don't worry, I've prostrated myself a lot, and also promised to pour the entire next week of my life into twisting Anthony's arm to marry one of the candidates."

"I love you," I say, running my finger over the earrings. "I love you so much it fucking hurts."

"But I don't want it to hurt," he says, trailing his hand down to my throat, and pulling me lightly closer. "I just want it to feel really, really good."

And it does. It does again, and again, and again beneath the Christmas tree, with the lights twinkling above us and our cats yowling somewhere in the house.

And maybe I stole this life—from the universe, from fate, or possibly even from the kindness of my friends—but I am never, ever giving it back.

ABOUT THE AUTHOR

ANGELA CASELLA is a romcom fanatic. Writing them, reading them, watching them—she's greedy, and she does it all. In addition to her solo releases, she was lucky enough to collaborate with Denise Grover Swank on three complete series, with more co-written projects to come.

She lives in Asheville, NC. Her hobbies include herding her daughter toward less dangerous activities, the aforementioned romcom addiction, and dreaming of having someone else clean her house.

Visit her website at www.angelacasella.com or Angela and Denise's shared website at www.arcdgs.com.